With his knuckle, he lifted her chin. He kissed her lips. "You fool," he said, his coal eyes unfathomable. "Why did you come?" And he held her close, not seeking an answer, but she gave him one anyway.

"Because I love you," she said simply.

His arms tightened around her. She felt the deep heat and erotic tension of his lips against her flesh. "If you love me, too," she whispered, "if you take my blood, drain me to the point of death . . . the chemistry can combine, the stars can collide. Something can happen that can . . ."

He'd gone still. Dead still. "Something that can make me human again?"

"Yes," she said softly.

He rolled, his fingers sliding against hers as he brought his weight atop her, his body and eyes pinioning her in the night. "And if not? If the chemistry, the stars, the feeling . . . the *heart* just isn't enough . . . What if you're damned, and no more?"

She felt the power of his strength. His hold was almost painful. She didn't know if he meant it to be so or not. She didn't flinch.

"I am willing to risk it," she said.

Books by Heather Graham

Beneath a Blood Red Moon

Deep Midnight

Night, Sea and Stars

Queen of Hearts

Realm of Shadows

Tempestuous Eden

When Darkness Falls

Published by Kensington Publishing Corporation

WHEN DARKNESS FALLS

HEATHER GRAHAM

ZEBRA BOOKS
KENSINGTON PUBLISHING CORP.
http://www.kensingtonbooks.com

ZEBRA BOOKS are published by

Kensington Publishing Corp.
119 West 40th Street
New York, NY 10018

All Kensington titles, imprints and distributed lines are available at special quantity discounts for bulk purchases for sales promotion, premiums, fund raising, educational or institutional use.

Special book excerpts or customized printings can also be created to fit specific needs. For details, write or phone the office of the Kensington Special Sales Manager: Kensington Publishing Corp., 119 West 40th Street, New York, NY 10018. Attn. Special Sales Department. Phone: 1-800-221-2647.

ISBN-13: 978-1-4201-3146-8
ISBN-10: 1-4201-3146-X

First Printing: October 2000

Previously published under the name Shannon Drake.

20 19 18 17 16 15 14 13 12 11 10

Printed in the United States of America

Prologue

The Tomb

"So you want to be scared, eh? Really scared? Then it's darker, deeper, into the bowels of the earth!" the tour guide exclaimed, dramatically sweeping a section of his black cloak over his shoulder. He had a pleasant, cultured Edinburgh accent. *R*s that rolled. Clean enunciation. "Yes. Deeper. For those of you who scoff at the ghosts of simple murderers, at the haunting mewlings of their victims, we will go onward."

"Can't hardly wait!" intoned Jeff Dean, a dark-haired, good-looking college kid.

"Yes, onward, lead us onward, for heaven's sake—I'm just shaking in my pants!" his date, Sally Adams, added. She was a pretty blonde who managed to ruin the effect of her youth and beauty with a skintight blouse and short, short skirt. Her lipstick was way too red for her coloring and covered more of her face than just her lips. She pretended to be bored, but she was hanging on to Jeff's arm.

"For heaven's sake, yes, please do something scary!"

That came from another of their companions, a tall, skinny, red-haired boy-man named Sam Spinder. His attitude was bored and taunting as well.

Jade MacGregor had come with the three of them and six other college-age visitors. She had met up with the group earlier while touring the castle; they had suggested the night excursion. Though they were a younger group—rich kids visiting Europe on their folks' money—and she was a brand-new publisher and writer, working on a travel piece about medieval lifestyles, she had found the thought of the tour intriguing, and important to her work, so she had joined the group. She had come to Scotland on her own, something she had wanted to do, but touring a foreign country alone could be quite lonely. The young people in the group were twenty-one and twenty-two to her twenty-five—not such a great distance in age—but she was already feeling as if she were fifty and they were living in a perpetual realm of adolescent football, fraternities, drugs, and rock and roll. She'd been dismayed to discover the extent of this group's recreational drug taking—they had come with an arsenal of pills and a variety of things to smoke. That they took such chances in a foreign country seemed exceptionally worrisome to her, and they had razzed her about not joining in.

Still, the tour was proving to be fun and entertaining. The night was beautiful, a full moon rising. It was fall, and the commercial significance of Halloween had touched Edinburgh along with ancient superstitions. The streets were dressed for autumn and for Halloween; ghoulies and ghosties adorned shop windows. It was a good night to be out.

Her companions, however, were somewhat wild.

They were proving to be rude as well.

She wasn't quite sure what they were on tonight, but it was making them bold and brash—and insultingly cruel.

They were enjoying heckling the tour guide, who seemed to have the ability to take it all in stride.

"I'm shaking in my boots already!" Jeff said, faking a shiver. "Where did you get that spiel, that accent—that look? High school drama? Ooh, I do shake!"

The sarcasm directed at the hardworking tour guide was unfair, Jade thought. Their guide was good—thirtyish, tall, lean, and yes, dramatic, perhaps a would-be Hamlet who had found his living as a tour historian, adding pathos to his recitations about the long-ago evil that had plagued the streets of Scotland. He had taken great relish and delight in extolling the inhumanity of man, explaining deaths by plague, by execution, and by murder most foul. They had gone underground, where the modern city had grown up over ancient closes, roadways that once housed homes, shops, taverns, and the everyday life of a people. No more. Now, by night, the underground was empty— except for the tours. Ghosts were introduced in different rooms; grisly murders were described in detail. This was, after all, the city of Hare and Burke, royal murder and espionage, and the utmost butchery imaginable—and unimaginable—in the medieval world. The tour guide's grasp of history was very good, Jade knew, because she had studied much of it.

The guide had led them from the rear of Saint Giles— where children were hanged once upon a time for so much as stealing a loaf of bread—around dark and shadowy streets, and then down into the closes. An older couple with them had appreciably *ooh*ed and *aah*ed at the proper places; a young couple with boys of about nine and ten had asked questions and received answers, totally enjoying the tour. There was a single man on the tour, older than the college crowd, but by how much, Jade couldn't exactly say. He was extremely good-looking, with fascinating dark eyes, the kind that could seem ebony one minute, then

suddenly lighter the next, a curious brown shade, even
. . . red. He was tall, very tall, perhaps six-foot-three, and
because of his height, he appeared lean, but having stood
behind or near him at various stops along the tour, Jade
knew that his shoulders were very broad and that beneath
the fabric of his well-cut suit coat, he was probably nicely
muscled. He watched the tour guide with interest. He
hadn't jumped at all, or *ooh*ed or *aah*ed, but he had listened
to all the tour guide had to say with a respectful silence.
He had kept somewhat to the rear of the group, in the
shadows, never speaking. Actually, only the college
crowd—nine in the group—had hissed and mocked and
heckled. The young couple and their children had been
totally intrigued.

"Where are we going?" Tony, another of the boys, asked.
He'd been among the worst of the hecklers, a football
player with a shaved head and shoulders the size of Cleve-
land and no neck between them. He seemed to consider
himself too tough for the concept of fear. He and Jeff had
already agreed to be volunteers. Pretending to be men
branded as traitors, they had been lightly flogged with the
guide's cat-o'-nine-tails, and had turned their backs on the
crowd for a pretend disembowelment and hanging. They
had made a huge joke of the proceedings, but the guide
had gone along with all their foolery.

"Maybe we're not supposed to ask," Marianne, Tony's
girlfriend and, oddly enough, the shyest and sweetest in
the group, suggested hesitantly.

"Don't be ridiculous," said Ann, a tall, thin redhead
with the impatient air of a bored scholar. "If you don't
ask . . ." Her voice trailed; she lifted her palms.

"You don't get to find out," Marianne said.

"And know if you really want to go or not," Ann said
sagely.

"Hey!" Tony repeated. "Come on, she's right. Just where is it that we're going?"

"You said you wanted to be scared," the tour guide reminded them.

"Yeah, damned right, better than what we've seen so far," Jeff said. "So tell us, where are we going?"

"Down to the dead," the tour guide told them dramatically.

"Down to the dead!" Jeff repeated, using his best Boris Karloff imitation.

Jade happened to notice that the tall, silent man on the tour frowned slightly. He seemed to realize she was watching him. His eyes caught hers. They were dark, incredibly dark. Black as the night. No . . . lighter again, weather eyes, every-changing eyes. They were brown again. A brown touched by fire. For a moment she felt as if she couldn't turn away. A strange sense of warmth filled her. It wasn't just a feeling; she couldn't turn away. Or was she simply doing this to herself?

"And where is that?" Sally, the blonde with the skintight blouse, asked loudly, breaking the strange sense Jade had experienced of being like a moth drawn to a flame.

Yes, a moth to flame. The flame was in his eyes. Now they were amber eyes . . . fire eyes, the eyes of a wolf at night. Arresting.

Sexy! she thought.

A stranger in a strange land, she reminded herself, uncomfortable suddenly with the way she had felt about a stranger. *Hey,* she warned herself. She was smart and savvy. Intelligent, friendly, but streetwise and careful. Not the type to fall for a total stranger under strange circumstances. Still . . . he was compelling.

Very sexy. Not just good-looking, sensual, sexy.

Those eyes . . .

Um, those eyes. They caught hers. Yes, she was watching him.

He knew it. Did it amuse him? Perhaps not.

For yes, he was watching her as well.

"You'll see. First we're for a stop at Ye Olde Hangman's Tavern—for a wee bit o' Scots whiskey—or an ale, or a gin and tonic, or even a swallow of fine wine, if ye've a mind, mum!" the tour guide said to Sally. Sally sniffed, indicating her doubt that Ye Olde Hangman's Tavern might have wine that she would consider drinking, much less enjoy. Sally turned away. Jade, still watching their tour guide, was slightly unnerved to see the way he looked at Sally.

Chilling. And odd. Throughout the tour, he had handled the heckling well, appearing hurt and wounded rather than insulted by the jibes cast his way. He didn't look exactly angry now. No, the look was more . . . calculating.

Like a hunter stalking prey.

"Follow me!" he said.

Jade gave herself a mental shake. His smile was back in place.

As they walked, Jade saw the tall, amber-eyed man talk to the couple with the young boys, warning them that the graveyards could be unsettling. The woman started to argue, telling him, "Oh, the boys are fine. They know myth from history, the present from the past—" She broke off, looking at the man. Then she told her husband, "Peter! We're leaving the tour here."

"Mary! This will be the best part—"

"A big tankard of ale will be the best part for you, Peter," Mary replied. "After that, we take the boys back to the Balmoral Hotel!"

They reached the tavern, easy access off the Royal Mile. The tavernkeeper, seeing their guide, nodded and called to one of his girls to see that they were quickly served. Jake chose an ale on draft. Sally and Jeff sat across from her at a dingy bar table in the center of the tavern. "Think he can scare us 'among the dead'?" Sally queried, giggling. Still, Jade thought, she sounded a little uncomfortable.

"He's nothing but a pile of hokey baloney," Jeff said disdainfully. "No doubt we'll see a few old tombstones. And maybe the statue of that little dog."

"Ah, my friends!" their guide said, spinning around them, his black cape twirling. "I have disappointed you throughout the night! Angus!" he called to the bartender. "Send these youths each a shot of your best—Johnnie Walker Black, if you will. Drink up, my friends, on me. I promise, a taste of Scotland's finest in your veins and what I am about to show you will curl your toes! The saints preserve me!" He laughed on the last.

"If the Scotch is on you, buddy, I'm in!" Jeff declared, raising the shot glass that had been brought to him. He downed the liquor in one swallow and chased it with his beer. Jade ignored the shot that had been set before her. She felt the tour guide staring at her. She smiled. "You've scared me just fine already," she assured him.

He inclined his head slightly and turned to the others. "I'll tell you a tale then, about the crypt we'll explore. It's the vault for the de Brus family. Ah, now I see the historian among you looking at me!" he declared, catching Jade's eyes. "Aye, 'tis true that de Brus on the one hand became Bruce, as in our famous good king, Robert the Bruce. But there was another family—one that stubbornly remained de Brus, and none other. Aye, and when first they came, there was, they say, an illegitimate cousin among them, and he was cursed with the illness more than most. Some say the family curse was syphilis; some say that he was a hemophiliac. Whatever, this cousin went mad and was killed by his own family. Now this was early in time, around the year 1080. He left behind a daughter, a rare beauty, but the family had her locked away in a tower. Still, as young men will do, suitors came to the tower, and some would find entry. . . .''

"And then?'' Sally demanded impatiently as his voice trailed.

"Then they tried to get into her pants!'' Jeff said flatly. The group all laughed.

"Did they wear pants back then?'' asked Tom Marlow, another young man in the group of teens. Of the boys, he was the quietest—it was the first time Jade had heard him talk that night. She had a feeling he wouldn't have said a word at all if it hadn't been for the Johnnie Walker Black.

"Shush!'' Sam Spinder said. Apparently Tom Marlow didn't get to speak often. "Then?'' Sam demanded of the guide, downing his own Scotch with a grimace and a swallow.

"Then they were never seen again,'' the guide said with a shrug. "But bones would be found out on moors and marshlands. And young women would disappear as well. It's said that the poor beauty de Brus would cry, and her anguish would be like a howling in the night, like that of a million demons, like banshees coming for the dead; oh, she would cry in such agony that her kinfolk would find some poor peasant girls and bring them to her . . . and likewise, they would never be seen again, for 'tis said she liked to bathe in blood, the younger, the purer, the better.''

"That's the Countess Báthory story!'' complained Hugh Riley, another of the football players. He wasn't quite as big as the others—maybe not quite as solid on the field. He did seem to know his history. And he had listened and paid attention throughout the night. *An interesting fellow.*

"And Countess Báthory is a very real historical personage, cruel, remorseless, and without conscience.'' Jade said sharply. "She caused the deaths of hundreds—perhaps thousands—of young women. She did bathe in blood, and her appetites were cruel and voracious."

She felt a strange warmth again suddenly, as if she were being watched from behind. She turned. He was there, yes, at a table in the corner of the tavern. He sat alone. He drank a beer so dark it looked red. Maybe it was wine, a very large glass of dark red wine. He raised the glass to her, as if he agreed. She could almost hear his voice in her ear. It would be deep and cultured. *Yes, evil does exist in this world; the cruelties of man to man need not be exaggerated!*

He didn't speak. He inclined his head toward her and drank.

She turned away quickly.

"Great story! So this bitch like the blood of virgins, eh?" Sam asked.

"That will make you safe from any danger, Sally!" Jeff told the blonde.

"You all know what you can do with yourselves!" Sally said, drawing away from Jeff.

"Ah, come on now, Sal!" Jeff said. "We're teasing. I mean seriously—where do you get an adult virgin these days? Unless it's the teach over here—eh, teach?" he teased Jade.

She didn't have to answer. Their guide had swooped down on them again. "Our lady just liked young blood, my friends, the more tainted the better! Aye, she was a sensual one, she was!" He widened his eyes at them and winked. "Drink up, drink up, my friends! It's time to venture to the crypt!"

The young couple and their sons departed, Mary tipping the guide well. "The boys have loved this," she told him.

He smiled. "Sweet dreams, and many thanks."

The older couple bowed out as well.

Jade thought about calling it a night herself, but she had the feeling that this particular tour wasn't offered often, that the hecklers had goaded the guide into a special excursion, and that it might be her one chance to see something really unusual.

The dark-eyed stranger, she saw, was staying with them as well.

They left the tavern, walking darkened streets, taking all kinds of twists and turns. Jade had wondered what cemetery they were going to—she thought she knew most of them in the city. But they came upon a derelict church that seemed to rise high upon a hill. It was surrounded by unkempt graves—broken stones, slanted stones, lichen-covered stones, and those that seemed bone white and glowing beneath the light of the moon.

Jade looked up as they walked through wrought-iron gates and into the churchyard. There was a full moon tonight—perfect for such a tour.

"And it's nearly midnight!" a girl named Julie said. She giggled and clung to Hugh. Like Sally, she was wearing a top that clung to her ample breasts and displayed a cavern of cleavage. She seemed sweet enough to Jade—just young and a little vacant.

"The midnight hour!" their tour guide exclaimed, lifting his hands to the heavens. "The traditional time for all witchcraft, for demons to rise, for the bloodlust of the undead!"

Sally giggled nervously. "It is pretty dark."

"There's a full moon! You can see like it's broad daylight!" Jeff assured her.

"Come, see the crypt," the guide invited.

They walked over uneven ground. Jade turned as they walked, to study the architecture of the old church. Built of stone, it was Celtic in design. The windows all seemed blackened, like countless vacant eyes staring out at the night. Staring back at the church, Jade suddenly tripped over a gravestone.

She felt herself steadied by a pair of strong hands. Startled, she turned to see the face of the tall, aloof stranger with the curious fire-and-darkness eyes.

"Are you all right?" His voice was deep, slightly accented.

Scottish? She wasn't sure. It seemed strange to hear him speak. He did have a deep and cultured voice, husky, compelling . . . as sensual as his eyes. And yet, though he certainly sounded as arresting as he looked, he also sounded perfectly normal.

What had she been expecting? "Am I all right?" she repeated, and felt like a fool. She knew she blushed. "I . . . of course. I'm just klutzy, I'm afraid," she said.

"This graveyard is not a good place to be at night," he told her. He was still staring at her, his amber eyes strange and disturbing. He didn't just look at her; he studied her. He smoothed back a lock of her hair. It seemed a very intimate gesture.

She should have drawn away.

She didn't.

"Why?" she asked him. She smiled. "Do you think that ghosts rise from their graves to take vengeance on the living?"

"I think there are many things on this earth that defy explanation, that is all," he said. "You're an American." Did he sound just a little bit disappointed? As if he had thought that he had known her, as if she might be someone else?

"Guilty. I am an American. But of Scottish descent." She shrugged. "MacGregor," she said.

"A Southerner?"

"Guilty again. Louisiana."

"New Orleans?"

"Yes. You're familiar with the city?"

"I am," he said, then pointed to the stone she had tripped over. "How curious."

"What?" She looked down. The stone lay in pieces next to an aboveground sarcophagus, similar to those in her hometown cemeteries. Though the smaller stone was broken, it belonged in the group that surrounded the aboveground tomb. And on the tomb, clearly legible in the moonlight, was etched the family name MacGregor.

Chills shot through her. It was uncanny. She felt the blood drain from her face. She had never been afraid of the dead before, of a cemetery, a church, a "haunted" place. She loved history far too much, and often, the poignancy of death. But now . . .

Fear began to dance in hot little steps down the length of her spine.

"I should really go back," she murmured. "I thought the tour was fine so far. I'm really tired, I guess. Not paying attention to where I'm walking."

"No," the amber-eyed stranger said, taking her arm.

She looked up at him, frowning. "I said that I think I should just go—"

"It's too dangerous to leave now, alone."

"Too dangerous—" she began.

"Scotland has its share of thugs," he told her with a shrug. "This isn't the best neighborhood."

"You're from here?"

"I was. Once upon a time. Long, long ago."

"Come along now, come along!" the guide called to them.

They had reached the far side of the graveyard. Here tombs in stone and steel rose above the ground like haunted houses of the dead. In places stones were broken away. Wrought-iron gates stood half-open. Vines grew everywhere.

Turning around, Jade could no longer see the winding street they had traveled to come here, only the old church and the grave markers, glowing golden beneath the light of the full moon.

As if on cue, a mist started to rise.

"Will you look at that!" Julie said with awe.

"He's got a fog machine going out here somewhere!" Tony told her. "Any minute now we'll start to hear the theme from *The Twilight Zone*."

"Or *Jaws*!" Jeff said with a laugh. "Land shark—cemetery shark, coming this way!"

"The tomb lies right ahead!" their guide called out, spinning around with a sweep of his cape.

And indeed it did. It was a grand tomb, if a decaying one. Beautifully carved gargoyles guarded the four corners of an intricately designed wrought-iron fence. Lichen and vines covered the walls and the steps that led to the gate.

"Come, come!" the guide said, mounting the steps and beckoning to them.

They followed.

From outside the gate, the tomb had appeared old and abandoned and decaying. Dry leaves covered the floor.

But once they were inside, it was evident that the walls were lined with coffins. They weren't bricked in; they lay on shelves, covered with debris and spiderwebs.

"Oh, spooky, spooky!" Jeff intoned.

"It gets better below," the guide promised. "I promised to scare you," he added with ominous dramatics, sweeping his cape around his shoulders again to lead them toward the rear of the tomb, where damp, ancient stone steps led below the ground.

Jade wasn't sure if she was glad of the stranger's protective hold as they walked down the damp steps into the stygian darkness below—or if he made her even more afraid. She thought that she should pull away and take refuge behind a pinheaded football player. But the guide lit a match off the stone wall and set fire to a torch, illuminating the underground vault they entered.

Julie was the first to let out a little scream.

The dead lay in various stages of decay beneath tattered shrouds. Skulls stared into the abyss of endless night; bony fingers clasped one another over chests covered in the remnants of silk and linen. Here and there bones littered the floor. Rats squealed and darted at their entry; a bat flew across the great underground tomb, drawing a startled scream from Sally.

"This is pretty cool, great to see, but I'm not scared yet!" Jeff told their guide.

"Because you haven't seen Sophia," the guide said. "And, young sir, I think that you should meet her first. Come here. You'll volunteer again to be the ancient victim, won't you?"

The guide crooked a finger at Jeff.

Jeff swaggered forward. "Sure. Bring it on. Beat me. Torture me."

"How about your girlfriend?" the guide queried.

"Oh, I don't know. . . ." Sally began.

"Come on, Sally, be daring. Fulfill my fantasy—ménage à trois!" Jeff teased.

"Oh, baby!" Tony hooted.

Sally made a face at him.

The guide smiled and led them to a sarcophagus that sat in the middle of the floor. It appeared to be sealed with a heavy stone, but the stone gave with a nerve-tingling, squealing sound as the guide shoved it to the side. Within it lay an elaborate wood coffin that had somehow withstood the ages. It, too, was decorated with an abundance of gargoyles and demonic-looking creatures.

"Sophia and her minions!" The guide hovered behind Sally then, lifting her blond hair, his fingers moving around her neck, fluttering over the exposed rise of her breasts, sliding along her neck again. "The place . . . for the dead to dine!" he said. "For here life beats so strongly!"

His touch on the girl was almost indecent, Jade thought, ready to say something, to put a stop to it all. The girl looked as if she were mesmerized, awaiting his touch. She turned to the guide, her head falling back. He smiled at the rest of them, catching her with one arm, delicately touching her then with his knuckles, that touch running from her throat down through the cleavage of her breasts. He tore away her top; no one moved. She smiled up at him. Jeff, her boyfriend, stared at him.

Enough. Jade was going to start forward.

The stranger pulled her back.

"Don't," he whispered. "Don't interfere now."

Was it part of the act? Was this the adult version of the tour?

She would have shaken off the stranger's touch, except that she felt the chill along her spine again. An inner voice warned her: *Don't speak! Don't move. If you do, you'll be in danger!*

Run. . . .

No, she couldn't run. The guide would see her run; he would drag her back. . . .

"Open the coffin lid," he commanded Jeff, who did so, apparently oblivious to the fact that the man he had ridiculed had now nearly stripped his girlfriend, who smiled at him, almost purring as he caressed her naked flesh.

Jade was rooted to the ground with fear.

Jeff ripped the lid off the coffin. There was a woman within it, young, beautiful, with raven black hair, wearing a white linen gown with fine lacework. She wasn't in the least decayed; her eyes opened. She stared at Jeff and smiled—a damning, come-hither smile. . . .

She rose in the coffin.

It's an act; it's all part of an act.

Their guide began to talk again. "They feared her; they feared Sophia as they feared neither God, the devil, nor even the English king, Edward, Hammer of the Scots, when it came time for him to ravage Scotland! They feared her, God, yes; her kin feared her, and so, to keep her happy and away from them, they brought her youth and beauty, and they fed her. They brought the blood of young flesh to her and her company. Jeff, volunteer . . . show her the blood that pulses through you; give her your throat."

And Jeff did so, reaching out to the woman, helping her from the coffin, smiling like a fool as he stepped into her arms. She kissed him, the kiss erotic, and then he inclined his head. . . .

And she bit into him.

He screamed.

"Scared yet?" the tour guide demanded. "Are you scared yet?" He smiled. And with this smile his drama had reached its peak, for he now had huge, glistening white fangs where his canine teeth had been. They glowed in the torchlight. . . .

Then he started to laugh—and he leaned forward and bit into Sally's neck.

She screamed; a cry of the anguished, a shriek of the damned. Blood began to spurt everywhere, spilling over the coffin, the ground.

It's real, oh, God, far too real.

The others began to scream and shout, to panic, to head for the steps. But from the shelves of tombs, the dead began to awake. Corpses, half-clad in their shrouds, misted in spiderwebs, suddenly rose, blocking the steps. Shrieks and screams of terror went up. The dead reached for the living.

Jade, as panicked as anyone, disbelieving, in terror, tried to run.

The stranger shoved her back. "No! Stay here, quiet, in the corner—wait!"

She would have disobeyed, but the tour guide was suddenly in front of her. He was covered in Sally's blood, smiling. She backed away.

And suddenly the stranger was between her and the tour guide. And the tour guide breathed with a deep rattle and made noises like spilling lava, as if he already tasted blood. He jumped toward the stranger with the dark eyes. . . .

He said something, a name she didn't quite catch. "I thought it was you. Bastard, you would interfere—"

"And you would destroy everything."

The tour guide tried to strike out, to hammer him down.

The dark-eyed stranger repelled his blows and parried them. The tour guide flew across the room, hit with a terrible force. . . .

People were screaming loud enough to wake the dead! Jade thought hysterically.

She had to get out.

How?

An exit.

Where? Everything was shadowed. . . .

And everything was red. Because blood was everywhere.

A corpse was attacking Julie.

A corpse!

Somehow Jade came to life. She grabbed the burning torch that had given them light here beneath the ground. She attacked the corpse, which backed away.

Another was at her rear. She spun around, whirling the fire before her.

Then suddenly it seemed as if they were all after her, stalking her, coming closer, and closer, and closer. . . .

They were wrenched away one by one. They went flying, shouting and hissing in fury. She felt their eyes, felt their hunger and their hatred. She was losing her mind. This wasn't happening.

She saw the tour guide coming for her, still smiling, pleased. He reached for her. She struggled. He was incredibly strong. She couldn't twist or turn. He smiled while she screamed and struggled, tearing at the tailored white blouse she was wearing.

"Shh ... shh ... you are the cream of the crop, this midnight hour!" he told her.

She saw his fangs. . . . He was coming closer and closer to her throat. . . .

Then his smile faded.

He was right in front of her face; then he was gone, torn away again by an incredible force that wrenched him cleanly from his feet.

And she was dropped. She fell on the floor hard, striking her head against the stone. She heard the tour guide scream with rage, protest, hurl obscenities at someone named . . .

She saw the stranger again, bending over her. Saw . . .

His eyes. Deep, dark eyes. Eyes that burned with the red fire of the torch, with a strange golden touch of flames and moonlight.

Then she felt the pain in her temple deepening. Stone, yes, she had struck the stone, and the world was fading. . . .

The torch she had held still burned on the nearby ground.

She thought that, distantly, she could still hear the sound of screaming.

And she began to fall, fall, into eternal darkness. . . .

Stygian darkness.

Like his eyes, with the fires gone out . . .

* * *

They found her upon the tomb that bore her family name, MacGregor.

She was laid out atop it, stripped, but swathed in white linen.

A shroud.

She was barely aware of her surroundings when she first awoke. The police were there, and she could hear the sound of a siren. She drifted, then realized that now the siren was being blared by the ambulance that carried her.

She fell in and out of consciousness. She tried to tell the police what had happened; she talked about the tour guide, the tavern, the monster, Sophia de Brus, who had risen from the coffin.

The police believed that she had been under the influence of a narcotic—as the other survivors had been.

Yes, there were other survivors. Several of them. Four had been killed. She, along with five other young people, had been found alive. Hugh Riley had lived, as had Tom Marlow, Tony Alexander, Ann Thorson, and Marianne Williams. All had been found among the headstones, some naked, some in torn clothing, injured, rattling on in confusion, half maddened, but alive.

She was glad that they had survived, insanely sorry about the others. *See? That's what happens when you're cruel and taunting to a tour guide!*

But no one had deserved such a death. . . .

Little by little she learned what had happened—according to the authorities.

The police had determined, through careful investigation, that cultists earning entry into a Satanic sect had been responsible. Jeff, Sally, Julie, and Sam had been drained of blood, their throats slit ear to ear, their heads . . .

Two had remained attached by a few threads of flesh.

Two heads had been missing completely—she had never found out precisely to whom those missing heads had belonged. The others, those lucky enough to make it out of the vault, had been found just as she had been found.

Unconscious.

Then incoherent.

And they had finally admitted to the drugs and alcohol they had ingested.

Jade reminded the police that they had tested her blood and urine; they surely knew she hadn't been on drugs.

But no one had wanted to believe her. They wanted to move on, to look for the murderers, to pray it never happened again.

She needed to go home. To let the police do their work.

She had been lucky, incredibly lucky.

Lucky, yes, except that the police were wrong.

She couldn't remember everything . . . because what she remembered was so preposterous. What she did remember couldn't be true—what the police were saying certainly could be. Much of it had been an elaborate act. Illusion. *Of course. It had to be.* Corpses didn't just come to life.

There were no such things as vampires.

And still . . .

They had questioned her relentlessly, so she persisted with her own questions. Something wasn't right. And she hadn't been on drugs. Whether they admitted it or not, they knew that she hadn't been.

Neither had the man with the haunting eyes.

What man? they had asked.

She described him.

The police hadn't seen him. Such a man, as hero or demon, could not be found. And she hadn't known his name, or where he was staying, or if, indeed, he had been a native or a foreigner. *Yes!* He had said something about having come from there . . . at some time. Whoever he was, wherever he had come from, he had fought the corpses—and the blood-drinking guide—she was certain.

The police, again, thought the terror of the evening had unhinged her thought processes.

The corpses in the tomb were nothing but corpses, the police assured her. Ashes, decaying, falling apart. There was no Sophia de Brus in Scottish history. What had happened was terrible, terrible. She needed to go home, to forget all about it. . . .

They needed to find the murderer. The guide, the young man who had created such havoc.

The truth—the bizarre truth as she remembered it—began to fade in her consciousness. Her mind protected her sanity. The police continued to question her endlessly, trying to make some sense of it themselves. Where had she been before? Why had she come on the tour? What had the guide been like?

There were many tours in the city—but none by the name the guide had given them.

And there was no tavern called Ye Olde Hangman's Tavern.

The police had to be right—that what she remembered was an illusion. What she thought she had seen could not have been real. A ritual, yes, a sick ritual. Tragic murders perpetuated by human beings who were sick themselves . . .

But the tour guide, who had led them to death and terror and mayhem, had managed to totally disappear without leaving a clue as to his identity or whereabouts. If there were cult members involved, who were the rest of the cult members—who had helped the tour guide in his murder spree?

The man with the amber eyes.

If only she could tell them more.

But she couldn't, nor could any of the other survivors. Blood was scraped from the headstones, and corpses were studied. The killers had left behind no clues. Not a drop of their own blood, not a hair, not a follicle.

The more time that went by, the more it all became unreal. Confused. Enwrapped in a mist of total, surreal darkness and shadow.

There was nothing more she could give the authorities, and nothing more they could tell her. They would handle the matter, call in Scotland Yard—even invite the FBI over to perform their own tests. Every possible clue would be followed; every like crime across the country and the civilized world would be checked by computer for comparison.

They didn't want any more of her opinions.

She was lucky; she had been spared. She had to forget, or go mad. She needed to go home and get back to living her life.

Her sister, Shanna, came to Scotland to get her so that she wouldn't have to travel home alone. They used mileage awards and traveled home in first class. Shanna was wonderful, letting her talk and talk, to try to sort things out in her own mind.

Of course, Shanna was certain that it had to have been cult members as well, horrible people with no regard for human life. Jade had been lucky.

She needed to be glad she was alive.

And she was going home. Far from the horror.

And she *was* glad, so glad, and grateful.

And yes, life would return to normal. . . .

A year later it had almost done so. She started dating a cop named Rick. She published a small history and photo book on medieval churches.

And it was almost exactly a full year from the date . . . on the night of the full moon, when she began to dream about the man.

The man.

Not the tour guide, not the woman who had risen from the dead, not even the other corpses that had come to life in the vault.

It was dark in her dream, and she stood in the darkness that was illuminated only by the golden glow of the moon. Shadows crossed the land; mist rose. . . . She stood there, chilled, for the breeze was cold and she was vulnerable, she knew, naked—no, clad only in the white linen of a dead man's shroud. . . .

And he was walking toward her.

The man with the fire-and-ebony eyes.

She awoke with a violent start, shaking.

She looked at the luminous dial of her bedside clock. It had just struck twelve.

The midnight hour.

Chapter One

"Ah, good morning, madame sister stupendous!"

Jade didn't need to look up to know that Matt Durante had arrived at her table. She was as familiar with his voice as she was with his cherubic cheeks, broad smile, and ever-sparkling powder blue eyes. Everything about Matt seemed to be an eternal contrast—she had never met anyone with such a light and cheerful attitude toward life. He was continually smiling, never down, and ready to do a good turn for a down-and-out bum on the streets as well as for a friend. His writing, however, was dark, darker than the stygian abysses of any ancient mythology. He created tales of the shadow world, scary, haunting, the type of work that left a reader chilled, afraid to walk down a dark alley at night, and equally afraid to be alone.

She set her paper down and looked up at him, adjusting her sunglasses. "Good morning, sister stupendous? Does that mean that my ever-so-slightly younger sibling has been up to some evil deed this morning? Did she find fault with your latest chapter about the lives of the wicked and lucky?''

He grinned, taking a seat beside her as if he had come here just to find her. It was no great secret that she usually spent her mornings here at Café du Monde. Yes, it was the tourist trap of the early riser in New Orleans. It also offered what she considered to be great coffee and terrific beignets at an incredible price. Tourists were fun to watch as well; there was always a lot of talk and activity. Speech could be heard in a wide variety of languages. She loved the busyness that went on here in the morning, even though she liked to come alone and read her paper. Just as she had, especially in the last year, enjoyed the brightness of the morning sun and the bustle of hundreds of people and their chatter. Her friends always knew where to find her. And many of her friends, like Matt, were writers. They had become friends because they were all part of one of the most eclectic writing groups ever to come together. She specialized in travel and history; Matt loved the macabre; Jenny Dansen wrote comedy, slice-of-life tidbits. Jade's sister had recently taken a turn toward fantasy, and so on. They had begun as the Wednesday Eve Group, calling themselves such a simple name because they had come together for no other reason than a love of the written word—without it mattering too terribly much what the written word might be about.

''I saw your errant younger sibling just last night. We had dinner at the new Cajun place off the highway, and went shopping for Halloween decorations. Your sister is gorgeous, and glorious. Sweet as pie—and shaped like pure sin. And even to me, awkward cad that I am, she was as kind as can be.''

''Ah. Well, forgive me, but my sibling sounds pretty darned good. So why then am I suddenly so stupendous?''

"Oh, well, you're sweet and gorgeous and shaped like sin, too. But this morning you're also so talented."

"Oh?"

He tossed a stack of computer sheets on the table in front of her, grinning, taking a seat, and running his fingers through his hair. "You know how obsessed I am."

Matt was the biggest commercial success among their group. He was fairly well paid, and fairly well known. His books continued to climb on the important lists—those put out by the major bookstores, *USA Today,* the *New York Times,* and so on. But he was obsessive. Each time one of his books came out, in hardcover or paperback, he was just like a little kid. He worried himself sick, and constantly called the Internet and any other possible source for the position of his book that week.

What he had set down before her were printings he had done of the morning's *USA Today* list. Not just the first fifty, which regularly appeared in the paper, but the list of one hundred and fifty that could be found on-line or through the paper itself.

She stared at the pages, then at him.

"One hundred," he told her.

"One hundred?"

"Your little self-published *Divinely Wicked* book on cathedrals and churches made it to one hundred. Jade, that's almost unheard of! That's an incredible coup."

Not believing him, she met his eyes, then picked up the paper. Her type of book didn't tend to be a popular success, though she had done well enough because she was her own publisher. The Internet had given her the ability to reach markets she might not otherwise have touched. Because of the Internet access, she had also been picked up by the bookstore chains, as well as by a number of the remaining independent bookstores that specialized in history and anything medieval.

"Fine, don't believe me. Look!" he told her.

She looked. And there was her book and her name.

"You don't think there's been a mistake?" she asked him.

He laughed. "You sound like me."

"No," she told him, flashing him a smile. "You're a total neurotic. You can't believe in your talent because you are successful, and you're always terrified that you're not talented enough to be successful, and no matter how often we all pat you on the back, you're still neurotic."

He nodded cheerfully. "I know. You sound just like me," he repeated.

She sighed, looking at the list again. "I'm just amazed. And happy, of course."

"It's a great book. Fabulous photography. And you did it all yourself."

"Most of it. But Shanna did some."

Jade's waiter came back to the table. Jade ordered more coffee; Matt ordered beignets and coffee.

Jade continued to stare at the list.

"It is unbelievable," she said, flashing him a smile.

"So when's the party?"

"Party?"

"Naturally you're having us over—the Wednesday Eve Group—tonight."

"It's Thursday."

"I know that. But you're buying lots of champagne—and no cheap stuff—and maybe even some caviar."

"You told me once that you hate caviar."

"That's beside the point. At such an occasion in life, you should have caviar. And we're all going to toast you and say good things and celebrate."

"Maybe we should. But do you think there's time to get hold of everyone?"

"Jade, Jade, Jade," he said impatiently. "Why do you

think I'm here so early? We'll start calling everyone right away."

"We?" she queried.

"Well," he said modestly. *"The Ripper of London,* hard-cover by yours truly, is in the top ten," he told her casually, pulling the actual paper from his back jeans pocket and tossing it on the table.

"Matt, really?" she inquired, excited for him. He already had the Arts and Entertainment section opened to the right page. His book, number eight, had been circled in bright red, and the word *yeah!* had been written around it several times. "Congratulations!" she told him.

"Thanks!" he grinned happily.

"So . . . you're higher up. Why am I having the party?"

"You have the nicer apartment."

"You think?"

"Town house in an actual old antebellum colonial with a French restaurant right next door that serves the best desserts known to man? Beautiful, flower-filled, vined brick balcony on the second floor overlooking the street, with a view of a great jazz club and beautifully kept streets? Um. Let me rethink this. I have a third-floor walk-up in a part of town where they tell the tourists not to go. Yes. I've thought it through. You have the nicer apartment. You have the party."

"You could move," she told him.

"Are you kidding? I live next to the best, craziest voodoo practitioners I have ever met. My neighbors are totally insane. I love them all. Including the one-eyed, one-balled Jack Russell owned by old Mammy Louise upstairs."

"He pees on your shoes all the time."

"How mad can you get at a one-balled dog?"

"I have nothing against the little fellow; he never pees on me. And hey, I like your place myself," she assured him. "You were the one complaining."

"I wasn't complaining. Yours is simply the better place for a party."

"Fine. I'm happy to have a party. I'll invite everyone."

"Just call your sister." He flushed. "I already made a few phone calls."

She arched a brow. He grinned. "Well, you had to agree. You had to be excited. You had to want to celebrate!"

The waiter brought more coffee and beignets. Matt pushed the basket toward her. "Fresh and warm!" he said hopefully.

She pushed the basket back. "I've had plenty. Thank you."

He accepted her refusal, quickly gobbling down one of the powdered-sugar-covered breakfast rolls. He let out a little sound of sensual pleasure at the taste of the food, and licked his fingers.

"I'll buy the caviar," he told her.

"Good. You should. I don't like the stuff, and neither do you, so if you want it, you go find it."

"You'll do the champagne?"

"I will."

He snuffed a second beignet in his mouth, chewed, and swallowed in seconds flat. He gulped his coffee and rose.

"You're in a hurry," she said.

"I have to speak with my agent. Strike while I'm hot. I've got work at home, and bills to pay, and caviar to buy."

"What time am I having our party?" she asked him.

"Eight. After dinner—didn't want you to have to cook."

"How kind."

"Not at all. It was just fast thinking," he said.

"Chips and dips and—"

"A few desserts from the French restaurant would be nice."

"I'm sure they will be."

"Don't forget the little éclairs, okay?"

"I'll try not to."

He grinned and started to weave his way through the tables and the crowd to the street. Realizing she still had his paper, Jade called him back.

"Matt! Your *USA Today*!"

"Go ahead. Keep it. I bought twenty of them!"

She glanced down at the listings again. She had to admit that she was pleased. And naturally she was proud of Matt. He was making his way to the top in a tough world.

She sipped her fresh cup of coffee, not in such a hurry herself this morning. She wondered if she would invite Rick. Sergeant Rick Beaudreaux. He knew everyone in the group; they knew and liked him. She'd been dating him now for three months. He was everything she'd been looking for all of her life—until now.

What the hell was the matter with her? she wondered.

He really was wonderful. Beautiful blue eyes, sandy blond hair, bronze, muscled physique. All exterior, of course, but he was simply an all-around great human being, pleasant, soft-spoken, with the easy disposition of a confident person. He had worked Drugs in Miami before returning to New Orleans, the city of his birth. He told her that he had worked Homicide for a while, but now he worked Drugs again, spending a lot of time with kids in the schools, and also doing press releases for the department. He was polite; he was kind. He was clean—and always smelled good and inviting. He danced, biked, Rollerbladed. . . . He liked Sunday walks—around Sunday football, of course, but that was okay. He would miss a game when necessary. He liked a drive in the country, a picnic in the cool days of autumn. He had a smile that could devastate; he really cared for her, admired her work, and was always willing to pitch in—no matter how tired he might be.

He hadn't said so yet, but he must be wondering why

she wouldn't sleep with him. Why she didn't seem quite ready.

She wondered that herself.

"Yes, I'm inviting him," she murmured aloud.

A woman, a tourist who appeared to be from the north—she had very white legs, a sunburned nose, and was wearing a straw hat—looked at her oddly from a nearby table. "Sorry!" Jade said, and grinned.

The woman grinned back. "I talk to myself all the time, honey. You get better answers that way!"

Jade nodded and turned her attention back to the newspaper. Yes, she was inviting Rick. When the others were gone, Rick would stay. She didn't want to lose him. Not that he seemed to be pressuring her. She had told him what had happened in Scotland. He was a cop. He had understood. It had all been traumatic.

She hadn't told him about the dreams, though. . . .

She took a big swallow of coffee. She was having him stay. That might take care of the dreams. Maybe she was a victim of her own Victorian frustration. Too bad they didn't have a psych major in their crowd.

And then again, maybe not. She wasn't so sure she wanted to share her dreams with anyone.

The coffee was good. Still hot.

She set down the Arts and Entertainment section of the paper and picked up the front page.

Her heart seemed to stop right there in her chest.

The headline read: SLAUGHTER IN THE BIG APPLE; RITUAL KILLINGS STUN RESIDENTS

He watched her from across the street.

It was easy enough to do so.

She sat out in the open-air section of the café, near the street, near the sun. There was a roof over the outer section of the café, but she sat as close to the street as she could, and she tilted her face toward the sun frequently.

She loved the sun, the brightness. She smiled when it touched her face, the planes of which were delicate and beautiful in a perfect, classical sense of the word. He could remember the smell of her flesh, the softness of her skin. Her perfume, subtle in the darkness and the shadows. To him, she was such a beacon that he knew where she had been every second.

She had beautiful eyes, wide open now to the daylight. Blue eyes, deep eyes, touched with a hint of green. *Sea eyes,* he thought with a strange shudder. They were framed by flyaway brows and hair the color of sunshine and shadow itself, light brown, highlighted with natural streaks of pure gold and here and there a strand of red. So familiar. So different, and yet . . .

Maybe it was the color of her eyes. So much like the sea.

Like a cat, she moved slightly—and sensually—to the light. She obviously loved the outside, the heat of the sun.

He sat inside, where the doors were closed, where the air conditioner hummed, where the light from a cheap bulb illuminated the menu and the inner world of the little restaurant. Dark glasses protected his eyes, but from the glare of day, not from her. It was simple logistics. He could watch her. She could not see him.

He had followed her for a few days now.

Funny, the temptation to do so had been there a long time.

He had resisted. Until now.

Because his enemies were surfacing again.

She had asked him once if he knew this city.

Did he know it? Yes, certainly. Very well. It was one of his favorite places. It had been easy to find her. He knew where she lived. Knew who her friends were, where she went, what she did. He knew her habits. And if *he* knew . . .

Others could know as well.

"More coffee?"

He looked up. His waitress, an easy smile on her pretty face, had made the inquiry. She was young, with short blond hair, big brown eyes, well-muscled legs—and a uniform that showed them off very well. Once upon a time she would have been as delectable and tempting a treat to him as a truffle to a chocoholic. She wasn't from New Orleans. He'd learned, over the years, to place accents, especially American accents, rather well.

"Yes, more coffee, great. Thanks."

She poured it, smiling. "You're not from around here," she told him.

"No," he agreed, allowing a smile. He lifted his cup. "Neither are you. Pittsburgh?" he asked.

Her eyes widened. "How did you know?"

"It's a fairly easy one."

"Well, you're right." She was surprised at first, and then distrustful. "Hey, my folks didn't put you up to this, did they?"

"Put me up to this . . . ?"

"Watching me, following me?"

She was staring at him suspiciously. He grinned, shaking his head. "No. I wasn't watching you or following you. I'm afraid I don't know your folks."

She blushed furiously. "Sorry. I'm really sorry. I just . . . I'm going to Tulane. They think it's a party school. I love it, and I'm serious, and I'm working hard . . . and they think the better schools are back north."

He felt rather at a loss. "Ah. You're doing well at Tulane?"

"Dean's list," she said proudly.

"Stick to it, then. Your folks will see the light."

She nodded, still embarrassed. Then she smiled. "You're not even from this country," she told him.

"Not originally."

She offered him a hand. "I'm Cathy."

He accepted the intro, but hesitated slightly. "Call me Luke."

"Luke." She said the name as if she were tasting it. "Well, nice to have you here, and I hope I didn't make too much of a fool of myself." She studied him a moment, grinning. "You're too pale to be a Southerner, too, you know."

"Actually, I have a lot of friends from the North who look like Floridians or Californians—tanning beds," he told her.

"Right. Of course. Well . . . be seeing you, Luke."

"You bet."

She walked on by. He sipped his coffee, staring across the street again.

Something had happened. She was standing up. Her coffee cup had spilled; she hadn't noticed. She was staring down at . . .

He had to rise himself to see. A horse-drawn carriage bearing a rowdy family wheeled between them on the street.

He threw money down on the table—way too much, but he was sure Cathy could use it—and exited the restaurant. He hurried across the street.

She was gone.

He walked to where she had stood, and saw the headlines on the newspaper strewn over the table, covered in the spilled coffee.

"You're taking this far too seriously!" Shanna called to Jade.

Jade walked back into the living room/dining room, where Shanna was busy folding napkins for the buffet table.

In a light cotton blouse and form-hugging jeans, her sister was beautiful. She had tawny hair, the color of pure honey, with sun streaks thrown in. Her eyes were huge and deep blue. She was Jade's junior by just one year, and though they had fought like cats and dogs through eighteen years of home life, they had become best friends when Jade left the family colonial in the Garden District for college in New York City. Shanna had gone to UCLA the next year, but after obtaining degrees, they had both returned to New Orleans. Shanna had modeled her way through school and still did photo shoots, but to her own surprise, she had found out that, like her sister, she loved the written word more than anything else. She had dabbled with screenplays, sold a few, then fallen head over heels in love with Tolkien and turned to writing novels in the fantasy genre. She was a financial realist, and quick to drag Jade into print work when it was available, which was fine with Jade—she liked the extra income. Not that they were in danger of being destitute; though their mom had passed away from pneumonia when Jade was sixteen, their father was still living in the house in the Garden District, and making a decent income as a newspaper man. He had remarried, and so Jade and Shanna now had brothers at last—two-year-old twins Peter Jr. and James, or Petey and Jamie. Peter MacGregor continued to adore his daughters, and his new wife, Liz, was willing to turn somersaults to make them a full family. Still, neither girl wanted to rely on her father—he now had two new babes to get through to college and adulthood. They had both worked to get through college, and their work ethic was a good one. Jade had also wanted her publishing concern to be her venture and her venture alone—except that she had been more than happy to bring her sister in on it. Other than the devastating loss of her mother, she'd had a life filled with normalcy and love, and she knew that she was lucky.

Lucky, yes.

She had a great family.

And she'd survived a slaughter.

"Shanna, did you read—actually read—that article?"

Shanna set down a napkin and stared at her. "Yes. Four people were brutally murdered in New York City. Jade, do you know how happy New Yorkers would be if they could say that murder almost never happened there?"

Jade sighed. "Murders happen. Yes, we know that. But murders in a graveyard? Corpses found naked, torn to shreds—and beheaded!—on the gravestones?"

"There are very sick people in this world, Jade." Shanna turned back to the napkins.

"It could be related," Jade insisted, heading back into the kitchen for champagne glasses. When she returned, Shanna wasn't folding napkins. She was leaning back against the antique buffet, waiting for Jade to return.

"Jade, when you came home from Scotland, you really scared me. I thought we were going to have you under psychiatric care for the rest of your life. You were convinced that evil creatures came to life out of the graves—"

"Wait!" Jade said, lifting a hand. "I woke up hysterical; I know that. So frightened I didn't know what happened. I said many things that were very wild. But Shanna, I awoke in a shroud—on a gravestone! They never caught the people. Don't you think they might be the same?"

Shanna looked as if she didn't want to answer. Then she said, "I've heard that they have excellent Homicide detectives in New York City. Not to mention the fact that the FBI will be in on it all."

"But maybe I can help in some way."

"How? By drawing attention to yourself? By saying, 'Hey, here I am, guys; you missed me last time!' Jade, I just . . .'"

"What?"

Shanna shook her head. "Do you really remember anything? Could you really help? It's not as if they have any suspects now." She hesitated. "I read it, really read it. Yes, I see why you're upset. Hell, no, I don't want you involved again."

Jade shrugged. "It's unnerving."

"I agree," Shanna said. She studied Jade, then grinned. "So sleep with the cop. Heaven knows, I've been thinking you are entirely insane for a long time now, holding that puppy off! Honey, he is . . . yummy."

"Oh, really? You think?"

Shanna sighed impatiently. "Well, I don't know it for a fact, but I sure am assuming. He's cute as hell. He's got a steady income. He's built like the Hulk. And he's not even a jerk or an asshole. If I had him, I guarantee you I wouldn't risk letting him go."

Jade smiled. "Shanna, men trip over themselves to get near you. Cute ones. Rich ones. Built-like-Hulk ones."

"Yeah, but the ones after me thus far have been assholes. Sleep with the cop. You get good guard coverage during the night, and a bunch of orgasmic pleasure as well."

"I've been thinking about it."

"Good for you."

"You invited him tonight, right?"

"Yes, I did."

Shanna started folding napkins again. "When's the group coming?"

"Eight."

"Is Matt's head as big as a pumpkin yet?"

Jade laughed. "No, he's like a little kid, all excited. He's buying caviar, despite the fact that he hates it."

Shanna grinned, then turned back to Jade. "And you! Hey, am I glad I'm a partner in MacGregor Publishing Company, L-T-D. All right!"

"Thank you, ma'am. Thank you. Soon we'll be publishing you, with your fiction."

Shanna laughed. "No, thank you, not soon. I want to stick with the big commercial guys at first, get zillions of readers—and hit the lists topside like our buddy."

"Hm. There are people who think you should work long and hard and pay lots of dues to do that."

"And there are people who pick up Lotto tickets off the floor and become millionaires overnight," Shanna said. "Let's pop a bubbly, though. I'm restless. In the mood for champagne."

Jade shrugged. "All right." She headed back into the kitchen once again.

"Hey!" Shanna called after her.

"Yeah?"

"We're celebrating tonight. We're not going to get psychotic over what happened in New York!"

"No, we're not going to get psychotic over what happened."

He knew her address.

He had come before.

He stared up at the balcony for several long moments. He felt the breeze touch his cheeks, felt the night, the gentle, gentle kiss of the moon.

The doors to the balcony were open. The breeze stirred the curtains there.

He could go up. Touch the night there on the balcony. Know more.

He would watch. Stand sentinel.

He closed his eyes, then opened them, aware that she had come out to the balcony. Oddly enough, he felt that she was looking for him.

He stepped back into the shadows.

She leaned her arms on the railing, rested her chin on

her hands, just staring down to the street. *Let me in,* he thought.

She would have done so.

No. Stay away.

There had been a time when he had known a pain and fury and an absolute sense of power that would have allowed him any action. He'd always had a certain restraint, an ability to rule his world, and himself. But he might well have taken what he wanted: a tease, a taste, no great harm done. There and then gone . . .

He stayed in the shadows.

Watching.

He had come to . . .

Guard. To protect.

Then . . .

He felt it. The strange disturbance.

And he knew. He closed his eyes.

Yes. They were in the city. There had been a time when he felt any rift, any change, any disturbance. He could have summoned any of their own kind, settled disputes, spoken the law, and his word and would have been the end.

But now . . .

She was free. Sophia, with her wretched—but powerful—fool Darian. They walked the world again. And they were able to hide from him, despite the damage he had done—again—on that night in the old homeland. And he could only think, *She has found the talisman, the locket, and I must somehow wrest it back!*

Jade MacGregor stood on the balcony, looking out to the night. She lifted her hair from her neck, feeling the breeze against her flesh, then let it fall back.

He had to leave. To take action. The feeling of upheaval was growing stronger and stronger.

Why were they here, in this city?

He had not meant to come back here, no matter what his feelings for New Orleans. The not-too-distant past was still keen in far too many memories.

In his own.

What had finished had been just that—finished. He had played his part then, and moved on, only vaguely aware of the force reemerging. Reckless, harsh . . . ironfisted, iron willed. He had changed; he had not changed. No man was immune to those around him. He had learned. The world, in the light, out of the light, taught the simple lessons of survival.

He was evil himself.

But by all the fires of hell and damnation, there was one evil he would not allow to walk again.

There she stood. The American girl. Jade.

I wish I could touch you, he thought. *Just touch you. Feel . . . Remember.*

The disturbance was growing, becoming ever stronger. If he closed his eyes, concentrated, felt his power . . .

He could see . . .

His enemies were busy.

Time was now of the essence.

He turned into the darkness.

And toward the evil he knew too well.

"But did you see *this*?"

Renate DeMarsh, a tenant in another part of the old antebellum house and the creator of the *Miss Jacqueline* mystery series, had come to the party armed with a pile of New York papers. Shanna had tried to stop her at the door; Renate had barreled on in.

At thirty-eight she was respected and had acquired critical acclaim for her mysteries, referred to in the genre as cozies. Cozies were great. They were the mysteries solved by the fireside by a sweet, gray-haired grandmother. They were loved and cherished by readers. Renate was petite and beautiful, with platinum hair and Liz Taylor blue-violet eyes. She was constantly on talk shows. Seven of her fifteen novels had been optioned for television and feature films—none had as yet been made. Although she lived well, Renate was frustrated. Her novels, though popular and acclaimed, still hadn't made her the fortune she thought she deserved. She liked to tell Matt that he wrote sick books for far too much money, while she wrote good, quality, literary books for far too little money. Her comments never offended Matt—he was very fond of making money and didn't give two figs about talk shows. Still, he admitted that sure, he'd like her critical acclaim, and she'd turn around and tell him that she'd like his cash flow. They were great commiserators for one another.

But now Matt was annoyed. This was, after all, his big celebration as well, and it was filled with nothing but talk about the murders in New York—and those Jade had survived in Scotland.

"Renate, I hadn't even meant for Jade to see what happened!" Matt said. "I forgot about the headlines when I left her the paper."

"Yeah. Pumpkin head!" Shanna murmured.

"What?" Matt said.

"Never mind," Jade said quickly.

"No, no, no," Renate said impatiently. She stood before him, hands on hips, very dignified and regal—she had a flair for just the right clothing. Her eyes were large and sharp, demanding that she receive her just attention, and she was determined that Jade was going to read every word in the articles on the murders.

"It's important that Jade read all about this!" she said indignantly.

"Why?" Shanna demanded.

"The same sick people could be involved."

"Oh, Renate—" Matt began.

"You people all deal in the fantastic," she interrupted sternly. "Whereas I deal with real police procedure. There's always a motive, you know."

"Yes, but there are cult members all over the world," Jenny Danson put in. She was pretty, buxom, and plump, and, like Matt, almost always cheerful and pleasant. A mother and nurse for twenty years before she ever started writing, she had made a quick success with stories about the struggle between career and family and the foibles of everyday life. Nothing got Jenny down.

And now she was facing Renate. She wasn't going to allow any of them to tear down Jade's hard-won grip on normalcy. "Oh, now, Renate, you don't read newspapers any better than the rest of us! You're not a homicide detective or a behavioral scientist. Jack the Ripper is gone, Bundy is dead, but there will be more serial killers. New Orleans was ravaged by a monster not long ago at all! They are not all going to be the same, and they are not all going to be after Jade."

"Did I suggest such a thing?" Renate demanded.

"Well, sort of," said Danny Thacker. A lean young man, he *looked* the part of the starving artist; Danny had published several papers and some articles and stories in magazines, but he hadn't yet managed to sell his novel.

He did work part-time for the coroner's office. A good credential at the moment.

"I suggested no such thing, Daniel Thacker," Renate said firmly. But she looked at him and smiled. He helped Renate out a lot—he didn't seem to mind that she had an ability to use him. He liked Renate, and he liked being with her. Why she chose to be with him didn't matter.

"Renate, come on, seriously, we can all read, and we all know what happened. You'll scare Jade!" Matt said.

"Knowledge isn't going to scare me," Jade said. "*Not* knowing things is very scary."

"But there's surely no need to know more about New York City," supplied Todd, Jenny's equally cheerful husband. "Jade, you're in your home city, you know. In your home."

"With us," Jenny added.

"Oh, boy, now there's a piece of security!" Shanna said lightly.

"You all are getting into a tizzy!" Renate argued. "Jade is right, and Jade is sensible. Forewarned is forearmed, I always say."

"Yes, you do. Over and over again in every book," Matt noted.

Renate cast him a withering glare. "All right, all of you," she insisted. "Just let Jade see this one article. After that I'll say no more. She can decide for herself whether she should worry or not. You know, I have a friend with a large bulldog. A pit bull. One of the meanest I've ever seen."

"All pit bulls are not mean," Matt protested.

"This one is. And it would probably maul each and every one of *us* to a pulp, dear," Renate said.

"Renate, Matt, mean or not mean, I'm not getting a pit bull," Jade said.

"Jade," Danny commented, "those little cheese-puff things are delicious. Did you make them?"

"No, they're from the restaurant below."

"Wow."

Again, Renate sighed.

"The hell with the cheese puffs! Jade, I mean it; it's important—read this!"

Jade arched a brow. The others fell silent. She stepped forward and picked up the article that Renate had indicated.

She read about the murders. Black-and-white, no-nonsense, nonsensationalist reporting. Cold, almost. Blood and guts, horror and terror—stone cold. *The facts, ma'am, just the facts.* And then she saw *the* fact that Renate had been so determined she notice: the list of the dead.

And the name Hugh Riley. It seemed to jump out at her. It seemed to scream.

"Hugh Riley!" she said it out loud. And she remembered him. The boy with the mile-wide shoulders who had known his history, quiet most of the evening, coming to life when he knew all about Countess Báthory. She remembered his face, his eyes, his walk. . . .

He had survived that night in Scotland. He, too, had been found in a shroud among the gravestones.

He had been found among the gravestones once again. In New York.

Only this time . . .

His head had been missing.

Chapter Two

Cathy Allen left the restaurant late that evening, long after dark.

She worked most mornings, and a few lunch shifts, but this was the first time she had ever helped out with the dinner rush. But Loren and Jeffrey had both called in sick, and so she had stayed. She was missing a class, but it was Spanish, and thanks to a summer in Spain she had an excellent grasp of the language, so she wasn't too worried. She needed the money more than the class, since she was doing school on scholarships and what she could make working—and Tulane wasn't cheap.

Her last table was a single guy. He didn't seem too young—more than college age—but neither was he old. He was dressed in black jeans and a black denim jacket, and though it was getting dark, he was wearing sunglasses.

His hair was reddish, he had freckles, and he was decent when she spilled a little of the wine he had ordered, smiling and licking the drop off his hand.

"I'm so sorry."

"It's cool."

"Thanks."

"The management give you a hard time here?" he inquired. She realized he had an accent. It was her day for foreigners.

"No, they're fairly decent, but no one likes it when the customers complain."

"I guess not. Hey, you know anything about the groups around here who give tours?" he asked.

"Well, there are a few companies at the moment. Some have been here forever. Some come and go. Folks like ghost stories. And we've had lots of grisly murders here in New Orleans."

"So I've heard," he said, still smiling.

"This time of year, with Halloween coming up, there may be a lot of new tours going on."

"Yeah, maybe. Hey, why don't you go ahead and give me my check? I saw you talking to that girl over there before, telling her you needed to get going, that you were exhausted."

"You heard me?" she said incredulously.

"Yeah."

"I must have been talking louder than I thought. I didn't mean to be offensive."

"You weren't. You've been helpful."

"Oh, about the tours—"

"Yeah." He shrugged. "I'm an out-of-work actor. Getting some dramatic storytelling work at the moment would be fun."

"Most of the groups make you take a test to prove you know the history and can tell the stories."

"Oh, I know history. And I can spin a good yarn. Give me my check, so you can get out of here." He smiled broadly. "You need a ride anywhere?"

"Oh . . . I . . . uh . . ." she stammered. He was pleasant enough, but she knew better than to accept a ride with a stranger.

"Never mind—bad question," he told her. He took his check from her fingers and gave her some money. "I'll be seeing you," he told her.

"Thanks," she said.

He started walking away. She realized how much money he had given her. She turned to thank him.

He was already gone. As if he'd disappeared into thin air.

Twice that day she'd gotten lucky with men.

Or so she thought.

When she stepped outside, the streets were still busy. It was New Orleans. The streets were always busy.

Jazz always played.

She loved that about New Orleans.

The problem was, of course, that she had a bit of a long trek home. She had a car, an old—very old—Chevy Nova. Bought for a mere one hundred dollars, it was good for the few miles a week she drove between the college and the French Quarter.

She had to park it outside of the Quarter because space inside was so very dear. She couldn't begin to afford a garage. And so she left the bustling tourist area of the old sector each day for streets beyond that weren't considered at all safe. During the daytime, they were all right. But at night . . .

Today her car was almost all the way down by the cemeteries. They didn't usually freak her out. In fact, she loved the history of the place. Not that Pennsylvania didn't offer history—it certainly did. But New Orleans was just so unique. The different accents, the different cultures, the weird, aboveground vaults . . .

So haunting in the moonlight.

Moonlight that played with shadow.

There were clouds overhead. Every now and then the streets were pitched into darkness.

She was halfway toward her car when she first heard the footsteps.

Not her own. She had been listening to that swift, rhythmic echo since she had started out.

She clutched her purse tightly to her chest. *Great.* She was going to get mugged the first day she'd made real big bucks working. Both the solo guys—the one first thing in the morning and then her last customer of the evening— had been generous to a fault. The first guy had put down a twenty to pay for a cup of coffee!

After working all day and running herself ragged, she had about a hundred bucks. Good, necessary money for her.

Clip, clip. She swung around, trying to see who was following her.

Your life is worth more than any amount of money!

She could almost hear her mother saying the words. She bit into her lower lip. They were true words. She had never realized how true until this very moment.

She quickened her pace.

She heard the footsteps again. She spun around.

Spun back.

There . . .

Behind her! Black shadow.

No! There—in front of her! Shadow, flying. No, the moonlight, haunting, teasing . . .

Then again . . .

Clip. Clip . . . The sound of footsteps. Furtive. Menacing.

"Hey!" she cried out suddenly. "I carry pepper spray!"

Pepper spray? What kind of an idiot was she?

"Pepper spray—and a fifty-seven Magnum!" she shouted.

Laughter . . .

Did she hear laughter, or was it a haunting echo in her own mind?

She looked and looked. . . .

Spun around.

There was no one, no one . . .

Shadows, laughter, footsteps . . .

She began to run.

And the *clip* . . . *clip* . . . *clip* came faster and faster, too. The shadow . . . it flew, rose like a giant black bird. It swept into a canopy above her head.

The moon, the glorious moon, covered by shadow, darkness falling . . .

And then . . .

The touch.

She began to scream.

Rick Beaudreaux arrived late, and he looked tired, Jade noted immediately.

It was obvious that he'd seen the newspaper article. His eyes caught Jade's quickly, and there was a question.

He knew what had happened in Scotland, and he had assumed that Jade was going to be upset.

But he had been greeted at the door not just by Jade, or even by Jade and Renate, but by a small throng of people. Every one of Jade's celebrating guests—the Wednesday Eve Group—was there to watch him.

His brows rose as he remained in the doorway; he looked at Jade and smiled, and her heart pounded a little bit— he really was a perfect heartthrob, a guy with all the right stuff. *Yes exactly, he is the right stuff!* she told herself somewhat angrily. She was glad to see him; she wasn't glad to see him. He was everything she had wanted in life . . . and strangely, she felt as if a relationship with him would be like betraying someone else. *Who, idiot?* She didn't know. But she'd had the most bizarre feeling, standing on the balcony earlier. As if someone was out there. She almost felt . . . touched. The breeze had been almost unbearably sensual. *Yes, I am waiting. . . .*

Alone, she had almost said the words out loud. Then she had heard Shanna calling her in and she had felt like an idiot, having sexual fantasies with a breeze when a perfectly good—no exceptionally fine—man wanted in on her life. Tonight.

Yes, tonight, definitely. None of this insane stuff in her head!

"Come in—if they'll let you," she told Rick, her lips curling into a smile.

He grinned, glad to see that she seemed to be okay.

"Hi, guys."

"Don't 'Hi, guys' us," Renate commanded immediately. "I know you're a cop and that you can read, and that you can see between the lines. These little darlings are pooh-poohing everything I say. And Jade is scared—"

"I'm not exactly scared," Jade murmured.

"She'll be psychotic if Renate keeps it up," Shanna said dryly.

"She needs to be careful," Renate said.

"Hey, champagne, Rick? We're celebrating here tonight," Matt reminded him.

"Champagne, sure, great, why not?" Rick said. "Congratulations, Matt. Big-time. You're the next best thing to knowing Stephen King."

"I'm far humbler," Matt said mildly.

"King's written far more books," Renate noted.

"So what do you think, Rick?" Shanna asked.

He hesitated, staring at Jade. He shrugged. "I think New York is far away."

"One of the survivors from Scotland was killed in New York," Jade said. "Hugh Riley."

"Hey!" Matt suggested suddenly, gulping down a bite of éclair. "Maybe it's just the same name, and not the same man."

"Strange things do happen," Jenny Dansen told them. "We were just reading an article in a magazine—Todd and I, that is—about a man who survived two plane crashes and then died in a third. I mean, really, such things do happen. Chance, circumstances. I mean, obviously the planes weren't out to get him or anything."

"The Vikings believed that our futures were woven from the moment of our births," Danny said. "That's why they were so brave. Fear would avail them nothing. What was going to happen to them would happen to them. And then, of course, they would simply go on to Valhalla and live there in their heaven. Not a bad concept, eh?"

"How old was the guy you met in Scotland, Jade?" Jenny asked.

"Twenty-one or twenty-two."

Renate picked up a piece of newspaper. "Big-time coincidence. This one happened to lose his head at the age of twenty-three."

"I can check into all of it," Rick said. "We don't need to stand here and speculate."

They all stared at him.

He cleared his throat. "I meant later. We're have a party tonight, right?"

"Right. To success, in all its forms and guises."

Shanna came forward, carrying a crystal flute. "Right. Champagne for the cop!"

"Why, thank you, Miss MacGregor."

"My pleasure. A toast! To Jade, and to Matt!"

"Hear. Hear!" Danny exclaimed.

"To thrills and chills and commercial success!" Jenny told Matt. "And to history and our own evil dead and the great cathedrals and churches where they attempted redemption!" she continued, lifting her glass to Matt and then to Jade.

"Indeed!" Danny laughed. "To my rich and famous friends! May their luck—and their talent, of course—rub off on me.!"

"Danny, you are wonderfully talented," Jade said.

He grinned with good humor. "Thanks. I think so, too. But even if no one else ever does, the two of you will still act like you know me, right?"

"How can you all stand there and act so silly when something so terrible happened!" Renate exclaimed with disgust. "And you, Rick! You're a cop."

Rick drew in a deep breath, his eyes steady as they fell on Renate. "That's just it, Renate. I am a cop. I either see or hear about awful things every day. You just keep on living and enjoying life, because you know it's fragile."

"Can't you find out more now—"

"Renate!" Jade admonished.

"No," Rick said. "I have to go back in for a few hours tonight."

"You do? Why?" Jade asked. *No, you're kidding!* she thought. *I was finally going to ask you to stay, despite what . . .*

Despite what I felt on the balcony. Or maybe . . . just partially . . . because of what I felt on the balcony.

"There was a bad accident tonight just outside the French Quarter. I'm heading on down to the morgue to find out more about the kid involved."

"Kid?" Jade said softly.

"College kid. I need to find out if drugs were involved, deal with the family. . . ."

"Wow, what a shame," Danny said.

"What a downer," Matt added sorrowfully.

"Yeah, well, that's what I mean."

"Life's a bitch, and then you die," Renate announced.

"Mm, to some. Others say, Life's a bitch; then you get fucked by one; then you die!" Matt told her, smiling.

"Don't you just wish, pumpkin head," Renate said sweetly in return.

"I think I need some air," Jade said. Slipping her arm through Rick's, she eased him out to the balcony with her. She leaned against the brick rail, looking back.

"Oh, thank God, they're not following!" Rick said.

She grinned. "By God, they took the hint."

"And accepted it."

Some really great jazz was coming softly from a place across the street. The moon was high. October. It was a great fall night. Not cold, just cool.

Rick leaned against the brick as well, rolling his champagne flute in his hands, studying her eyes. "You really okay?"

"It was startling to read those headlines."

"Yeah. That is pretty bizarre. You know, Jade, the same people might be involved. They never caught the murderers in Scotland."

"Edinburgh to New York. Seems far-fetched, doesn't it?"

"Yes, and no. It depends. There are serious cults out there. You know that. And if someone backing such a thing has money . . ."

"And the murders occurred in a cemetery again."

"Yep." He watched her. "You don't spend your days crawling around cemeteries, do you?"

"Days . . . well, I admit, I do sometimes. It's hard to write about old cathedrals and churches without walking through a few old graveyards. So days . . . yes. Nights—no.

Not anymore. Rick, do you really think it could be the same people?"

"No, I don't really think so. But it's not impossible."

"That's so bizarre about Hugh Riley. If it is him."

"Well, there are lots of colleges in New York. You told me they were all college kids, remember? Frat fellows, football players, smokers, druggies, jokers."

"They were just kids. Wild kids," she told him.

"Unfortunately, the young are not immune to disaster— though they tend to think they are."

"I can't believe you have to go back to work tonight. I was . . ."

He moved closer, his eyes bright and expectant. "You were . . . ?"

She met his gaze squarely. "I thought you might stay."

"Oh, yeah?"

She nodded and grinned suddenly. "You know, you heard Matt; 'Life's a bitch; then you—' "

He interrupted her with a groan, then went to set the champagne flute on a wicker table. It fell from his fingers, crashed to the floor.

He swore.

She laughed. From inside, they heard the sudden sound of music. And laughter. The party was going to go on without them.

Shanna had seen to it, Jade was certain, that they wouldn't be followed.

"Your beautiful glass," he said.

"It's just a glass," she whispered.

"Right. The hell with it," he murmured, drawing her into his arms. His fingers threaded into her hair. He drew her against the hard warmth of his chest. She felt his heartbeat, felt it quicken. His fingers moved. His mouth found hers. They'd kissed before, petted before. He was good. Hard, demanding, sensual . . .

She kissed him back, moving against him, open-mouthed, ready, waiting, wanting. . . .

A sense of arousal.

It didn't come.

It should have! Damn, it should have, should have . . .

She didn't care. One way or another, it was going to happen.

He drew away from her, his eyes hard on hers. She felt air against the dampness of her lips. She met his gaze, her own heart thundering. *Please, God, don't let him see that there's nothing there; don't let him know that I'm answering him with a lie, that I'm losing my mind, wanting . . .*

"Come back when you finish," she told him.

"I could be really late."

"I don't care."

"Crack-of-dawn late. Into-the-A.M. late. And God knows, I shouldn't be with you. I shouldn't have kissed you. I'm coming down with something."

"A cold?"

"I guess. I'm just wiped out. Really tired." He shrugged awkwardly. "Can't seem to shake it off, but I—"

"I don't care if you have a cold."

"I wouldn't want to—"

"I'll take my chances."

"You don't mind me being really late?"

"I'll give you a key."

"It's a deal."

"Kiss me good-bye."

"I shouldn't. . . ."

"Let's live dangerously."

He grinned.

He kissed her again. It was stirring; it was passionate. The way he touched her, on a balcony, was almost indecent. . . .

He breathed deeply against her hair. "I think I'll go now. And I'll try to get back earlier."

She nodded, feeling numb. Hand in hand, they walked back in. Shanna had put on music. She was trying to teach Matt how to tango. Danny, slumped into an overstuffed antique chair, was giving instructions; Jenny and Todd were laughing, doing their best to follow the movements.

On seeing Rick and Jade, Danny leaped to his feet.

"Jade, I was hoping you guys would come back in. I needed to say thanks and good-bye."

"You're leaving already, too?" she asked him.

He nodded, looking at Rick. "I got paged. They need some extra help at the morgue."

"Oh."

The tango music came to a sudden halt as Shanna turned off the disc player.

"Well, it's a Thursday. Work night," Todd said. "I guess we should get going, too, eh, there, Ms. Voice of America?" he queried his wife.

"I suppose," Jenny said. "Jade, thank you." Smiling, she stepped forward, hugging Jade, kissing her cheeks. "Congratulations! And enjoy the moment. Don't start dwelling on the past, on anything bad!"

She gave Renate a stern glare.

Renate glared back. "Good night, Jenny."

"Good night, all," Danny said, taking his jacket from the ebony hall tree by the door, and exiting.

Rick followed him, telling Jade, "Might as well catch a ride with Danny." He brushed her lips with a brief kiss, paused, and kissed her once again.

He left with a grin.

Jade was sure her sister saw it.

The Dansens followed. Then Renate decided she had spent the evening with a group of pigheaded, dumb people, and announced she was leaving.

"I guess I'll get going as well," Matt said. "It was a great party, Jade. Thanks. And to both of us, really.'' He hugged and kissed her.

"Hey—take the caviar,'' Shanna suggested, making a face.

"Bring it to my place—I love the stuff,'' Renate said.

"Yeah? Are you actually inviting me to your place?'' Matt said.

"Don't go getting too excited—it's just across the main hall,'' Renate told him. He stood still, looking uncertain. Renate sighed. "Yes, I'm inviting you to my place. Bring the caviar. Hey, Jade, can we grab one of those last bottles of champagne?''

"Sure, knock yourselves out,'' she said, trying not to grin.

She couldn't help it—when the two left, she and Shanna looked at one another and burst into laughter.

"Shh!'' Jade covered her sister's mouth with her hand. "They'll hear you.''

"You shush!''

They both went silent, then started up again. Shanna swept a champagne bottle from a side table and swigged straight from it, then passed it on to Jade, who followed suit. They collapsed into the large central sofa side by side and passed the bottle back and forth.

"She takes herself so seriously!'' Shanna said.

"Renate?''

"Who else?''

"She can't help it. She feels unappreciated.''

"How can she? People rave about her all the time. She's the only one of us whom most people have ever heard of!''

"Because she does talk shows.''

"Yeah, well, that's good.''

"But how many people do you know who actually buy her books?'' Jade asked softly.

"Someone must buy them."

"Some people do. But not enough to make them real moneymakers."

Shanna lifted the champagne bottle. "You can't be judged in a literary world, dear girl, by how much money you make!" she said in perfect imitation of Renate.

"Which really means she wants more money."

"Why doesn't she just always admit it?"

"I don't know. We all want something we don't want to admit, I guess."

"I'm not at all averse to admitting what I want," Shanna said.

"And what's that?"

"A decent male." She looked at her sister and grinned. "I used to want a fabulous male. Now I just want a decent one. We're willing to settle for less and less as time goes by. Isn't that sad?"

"Shanna, you're twenty-four."

"Twenty-five next month."

"That's young."

"That's right. I want a life now, while I'm young, while I've got the energy to enjoy each and every second of it!"

"Shanna—"

"I want to meet, date, fall in love, get married—and have kids before I'm thirty. Okay, so I've got a little time left. But if I can't even find 'decent' to date, how am I going to find the love of my life to marry? Of course, I suppose I could just get married, have children—and get divorced, get rid of the bum, as seems to be the fashion these days. Or maybe the bum can just run out on me. But hey! You do have Mr. Perfect—and he's coming back, right?"

"Yeah, but late."

"Hell, I'm leaving."

"He's not here now."

"But you'll want to chill more flutes."

"He's a beer man at heart."

"So chill a stein. But get in that bubble bath. Make it special!"

"Of course, I intend to."

Shanna was already on her way to the door. Jade rose to follow her. Shanna kissed her cheek, gave her a hug, then stared into her eyes.

"What's wrong?"

"Wrong? Nothing."

"Are you afraid?"

"Of what? Oh! If you mean about the newspaper articles on the event in New York, no. I'm all right. Seriously."

"Of course. Your cop is coming back."

"Um."

"He is special."

"I know."

Shanna studied her another long moment. Jade felt as if her sister could read her mind, as if she somehow realized that . . .

She wasn't feeling a thing; she was just desperate to make it work.

Jade widened her smile. "Thanks, sis. Thanks for everything."

"Thank you. I can't wait to talk tomorrow! Call me the minute you're alone. I mean it!"

"I promise."

She closed the door on her sister. She leaned against it for a long moment. Then she locked the door and pushed away, determined.

She set steins in the freezer to chill.

Then she headed for the bathroom, determined to enjoy a good, long bubble bath.

She started the water. Hot steam rose as she studied the

various bath fragrances in the wicker toiletry cabinet. She chose an Oriental bath oil and poured it into the water.

She crawled in, closed her eyes, and leaned back. The heat permeated her. Silence surrounded her. She *felt* the silence as if it were as soft and sleek around her as the scented water. Sweet, sensual. As if it caressed. The water was luxurious; it lulled and seduced. She so nearly slept; she so nearly dreamed. There was a figure in her dream, walking through the mist and steam that rose above the tub.

You are there, in the water.

I am here.

I am coming.

I am waiting. . . .

The words weren't real, just part of the steam. But she could see him, the lover that she awaited. He strode with smooth, sleek confidence, he had the fluidity of a cat, a muscled cat, agile, sinuous, grand. . . .

"Come, yes, come to me. . . ."

She jumped, startling herself to full attention by speaking aloud.

The water was cooling.

The steam had faded.

"I'm going to drown in here," she said with exasperation. "Jesu, Jade what is the matter with you?"

She sat up, cupped her hands, and swept the scented bath oil around her, then rose, grabbed a big terry towel, dried off, and wrapped it around her. She saw her reflection in the mirror over the sink. She was pale and drawn.

"Am I losing it because I'm afraid?" she whispered to her reflection.

But she wasn't afraid—not to any kind of a panic point, certainly. With that thought, she opened the door to her bedroom, glad she had left the lights on in there. Nothing.

She walked out to the living/dining room, into the kitchen, then into the second bedroom—her home office.

She walked back to the doors leading to the balcony and thought back.

Yes, she had closed and locked them when Shanna left.

She tested the doors. Yes, still locked.

The front door was bolted.

Rick had a key.

With a sigh she walked back to the bedroom and turned on the television. One of the premier cable stations was showing the old Errol Flynn version of *Robin Hood*. She halfway listened to the movie as she contemplated the grave question of what to wear when Mr. Perfect spent the night for the first time. Short or long? Somewhat concealing or totally revealing? Flat-out sexy or subtly sensual?

Long, somewhat concealing, subtly sensual. She didn't really have anything out-and-out revealing. Amazing, when she lived in a land of adult-toy shops. She hadn't come upon the occasion to warrant such an outfit.

She did have a long, black, low-cut gown. Silk. Soft as a whisper. Perfect. Not too obvious. Of course, how much more obvious could she be? Still . . .

She doffed her towel, donned her gown, brushed her hair and her teeth, powdered, lotioned, and at last realized that she was nervous as hell.

She crawled into bed, determined to watch Errol Flynn. He had been a great Robin Hood.

Her eyes began to flicker. She had awakened early that morning. It had been a long day.

It was late. . . .

I really need to wait up! she admonished herself. She had given Rick the key, but . . .

This was it. A big night. A big, big night. She needed to be awake, to greet, to charm, to seduce, to know the man who could just be the rest of her life. . . .

Something just hadn't been right.

It would be right. She would make it right.

She was tired. So tired.

Concentrate on Robin Hood, she told herself.

Robin Hood. Errol Flynn was great. His leading lady a perfect foil . . .

Her eyes began to close. Too much champagne.

Or not enough . . .

Stay awake . . . stay awake. . . .

Daniel was accustomed to the morgue.

New Orleans could be a tough place.

He hadn't minded being called in to assist; he had learned the job, following the orders of the medical examiners, having the right tool at the right time.

There was no real pressure that he might make a horrible mistake.

He was good at his job, but it was a job. He needed the income from it, and he didn't mind odd hours when the M.E.s needed to work late, when something was so horrible it couldn't wait, when someone just felt they had a huge caseload and wanted to get cracking.

He'd seen old men and women, some as peaceful as if they slept, some contorted by the final pain of a heart attack, or racked by the ravages of cancer and emphysema.

He'd seen children, so sad.

Babies. Two that had been shaken to death by parents.

Murder victims. Husbands with knives in their gullets. (*No problem determining cause of death there, eh, Doc?*) Wives beaten black and blue. He'd seen it all in the three years he had worked there.

He'd seen it all.

No.

When the sheet was pulled off the young accident victim, he almost vomited on the spot.

He hadn't seen anything. He'd seen nothing at all.

Not until that moment . . .

Jade became slowly aware of a change . . . something different around her. Had she awakened in the night? If so, she didn't know why at first. The room around her remained in darkness, the only light in the room coming from the television. *Robin Hood* was no longer playing. Not unless they had added footage in which Robin and Marion were . . .

Sighs and whispers. A man and woman together. Making love.

Fog filled the room. She lay within it, wrapped within it. Soft and warm, it encased her like the silk. She heard music, a sound so soft it might have come from within her; the beat could have been her pulse. She had been waiting for him. *Yes.*

And he was there.

With her.

She felt him touching her, felt his face against her flesh, breathing in her skin. There was something incredibly sensual about the way he appreciated the scent of her, the feel, the taste. His fingers brushed her flesh, and they might have been a hundred degrees. She moved against him, amazed that it was so easy, astounded that she could want him so much. Her body rippled, ached, burned. His fingers moved, liquid lightning, touching, stroking, a seduction so slow . . .

"You're here," she whispered.

Should I be?

"I invited you."

You've been inviting me, you know. I shouldn't have come. I shouldn't be here. But you have invited me.

"I've waited; I've wanted you."

The silk moved against her. Silk and shadows and fog. She felt his weight, the brush of knuckles against her cheek, silk rubbing against her flesh, his body, the subtle power of his chest . . . his kiss. . . .

It aroused as she had never been aroused before. Life awakened within her. She felt *colors* all around her, shades of red and flame, searing, dancing, leaping against a field of fog and darkness. The coolness of mist and breeze touched her, fire lapped her, and the fire was his kiss, traveling the length of her. Fire, color, mist undulated; she felt his strength, his warmth, his chest. . . .

A pulse.

The beat of his heart.

No, the beat of her own . . .

Then . . .

Lightning.

The sun, the stars, the burst of a nova . . . Fire exploded within her; she couldn't breathe, couldn't think; the searing was sheer decadence, fierce, pulsating, undulating. . . . She could barely keep afloat in the sea of sensation, yet she was aware of a whispering. . . .

Why are you with me?

"Because you're perfect."

I'm far from perfect.

"Perfect, so decent . . ."

Dear God, no, I'm so far from decent you couldn't even begin to imagine. Nice? No, my sweet, don't go there. My sins are like the weight of the world. . . .

"You're not who I think you are."

I'm exactly who you think I am. You've seen, you've known. . . .

"No."

You can't close your eyes. . . .

But her eyes were closed. She shook her head. She didn't want to think or talk; she wanted to feel. The sun and the earth and the sky were within her, novas bursting, and she had never expected that anything could be so sensually, sexually, wildly . . . good.

She awoke drenched, and with memories that brought a flush to her cheeks and confusion to her heart.

The room was in shadow. It was very, very early in the morning, she thought sleepily. The sun hadn't quite come up.

She heard strange noises.

The television was still on.

Moving damp, tangled hair from her eyes, she squinted at the television. Yes. The soft porn that came on the respectable cable channel late at night was still going. She shook her head, amazed at herself.

Embarrassed.

She reached out, certain that Rick had to be next to her. She knew that he had arrived in the night, and that her fears had been ridiculous. He was perfect. Everything that she had wanted in a man. Bright, decent, and . . .

Could she face him?

"Rick . . ."

She stretched out a hand. He wasn't there.

Frowning, she started to rise. Her black gown was on the floor. Her covers were twisted halfway from the bed.

"Rick?"

Had he gotten up to make coffee? Or, since it was still nighttime for him, had he grabbed a beer and found one of the icy steins?

She crawled out of bed, hurried into the bathroom for her terry robe, and started back out to the living room.

"Rick?"

No answer.

Then she heard the key twisting in her lock.

She frowned.

Rick stepped in. He looked beat. Absolutely beat. She stared at him. He stared back. He fumbled with the collar of her terry robe.

"I'm sorry, so sorry."

"Rick?" Her voice was a bare whisper. "You've been here."

"I told you it would be late. Really late. Or early," he apologized. "I shouldn't have come here, Jade. It's so late, the night was awful. I'm getting sicker and sicker, I think. I can barely stand. I think I have to get home."

"Get home . . . but you . . . you haven't been here?"

"You just saw me open the door."

Her body went cold. Rigid. She thought she would fall.

"Jade?"

She barely heard his voice.

The world filled with . . .

Fog.

And she crashed to the floor.

Janice Detrick yawned.

She liked the early shift at the hospital, but this morning she was tired. Still, she wouldn't have traded her schedule for anything later, not even for a fair-size raise. She got off early—she was able to pick up her first-grade twins from school, have dinner, do homework, and even go shopping now and then. Granted, she shopped at the discount stores, but she valued her time. She was a single mother. Thanks to her own mother—who had raised six kids without a man in sight, cleaning house for rich white folks—she had gotten an education. She was a registered nurse with a good job, great kids—even if she, too, had made a foolish choice in men—and had an ever-abiding affection for her mother. Jennie Pritchard would never—no, never—go into a nursing home. Not while Janice had breath in her body.

This morning, though . . .

Getting moving was a little rough.

She'd seen some med techs downstairs at the emergency entrance; everyone had been talking about the awful accident that had nearly decapitated some college kid. Strange things were happening. *Look at those murders in New York.* Not that New Orleans couldn't be crazy. Mostly, nowadays, voodoo was a big tourist industry. But there were still those—her mother included—who saw it as pure religion, who believed in zombies, the power to raise the dead, to cast spells, throw curses—*do weird shit!*

Nursing wasn't weird, *thank God.* Just humdrum. She was a good nurse.

She went up to the third floor, where she worked in surgical care. The night crew was filling out paperwork, getting ready to leave. As usual, the incoming nurses chatted with the outgoing. They discussed their patients, new and old. "You have a new hernia in three forty-seven," Andrea, the girl she was replacing, told her. "Let's see—the tonsillectomy could have gone home yesterday, but the kid's a little wimp—whined all night. Told him whining would hurt his throat more; he didn't care."

"Oh, I can deal with him," Janice assured Andrea. She could. Her tonsillectomy was Tommy Hart, her twins' age. She teased him, laughed with him, and brought him little presents—today it was the newest kids' lunch toy from Burger King.

"Yeah, well, you're a saint."

"Not at all," Janice said. Andrea lifted a brow and turned back to her paperwork. "Most else is just status quo," she murmured.

Janice thought that she saw something.

A black shadow . . . sweeping past the nurses' station. She had the strange sensation of . . . wings. Great, sweeping, broad wings.

Shadows . . .

Silly. It was very bright here.

She started down the hall that angled to the left of the nurses' station. Now there were some shadows. The bright lights from the work area faded out here, and they hadn't started the whole let's-get-moving day yet; medicine runs and breakfast wouldn't begin for another half hour. Outside, the sun was still struggling to rise.

Still . . .

Something seemed to draw her down toward the supply room.

She stopped dead in the hallway.

There, right before her, not twenty feet away, stood a man. He seemed to be in shadow.

Or he *was* shadow.

Wearing a cloak? What was he doing, and who was he?

Mr. Clark, from 322, sleepwalking again? No, Mr. Clark was seventy if he was a day, and this fellow was young and virile. How could she tell from a damned shadow? she wondered.

He buckled over suddenly, like a man in serious pain.

She rushed forward, always a nurse. "Here, here, let me help you! What's wrong? We'll get you back to your room."

He had never been in a room, she was certain. If she'd ever seen him before—ever, even a glimpse of him!— she would have remembered him. He was so different. So compelling, so tall—striking, virile, attractive. . . .

Cold.

Cold as ice.

How did she know he was cold?

She could feel cold. Waves of cold.

He was pale, bruised. Stabbed? Bleeding?

"You're hurt," she said. Compassion overrode any sense of unease.

For a moment he smiled. An oddly charming smile. Chilling . . .

Charming.

"Shucks. You should see the other guy. And then . . . well you know. I thought I was okay, and I stopped to see this girl . . . too much exertion, huh?"

"Let me help you!"

She tried to get his arm around her shoulder. He really was charming. What a smile. She envied the girl. But then, he clenched his teeth.

"No! Get away!" he insisted, suddenly shaking his head fiercely. His voice was deep, rough, edgy—but commanding. He was accustomed to authority.

"You're hurt—"

For a moment she thought she saw his eyes, his face. She felt ice creeping around her. He was so ashen. He smiled again, but his smile faded.

His eyes were focused on her.

Focused on . . .

Her throat.

She felt a deep, swift shaft of fear along her spine, yet she was mesmerized. She thought he smiled still, despite that razor-sharp gaze he kept hard on her.

A rueful smile.

He hadn't meant to be seen, she thought.

She could feel her heart pumping. She could feel her veins. Pulsing. It was like . . .

Music.

Childhood stories came to her mind.

"Grandma! What gold eyes you have!"

"The better to see your veins with, my dear."

"Grandma! What big teeth you have!"

"The better to suck those veins dry!"

"Go!" he said gruffly, speaking at last. She couldn't move at first. Then, "Go!" he repeated. "Yes, I'm hurt; get help!"

He shoved her. She lurched forward, then stopped. He was crumpling to the floor. The strangeness she had felt faded. Help, she needed help. He was too big for her to handle.

Jasper, one of the male nurses, had just come in. He'd played football until a shoulder injury sidelined him for good. He was great friend, and his strength came in handy at the hospital.

"Jasper, quick, we've a patient, or maybe not a patient—" she said as she approached the nurses' station.

"What?"

"There's a man in the hall who is hurt—"

"A patient is up and staggering around?"

"Maybe he's not a patient; he's just a man—"

"He is or isn't a patient?"

"I'm not sure, damn it. Now, Jasper, there's a man in the hall hurt, and he's a big one. He's . . . he's too much for me. Help me."

"Sure, I'm coming." Jasper said, his dark eyes confused, but not doubting. He gave himself a shake, as if he'd realized he should have moved much faster. He followed Janice as she started back to find the man.

She came to a dead halt. He was gone. There was no one there. Nothing. Not a drop of blood, not a speck of torn flesh—not a hint of the man.

"Couldn't have been hurt too badly," Jasper commented.

"Jasper, I swear, he was here."

"I believe you. I guess . . . Hey, maybe he was a gunshot wound. He chickened out and disappeared. What was he? White man, black man? Kid? Senior? What did he look like, Janice? Maybe he's already a patient. Hell, maybe he's from the loony ward!"

Janice walked forward. "He couldn't have been a gunshot wound . . . there's not a speck of blood anywhere."

"Hey!" Jasper said suddenly. "Look."

The door to the supply room, always locked, was open. Drugs were kept in this particular room. And the blood they used for transfusions.

She looked at Jasper; he looked at her. They started forward together.

The supply room had been devastated. It looked as if a hurricane had gone through. Shelves had been broken, cabinets overturned, drawers emptied.

Yet . . .

Drug vials lay everywhere.

"Jasper . . ."

"Janice," he answered softly, and he looked at her, his dark eyes wide. "There's not a drop of blood left in here!"

Chapter Three

Soon after seven A.M., Lucian was seated at his table at the restaurant. His face was washed; his hair was neatly combed. His features betrayed weariness.

His eyes were wary.

Jade wasn't at Café du Monde, and Cathy had not come in to work.

He hadn't really expected either of them.

He had come here because of Daniel.

After the full light, weary and worn, he had spotted the young man leaving the morgue, and had followed him, knowing his association.

They liked the same restaurant.

He watched the young man. Time and again, Daniel dragged his fingers through his hair, then pressed his temples, then shook his head. He ordered coffee and eggs.

When the eggs came, he pushed them aside, stared at them, then covered them with his napkin.

As if giving them a decent burial.

Lucian's server came by. This morning it was a girl named Shelly. He asked about Cathy. No, she wasn't coming that morning. No, Shelly wasn't sure why.

Daniel noted the two of them talking. Lucian met Daniel's gaze. Daniel offered him a weak smile. "Hey, sorry, didn't mean to eavesdrop. Caught your accent. You're not from around here."

"No, not originally," Lucian agreed.

"British?" Daniel inquired.

"Scottish," Lucian said.

"Yeah, British."

"Ah, well, there is a distinction there—ask any Scot or Englishman," Lucian said lightly. He never answered questions, especially about his background—no matter how innocuous.

Daniel sipped coffee, his hands shaking. "Scottish," he said, agreeing. He would have agreed to anything. He wanted company. Someone to talk to.

"You're from here?" Lucian asked politely.

He nodded. "Well, close enough. Metairie. Just up the road."

"It's a good town."

"I used to think so." Daniel hesitated a moment, then looked somewhat longingly at Lucian. "I had a rough night," he said.

"Really?"

He nodded, still looking hopeful. Lucian indicated the chair opposite him at his table. "Feel free to come tell me about it."

Daniel got up so quickly his chair toppled over. He reddened, picked it up, straightened it, grabbed his coffee cup, and moved over to join Lucian.

He offered his hand. "Daniel Thacker," he said, introducing himself.

"Lucian. DeVeau," he added after a moment. The name tasted strange on his lips. He hadn't used it in a long time.

"That's not Scottish," Daniel commented.

"French—Norman, rather. Around a thousand years ago, it seems, my family moved north. A great-great—I don't know how many greats—grandfather left Reims on a merchant ship, was attacked by Norsemen, and joined them in their pursuit of Celtic gains. He settled there."

"Cool," Daniel said, staring at him blankly.

Lucian grimaced inwardly. He seldom offered information about his surname. He had given Daniel more than he was actually ready to comprehend.

"Have I seen you before?" Daniel asked.

"Maybe. I come here sometimes."

"So do I. I feel like I know you. Wow, that sounds strange, doesn't it? I don't mean anything by it. I'm not trying . . . I mean, I have a girlfriend. Well, not really anymore, she kind of broke it off, but what I mean is—"

"It's all right," Lucian said, lifting a hand, amused.

Daniel nodded.

"I'm trying to be a writer. I think I'm pretty good. My friends think I'm pretty good. And they're writers themselves, successful ones." He ran his fingers through his hair again. He had the start of a wispy, pale blond beard on his cheeks. His clothes—jeans and a tailored cotton shirt—were neat and clean, but showing signs of a few wrinkles.

Lucian lifted his coffee cup. "Keep at it then. I'd like to write myself."

"What do you do?"

Lucian hesitated briefly, then met Daniel's eyes. "Travel."

"Ah. So you're independently wealthy. You have a castle back home?"

"Not exactly."

"I'll bet you have a title."

"Not much of one."

"A great estate, at the least, huh?"

"All that's changing these days, you know," Lucian said casually. "They've even done away with the House of Lords."

"Yeah, of course, well . . ."

Lucian leaned forward. "So what upset you so badly?"

"Oh! Oh, well, I . . . uh . . . I have odd jobs to make ends meet. I work at the morgue, and it's been interesting, and I've learned a lot, but Jesus! Last night . . ."

"Last night?"

"We had an accident victim. A kid. Went right through the front window of a car. Man . . ."

"Ripped up, I take it?"

"To shreds. But the oddest thing, the most awful, was . . ."

Daniel looked down, breathing in.

"The most awful was . . . ?"

"The head."

"What about it?"

"It was"—he moistened his lips—"off . . . but not completely. It was hanging by shreds of flesh and sinew and . . . there were smears of blood, but not pools of it, and the eyes, oh, God, the kid must have seen it coming, the eyes . . ."

Lucian was very still for a moment. "They're convinced he was the victim of an accident?"

Daniel exhaled. "What else? What the hell else? They found the car in a tree. The kid was through the window, half wrapped around the tree. It happened not far from here. Near the Saint Louis Cemetery. God, it was awful.

I've seen little kids, poor old people mugged and battered . . . I've just never seen anything like this kid's eyes."

"You should go home and get some sleep."

"I'm not very tired," Daniel said, looking down into his coffee. "Or maybe I am tired. I just can't seem to shake this. I'm . . ."

"What?"

Daniel hesitated. "I'm tired. But I can't sleep."

"Yes, you can."

He looked up. "I—"

"You can."

Daniel nodded. "Yeah, thanks. I'm going home now. I'm going to sleep." He stood, started to leave, then turned back awkwardly. "Nice to meet you. Thanks again. See you around."

Lucian nodded.

Daniel left. Thoughtfully, Lucian stared after him.

Jade awoke to find herself on the couch, Rick at her side.

"You okay?"

A sense of panic seized her. What had she said and done? Nothing, nothing—he had walked in; she had passed out. He had come in very late—or very early, depending on how you looked at it. He hadn't been in her bed.

She had dreamed that he was.

No, not him.

Yes, it must have been! Who else would she allow into her dreams, and such a dream?

"You really are upset, huh? I don't blame you, of course," he said kindly, his blue eyes gentle as he smoothed hair from her face.

Upset? She was losing her mind!

"I . . . um . . ."

"No offense, but you look like hell. And I feel like it."

She looked like hell? She believed him. And she believed that he felt like it as well. He was drawn and haggard. She had never seen Rick in such sad shape.

She reached out and stroked his cheek. "You must be exhausted. Bad night?"

"Terrible." He shook his head. "Even your buddy Daniel was turning green."

"I'm so sorry. It was a teenager?"

"A young man, a student. A transfer student with a bit of past history, but still . . . young." He looked at her awkwardly. "Look, I, um . . . well, I've never been so thrilled in my life that anybody wanted to be with me, but . . . I think I gotta go home. I'm really feeling lousy. I can't keep my eyes open. I want to thrill you to no end and make you see that the world will never be the same without me. But I'm not so sure I could accomplish that at this moment."

"I understand," she told him softly. "I'm . . . uh . . . not so sure I could thrill you to no end myself right now."

"You couldn't sleep. Nightmares, hm?" he asked kindly.

"Um, yes, dreams," she said.

That wasn't a lie. Was it?

"I asked for details from the crime scene in New York," he told her. "Gavin will be getting everything in today. When I wake up we can go to the station together and get the information he's received over the wires."

"Okay, thanks, Rick, you look . . . drained. You know," she offered, "you could just get some sleep right here."

"I need to get home. I want clean clothes. I need clean clothes. After the morgue . . ."

"I see."

"I just can't begin to explain how exhausted I am. I'm sorry."

"No, no, it's okay, really okay," she said quickly. What

had she been thinking? Her room looked as if she'd invited a dozen friends to an orgy.

"I'll make it up to you."

"No. I'll make it up to you," she promised.

He nodded and rose. At the door he hesitated. "Even in the day, keep the doors locked. I mean, what happened was in New York. Far away. There are lots of madmen in the world, no reason to think this is part of the same insanity. But still . . ."

"Hey," she said. "This is New Orleans. I'm a street-smart kid. I always keep my door locked."

He nodded. "Talk to you later."

She brushed his lips with a kiss. She felt odd. As if she'd cheated on him.

Or as if she were cheating with *him.*

"Rick," she murmured, feeling guilty. Shamed.

"Yes?"

"I do love you, you know," she whispered very softly.

He cupped her chin. "I adore you." He smiled, caressed her jaw, then stepped out the front door.

"Lock up," he told her.

"Right."

The door closed.

Rick Beaudreaux heard Jade lock the door behind him.

He stepped away, starting down the hall. He hesitated, looking back. *Idiot!* He told himself. *Go back.*

That was nuts. He'd waited this long. She was a strong character, but she had been damaged by the horror she'd witnessed in Scotland. He understood that. He'd fallen head over heels for her, though, and he'd been willing to wait. She never played games; she'd been honest, affectionate, fun, charming—and beautiful—from the start.

He could wait a little longer. She was unnerved.

And man, but he felt like shit.

He didn't remember ever feeling so bad. Hell, yes, a lot of it had been the corpse. But then, actually, it had started before that. It had started when . . .

When that woman in the street had asked him for directions on his way to Jade's last night. She'd been really good-looking. Not that her appearance had really swayed him.

Jade was gorgeous.

But she had been a charming and lost tourist—a beauty with a soft accent and a way of getting a cop not just to show her the way to where she wanted to go, but to lead her in the right direction.

She had sneezed. He must have picked up a bug from her.

And so, at this moment, he was in sad shape. Totally unworthy.

And yet . . .

As he left Jade's house, he had the strangest feeling that he had let something slip through his fingers that he couldn't quite touch, and in doing so . . . he had lost something.

A strange fear closed around his heart.

Go back! A voice urged him.

He shook off all his strange feelings.

He was a cop, for God's sake!

The young woman slid into the chair in front of Lucian—the chair so recently vacated by Daniel Thacker.

He looked at her, surprised to see her there. Maybe he shouldn't have been, and maybe he shouldn't have cared. God knew, he'd gone through his times of darkness.

Times of cruelty.

And there was nothing different about what he was now:

a survivor. The one who upheld the laws, kept the balance. The keeper of the keys, so to speak.

But the world had changed for him that night in Scotland. He'd felt the threat of his enemies again for the first time in eons.

They had waged battle, and he had won the fight, but he knew that it was a war—and for them, a war of vengeance. He knew his own strength and power, which had been savagely won.

Yet there was something else he knew again. Something he had once managed to put down, along with his enemies.

Fear.

She smiled and reached out a hand, touching him.

"It was you last night, wasn't it?"

"Hey, Cathy, you came in after all!" Shelly said, walking by. Cathy shook her head. "I'm not working, Shelly. I just came by to . . ."

Her voice trailed. She looked at him.

"It was you, wasn't it?"

"I'm not sure what you mean."

"Yes, you are. I'm certain I saw you . . . no, I think I saw you. Or I heard you. I was terrified and I knew I was about to be mugged or murdered and you . . . you stopped him. The shadow, the fear, the footsteps. He never got me. You told me to run. And I did. God, I ran so fast! I reached my car, climbed in, and gunned the motor. I was out of there so fast. . . ." She stared at him. "I would have been killed if it hadn't been for you, right?"

"You were followed," he told her simply.

"You saved my life."

He shrugged his shoulders impatiently. "You shouldn't leave this place late at night alone."

"I won't again. Ever. I swear it."

"Good."

"God, you're wonderful."

He rose impatiently. "No, Cathy, I'm not wonderful. But you need to listen to me right now. You've got to be careful. Really careful. It's that simple. Get off in the daylight. Be careful at night; stick with large groups." He started to walk away; then he turned back to her, shaking a finger beneath her nose. "And don't go inviting any strangers in, you hear me?"

She nodded, somewhat taken aback by his ferocity.

He started out to the street, anxious to be away. The sunlight was very bright. Too bright. He doubled over suddenly, caught in the vicious grip of a gnawing agony. Home. He needed to get home. Quickly. Now. He needed rest today. His customary strength was more than admirable, but the sun was bright this October.

You should see the other guy! he had said earlier.

And that had been true enough.

He had known they were there; they had wreaked carnage in New York and come here. Quickly. Last time, he had ripped them both to shreds. . . .

But they had healed.

This time he hadn't seen Sophia. She was keeping her distance, ready to sacrifice that fool, Darian. And he had stopped Darian, torn into him again. . . .

But . . .

Darian had escaped. Lucian had kept him from Cathy, but he had escaped Lucian's hold.

And this morning Lucian could still almost hear the taunting voice of his adversary.

Just who do you think you are? Just what do you think you are? To the others, are you any less fetid, horrible, repulsive?

I think I'm the king, the ruler; that's what I know.

You have to hold on to power.

And I will, my friend.

You grow weak, and I grow strong. And she, *she grows stronger still.*

You are a fool. You will never be stronger than I! I will never allow it.

And to himself he added, *Because my hatred is greatest, my bitterness the deepest. I will hold my power with my will, and it is not weakness that governs me, or a conscience, but sense and logic and the will to survive.*

We are what we are, Darian taunted. *Hunters. Wolves. And wolves will hunt sheep.*

Not when meat is provided. And not when hunting the sheep will bring upon us a hundredfold the vengeance of the sheep farmers.

Farmers, bah!

Farmers. You've seen through time. We will all fight to survive. The farmers just as fiercely as we do.

You are growing foolish and sentimental and weak. We bided time. We healed. We grew strong. And in the end, we will best you, and I will be king. She made you, and she will unmake you as well. What she created, she can destroy.

Never . . . never . . . you think you know hatred, you think you know anger? You have no idea what hatred is, fury, loss. . . .

Because you think you have found her again, you think you have a soul. You see Igrainia in that woman. But what would she see in you? You are a creature of the night. Foul. Loathsome. You are heinous. You have sinned as few others, raged, killed . . . you are darkness, you are death, you are the very flames of hell. . . .

His head was nearly bursting. The sunlight was staggering. He gritted his teeth and straightened, his shoulders squared beneath the sunlight. He seldom needed help. He kept no one close. He had spent a great deal of time taking the gravest care, trusting no one.

The talisman!

It was all he could think.

She must have the talisman again.

Damn, but the sun is bright! He needed his home here, rest, a place of darkness. . . .

No, he needed more than home. He needed help. And though he had sworn to stay away, he had an old friend in the city. A very old friend . . .

He walked with the crowd.

And then he was shadow.

By the bright light of day, Jade was convinced that she needed a psychiatrist. She tried to analyze herself, and could only come up with the fact that she must be frustrated, afraid since Scotland.

Not wanting to dwell on her thoughts, she decided on a trip down to the police station. Gavin, a friend of Rick's, worked in Homicide, and was a really nice guy. If he knew something, he would surely share it with her.

When she was just about ready to leave, Renate appeared at her door.

"You were on your way out?"

"Yeah."

"I thought Rick was here." Renate looked over Jade's shoulder, into the living room.

"He was. He left."

Renate wedged her way into the entry.

"He's really gone?"

"Yes, he's really gone."

"I was hoping to learn more."

"About?"

"The kid killed in the accident," Renate said impatiently.

"Sorry. He's really gone." She hesitated, then added. "He came in, but he's sick. He's in bad shape. He's a good cop, you know, and he went back in to work last night just because of the kid."

"I thought he could tell us about it."

"Well, he's not here."

She didn't tell Renate that she was about to head off for the police station. She didn't want company, not Renate's, at any rate, not right now.

"The story about the accident is in the paper. The alcohol level in the kid's blood was off the charts. Not that they found that much blood. Not even on the car—or on the tree he hit. He shouldn't have been driving. He'd been drinking, beating up his girlfriend. . . . I know Rick is really fond of kids, that he prides himself on his work, but this one . . . Jade, he hadn't even been at LSU a semester, and he was in trouble for outrageous stunts. I'm telling you, this kid—I know how you usually feel—but this one . . . this one . . ."

"This one what?"

"He was bad."

"It's still a terrible death," Jade argued. "And if he was young, he might have changed; he might have grown out of being a delinquent."

Renate looked skeptical. She cast her head at an angle, studying Jade. "And he might have killed other people as well. Thank God he didn't kill some little girl or boy."

"Renate, once in a while—"

"I should look for the good. Yeah, yeah. But I write mysteries. All about crime. And I do research, and I know that people can be really terrible. They can be terrible more often than they can be good. Even people we think are good would probably be terrible if they thought they could get away with it."

Jade lifted a brow. "Renate, there are good people and bad people, and there are all kinds of gray in between as well."

"Yeah, sure."

She stared at Jade, waiting for something, expecting something. "Well?" Jade murmured.

"Well?"

"Is Matt still at your place?" Jade queried, suddenly determined to turn the tables.

"What?" Renate demanded.

"Matt. Remember, you two left here with champagne and caviar."

"Oh, yeah. No, Matt is long gone."

Jade grinned, looking at her. "Did Matt get lucky?"

"Jade!" Renate smoothed back her perfectly styled hair. "Really, Jade, how could you ask such a thing? That's repulsive!"

"Renate! That's cruel."

"I said no such thing to Matt," Renate said regally, "so it's cruel only if you repeat it to him. And of course I'd call you a liar, and insist I never said such a thing."

"Matt is not repulsive—and I would never hurt his feelings by repeating such a thing to him."

"Okay. He's not repulsive. He's just not . . . sexy."

"He's as nice as can be."

"I don't see you having an affair with him."

"I'm seeing someone else. And Matt is my friend."

"Yeah, well, Matt is my friend, too."

To Jade's great relief, her phone started ringing. "Oh, hey, excuse me, Renate, will you? I've got to get that."

"Um. Well, if you get any good, usable information, you'll share, right?"

"Sure thing."

Jade got Renate out of her apartment. She went flying to the phone. It might be Rick. She hadn't thought of that at first, but it might be. He might be feeling really awful, even worse than he had been, and he might need her.

When she reached the phone, her machine had already picked up.

"Hello?" she said quickly.

"Jade? Jade MacGregor?" It was a woman's voice. Soft, hushed.

"Yes?"

There was a silence.

Then a click indicated that the woman had hung up.

He could have entered at whim.

He didn't.

He stood in front of the fine antebellum mansion and hesitated. He'd never meant to come here again. To see Maggie. Their history together had been long and rich, but it was now over. He had thought that one day he would hear of her death, that of an old grandmother, and he would come and cast roses upon her coffin.

She had found what she had wanted: a new life.

And the certainty of death.

He stood there several minutes, then reminded himself that he needed to knock at a door, and he did manage to do so.

She opened it.

And seeing him as he was, she gasped.

"You!"

"Aye, it's me. And I'm sorry."

"My God—"

"Look, I haven't come to interfere with your life."

"I know."

"There's more trouble afoot, and—"

She caught him by the shoulder, looking up at the intensity of the sun. "Come in, you fool. My God, you look like hell!"

They were old, old friends. And old, old enemies.

She could say that to him.

He smiled. He almost laughed. For the second time that day he said, "You should see the other guy!"

"I've been afraid. So afraid. The things in the papers, the things happening here . . . I saw the write-ups last year about the murders in Scotland. And now in New York . . . Lucian, just what is going on?"

"Rebellion," he murmured. "The past rising. A past I had done my best to bury for all time. I never explained to you how I came to be—"

"Lucian, you wouldn't have explained anything to me. You were the power, and you made the rules. But I heard things throughout the years."

"Oh?" he queried.

"Vampires talk," she teased. "Apparently death does nothing to still the urge to gossip."

"Then you heard about Sophia."

"Yes."

"Well, she has awakened, and Darian, her lackey, goes before her, protecting her from harm."

"So you fought Darian?"

"Yes."

"But he isn't—"

"Dead?" he supplied. "No," he admitted bitterly.

"But you can't really kill him, can you?"

"Not by all the ancient laws. And I am the keeper of the laws. But their depravities might well jeopardize us all, and if that is so . . ."

"You can twist the law," she suggested.

He nodded. "But I still risk the wrath of an uprising." He spread his hands before him, suddenly noting the length and strength of his nails with distaste. *The king of the undead!* he mocked himself. Dimly he could remember what it had been to know a simple life.

And he could remember becoming what he had become. Hating it.

Accepting it.

And all the years.

Oh, God, all the years!

Since . . .

Maggie reached out and touched him. "I have never seen anyone with your strength," she told him.

He lifted his hands. "Darian just escaped me. I might have been too confident. In Scotland I didn't know until we came to the tombs that he was indeed with Sophia. I hurt them both there, but not enough." He hesitated. "They've been like weight lifters before a bout, gathering strength, drinking huge quantities of blood. . . . Sophia has now spent centuries gathering strength to topple me. And there was a talisman . . . a locket. A gold locket; she wore it at all times. It was filled with the blood of a fallen angel."

"The . . . devil?" she inquired.

He lifted his hands. "I don't know. Christian popes are buried with their gold enclosures carrying the relics of long-dead saints; altars are built encompassing a drop of blood, a bit of bone. Sophia was ancient when I first knew her. She claimed to come from the beginning of time. She wore her locket always. She believes it gives her power. Perhaps a strong enough belief is as powerful as the truth."

"Where has this talisman been?" she asked him.

"At the bottom of the sea."

"But then how has she—"

"Retrieved it? I don't know. I don't know for sure that she has the talisman, but she claimed that it was her greatest source of power. But whatever the reason, she has healed—they have healed, and regained strength."

"You've tried summoning them?"

"They block me. They mean to seize complete power."

"You can't let that happen. You need to sleep, to regain all the strength you can," she said.

"I can betray no weakness," he murmured. Weakness! He was as frail as a kitten at this moment. Exhausted.

Her eyes studied his. "That's the truth. You can betray no weakness," she said softly. She touched his cheek, a gentle touch. "You've learned so much. Learn to trust an old friend. It's why you've come here, isn't it? Come in."

He nodded and came into her home—a mortal home, filled with warmth now. A rich, tempting aroma from the kitchen. The sound of a baby's cry. The softness of a mattress. The cradle of a pillow.

"Earth?" she asked quietly. "A wee bit of the old country?"

"In my pockets."

"Guest room," she told him.

He paused. "Thank you. I should explain that—"

"Later. Sleep now. You look as if you must have some time to heal." She eyed him carefully. "Have you . . . eaten?"

Had she sounded just a bit afraid? he wondered. She lived a different life now. He had left her to that life.

He grinned. "Yes."

"Lucian . . ." she murmured, then hesitated. "Lucian, please tell me that you haven't been seizing upon the innocent. Tell me that you've been gnawing on vicious dictators, convicted killers, child-molesters—"

"No."

"Lucian—"

"I didn't gnaw on anyone. I went to the blood bank at the hospital."

She smiled, looked down, laughed ruefully. "I'm sure that will be in the papers."

"I'm sure it will."

"Well, I married a cop, remember? You may be all that stands between us all and total insanity. Sleep. You will need all your power."

"Thank you."

"Later Sean will be home. He'll know more. He can help you. And you . . ."

"Yes?"

"You can help him," she said very softly. "For now, come with me."

They walked up the grand staircase, past the remarkable Civil War picture on the landing. "Have you hurt Darian enough to buy some time?"

"Yes. I don't think he'll risk another encounter with me again soon. But he is not alone. He has Sophia—at the least."

"Still, injured . . ." She inhaled, looking at him. "You're right. He won't want to tangle with you until he's gathered his own strength again. He—they—must find prey elsewhere."

"I'm afraid that might be true."

"Maybe you'll be able to find them."

"Maybe."

She smiled. "You could always find me."

The slightest curve took his lips as well. "I was infatuated with you."

"If I'd given in, you'd have tired of me immediately. I wasn't really the one you wanted. I was a toy, a plaything for you."

"An enchantress, who suddenly found herself in need of guidance."

"Pygmalion?" she teased.

"Magdalena—"

"Get some sleep. We'll talk later."

In the deep, dark luxury of her guest room, he dared to close his eyes.

And to sleep.

And it was then that the years rushed back—eons, decades, centuries.

* * *

His hostess, watching him, tenderly smoothed hair from his forehead. She remembered hating him with a passion. He'd had his time of being all-powerful, as autocratic and demanding as any ruler versed in the divine right of kings. He'd taken what he wanted, taught, mocked, demanded. . . .

And come to her rescue, risking his own position.

She bit her lip. Even then, he had probably risked more than he knew.

In sleep he was gorgeous. Long, lean, hard muscled, the sleek, dark hair veering over his head no matter that she swept it aside. His facial planes were striking . . . his eyes.

How she remembered those eyes.

His lips moved.

"Igrainia."

He whispered the name out loud. And she knew.

Even vampires dreamed.

Dreamed of the past.

Of mortal days gone by.

Chapter Four

"Dragons! Dragons on the horizon! Deliver us, oh, God! Dragon ships sail the horizon."

Lucian heard the cry while studying the delicate gold workings of an Irish metallurgist at the spring market. Igrainia was at his side; she had just let out a soft cry of delight at the beauty of a jeweled cross. Having just haggled over the price of the work with the artisan, Lucian had barely hooked the piece around her neck when he heard the alarm. He looked up sharply. From where he stood he could just see the high mast of the ship coming into view above the cliffs before the harbor.

It was the year of our Lord 985 A.D., and he was well aware of the meaning of the dragon ships on the horizon. Like that of many a Scotsman along the coast, his blood was mixed with that of earlier invaders, mainly Norman, English, and Norse. Though the attacks had somewhat lessened in the last fifty years, they still came frequently. There were great prizes to be found on this coast, for like the Celtic Irish across the sea, the people here, led by monks and their students, were undergoing a great age in the creation of jewelry, church relics, and bound and gilded manuscripts. True though it might be that the average young man eking a living from the craggy soil did not read—and that superstition and the old ways persisted side by side with the teachings of Christ—the priests and clerics learned God's word from the beautifully crafted books the monks labored so hard to produce. Necklaces, earrings, rings, and more were fashioned by a rare breed of talented artists, and so there were many such riches to be plundered.

Screams went up, rising higher and higher on the wind, which suddenly seemed to blow with a tempest—an omen of what was to come. Fire pots fell over, canopies fell, and Lucian gripped his bride by the shoulders. "Go!" he told her.

Her eyes met his. They were a blue-green color, as beautiful as the sea beneath the sun. They met his with simple understanding. She was to run to the cliffs; as wife of the chieftain she would gather other women and children as best she could, and stay until the danger was over. A daughter of ancient kings and Viking lords, she was proud, and a fighter, but she knew as well that men too often gave their lives to save their women, and that her greatest contribution to the fight would be to leave him with the assurance that she was safe.

"Husband!" she said softly, rose on her toes, and kissed his lips. The word was still precious to her. Then she spun around, calling out that others must follow her.

"Stand stalwart, sons of MacAlpin!" Lucian cried out, reminding them of the first king to draw the great tribes of Scotland together as one nation—a nation that now only faced the dissidence of the Viking colonies settled firmly upon certain of the isles and lands they had wrested from the tribes previously established here. They were kindred; they were enemies—they all sought a livelihood, and violence was part of life.

As much a part of life as the delicately worked beauty of the gold and jeweled cross that Igrainia now wore as she raced to their lair.

"Stand!" Lucian roared again, running through the crowd to reach Malachi, his great black warhorse. He mounted while drawing his sword. The huge black horse reared, and he allowed it the freedom, drawing the attention of his people to him. "Stand!" he shouted again. "Stand—or die! And give over to the heathens all that is yours!"

His cry roused the courage of his men. They ceased to run like scattered ashes, and those who had fought as warriors before came to their arms and their horses, and those who were farmers and herders went for their pikes and their scythes. "Archers, to the cliffs!" he ordered, and though the wind continued to blow, and a clap of thunder raged across the sky, there was order as men rushed to do as he had bidden. He dug his leather-clad heels into Malachi's haunches and rode for the cliffs, ordering the men to positions, watching as the Viking ships neared. There were three of them, each dragon-prowed and filled with men of the Scandinavian nations, warriors, berserkers, adventurers who believed that death in battle would do nothing but bring them to the halls of Valhalla, their heaven, to sit at the side of Wodin, their great god.

"Now!" he cried to his clansmen who had scrambled up the craggy rock to attack the foe while still at sea.

Arrows flew.

Vikings, startled by such a land attack, screamed. And many died.

"Again!" he shouted.

And so again arrows flew, and again invaders died.

But not enough.

The ships had reached the harbor. The enemy plunged off their ships into the shallow waters; they defied the cold and the wet and the wind and the rain of death.

Lucian rode out to meet the coming horde.

It was then that he first saw her.

She stood at the bow of one of the great ships, as straight, defiant, and stalwart as the fierce dragon-headed prow of the vessel. She was startling there, for though there were a few darker-headed men among the warriors, her long hair was raven black, and contrasted sharply with that of most of the men who plunged to the shore.

Beneath a rich cloak of fur, she wore a gown as black as the raven's wing of her hair. A vee in the cut of the dark linen revealed the long, graceful line of her throat and the swell of her breasts. Between them, even at this distance, he could see the fine gold work of the pendant that dangled between her breasts.

But his eyes were drawn to her face.

Her chin was high; her eyes were wide, sparked with the fire of battle—and amusement.

She ignored the rain of arrows that whistled through the air, arcing and falling like a great thunderstorm.

Equally, she ignored the screams of men and horses, the agony of the dying.

She stood clad in her cloak of ermine, and watched the carnage without blinking, never once shrinking from the threat of any danger.

A great berserker with fire red hair charged Lucian. He brought down his war sword—a Viking weapon itself, inherited from an antecedent—and felled the man with a powerful blow to his back. His father had taught him the advantage of staying mounted when men on foot attacked—the power of a blow delivered from on high.

And so he kept his seat upon Malachi, hacking and slicing those who would unhorse him. The redhead was followed by an ice blond, an old warrior—ready to fly to Valhalla, he determined. A young man then—followed by a maddened berserker whose mouth was flecked with foam as he fought. They died. The shallows before him had become a pool of men, blood, and churning sea.

The attackers lay before him. He tensed for the next assault. He looked again at the ship, and saw that she was watching him, her lips curled with amusement. The fight was great entertainment for her.

He hadn't realized that he had not been able to draw his eyes from hers until men assaulted him from the rear.

Malachi kicked and reared, downing a screaming man, thrashing him in the water. But there were half a score of men upon Lucian now, and despite his experience in the saddle and his fury with the sword, he was dragged from Malachi. He struggled, slashed out, and when he lost his sword, he fought with his fists. His attackers dragged him down in the water, and his lungs began to burst, and he fought free. Fumbling in the frigid water at the shoreline, he found his sword. He stumbled up. The cold water chilled the small coat of mail he wore, and made his leather coat and boots heavy. But bursting to the surface, he saw that he was surrounded.

And worse. With his back to his ships, his eyes on the shoreline, he saw that the Vikings had broken the farmers. He and his men had fought well, but there had been too many of the enemy, and not enough time for help to come from up or down the coast, or inland.

And they had caught up with the fleeing women and children.

"Give over, Chieftain, and we will let them live."

He heard her voice. She spoke Scots Gaelic with a melodic rhythm to her voice.

Oddly, she was no longer on the ship, but stood before him. Or seemed to stand. The hem of her black gown appeared to ride above the surface. He thought he must have received a tremendous blow to his head, because she seemed to be standing on water.

"What guarantee?" he demanded.

She arched a brow, still very amused. She turned back to the shore with a shrug. "Free the children . . . let those flat-footed farmers there run with them. Let go the silly peasant lasses there, and the women . . . except for that one."

She had pointed to Igrainia.

Could she recognize the wife of the chieftain?

"That one!" she commanded to one of her warriors. "Take that one and behead her, so that he will know we have no mercy."

His heart slammed against his chest.

"Let her go, or I swear I will kill you myself. I, too, can have no mercy."

She looked back at him, a winged dark brow rising. "Chieftain, I do find you . . . curious." she said. The sound of laughter was in her voice. "Let us barter with the chieftain here. He desires it, so leave the lass her head!" she ordered.

"Lucian! Give over nothing for me! Barter nothing for my life!" Igrainia cried fiercely.

"She asks to die!" the woman said.

"Don't touch her!" Lucian commanded.

The woman smiled slowly. There was a curve of cruelty to her lips. With the wind now raging around her, she seemed a greater menace than any storm.

"I will try to refrain," the woman said. Her fingers curled around the gold pendant she wore.

He was as still and silent as she.

"Now—give over your sword."

"Let her go with the rest of them," he said, indicating his wife.

The woman watched him a long moment, then walked toward him. It seemed that she barely stirred the water. He did not believe in such things, but by God, she walked over the water.

Sorceress!

He heard the whisper rise from the shore. Christianity had come here, to the British Isles, several hundred years ago.

But old superstitions remained.

Witch! Aye, she was some kind of witch. She practiced magic, the darkest kind.

Illusions! he told himself.

Don't believe what you see!

"You do not need her," the woman told him. "You will have me."

Illusion! he reminded himself. *Deny her!*

But his lips were heavy; his throat seemed rigid; words would not form. He looked at her, and fought to shift his gaze.

He managed to speak at last. "I have no need for a witch such as you."

Her subtle smile deepened.

"You lie."

And he did lie.

She had a power.

There was something about here . . . something that created a fire in his groin, a hunger unlike any he had known. He wanted to touch her. With his wife, whom he adored, standing in peril before him, with an audience of warriors and farmers and children, with God above . . . he wanted her. In the water, the dirt, the mud. Now. He burned.

He fought for his senses. Strained, ached. "Let her go. Let her run after the children then."

She cocked her head at him, her eyes amused, ever more intrigued.

"Tell me to come to you."

"What?"

"Invite me . . . to know you."

"Know me, madam, have what you want; do what you will. But let the woman go!"

Her smile deepened with wicked triumph and she turned. "Let her go."

The men released Igrainia.

Her eyes met his. For a moment he was released from the woman's uncanny hold. God, how he loved his wife! Her eyes, her laughter, the softness of her voice, her quest for knowledge, her love of books, learning, art . . .

He inclined his head. *Run! Help me fight for my own life, knowing you wait for me.*

Igrainia's eyes held his a moment longer.

Then she ran after the children. He knew that the Viking warriors could easily run after them again. His men were dead, broken, injured, shattered. The Viking crew knew it, too.

But they knew as well that the longer they tarried, the longer they faced the danger of other clans hearing of their arrival on the coast, and coming en masse in fury against such an invader.

"The woman has gone," the raven-haired witch announced; then she turned to Lucian, irritated at last. "Perhaps I should take your fool head to prove to all that we will take what we want."

He stared at her, his anger a sudden wall against her.

"Perhaps someone should take *your* fool head, and you'll see that the world is not your playground alone."

"Your sword, chieftain," she said.

He held still.

"Is your word no good then?" she demanded.

Slowly he stretched out his arm. His sword fell into the water. It glittered beneath it.

She nodded and started to walk away. He heard a noise to his rear.

He spun around. Vikings had moved behind him. He felt a crack of steel against his head, and went crashing down into the water. Pain went into a land of darkness. . . .

He knew that he remained in a strange place, a place of darkness, as time passed. No time at all, eons of time. Dreams began, and he fought those dreams. He ached, he burned, from head to toe.

I will heal you. . . .

She was there. The dark-haired witch.

His teeth gritted. *Get away, vile, fetid witch.*

Her laughter seared him.

I will heal you as you have never known yourself healed. I will give you a strength you have not ever imagined. You invited me.

Never.

Ah, but you did invite me. . . .

Then he knew a pain that caused him to scream like a child, like a woman, fierce and exquisite, horrible and thrilling, climactic and terrible. Sweat saturated his body, pleasure—deep, decadent, shameful—wound up with the pain. He was strangling in the length of her dark hair, in agony, shuddering with desire, and still, he was certain none of it could be real. It was all part of the darkness and the nightmare.

It was his head, nothing but the blow to his head.

Because she was there, too. Igrainia. Calling to him, a siren's song. She stood out on the water, and her arm was outstretched, her palm was up, she reached to him, called to him. Her honey-colored hair billowed behind her in the breeze ... or floated in the water, he was not sure which.

She could touch the sea.

For some reason, he could not.

Igrainia!

He called her name in his soul. He could not reach her.

He awoke later, aware of the lapping of water against the hull of a boat. His head thundered. He ached all over, his muscles ravaged and worn and strained. He opened his eyes. Wood above him. He lay in the covered hull of a Viking dragon ship, on a bed of furs. His arms pained him, his shoulders ached ... his neck, sweet Jesus, he felt as if it had been sliced from his body. Wet, sticky ...

"You are with us."

His eyes focused. She was there, sitting at his side.

"I live, it seems."

She smiled and shrugged. "You rested well?"

He had no intention of sharing his dreams with her. "Go to hell, madam, and burn there forever."

"Are you hungry yet?"

"No."

He lied. He felt as if rats gnawed at his insides. He was painfully hungry. It was a hunger that seemed to hurt all of his flesh.

"Drink."

She handed him a skin.

He wanted to refuse her. His mouth was dry, his lips

parched. If he didn't seize the skin from her, he was going to die.

He took it and drank deeply, not even thinking of the contents. They spilled down his chin, dropped upon his hand. He stared. The drop looked like blood. Something inside him seemed to curl in a knot.

He looked at her sharply.

"Where are we?" he asked coldly.

"About to make landfall," she said.

She stood, leaving him with a sweep of fur behind her. Darkness had fallen. Her crew was awake, laughing, riding the waves that rose high in the night.

He didn't know how long he had slept, so he didn't know how far they had come.

He staggered up, holding fast to a support beam to stand.

The warriors were aboard, donning mail or armor, grabbing their weapons. Talk and laughter filled the ship as sails were brought in, and they slipped as far as they dared into the channel to disembark.

Suddenly the talk and laughter rose to a deafening pitch; horses were brought from below; men and animals leaped from the ship to the shallows, making for the shore.

Only a few stayed aboard.

The settlement had slept.

It was awakened.

Fierce, high battle cries went out on the night air.

And the attack was begun.

Screams rose as homes in the small fishing village were raided and sacked. He heard prayers, and they were not spoken in the Gaelic of his homeland, nor they were cried out in that of the Irish.

Norse!

They had come to the edge of the Hebrides, he thought. Islands held by Viking jarls.

They attacked their own kind!

Attacked hard and viciously, showing no mercy. Men ran in the night, screaming, to be brought down with the weight of battle-axes in their backs. They were not his own people, but he gritted his teeth and could have wept, the carnage was so swift and terrible. He longed to fight, even to die, rather than witness such senseless, cruel brutality.

Then suddenly he saw that the survivors were being herded onto the beach. The raven-haired woman was there, walking among them.

Oddly, at his great distance, he could see the eyes of men. See their hatred, see their longing to strike out at her as she stepped so lightly among them. He could see so clearly. Hear them, Lord God, it seemed he even heard their thoughts, knew their sweat and their fear. . . .

It became a clamor in his head. He pressed his palms to his ears.

She walked among the men, and from behind a white-haired warrior she suddenly caught the hand of a girl. The slender beauty had hair that was gold in the moonlight and spilled below her back. The woman dragged her away; the old warrior would not bear it. He stepped forward, drawing his sword.

The woman turned. One of her men stepped forward. The old fellow didn't have a chance. A sword flew hard and sure.

The white-capped head departed the body and bounced onto the sand.

The girl seemed not to see her father die. Her eyes were on the woman's. The woman touched her chin, and the girl lifted her head. She loosened the tie at her throat, and the simple wool shift she had worn fell to her feet.

The whole of her seemed to shimmer silver and gold and innocent in the moonlight.

The woman leaned over to her throat, stroked it, bit into it.

Lucian was horrified. But . . .

His loins throbbed, his lips were dy and parched, the gnawing had begun, a gnawing like rats in his abdomen, scratching, clawing. . . .

He thirsted.

God, he thirsted. . . .

He could hear her, hear the raven-haired beauty drinking, hear the blood spurting, the girl's heart pounding, and that pounding coming slower . . . and slower.

The woman finished and tossed the body aside. She said something to one of her men. He turned, lifted his battle-ax, and took off the girl's head.

Lucian reeled, staggering over, feeling the gnawing, the desperate hunger, the sexual need, the scratching in his stomach. Feeling shame—*oh, God*—such a sense of shame, of horror. He wanted to move, to fight, to die, but he had no more power than those caught on the shore still alive, seeing their friend, dead, the girl . . . drained. . . .

The raven-haired woman turned to the ship in the harbor. She lifted a hand.

Suddenly three men who had remained aboard were ashore.

He did not see their feet touch water.

They walked among the crowd and made their picks, selecting their victims.

Lucian cried out in pain, hearing the spurt of blood again, the slurping as the warriors-who-were-not-warriors drank. He felt blood, smelled blood, knew agony. . . .

He gripped his hands into fists, grated down on his teeth, strained every muscle in his body, fighting the overwhelming agony, the hunger. . . .

Then he looked up, forced to do so. She was staring at him, and he could see her eyes. And she smiled.

And suddenly he was there with her.

He didn't remember moving. He was on the shore with her. And she was beside a . . . body. He refused to look, to see if it was a man, a woman, or a child. She had her victim by the hair, and the victim was down, the throat offered as if she had come upon a lamb ready for slaughter, rather than a human life. She stared at him, and he was suddenly on his knees. He tried to close his eyes, his ears. He heard blood. Heard it racing in the victim's throat. He was freezing and starving, and the blood would be warm and filling. And he would ease the agonizing pain that ripped into him.

Bite. . . .

She didn't say the word out loud. He heard it anyway.

No.

She bit into the victim's throat, into pale flesh, creating a bright spill of red blood. She licked; she slurped, sucked. . . .

And he could bear it no more. Her hand was at his nape, her fingers tearing into his hair, and his lips were forced to the victim's throat. And the blood was on his mouth, and he could taste it, and he could feel that pounding, that pulse, the warmth. . . .

His mouth opened.

And he was desperate. In agony, frozen, thirsting unbearably.

Then he began to drink.

And drink, and drink . . .

And he was holding the victim himself, bearing into the throat, feeling the blood spill from the veins and into him. He drank sloppily, with great, gulping sounds, drank, drank, and drank until he was filled and . . .

There was no more pulse. No heat within the flesh he held. No life.

He held dead still, then roared with a sudden anguish

of the soul. It was a woman. A young woman. Lovely, blond, perfect . . . life, family, home, future ahead of her.

Lifeless.

He roared out his pain again, and he heard her laughter.

"Bitch!"

He cast down the lifeless body and rose, raging at her, ready to tear her apart limb from limb, heedless of her sex. She was not a woman but a monster.

Yet as he tore at her, she moved, and he plowed into one of her monster-henchmen. He was shoved back, amazed that his strength meant nothing at all against these men. Half-maddened, he went at her again. He reached for her, and she caught his arm and twisted it, and he was amazed, stunned by her strength. He was brought to his knees, rage and venom tearing from his lips.

She released him.

He rose, charging again.

She fought back.

And he flew. . . .

And this time one of the three men who had remained on the boat strode toward him, picking him up, slamming him down again. He fought, finding some strength. He had once been a great warrior. A chieftain.

Once.

He slammed into the side of the tree.

Stunned, he fell.

He landed hard upon the sand of the beach. He struggled up on an elbow and saw, amazed, that the survivors from the village still mingled there, no expressions on their faces. They were like sheep, unaware of the battle before them, or of the horror they had just faced. Body parts lay about; the head of the white-haired old father of the first girl lay just by Lucian's elbow. . . .

She was suddenly standing over him, her smile deepening.

"Bitch, monster," he told her.

She smiled. "The blood was delicious, wasn't it?"

"No."

She started to laugh, entirely entertained.

"It will seldom taste so sweet; she was young. Truly an innocent."

She stared down at him.

Her lackey, the man who had come in on the fray to beat him for her, stood by her side. Tall, lean. His hair had a touch of red and was not too dark. His eyes were a light brown.

"Understand it. You are a monster, too, chieftain," the lackey told him.

"No."

Even his denial made him ill. The blood had been good. So good. Water on the desert, meat to the starving. It had tasted sweeter than any mead, ale, or wine; it had filled him, warmed him, it had . . . *Oh, God* . . .

It had stopped the agony ripping at him, tearing at him. The unbearable pain . . .

"Get up," she told him.

"No."

"You will do as I say."

"I will never be your arse-kissing slave, you witch. Such as him." He indicated the fellow at his side.

The man started forward, ready to tear into him again. She stopped him, just lifting her hand.

"But you will," she told Lucian. She set her palm upon the chest of the other man. "Darian is my right-hand man. Touched by power. Protected . . ."

Her fingers touched the locket she wore around her neck.

"Protected by my power," she said. "I will let you exist for now. Perhaps you will learn. We do not destroy one another. Such is written in the ancient laws. But, I am above the law, chieftain. I am the law. I made you; I will destroy you, if you learn too slowly."

Lucian knew what he had to do.

He rose and suddenly turned on one of the Vikings, seizing his sword. The lackey—Darian—panicked, thinking he meant to slay the woman. He dragged her back.

Lucian thrust the weapon hard into his own stomach.

Pain. Blinding pain. He fell to his knees.

And heard her laughing again.

"Darian, get him up and back to the ship."

Again, he wasn't quite sure how he got there, but he was in the ship. He should have been dead. He wasn't. He should have bled to death.

The wound was almost healed.

When she stood before him next, he was no longer in pain. Just exhausted. He couldn't move.

"What are you?"

She watched him a moment. "I am everything. Your sun, your moon, your stars. I am your ruler; I am your god."

"You are nothing to me."

"You're stubborn, chieftain. But you do tempt me. I'll give you far more of a chance than most." She shrugged. "I believe you will learn in time. You must."

"You make me vomit."

She started to laugh again, that awful, deep, cruel and taunting sound. "You lust for me, and lie to yourself. You think you have a soul still, or such a thing as a heart. You do not. You will forget your little honey-haired bride—"

"Forget her? For you?" He found strength and spoke with a raging contempt, sitting up. "Forget the sound of her laughter for the cackle of a witch?"

"We'll see." She smiled again. "You want to know what I am, chieftain? Some men call me *lamia*. That is the name they give creatures such as myself in the East. Among the

Tartars and Huns and Gauls, my name is whispered, no more. *Vampyr.* But I am not just such. I am the oldest, and the most powerful. I rule. I create, and I destroy. Take care, chieftain, or I will tire of your whining. Believe me, I will destroy you."

"You have already destroyed me."

"I have given you strength, and life that can last forever."

"I am a dead man."

"Your hunger will keep you alive."

She left him.

The lackey suddenly knelt down beside him, sneering.

"She wants you now. You are a fool. But she will tire of you. And when she does, rest assured, I will destroy you."

Pale streaks of day touched the sky.

Dawn was coming.

The lackey left him as well.

He couldn't move. He had no strength then, no power. The sun was rising. He closed his eyes and felt the deepest pain and anguish.

He thought that he was dying.

And it didn't matter; he was glad.

He only slept.

Chapter Five

Rick Beaudreaux felt as if he were burning up. He was sicker than a dog, sicker than he could ever remember being.

And all this . . .

Right when he was falling in love. He smiled, thinking about her. Jade. The great thing was that she'd understood. She didn't accept pressure, and she didn't give it in return. She was great; she was beautiful. She was sexy. And she was a friend. He wished he could be with her.

Oh, yeah. After all this time. And now, when she was ready . . .

He was a mess.

Not too much he could do.

He slept, he woke, he took medicine. He left off knowing whether it was day or night. He told himself that he needed to get to a doctor.

Cold, hot, hot . . .

It was October. Cool. The windows were open. He shouldn't be feeling this way. There were so many viruses lately that were really bad. Killer viruses. It made sense to go to a doctor.

As soon as he could get up and dressed, that was what he'd do. Hell, being a police officer, at least he had good insurance.

He was thirsty. No matter what he drank, he still seemed to be thirsty.

Laying in bed, he groaned. He had the urge to pee. He had to get up.

He made his way up, stumbled into his bathroom. The simple act of urination felt good. Except that he was even colder when he finished. Well, pee was hot. Body temperature. Something like that. He dealt with kids and drugs, and chemistry and physiology had never been his best subjects. Didn't matter. He was good with kids. Loved them. Wanted the best for them.

Thirsty again.

He started for the kitchen. His doorbell rang.

He paused, because he usually answered his doorbell. *Hell. Not today.*

He walked on into the kitchen in his briefs and open robe, shaking his head. He opened the refrigerator door and stared in. Water, beer, wine. Two-week-old milk. And a can of Bloody Mary mix.

To his amazement, he opted for the Bloody Mary mix. He shook his head, amazed that he could gulp down the two-liter can so quickly.

There was some hamburger meat in the lower shelf. He'd meant to cook dinner last week for Jade—the one dinner he did well: hamburgers on the grill. He hadn't gotten to it. The meat was probably too old now. It was raw, red, and wrapped in cellophane. He could see just how raw and red—and probably *bad*—it was.

He reached for it, suddenly as hungry as he was thirsty. He pulled out the hamburger meat, set it on the counter, and delved into a cabinet for a frying pan. It wasn't hard to find. There weren't that many pans in his kitchen. He seldom ate at home. He had a lot of talents, but cooking wasn't one of them. And he was surrounded by some of the best restaurants in the country.

He never bothered with the pan, or turning on the stove.

He ripped the cellophane off the meat and started thrusting it into his mouth. It didn't taste bad. It could have been fresher. It could have been . . .

His doorbell was still ringing.

"Hell!" he swore aloud. "A man is sick in here, sick as hell, I may be dying—go away!"

He caught a glimpse of his face in the aluminum surface of his coffeepot. He hadn't shaved; bits of raw and bloody meat were stuck in the pathetic blond stubble on his cheeks. He shook his head, disgusted, ran the water, and vigorously washed his face.

He looked at the remaining meat, shaking his head. Well, hell, people did eat steak tartare. This was kind of the same. Maybe his sick body was craving the iron or something.

The bell was still ringing.

"Shit!" he swore.

He started for it, shook his head angrily, and walked back to the bedroom. He closed himself in, pulling his pillow over his head.

He never took time off.

He always paid his creditors.

Whatever it was, they needed to leave him the hell alone.

Shanna MacGregor woke to the sound of her phone ringing.

She groaned, pulling her pillow over her head. She wasn't a morning person.

The answering machine clicked on.

"Shanna, dear, this is Liz. I'm so sorry to call. I was hoping to catch you in. I always hate to bother you girls, but . . ."

Shanna groaned inwardly. She knew that Liz hated to call.

She and Jade had both accepted Liz as their father's new wife. They had adored their mother, but they had lost her. And their father had grieved with them, long and deeply.

And though he was eight years older than his new wife—fifty to Liz's forty-two—he hadn't gone and married a woman young than his own daughters, something Shanna had seen men do.

For herself—though she adored her father—she knew she'd never marry an old fart.

But Liz was okay. She hadn't planned the twins, and she'd been embarrassed to tell the girls about them. And she tried never to be a burden on her new husband's first family.

Shanna adored the twins; so did Jade.

They were like practice. Almost like having her own little moppets without having all the poop and vomit all the time.

"But it's okay, I'll give Jade a try." Liz's voice continued.

Jade? No, no, not this morning. Jade should be sleeping with supercop. Not a good morning to leap out of bed and off to the home front.

She staggered up and answered the phone.

"Liz, I'm here."

"Shanna?"

"Yes, I'm here," she repeated, looking at the phone. Who else would it be?

"I'm so sorry, Shanna—"

"Liz, what is it?"

"I know this is terribly short notice, but Petey's got an ear infection, his temperature has just gone up and up, and he's got to go to the hospital, and your dad has been out since about four this morning. He's involved in a story for the paper, and I can beep him, but—"

"Liz, you need me to watch Jamie?"

"Only until I can reach your father."

"You don't need to get Dad. I'll be there right away."

"Oh, bless you, Shanna. I don't know what I would have done without you girls."

"No big deal, Liz. The little guy is my half brother. I'll be right over." *Just don't wake Jade up. Not this morning!* she thought.

She breezed in and out of the shower, hopped into jeans and a T-shirt, and ran out of the house with her sandals in her hands. Rather than go through the wait of getting her car out of the garage, she hailed a cab for the ride to the Garden District.

She made it to her old home in record time. Liz, a pretty, slender brunette, was in the doorway with a crying Petey in her arms. She looked very upset and worried.

"Don't you go trying to drive!" Shanna told her stepmother. "Get in that cab, and give me a call when you know what's up."

Jamie started to cry as his mother left. Shanna picked him up, letting him wail a minute, then telling him how she'd read him Dr. Seuss—he adored *Green Eggs and Ham*—and they'd make pancakes.

She kept her promise, reading first, then sitting Jamie in his chair in the kitchen, letting him stir batter with her, and keeping up a chatter all the while. He missed Petey already—he kept looking at his twin's empty chair. She knew what he felt; she and Jade weren't twins, but she couldn't begin to imagine life without her sister. They'd gone away to separate schools, and learned then just how close they were. When she'd gotten the awful call from Scotland a year ago—and had not known just what had happened to her sister—it had been the most awful thing in the world.

She poured pancake batter onto the griddle and thought about how strange it was to be here—home. It was a grand old house, and had been here at least ten years before the Civil War. The rooms were big, and there was a porch with large white pillars and an old swinging chair. Her rocking horse was upstairs in the attic; there were still pictures of her mother on the walls. Liz had never touched those. But the house . . .

The silver was Liz's. The cookware, even the griddle. The kitchen was different. For a moment Shanna missed her mother with all her heart.

The kitchen had been far more cluttered when her mom was alive. There had always been pictures all over the refrigerator, "artwork" by her and Jade. Their latest essays had been attached to the fridge as well by several silly, cheap magnets. Liz was not a clutter person. There weren't even snapshots of the twins on the refrigerator. Those were neatly kept in frames out in the parlor.

"Here you go, baby," she said, turning to Jamie with a plate of fresh pancakes.

"I'm not a baby!" he told her.

"I'm sorry, of course not. Want me to cut it up for you?"

He scowled at her. "I'm not a baby."

"I know. Silly me. You're almost three."

The great thing about a kid his age was that a scowl didn't last. Jamie beamed at her now. He pointed at the kitchen window with his fork. "There's a man, Shanny." He might be almost three, and not at all a baby in his own mind, but he still didn't have her name quite right. He always called her Shanny.

"A man?" she spun around. There was no one there. "I don't see anyone, kiddo."

The scowl came back. "Saw him! Looking in."

"I'll see," she said. She exited the kitchen, walking through the dining room to the open hallway and the front door. The wooden door had been left open; the screen door had been latched. She opened the screen door, stepped out to the porch, and looked around. "Hello? Is anyone there?" She saw no one. "Can I help you? If you're there, show yourself!"

The phone started to ring.

"Liz!" she said, running back inside. The screen door swung. Shut, open, shut.

Open.

She raced into the kitchen and checked to see that Jamie was still safely in his seat. She all but wrenched the kitchen extension off the wall.

"Hello?"

"Shanna! I was getting worried."

"I'm here."

"You're breathless."

"I was running a bit."

"It scared me when you didn't answer. So many awful things happen these days . . . that's why your father was out so early. His job is to edit these days, not walk the streets, but . . . well, never mind. I'm on my way home. They gave Petey some magical shot, then left me in one of the little cubicles in the emergency room with him for an hour. They told me that if the shot didn't help him, they'd have to admit him. But it worked; his temperature is normal, and he's much better.''

''Liz, that's great. But we're fine. You don't need to hurry.''

''Frankly, I'm exhausted. I'll be glad to get back home.''

''We'll be here.''

''Great. Keep the place locked up tight, okay?''

Shanna felt an odd, creeping sensation. ''Why? I mean, I will, but I grew up here, Liz. This neighborhood is as safe as they get.''

''Oh, I know. It's just that . . . I'm not sure what's going on, but something very bad has happened in the city, and your father is out because they're not sure what they want in the media. I mean, they're not trying to hold back freedom of speech or anything, but there was a murder, I believe, and they don't want the public to know the details.''

''We're locked up. We'll be careful. See you soon.''

She hung up, grimaced at Jamie, and went racing back through the house.

The screen door was wide open, welcoming any kook who happened to be walking by.

''Shoot!'' Shanna said under her breath. She quickly closed and latched the door.

She walked back in. Jamie was munching pancakes.

''Mommy's coming. With Petey?''

''Yep. Petey's a bunch better. They're both coming home right now.''

She shivered. She accepted the piece of pancake he insisted she take. "Only a sister would do this, kiddo," she told him, ruffling his hair.

She shivered and looked around.

The house had grown cold. Really cold.

No. She was imagining it.

"Cold, Shanny," Petey said.

"Ah. Cold, eh? We'll light a fire then, and wait for Mommy."

Rick tossed and turned, and tossed and turned, nightmare images of the kid who'd gone into the tree and then through the windshield filtering through his dreams.

The kid talked to him.

"Hurts, man. Hurts."

"I keep trying to teach you guys to stay away from drugs, and watch the alcohol."

The kid's head was detached from his body, floating above it. "You don't know. You really don't know. Man, I saw it. Bad scene. I wasn't so drunk. Just driving fast. Running. But you can't run fast enough, you know? No, you don't know, you don't know. . . ."

Go away, please go away, oh, man, kid, you look just awful!

"You don't know who I am. You don't know what I saw. How hard I ran . . ."

But the kid's image faded from his fevered dream.

Suddenly a different face was in front of him. Much better. It was the tourist. The beautiful, dark-haired tourist who had been so lost the other day.

"Hello, Rick. I'm so sorry to see you suffering."

Her voice was so gentle. Sweet. She was just stunning. All that dark hair framing the perfection of her face . . .

She was floating, too. Just outside his window.

It was a second-floor window, but that was okay. She was much, much better than the decapitated kid haunting his sleep.

"Just a cold, I think. Sore throat. Thirsty," he said politely.

"I'll just bet you are," she said sweetly.

"Did you get where you were trying to go the other night?" he asked.

"I'm getting there, bit by bit."

"It's a great city," he said. "You'll want to take your time. See everything."

"Oh, I think I will." Her tone was silky, so soothing.

"Rick!"

The kid with the detached head seemed to be floating by his bed.

"Kid, go away. She's a much better delirium."

"You don't know, you don't know, you can run—"

"Rick!" she said softly. "It's cold out here. I need to come in."

"Of course. Come in."

The kid was gone again. *Thank God.* His head floating . . . his neck all chopped up, his face bloated . . . it had been bad.

"I rang the bell, Rick," she said, climbing through the window. "You didn't answer."

"Sorry. I'm sick. Really sick. Sore throat. I just got it the other night."

"Poor dear."

"Well, of course you were cold," he told her, staring at her, amazed.

Now *this* was a dream.

She was naked. Stark naked.

"You have no clothes on."

"No clothes? Oh, dear."

"It's all right. It's quite all right."

And it was. *Wow.* She was stunning. Her breasts were swinging, perfect globes, peaked with rosy red, large, hard nipples. She had a will-o'-the-wisp waist. Flaring hips. Long, shapely legs. A black thatch of short, silky hair at her crotch.

She was . . .

"You can . . . uh . . . borrow a robe. Or a coat. Or a shirt," he told her.

She smiled. "That's okay. I don't think I'll need one." She sat by his bed, smoothing back his sweat-dampened hair. "Poor dear. You're cold."

"No, no. I think I'm burning up. And you're an invention of my fever." He looked her up and down again, amazed. "And I'm not usually this inventive. Wow. Wait till I tell the guys at work. No, maybe not," he amended.

"Um. Maybe you are hot. Hot-blooded, hum, Officer? Well, I'm cold, so cold. You'll share with me, right?"

She scraped her breasts over his chest, rubbed her body against him.

He sprang to with an erection that would have done a porn star proud.

"You are cold," he whispered as she crawled over him.

"And you're hot. . . ."

She leaned over him, engulfing him. "So, so, hot . . . thanks . . ."

"Thanks?"

She was moving over him. This was really delirium.

"Thanks for . . . ?"

"Inviting me in," she whispered against his lips. Then she was kissing him. Moving, bringing him to spasms, kissing him . . .

His fever must have worsened.

His hallucinations faded. . . .

He blacked out after thinking that his dreams were fantastic, but his throat hurt worse than ever.

When the phone rang later, he didn't hear a thing.

Shanna was really ready to run right out by the time Liz made it back. The day had worn on long enough now.

She could stop by Jade's house.

But Liz wanted to talk, and so she forced herself to be patient, playing with Petey for a few minutes, glad to see him so much better.

Then Liz put the kids down for a nap and made a cup of tea. Shanna declined, itching for a good, strong cup of coffee, but not wanting to wait long enough now to brew any.

"I really want to thank you. So much," Liz told her. She was already cleaning up her kitchen. Apparently, though Shanna had washed the griddle, she hadn't cleaned the counter sufficiently. "Sometimes I just feel so bad. . . ."

"Liz, why?" Shanna said, struggling for patience. She suddenly wanted to leave really badly. This wasn't her home anymore. It hadn't been for a long time. There wasn't anything wrong with Liz; she was a good human being, a good mom to Petey and Jamie. Shanna just felt acutely uncomfortable.

Cold.

The fire hadn't done a damned thing.

"I don't know," Liz murmured, mopping down the counter, then meeting Shanna's eyes. "Last year . . . your sister had given your phone as an emergency number rather than this number, your father's number. You went after her when there was trouble, and your dad didn't even know what had happened until Jade was home."

"Liz, Jade didn't mean to hurt anyone's feelings. The kids were really little then. Jade didn't want Dad leaving you when . . . when . . ."

"Jade's having survived a terrible massacre wasn't important enough for him to leave us for her?" Liz said softly.

"She never meant to hurt your feelings," Shanna said. "I never meant to hurt your feelings."

"Then . . . well, then, quit doing it!" Liz said. She suddenly squeezed her sponge out over the sink with enough force to cause it to become a gusher.

Shanna stared at the sponge, then at her stepmother. "Excuse me?"

"Quit being so polite to me. Treat me like I am a member of the family. Don't tiptoe around me all the time. Let your father know that you need him sometimes. Make the twins go without now and then so that you can have some of his time—or our time."

Startled, Shanna sat back. She nodded. "All right. All right then. You quit apologizing when you ask me to help with *my* baby brothers."

"I . . . well, I can hardly expect—"

"Yeah, you can. If you want to be a real family."

Liz smiled slowly, nodding. "Okay. But if you hadn't wanted to get up, I would have called Jade. She's more of a morning person."

Shanna grinned suddenly. "Oh, no, not this morning. I think she might have finally slept with that great cop she's been dating."

"Really!" Liz's cheeks suddenly turned very red. She looked down. "Would you have . . . would you have said that to your mother?"

Shanna thought a minute. "Yes, actually, I would have. But, Liz . . ."

"Yes?"

"I wouldn't say it to Dad. So that was between us, huh?"

Liz agreed, still blushing. A minute later Shanna told her that she really had to go. After giving the boys huge, sloppy kisses, she hugged Liz warmly. She had never felt closer to her stepmother.

And still, she was eager to go. The house was so cold. Colder than outside. And it was a bone-chilling, damp kind of cold today.

Liz offered to drive her back, but she insisted that she didn't mind taking a taxi. She was still so chilled, though, that when she reached the French Quarter she had the driver drop her at a coffee shop rather than at her home, or at Jade's, where she was heading next.

She walked to the counter, just wanting a rich, French-roast coffee.

Someone came up beside her. He was obviously cold, too. He warmed his hands before him. He looked pale, and he was slim, as if he had been ill awhile.

A good looking guy, though. Different from the muscle-bound, blond good looks of a guy like Rich Beaudreaux. This one was . . .

Hm. Tall—and wickedly lean. Cunning, maybe. Like a fox. All right, so his hair had a red tinge to it, and it seemed he had a few freckles.

A scholarly, sly red fox. He was cute.

And he offered her a very inviting smile.

"Darned cold out there for the Deep South, isn't it?" he said. Nice voice. Very nice voice. Deep, rich . . . exciting. She felt like getting closer to him, just because of the sound of his voice.

"It's all the water. The temperature isn't that bad, but it's damp."

"Yeah. Yeah, I guess."

Her coffee arrived. She curled her fingers around the cup.

"My name's . . . Dave," he told her.

"Dave. Hi. I'm Shanna."

"You're gorgeous," he said.

She grinned deeply, enjoying his blunt appreciation. "Thanks."

"I realize I'm a total stranger . . . but I'd like to see you."

"You might be fun to get to know."

"Oh, I can promise you—I'm different."

"I'll bet."

He smiled, but he suddenly started coughing and backed away. "Sorry, I guess I'm getting something."

"Seems to be going around. You look like you need to be in bed."

"I do," he agreed.

"Well, if you do get some sleep and decide you feel better . . . I'm going to the old Mel Gibson rerelease at the movies tonight," she told him.

She'd had no intention of going to the movies. Until now, of course.

Because she would like to see him again. And she wasn't fool enough to invite a stranger over.

"I'm sure as hell going to try to be there," he told her. "But you know . . ."

"My last name is MacGregor. My phone number is in the book."

"Great. Is that an invitation?"

"Sure. Please do call."

She didn't want to appear too eager. She raised her coffee cup to him and left quickly. She felt elated.

She looked back, though, and frowned to see that he had doubled over.

A laughing crowd of teenagers suddenly passed her blocking her view of him.

Worried, she hurried back to the coffee shop.

He was gone.

As if he had disappeared into thin air.

Chapter Six

In the days that followed, Lucian learned his first defeat at Sophia's hands.

A young Viking with a rich blond beard and bright blue eyes became his teacher, his mentor, his guide—and then his friend. Lucian learned that the woman Sophia had lived among their people for many years—the man's father's father's father had acquired her during a raid on the British Isles years ago. No one was sure where she had originally come from, but when they raided and ravaged her village, they found that they had seized far more than they had imagined.

They made peace with the captive who nearly slayed them all. Two of the other vampires at her beck and call were very old, nearly as old as Sophia herself, older than the Viking could remember. The third man, Darian, she had brought home from a raid not long ago. He was dangerous, more vicious than any berserker, crafty, cunning, mean. And learned. He knew history from all over the world. He knew about legends, gods, goddesses, sorcerers.

The Viking crew sailed the seas with the vampire and her followers. They gave their masters victims. In turn, they kept the riches they plundered.

And their lives.

Their families were allowed to live as well.

The Viking's name was Wulfgar. He was careful of what he said, but there were times when Sophia was gone— really gone from the ship—and at those times Wulfgar lowered his voice and told Lucian more.

Aye, Lucian was dead. Wulfgar said so sorrowfully, and regretfully.

Well, not exactly *dead*.

Now he was undead.

He must have blood to survive. Aye, it could be animal blood—he had seen Sophia drinking the blood of such creatures as seals, raccoons, and more—when good human sources could not be found. She was not happy upon such occasions. She looked at them—the living among them— in such a way at those times as to make their spines chill until they thought they would snap. . . .

She kept certain of her own kind with her at all times, thus the three men who were vampires as well. Always one was closest—a true protector, as Darian was now. There had been a leader before Sophia, she had told them once, but she had grown stronger, and destroyed him. She had learned from him, and though the bite of a *lamia* or vampire could create a new one of such kind, there was a law among the undead that no such creature could create more than two of their own kind every hundred years.

There were other rules.

They were not to kill one another. They were not to be

found, to be caught in the act of vampirism, by any great power or strong government. They were not to bring so great a wrath against themselves that stronger forces could defeat them. They did have their weaknesses; they could be killed. Their bite was infectious—they could create others of their kind with such a touch, and with their appetites their numbers had to be limited. "That is why the heads must be removed. Too many victims would awaken." Wulfgar shrugged. "As you awoke yourself."

"I had heard legends. The undead walk by night," Lucian told Wulfgar. "Sophia moves by night and by day—"

"While you lie exhausted," Wulfgar said. "She is strong, very strong. She is old. She has learned, tested, and taught herself. Time will give you greater strength." He hesitated. "Blood gives you strength. She is also best, more powerful, at night. Sometimes the sunlight drains her."

"But it doesn't kill her."

"Set her afire to disappear as dust? I fear not."

"But I had heard—"

"There are many legends. Some true. Most not. In time, you will need to feed. But not so often. Meat as other men eat can fill your stomach." Wulfgar shrugged. "It's easy. You will not care if your lamb is cooked or not. Your situation has its advantages. Lift a cow off a field and bite in, no cooking fires needed. Rain would not matter."

He tried to smile. Lucian did not.

"You could live forever and ever," Wulfgar told him.

"Despised, loathed, feared?"

"Great leaders are despised, loathed, and feared. But they wish they could live forever!" Wulfgar reminded him. "You have power. Power is always feared—and hated."

That night there was an attack again. Lucian remained on the ship, listening to the screams.

He felt her summon him.

And he remembered that Wulfgar had told him that he would grow strong. It was in the will, he thought.

He must make his will stronger than hers.

He managed not to go.

She didn't try to force him. He knew that she was certain that in time his hunger would drive him to insanity, and he would have to follow her when she led.

The next day the pain began.

Hunger. Anguish. It was more than just waking with a need for food. It was a need so fierce it made him ache throughout. He was so hungry he thought he would be sick. So hungry he felt his strength deserting him.

Off the bow of a ship, he saw a dolphin. The gnawing started up so fiercely he nearly doubled over, blinded with the pain. He could feel the mammal's warm blood, even at a distance.

It was then that he discovered his own power. He concentrated on the dolphin, closed his eyes, moved with it through the water. He felt the surge of the creature's muscles, its movements through the waves. He willed it nearer. And nearer . . .

To the edge of the boat it came. He could have reached out, seized it. . . .

He opened his eyes and saw, suddenly, the beauty of the animal, the trust it had given him. His hand was upon it, for it bobbed by the boat. He could have hauled it up without a thought.

Swim, he thought. *Swim away.*

It went off in a rush. He sank to the floor of the ship, shaking. He didn't want people; he didn't want a mammal. A different pain suddenly seared him. He looked at his hands.

The salt water had burned him!

Salt water could kill.

With that knowledge, he crawled back to the bed in the hold.

When he slept, she came to him. Daylight was the time. He had no power, and no will. No strength, and yet . . .

What she made him feel . . .

He had never been more virile, known such a violent climax. And when it was over . . .

He had never known such self-disgust and loathing.

The next day he stood at the bow of the ship. He kept a fur cloak around his shoulders, but it did nothing to warm him as the wind whipped around him.

He contemplated throwing himself in the sea. He stood for hours, thinking.

He heard Wulfgar at his side.

"Don't."

"Why not? I am a dead man."

"Don't destroy yourself."

"Why would I not?"

Wulfgar stared at him for a long time, puzzling out an answer. Then he found one.

"Because you should stay—to destroy her."

"One day, friend, I could turn on you," Lucian told him. "Lose control, rip you to shreds, tear you apart limb from limb."

"You could," Wulfgar answered evenly. "But you will not."

He heard the whistle of the wind and felt its great force. There were many things in the world that were evil. Few like her.

Living—if this was living—to destroy her. That made sense.

And later that night, he was glad.

*　*　*

He learned to curb his hunger with rats and birds and other small animals. He had learned that he did need blood, and he knew as well that the blood gave him strength.

He had also learned to move with his mind—to walk on water, as she had done.

Aye, indeed, he had learned to live his own wretched form of his undead life!

The best he felt in a long time had been after the day he had found the boar—the poor animal, though something of a brute itself, had surely never imagined such a savage death. He had left the ship alone, gone ashore, and hunted the boar. He smelled it on the air and felt his shape shift to that of a hunter, a wolf. He had run down the boar, attacked it, pounced upon it.

He had drained it dry of every last speck of blood, and he had consumed it, viciously tearing into it at first, then slowly savoring every drop of flesh and blood. He had eaten the meat, chewed on the bones, even gnawed the hide.

He knew he wanted human blood. And there would be times, he promised himself, when the right humans might appear conveniently before him. He had been a chieftain of a Highland people often besieged by battle. He had killed before.

He would kill again.

But if God could hear such a loathsome creature as himself, surely He would grant him power and strength. In nature there was a balance. Maybe he was part of that balance. If he fought for real strength, he could keep himself from the killing of innocents.

They traveled the sea, wreaking havoc from Scotland to Ireland, England, and Wales.

Sophia ceased to be quite as amused as she had been

when she realized she had created a being determined to resist her.

One night she accosted him.

"Why? You know what you are; you cannot go back. I offer you a chance to rule with me, to become my true consort. I am all-powerful in this world, I am beautiful, and I have offered so much to you! You are just a stubborn fool to reject me."

And he had been the one smiling then, amused. "You are the fool, you ridiculous woman. You think that all you have to do is take, and a man, once a human being, will be yours. You have no concept of beauty; you are hideous to me. You don't begin to understand the concept of what a man being with a woman means; you are devoid of love, compassion—and even reason. You rule? You will not do so long. Even in our world, the world of the hunter, there must be balance. You kill for the sake of killing, for the sport of cruelty. If you keep up such excesses, you will damn all our kind, and damn yourself!"

And he had turned away from her, taking pleasure in the fury he had seen in her eyes.

But she had still ruled the ship and her Viking crew. And so they continued to sail and to raid.

One day, late in the afternoon, just when the sun was falling and the strength of nighttime was coming on, they reached a village. He knew that there would be a killing spree. He ached for what he once had been. For the people who would die.

A time will come when I will rule. And I will know what I am, a creature, a monster, a hunter, but there will be rules to the hunt, and they will be followed, and there will be reason, and sanity, even within the horror. . . .

He heard the screams.

He smelled blood.

He hungered.

But he refused temptation. He remained where he was, and would not join in.

Then he heard her calling him. Sophia, her voice taunting . . . and threatening.

He came topside of the Viking vessel. A chilling, creeping horror settled over him.

He saw that they had returned to his own homeland. And as the warriors battled . . .

Sophia sidestepped the carnage. She had reached the women, running with the children.

She seized Igrainia.

"Sophia!"

He cried her name in rage, ready to head for the shore. But the battle had ended, the monsters victorious. Before he could reach land, Sophia returned to the ship, her men dragging Lucian's wife with them to the ship. Bringing Igrainia aboard, wet and shaking. Sophia forced her before him.

"Igrainia!" Her name was a whisper on his lips, a caress. She smiled, a smile that promised him that love never died.

Her eyes were on him. Her beautiful blue-green eyes, eyes the color of the sea, trusting, still,—*oh, God*—trusting him, his word, his thoughts. . . .

"She dies tonight, chieftain," Sophia said. She was to his wife's right, and just behind her. She lifted Igrainia's lush wealth of hair.

Then Sophia smiled, and started to part her lips, salivating.

He rushed forward, amazed at his own strength; he moved like the wind, like the power of the earth, with the fury of thunder. He caught her before her lips could rip into Igrainia's throat.

And they began to battle. . . .

He caught her by the hair and waist, tossing her hard

from her would-be feast; she faltered, staggered, and stood. Then, rushing him, she struck him with such power that his head rocked. He was thrown hard to the ground. He staggered up, catching her by the waist, swinging her around. She kicked him in the chin, spun, and struck him so that he heard his bones snap. Both desperate and enraged, he slammed his fist into her midsection, and as she doubled over, he finished with a blow to her jaw.

Again, he heard bones snap. Hers, this time, rather than his own.

She screamed, shrieked, crippled with the pain. The whole of the crew on board the vessel stood dead still, watching. She looked at him, then turned, plummeting down the length of the vessel, straight for Igrainia.

She tackled Igrainia. With him flying after her, hot on her heels, she hadn't a prayer for the seconds she needed to tear her teeth into Igrainia.

Yet she would not be defeated. She flew at Igrainia, catching her with a fierce power that sent her toppling over the bow of the ship.

And into the sea.

Lucian flew to the bow, grappling Sophia, seizing her up with such strength that when he threw her to the floor of the vessel, she stayed down.

But it didn't matter. Igrainia had gone into the sea.

He crawled to the edge of the rail, ready to leap after his wife, who had disappeared beneath the swells of the sea. Strong arms caught him by the shoulder. Wulfgar, blue eyes earnest on his.

"No! You'll die—"

"I care not."

"But *she'll* die as well. We will go for her. We will—"

Agony suddenly seared him. Stunned, paralyzed, he tried to turn.

Sophia's key lackey. Darian.

He'd brought a sword against his neck. The steel was imbedded there.

Lucian started to fall, his world pervaded by blackness.

When he woke next, it was to Wulfgar's cheerful face.

"So you've survived. You are a strong one. They nearly severed your head. That would be the end, you know."

He sat up, rubbing his neck. He looked around. He could smell the sea. Nets adorned the wall. The wood planking around him was rough. The cry of a gull met his ears.

They seemed to be in a small fisherman's cottage. He looked around, then at Wulfgar.

"Where are we?"

"An island off the coast."

"What island?"

"The Isle of the Dead."

"Isle of the Dead?"

"The weather is constantly fierce, and many will not come here. Many will. They say it is a place of the misbegotten. Of dwarves and knaves and hunchbacks. Lepers live here as well. It has been a home to Druids, witches, spirits, and more. No one will question that you should have power here."

"Sophia?"

We brought you here before she could awake. She thinks that you will soon die, if you haven't done so already. No one thought you could survive the depth of that sword wound. Sophia was furious. You injured her badly. She had to sleep in her shroud, surrounded by piles of her earth."

"What of Igrainia?" he asked, gripping Wulfgar's shoulder.

Wulfgar inhaled and exhaled slowly. "You know that she went into the sea."

"Aye, but you went after her, you swore—"

"Aye, you know that I did, I searched, I dove, over and over. The waves kept coming. . . . I couldn't find her, Scotsman."

He knew that Wulfgar meant it, that he had tried his hardest. Such a thought didn't ease the pain that swept over him. A darkness fell upon Lucian, seizing him in a terrible grip, worse than any anguish or agony he had felt thus far. Igrainia. Anything had been bearable when he had thought that at the least, his actions had saved her life.

"Don't despair completely," Wulfgar said quickly.

"Aye, and why not?"

"Some of the men swear that they have seen her walking the beach here. She comes by day, and disappears at night."

"What?" He grabbed hold of Wulfgar, wincing at the pain his sudden movement caused. "So she may be alive?"

"I don't know. Perhaps it is her . . ."

"Her what?"

Wulfgar looked at him. "Her spirit."

"No, if she has been seen, she's real. I don't believe in ghosts."

"And why not? All Norsemen believe in spirits. They guide us. Our ancestors have gone before us. They send messages in the runes, the bones. We heed the word of our oracles. There are many forces we cannot touch or see—those of the woods, the waters. The locals here are saying that she comes as a . . ."

"As what?" Lucian demanded.

He hesitated, then shrugged. "The island is Irish, my friend. And the Irish accept that you are dead, but still here. And they believe in the power of the water, the sea, as well. Legends abound. Aye, you are dead, but you spared the dolphin that day. Maybe the masters of the seas accepted Igrainia, and gave her new life as well.''

''What are you saying? You are daft, man!''

''They believe in selkies. Women by day, sea creatures by night. Saved by the sea, or born of the sea, they may walk the earth, touch man, but then . . . they must return to the water.''

''No. She must have survived. Perhaps she is here; she came to this island but is hurt, suffering, and doesn't know who she is.''

Wulfgar wasn't going to argue with him. ''Who knows? Perhaps you are right; perhaps I am right. Perhaps even such a warrior as yourself will leave this world one day, and still come and sit in the halls of Valhalla. There are more things in my own Valhalla, or your heaven and hell, and even in this earth we share, than any man shall ever know.''

''I don't believe—''

''You don't believe? In spirits, ghosts, sprites—or in bloodsuckers? In vampires?'' Wulfgar suggested innocently. *''Lamia?''*

''I will search for Igrainia. Unto eternity,'' he said.

''Later, perhaps you will do so. Long after I have gone to my own reward, whatever that shall be. For now . . . you will do nothing. You should have died. You must regain your strength.''

He had wanted to die—or perish as whatever evil thing he had become.

Now he wanted to live.

To find Igrainia, if still she lived.

To destroy Sophia.

But Darian had injured him badly. He was weak as a baby by day, and there was a time of healing when he could barely move, even at the midnight hour, even in the greatest darkness of night. But then, bit by bit, he healed.

He rode the island with Wulfgar. He established himself as lord of the misfits who dwelled there.

He started to walk the shoreline in the middle of the night, when his strength was the greatest.

He drank great quantities of sheep's blood.

He hungered for more, craved more. He knew, somewhere in the depths of him, that, injured as he was, he needed more.

There was a farmer on the island who viciously beat his wife.

Lucian heard their arguments sometimes when he rode with Wulfgar at night—seeking out warm-blooded mammals to attack. She was a tireless young woman who toiled hard with the soil, laundered, cooked, and served her husband. The husband had been a thief. He'd escaped Dublin—and the hangman—for the island, dragging her with him to this exile.

One night, as they were riding, Lucian heard her scream.

He glanced at Wulfgar, dismounted from his horse, and strode toward the house. The husband was drunk. She had spilled his ale on the raw wood table. He was beating her with a horse whip.

The hunger gnawed at Lucian.

He went after the farmer, wrenching the whip from his hands. And in his rage he bit into the farmer's neck. The wife watched while he drained the man of blood.

Lucian looked at his victim with revulsion. He staggered back, looking at his own blood-covered hands.

Then he remembered to cut off the farmer's head. Of all the men he didn't want coming back for eternity, this wretched bastard was surely one.

All this time the young wife simply stared at him. His eyes then turned to her. She didn't flinch.

"Thank you," she said softly.

"You know what I am."

"Most the isle know what y'are," she told him.

"You're not afraid?"

"Of many things, aye."

"But of me?"

"Should I be?"

"No," he told her.

The following day he had the strength to walk the beach while the sun was still up.

And it was there that he saw his wife.

Igrainia!

A ghost? He called to her. "Igrainia . . ."

A ghost . . .

Selkie, the Irish said.

He did not believe in such things. But could he create her with the power of his mind? Would she disappear if he raced for her, to touch her, feel her, to know the softness of her hair, the angel's breath of her whisper against his cheek?

He ran.

She stayed.

She was real. Flesh and blood and bone. He touched her. Her sea eyes touched his. "My wife, my love . . ."

He started shaking and fell to the sand at her feet.

She touched the top of his head.

"Husband . . ."

He looked up. She was smiling.

"My God, Igrainia . . ."

He stood, and he lifted her into his arms. He kept his eyes on hers as he walked with her to the fisherman's cottage he had made his home.

"How can you be here?" he whispered. He laid her on the bed. He loved her so much. And still . . .

He could feel her warmth, hear her blood. He would

never hurt her, could never hurt her—or could he? Would the agony seize him, overwhelm him? Would he slash her throat with his teeth, make love to her by stealing her lifeblood, her heart, her soul?

"I have to tell you—"

"No!" she pressed a finger to his lips.

"You must understand—"

"No."

"But I—"

"I know what you are. And I know you won't hurt me."

She lifted her lips to his, and he opened his mouth and kissed her and kissed her, more and more deeply. And he felt her body, and her warmth, her shape, her hips flush to his. He felt a burst of arousal, and with it lust and tenderness, and it was sweet, so sweet to know desire with love, and a longing that did not tear at whatever remnants of his soul might remain.

Insanely, he stripped away their clothing.

Sophia knew only violence, and the hungers of the flesh.

There were deeper hungers.

Hungers that hinted he might still have a soul.

He put his lips to her breast, down her belly, between her thighs. She writhed, wrapped herself around him. He tasted the sweetness of her flesh, of her being, of her sex. His body pulsed and groaned, he reveled in what he had, he felt the hunger gnaw at him, felt the ultimate ecstacy he denied himself, and still . . .

He nearly, so nearly, brought his teeth to the vein throbbing so sweetly at her neck. He fought down the desire, fought it with all the strength in him. She seemed unaware. Wild and wanton, hips locked to his, glued to his, breasts damp against his chest, her delicate fingers digging into his buttocks, her whispers, her words, the sweet wet explosion against him . . .

Climax rocked him. He bit down viciously on his own teeth. Fell to her side. Swept her into his arms. Held her . . .

"I thought I had lost you. I thought you had drowned. The sea was so cold. The waves were high that day, the wind sweeping. How can you be here?" he whispered.

"Does it matter? Love me. Just love me. As I love you."

He held her. The sun grew stronger. He grew weary. She sat against the hard wooden headboard, down pillow against it, and cradled his head to her breast. She stroked his cheek.

"Igrainia." He wanted to talk. To stay awake.

"Sleep, rest, heal," she told him.

Her fingers were magic.

In the darkened cottage, he slept.

When he awoke, she was gone.

Chapter Seven

Before Jade could start out again, the phone started ringing a second time. It was Shanna, telling her she was at a coffee shop, and that she'd be right up—if Rick was gone.

Jade assured her Rick was gone.

"When did he leave?"

Jade hesitated. "He never really stayed."

"What?" The word was incredulous.

"He never really stayed."

"Great! And I just soared out of bed and went off to Dad's house to baby-sit—so that Liz wouldn't disturb your little love nest!"

"You baby-sat already today?"

"Mornings are not my thing, you know."

"I know. I'm impressed. Is everything all right?"

"Fine. Petey had a fever, but they gave him a shot, and Liz brought him right home. I mean I leaped out of bed, thinking you were decadently busy! And you didn't even *do* anything!" Shanna moaned. "You're going to have to explain when I get there!"

"Shanna—"

The phone clicked. Shanna was gone, on her way over. When she arrived, she was impatient and disgusted.

"Nothing? Nothing happened?"

"How did you get here so quickly?"

"I was just down the street at a coffee shop. Tell me what happened. Did you fight? Why did Rick leave?"

"He was exhausted and sick. Really sick. He's got an awful bug."

Shanna looked down the hallway, toward Renate's door. "I wonder if our old buddy Matt at least got lucky."

"No, he didn't."

"How do you know?"

"Renate has already been over, looking for Rick."

"Why?"

"Who knows? She must think there's great info for her work in all this. But anyway, you're here now, so you can just come to the police station with me. Rick got Gavin to find out more about the thing in New York City—"

"Oh, God!" Shanna groaned. "What good is this going to do? Say you *are* in danger—you won't even make the effort to sleep with a good cop."

"Shanna, I told you—"

"He should have needed comfort."

"People can be just dead tired. And he wanted a bath."

"Did your water stop running?"

"He wanted it to be right."

"It's already *wrong*, if you can't just get to it!"

Shanna shook her head with disgust, turned, and started

out. Jade froze behind her, wondering if her sister was right. Had she felt that all along, or . . .

Had something changed last night?

I seem to have sex all by myself, and it's just great—better than it could be with him. And anyway, I couldn't make him stay, because he would see what my room looked like!

The whole thing was awful. Mortifying. She couldn't say any of it out loud.

Not even to her sister.

"I thought you were in a hurry?" Shanna said impatiently.

"Yes, let's go."

"I still don't see how you let Rick go home! You should have taken care of him. Run him a hot bath, given him a cold beer."

"He didn't have any clean clothes."

"He didn't need clean clothes for what you intended. Jade, if he's so sick, he should need you. If he's hurting, he should want to feel better."

"Shanna, he's *sick*, really, truly, rotten-feeling sick. Sex will not make it better. So stop. You are a pain in the butt!"

"Oh, all right, I'll leave off. You two can continue with your sweet, platonic, totally boring relationship. I won't torture you anymore."

"Promise?"

"No, but let's get going anyway."

The station wasn't far. They walked the distance easily.

Jade had known that she wouldn't find Rick at the station. She was glad to hear that he had phoned in and reported that he was really ill and was going to sleep all day.

"He's got an awful flu bug," the desk sergeant told her.

"I know. I'm going to make him go to the doctor if he isn't better by tomorrow. Would you mind giving Gavin a ring for me, though? I need to see him."

"Sure thing."

Gavin Newton was one of Rick's best friends. Squat and a bit chubby, he had an amazingly cherubic face and a slow, laid-back nature, which, Rick had told Jade, made him an exceptional Homicide cop—people *said* things to Gavin. He could draw a suspect's trust, and he could encourage the most reticent witness to talk. He was also a very nice guy, a truly concerned citizen, and nothing in the horror of the job had made him insensitive to the fears, cares, and concerns of others as individuals.

He greeted Jade warmly, welcomed Shanna, then stared at Jade again, sighing. "Come on back to my desk," he told them. "It was your guy, all right. I sent for information yesterday that was wired back to me, but if you take a look at most any of the papers floating around the country, you'd know that anyway now. Let's see. . . . Here's the fax on Hugh Riley."

He handed Jade a piece of paper. She scanned the information. It gave his name, height, weight, eye and hair color, and age. Apparently, when he'd left Scotland, he'd transferred schools. Then he'd signed up for a new fraternity.

The fraternity didn't demand any illegal or immoral offerings from its pledges—no beer guzzling, beatings, eating bizarre substances, no stealing the school mascot or trophies, and no flying underwear from the flagpole— but on the last night of pledging, the pledges were to tell ghost stories at the cemetery just outside the city.

And in the dark of night . . .

That was when the murders had occurred.

"At midnight," Jade said under her breath.

"Now, Jade . . . ," Gavin said softly.

"Gavin, it's exactly the same as what happened in Scotland."

"Jade, if there are real similarities, the FBI will be calling on you."

She gazed at him sharply.

"They'll definitely be called in on it." He shifted the papers on his desk, selecting one of the national dailies. "You're not the only one who remembers what happened in Scotland. This reporter comments on the fact that Hugh Riley had survived such an attack in Edinburgh, only to die in New York."

Jade met his eyes, then quickly scanned the article. "See?" she said to Shanna.

"Well, I might be able to see—if you'd just let me have the paper."

Jade let go of the paper. Her sister quickly read the article. Shanna stared at Gavin. "So what do think? Is it the same people?"

"Maybe," Gavin admitted.

"And maybe there's a major new cult at work in the world as we know it." They heard the deep, rusty voice of Al Harding, Gavin's partner, as he strode to his desk, which abutted Gavin's. Just as Gavin was short, squat, and round, Al was tall and as thin as a string bean. He was usually dry and quiet, standing back, listening, while Gavin did the talking. The Homicide detectives in the parish customarily worked in threes, two officers and a sergeant. Sergeant Bill Marceau usually worked with the pair, but he'd been out for some time after bypass surgery. With the department short, the two were still working without him.

"Don't you fear, little lady," Al Harding continued. "This is the United States of America. New York has top-notch, crack detectives. They'll comb that cemetery for every scrap of evidence, and mark my word—they'll get the psychos!"

Jade liked Al, but she felt she had to reply to him, "With all due respect to the New York police and the fine work of American agents, the Brits from Scotland Yard were no fools—they combed every inch of that cemetery as well. They found nothing.''

"Still, this is America.''

"God bless the Red, White, and Blue!" Shanna breathed softly.

Jade kicked her lightly in the shin.

"I wonder if I should call someone," Jade said. "Maybe I could help.''

"And maybe you could just relive a nightmare," Shanna said. "And maybe the media will get hold of your name again, and if it is a major cult and someone is after you, you might just put yourself into greater danger.''

"I'll talk to someone on the case, quietly and discreetly," Gavin told her. "And I'll make sure that if any agents or officers do want to talk to you, they'll be quiet about it. How's that?''

"That sounds good. Thanks, Gavin.''

Al cleared his throat suddenly. "Jade, from what I've read, and from what I heard from you ..." His voice trailed; he inhaled and tried again. "You talked about the man who disappeared, the one who saved you, and about the way people came from coffins to attack you all. Well, I mean, I just hope you realize ...''

"Yes?" she said.

"They were just sick people. Really sick people.''

"Of course.''

"I mean," he said, and his face turned red, "well, I heard you kind of went on and on about ... about ...''

"Vampires?" Shanna suggested sweetly.

"Yeah," Al said. "Well, you know," he went on impatiently, "you can't go to the FBI talking all crazy like that.''

"Maybe there *are* vampires, Al.''

They were interrupted again by another officer entering the homicide room. He was a tall, dark-haired, good-looking man who wore Dockers and a casual buff suede sports jacket. Shanna took note, straightening immediately, instinctively smoothing back her hair.

The newcomer nodded to them both.

"Ah, come on, Lieutenant Canady, just because of those old murders—"

"Al, excuse me," he said. He walked over to Jade, smiling, reaching out a hand. "Sean Canady. How do you do? If you're dealing with a cult, it may well be with people who really think they're vampires. And the human mind is a terribly strong thing to mess with—really bad things can happen when the mind wills it should be so. Not many people are going to believe you've come across a real cult of vampires. But I can promise you, if you know anything, if you think anything, if you remember anything—I'll be more than happy to listen to you."

"Thanks, thanks very much," Jade told him.

Shanna stepped forward. "She's Jade MacGregor."

"I know," he said quietly.

"You know?" Jade said.

"I saw some of the news articles after the murders in Scotland last year."

"Oh," she murmured uncomfortably. But he was staring straight at her, his eyes steady—and kind. He didn't seem to think she was a lunatic—or a dope addict.

"I'm her sister, Shanna."

He smiled, a nice, slow, curve of a smile.

"Shanna, Jade, nice to meet you. If these clowns are making fun of you, call me. I'll listen."

"I wasn't making fun of her," Al protested.

"See that you don't," Sean said. He hesitated, looking

at Jade. "I saw Hugh Riley was among the people killed in New York."

"And you remembered his name from the articles about the murders in Scotland?" Gavin said.

"Yep."

"Murders every day, around the world, and you notice the names of the survivors from a massacre in Scotland?" Shanna said suspiciously.

"I'm a detective," he told them with a shrug. But he was watching Jade, and she saw something very serious in his eyes.

"And he's a good one," Al admitted grudgingly. "They assign you to the kid?" he inquired.

Sean nodded, his eyes still on Jade. "There will be a task force, I've been told. Jade, Shanna, nice to meet you. If there's anything at all that I can do, let me know."

They thanked him. He walked away, leaving the room. Jade thought that it seemed—oddly enough—that he had come just to meet them.

Shanna exhaled. "There goes some good-looking testosterone."

"He's married," Al told her.

"He would be," Shanna murmured with a fatalistic shrug.

"Hey, I'm available," Gavin said.

"And you're a gem!" Shanna assured him quickly.

"But you're busy Friday nights," Gavin said, laughing.

"Gavin, you are a doll and a gem and—"

"And you're gorgeous and twenty-four and I'm . . . I'm not," he said after a moment, grinning. "Oh, well, if you ever get desperate . . ."

"A girl would not need to be desperate," Shanna assured him quickly and sweetly. Jade felt a deep surge of affection for her sister. For all of her cynicism, Shanna was almost always compassionate and kind. "To tell you the truth, I'd have grabbed you for a movie tonight—if we'd had this conversation just yesterday."

Jade looked at her sister curiously. "What happened since yesterday?" she asked her sister.

Shanna's eyes widened teasingly and she grinned. "I met someone."

"This morning?"

"Yep. At a coffee shop, on my way over to your place."

"You didn't tell me!"

"Well, I didn't get married or anything. I agreed to go on a date. Well, actually, I didn't even really agree to go on a date. I suggested that I'd be at a movie. Although, you know, this flu thing is going around. He was sick, too. He could be a no-show."

"Still, you didn't tell me you had met someone."

"Well, I was anxious to hear about your life at the moment." She grinned at Gavin and Al, who were watching the conversation between the sisters with interest. "Her life is just far more interesting than mine. At the moment."

"We need to leave," Jade said firmly, "and let these gentlemen get back to work. Gavin, thanks again. Al, thank you, too."

"My pleasure," Gavin assured her. "I'm delighted to help in any way. And listen. Although I have to say Sean is one good cop—" He broke off, shrugging. "You're sure there's nothing else I can do for you at the moment, other than contacting New York law enforcement?"

"Nothing, thanks."

"Good," Al interrupted quickly, drawing a puzzled glance from Gavin. "I saw the girls here and nearly forgot—we're needed at the morgue."

"What's up?" Gavin queried.

"The M.E. has made a curious discovery regarding the college kid in the accident the other night. You ready?"

"Yeah, sure, let me grab my jacket. Hey, great October, isn't it, ladies?"

"Beautiful, brisk, pleasant, great," Shanna agreed. "In fact, let's pick up a few pumpkins to carve, Jade, eh?"

"Sure. Well, thanks, guys, thanks very much," Jade said.

Twenty minutes later they were at one of the street markets, looking at pumpkins. Jade wanted to know about the guy Shanna had met. Shanna said he was just a guy.

"But you're going on a date with him."

"Not really. I'm meeting him for a movie. And that's a maybe."

"That's a date."

"I'm not having him pick me up or bring me home. We're just meeting for a movie."

"Tell me more."

"That's all," Shanna said, irritatingly evasive.

"Does he have a name?"

"Dave."

"Great. He has a name."

"He's cultured, cute, and charming. That's all I know right now. I'll tell you more later."

"I should go with you."

"No, you should stay home and sleep with your cop." She sighed, shaking her head with disgust. "The price on these is outrageous. You'd think these stinking pumpkins were made out of gold."

"We could drive out of the Quarter and buy a few along the roadside. They'd be much cheaper."

Shanna made a face. "No, thanks. I don't feel like driving anywhere."

"I'm going to take that one."

"Fine—I'll do that fellow over there."

They bought the pumpkins and went back to Jade's place. Coming up the stairs to enter by the living room on the second level, rather than through the courtyard and casual area below, they passed Renate's door. Shanna grinned. "Boy, I sure would like to know just how things did go for good old Matt last night."

"He's not Renate's type—and Renate never minds telling him that."

"Ah . . . but if she had enough champagne and caviar . . ."

"Well, she didn't."

"She should have. The poor boy was trying to celebrate."

"Go tell her that she should have given him a celebration one-night stand."

"All right," Shanna said, staring down the hall.

"Don't you dare!" Jade said, dragging her sister back.

Later, as they were carving out their pumpkins, Jade asked her, "Would you really have been that rude and brazen—to tell her she should have slept with Matt."

"Rude and brazen? How can you be more rude and brazen than Renate?" she said; then she laughed. "I don't know. Thank God you stopped me."

They talked about their Halloween plans, since the holiday was coming up quickly. "We need to have a party," Shanna said.

"New Orleans *is* a party. Every restaurant and every jazz club will have a party. And we have little half brothers, remember? We have to head out to the Garden District and see Dad and Liz and the boys. They'll be so cute—Liz always does such a great job with costumes."

"We could have a party at their house," Shanna said. "I mean, it was our house for years and years. When Mom was alive. Remember?"

Jade was quiet for a minute. "It's not our house anymore."

"Of course it is."

"No, something is different. But did you have a bad time with Liz this morning?"

"No. In fact, I felt pretty close to her."

"Then . . . ?" Jade said, puzzled.

"I don't know. Something just didn't seem right about the house."

"Well, still . . . let's think about it, huh?" Jade said. "It might be more fun just to ride out, see the kids, and come back and club hop."

"Yeah, maybe—ugh! I just cut the stupidest pumpkin teeth you've ever seen."

Jade looked at her sister's pumpkin. "They're pointed."

"I was trying to cut squares . . . oh, well. Thank God I never wanted to grow up to be a pumpkin artist. I've had it; I'm done. I've got to get going. I want to wash my hair . . . bathe in exquisite body salts, powder and perfume, and try on half a dozen outfits. Some of us know how to do this sex thing properly."

"You're going to have sex with a total stranger?" Jade asked, appalled.

Shanna grinned. "No—I'm going on a first date. You have to be beautiful, charming, devastating, and smell divine for just such an occasion. That way he'll probably ask you back out, and it will be your choice if you see him again or not. Understand?"

"I thought you said it wasn't really a date."

"It's not—it's still a 'first' kind of a thing. And you are so, so far from a first date with that cop! Do the bubble-bath thing tonight—"

"I did it last night."

"And you think it will last forever?"

"No, I just—"

"You asked him last night. You know he'll make it tonight."

"Probably," Jade agreed.

Shanna pushed her pumpkin back, stood, headed for the sink, and washed her hands. "I'm outta here."

She started straight for the door.

"Your pumpkin!" Jade said.

"Keep it. I think I have to start over. I messed up the teeth."

Shanna exited. The door closed, then opened again. "Don't mess it up with that cop!"

"I won't," Jade said. "And don't go accepting any more dates with this guy until we know more about him, until you let me check him out for you."

"Yes'm, big sister. Sure. And you lock this door when I'm out!"

"All right!"

Shanna had barely departed when the phone started to ring. It was Rick, and Jade knew immediately from the sound of his voice that something was wrong. "I'm not going to be able to do anything tonight," he old her regretfully. "We should be going somewhere great for dinner."

"Hey, I eat all the time," she said lightly.

"I've been sick as a dog all day."

"I'm sorry."

"I sure don't know what I picked up, but it's awful. I've been burning up, having chills, delusions, even. Slept all morning, and now I've got to head back to work. The kid who was killed in the awful accident—"

"What?"

"I have to go back to the morgue again. Terry Broom was the M.E. on the case, and he's a stickler. Seems he thinks there was some foul play."

She suddenly remembered Al asking Sean Canady if he had been assigned to the kid. There was going to be a task force on it, Canady had said.

"It is the kid from the accident, then," she murmured.

"Wait a minute—what do you know about this?"

She hesitated. "Shanna and I went down to talk with Gavin today."

"Jade," he said, sounding worried. "I told you I'd go with you."

"I'm all right with all this, really," she said. "I'm not going to lose my mind or go off the deep end or anything." She hesitated and added jokingly, "I even met a cop who told me there might be people who believed they were vampires, and if they believed it, well—"

"Sean," he said flatly, interrupting her. "Lieutenant Canady."

She was silent a moment. "Yes. Sean Canady."

He was quiet, then said carefully, "He's a good cop."

"Why do you say that so carefully?"

He hesitated again. "Well, there was some trouble right here in New Orleans—"

"I remember it! Those gruesome murders."

"Well, we've had lots of gruesome murders, but these were really specific. Sean had a lot to do with solving them, and then again, there was a lot that went unanswered and unsolved."

"You sound as if you don't trust him."

"It's not that I don't trust him, it's just that . . ."

"What?"

"I just think you might want to keep away from him. He could add fuel to the fire of past fears and . . . well, he's good guy. Just . . . just maybe not good for you right now."

She didn't answer. "So you're heading back to the morgue?"

"Then home again. I can hardly stand up."

"You should tell them that. You shouldn't have to work when you're that sick."

"Well, you've got to realize, the cop powers that be don't often care if we make each other sick as hell—they can't afford to. We have to worry about the general public we protect and serve, but I can hardly pass anything to the kid now," he said his tone even but with a sense of sadness beneath. "Forgive me?"

"Forgive you?" she murmured, confused by the sound of his voice. "For what?"

"For . . . for being entirely worthless."

"You're not at all worthless. There's nothing to forgive."

"You're just about the best thing that's ever happened to me."

"Same to you, Rick," she said softly. "Call me tomorrow."

"Will do."

She hung the phone up slowly, curious that she felt . . . Relieved.

No, I'm not relieved, she told herself.

But I am.

She suddenly wished she had asked Shanna where she was going. She could have shown up and seen this new man who might be entering her sister's life.

She went back to the dining room table where they had been working on the pumpkins, finished picking up the mess they had made, then took the pumpkins one by one and dried them out.

When she finished, she decided to put votive candles in the jack-o'-lanterns, and see how they looked.

Hers was okay, spooky enough once it was lit.

Shanna's pumpkin looked downright evil.

"Those are pointed teeth, little sister!" she mused aloud.

The pumpkin made her acutely uncomfortable. To her amazement, she found herself afraid. She blew out the candles and she set both pumpkins out on the brick balcony wall.

Coming back inside the apartment she loved so much, she realized that she felt very restless, and that she didn't want to stay home. She could hear music from the street

below, and laughter. Someone was having an early Hallo
ween party.

You're not invited!

But this was her city, and she knew it. She didn't need
a party to go out. The French Quarter was beautiful, and
she knew the shopkeepers in her neighborhood, and the
waiters at the coffee houses, and the bartenders at the
lounges.

She'd just go out for a drink or a coffee.

She brushed her hair, grabbed a jacket, and headed out.
A long walk alone might be just what she needed.

Terry Broom was young, fairly new to his job at the
medical examiner's office. He'd been hired by the head
coroner, Pierre LePont, he had shown LePont his findings,
and LePont had told him to bring in the Homicide cops.

Terry was six feet tall, very thin, and had a freckled face
and wild red hair. He was only a few years out of school—
although he was greatly relieved to be able to say that he
had turned thirty.

Still young compared to the more experienced doctors
here, but he knew his stuff.

He had always been at the top of his class. He had
learned from a doctor in Gainesville, Florida, who had had
such a passion for his work that he had all but branded it
into his students.

A medical examiner was really a victim's last great hope.

An M.E. cut into the dead and violated the body. That
had to be done with the greatest respect.

And done with every effort to bring a killer to justice,
or to put a terrible accident to rest.

This time Terry had nearly been fooled by what had
appeared to be obvious.

Glass everywhere. Huge chunks of glass, shards of glass.

Cuts everywhere . . . It was easy to see how going straight through the windshield might cause such tragic damage to a human being.

But since he had first examined the body, something had disturbed Terry. Something beyond the obvious.

So now, with skeptical cops encircling him, he nodded at Daniel, a motion that told his even younger assistant that they were ready for the sheet to be drawn back.

Daniel, looking very green, nodded in turn. The body seemed more horrible each time he viewed it.

The cops didn't move. They didn't joke. No one mentioned that it was Friday night, or that they were dying for their dinner, or cracked any kind of comment at all. They all stood still and stared.

Terry touched the gap at the corpse's throat with a gloved finger.

"If you'll observe my concern . . . I don't think that even the violence and force of the young man going through the windshield could cause these serrations," Terry explained.

He looked up. They were all staring at him. Lieutenant Canady was one of them. His partner, Jack Delaney, was at his side. The huge black cop was there, too, the third guy on Canady's team. His name was Mike Astin, and he was new to Homicide, though he had been with the force for some time. Across from them, on the other side of the gurney, were Gavin Newton and his partner, Al Harding—funny name for the man. The two cops were often referred to as Laurel and Harding—a play on words neither appreciated.

The sixth cop wasn't from Homicide. Rick Beaudreaux worked kids, drugs, and public relations.

He worked with the families.

He was the one who would have to explain this death to the boy's relatives—and to the press.

Rick Beaudreaux had a cold. He kept trying not to

sneeze. He looked even greener than the other men. He was probably going to vomit soon.

In fact, he looked almost as bad as the corpse.

"Serrations?" Canady said gravely.

Terry Broom pointed again. "You could have such a deep wound with that kind of force, but you see the flesh here. . . ." He hesitated, trying to point out the ragged edges of the flesh. "This you get by the glass going back and forth."

He felt frustrated, not sure whether they didn't understand, or whether they were a bit green because they did.

He sighed. "You see how it's like cut meat, like a steak? You get this kind of tearing by a knife—or sharp object—going back and forth, grating there, ripping the flesh—"

"We see." Sean interrupted quietly.

Rick Beaudreaux turned around, staggering out. He was going to be sick.

The other cops made no comment.

"Sorry," Terry said quietly.

"Rick has one hell of a fever going, but I'm pretty sure he understands what you're showing us," Canady said, then continued brusquely, "So, the kid was already dead when he went through the windshield?"

"Yes, that's right. That's what I believe." He hesitated, hoping that they trusted his expertise. "I've shown all this to LePont as well. His opinion concurs with mine."

"But how . . . ?" Al Harding began.

"He was killed, put into the car, and the car was either driven by someone else into the tree, or sent crashing into the tree," Sean Canady said, crossing his arms over his chest.

"But that doesn't make any sense—" Gavin began.

"Actually," Jack Delaney muttered, "it would make perfect sense if you were a murderer who wanted to get away with murder."

"But he was already dead, then sent through a windshield—and nearly decapitated with the glass from the windshield?" Harding queried.

"By someone using the shattered glass as a knife—to serrate," Canady said. "Is that it, Dr. Broom? Is that what you believe?"

Terry Broom looked at him, hoping that Canady was seeing past his freckles. "I know how it sounds, but . . ." Canady was looking into his eyes. "Yes," he said flatly. "If you doubt my abilities or my findings—"

"I don't doubt them at all," Canady said. He looked at the others surrounding the body. "Well, gentlemen, it's definitely a homicide."

"It's going to be one hell of a homicide to solve," Al Harding said, shaking his gaunt head. "The kid was scared, though."

"I doubt if we can even begin to imagine right now just how scared," Canady muttered.

Then he turned sharply and started out. At the door he paused, turning back. "I've heard the kid had a rap sheet, that he was kind of a rabble-rouser. Drinker, pusher, user. The newspaper articles used the name the kid had been going by. Did you get the court papers back yet so we can release his real name?" he inquired.

"Yeah, I got them back." Terry Broom looked at the kid's chart and answered him.

Canady suddenly looked worse than Beaudreax as he lowered his head and exited the room.

October meant party time in New Orleans.

Not as much as February. Fat Tuesday and Mardi Gras were the real celebrations. But New Orleans loved a good excuse for a costume party anytime. There were haunted houses open in various parts of the city, some run by charitable organizations and offering the talents of local drama students and teachers, and some open for the sheer pleasure of the profit to be made, and featuring fabulous costumes and world-class entertainment.

Then there were the usual attractions.

BATHE A BEAUTY FOR A BUCK, one window advertised.

PURE MALE AGILITY—MALE POLE DANCERS, advertised another.

A strip joint sat next to a toy store. A cappuccino/bookstore was next to a historical and respectable hotel on one side, and a sex-toy shop on the other. Jazz played on two corners. A handsome black man and a coffee-colored woman played spoons and sang on the street. A young drunk bumped Jade's shoulder and apologized profusely. She escaped him as quickly as she could—she was in danger of being entirely doused with his beer as he begged her pardon.

She slipped into Drake's, a neighborhood sports bar a bit off the beaten track. Derrick Clayton, the owner and Friday-night bartender, was an old friend from high school. He'd married one of her best friends, Sally Eaton, and every time she went in he had new pictures of their three-year-old daughter and infant son. Jade admired his kids, and he told her how proud of her all her old hometown buddies were, what with making a go not just of her journalism, but her own publishing company.

"Hey, Derrick!" she called, taking a stool at the end of the bar.

There was no big game tonight, and though televisions were playing around the bar, no sound could be heard from them. There was a great—if strange—Irish jazz band playing.

Derrick waved at her, finished with the beer he was pouring, delivered it, and came to the end of the bar. "Hey, gorgeous." He was a big man with curling brown hair, a red hint to his beard, and a curve to his belly. He looked as if he belonged climbing a mountain, fighting off bears.

"Hey, yourself." She leaned forward, kissing the cheek he offered her. "Got any new pictures?"

"Always. You know I'll make you see them. What are you drinking?"

"Black and tan," she told him. "In honor of the band."

"They're something, huh?"

"They're great. I've never heard bagpipe jazz before."

Derrick grinned, then delivered her beer and an envelope of photos. She accepted the photos, sipped the beer, and started through the pictures. She felt a small sense of loss, a maternal surge—and a chill. She'd found the right guy—decent, cute, employed, all the right things. Her business was a success. She could settle down and get married.

If she could just quit having erotic dreams about a stranger who had come and gone from her life in a night of pure terror.

Derrick finished refilling drinks along the bar and returned to her, grinning.

"What do you think of the baby's Halloween costume?"

"An infant werewolf. Perfect."

"He's so adorable. Great eyes. The folks are always calling him Wolfy, so we thought a werewolf costume would be just the thing."

"Didn't catch any of the new Disney flicks this year, huh?" she inquired politely.

He grinned. "I did, but what boy wants to be a little do-gooder?"

She shrugged. "I guess the evil do have more fun."

"Did you see Addie? She wanted to be a princess. Sally made that costume."

"Addie is the perfect little princess. Tell Sally I said the costume is beautiful. And your kids are beautiful, too."

He grinned. "Thanks. Thanks, a lot, Jade. Hey, how about you? Where is that copy you're dating? The two of you are like the A-plus gene bank. When are you going to start procreating, huh?"

"We're not married, Derrick. Not even engaged."

"Don't have to be, Jade. Don't you remember Human Sexuality? I think it was tenth grade."

"Funny, funny. Don't you remember Sister Ann Marie? She was the nun who wasn't supposed to teach us all about birth control—but did."

"Yeah. Cool lady."

"She was."

"Okay, so you're going to get married. Great. I love a good wedding."

"And I promise, when I'm going to have one, you'll be among the first to know!"

He grinned. "Cool—whoops, excuse me, Jade. Got a tour group coming in here."

"A tour group? I didn't know you were on that circuit!"

"I'm not, except that there are a lot of small companies out there right now—Halloween season, you know? Extra people working—cashing in on extra bucks."

He left her.

She continued to sip her beer, looking at the pictures.

The tour had crowded into the bar. She knew that, during the Civil War, the lady of the house had hanged herself in an upstairs room after someone in New Orleans spilled the beans about her liaison with a Union soldier.

The tour guide was telling the story.

At first, she was just aware of the drone of his voice. Then she became aware that . . .

He sounded slightly familiar. There was a roll to his *R*s. . . .

She spun around. The tour group was leaving the bar. A half dozen stragglers were blocking the exit.

She could see the guide ahead. He was dressed in a black cape. Her heart thundered. Lots of guides wore black Dracula capes in New Orleans. This was Anne Rice's city. Lestat's town.

But lots of guides didn't necessarily have Scottish accents.

He was ahead, far ahead.

She started running along the street, terrified but determined.

She was jostled into a group of costumed revelers, coming from or going to an early Halloween party.

"Sorry!"

"Sorry!"

"Sorry!"

She was passed from a white rabbit to a Tin Man and on to a dancing pack of cigarettes.

"It's all right, it's all right, excuse me . . ."

She kept running. A three-man band blocked her way. She sidestepped them.

On Bourbon Street the crowd became fierce. She ran, pushing and shoving, trying to keep up.

She reached a man wearing a black cape. She caught his arm, whirled him around.

His face was lined with weariness. His hair was gray; his eyes were powdery blue. She had never seen him before.

"Sorry!" she said softly.

He nodded and walked on.

She stood still in the middle of the street, feeling the rush of humanity go past her, hearing laughter and music and feeling as if it were all passing over her, by her.

Then the street seemed empty before her.

And up ahead, just up ahead, under a streetlight, stood a man.

The man.

She hadn't seen him in over a year.

Except in her dreams.

But he was here now. As tall as she remembered, dark, striking. His long-sleeved shirt was black, as were his trousers. His hands were casually shoved into his pockets. He might have been any striking young tourist. A businessman, out to see the sights of New Orleans. A musician, a politician, ad exec, plumber, electrician . . . any tourist.

Except that . . . he wasn't.

She started walking toward him, half certain that he would turn away.

Disappear.

It wasn't him. It couldn't be. . . .

He stood dead still, waiting.

He didn't walk away, and he didn't disappear.

And as she came to him, the noises of the city rushed to meet her. The jazz, the talk, the laughter, the footsteps . . .

She was fairly tall, but she had to look up at him. Yes, it was he. In the flesh. The dark hair, the slender-appearing but hard-muscled physique.

The eyes . . .

Like amber. Like fire.

"Hello, Jade," he said softly. "We have to talk."

They had to talk? He had been there during the night of her greatest danger and her greatest fear. He had probably saved her life—but then he had left her, leaving the police to think that she was crazy, leaving her to doubt her own sanity.

Then he had entered her dreams. Invaded her sleep, stolen into her soul. He had touched her, somehow. He had touched her; it had been real.

He had ruined—absolutely destroyed—her chances with the most perfect man she was ever likely to meet.

"Jade?"

"You bastard!"

She hauled off and hit him with every bit of strength she had in her.

Chapter Eight

It might have been a stupid thing to do.

He was a good six feet, three inches tall, and muscled like a son of a bitch. If he'd taken it the wrong way . . .

Fear or instinct caused her to draw up an arm again. He caught it. She attacked him with words. "Bastard. You were there. You saw everything. You just disappeared. And how amazing! I start to dream about you—"

He held her wrist; he had caught her flying palm in air, and now held it by her side. Gently? She couldn't feel the grasp, yet she knew that she couldn't have moved had she tried.

"What the hell is going on?"

He shook his head. "I don't know what you mean."

"I think you do."

He stepped back suddenly. "Look, I hardly know you. Excuse me."

To her amazement he turned and started walking away. She stared after him, mouth agape, hands on hips.

"Excuse you?" she repeated. *"Excuse you?"*

She raced after him. He was in black again. Black form-hugging jeans, long-sleeved knit shirt, casual black jacket. It rode his shoulders very nicely. His dark hair, still longish, curled over his collar. It glistened in the lights of the street.

"Hey!"

She caught hold of his shoulder, drawing him back. "You can't just walk away from me."

"Should I stand here so you can hit me again?" he inquired politely.

"No, no . . . but you . . . you have to talk to me!"

He arched a brow. She did want to hit him again. He wasn't just attractive; he was compelling in an almost frightening manner. Devastatingly good-looking, dark eyes, dark hair, and an air of self-confidence, assurance, even arrogance.

She knotted her hands into fists at her sides.

"Fine! Don't talk to me!"

She turned that time, and started to walk away.

He didn't follow. She stopped, turned back. He was waiting, a smile lightly turning the fullness of his lips.

"Who the hell are you?" she whispered. "What is going on?"

"Where's your cop?"

"What?"

"Officer Beaudreaux."

"He . . . he's sick. Wait a minute, what do you know about—"

"I've been in New Orleans a few days. Naturally I wanted to see you. I made a few inquiries."

"Oh?" She walked back toward him. "And whom did you talk with to make these inquiries?"

"A man never gives away his sources."

She was going to walk away again, but even as she thought it, her mind struggled—he was in front of her right now. No matter how impossible he was, she wanted to keep him there.

Maybe he sensed her flight. His hand was on her arm. She felt as if she were shaking inside. Remembering.

Being with him . . .

"I . . . I—"

"How about a drink?"

"Some little out-of-the-way place?" she inquired.

"No, let's go back to your friend's bar. Drake's? Is that it? Great music."

She lifted her hands. "Why not?"

She started to lead the way. Then she suddenly paled, pushing through the crowd, and turned back. She looked at him. "I thought I saw . . . I thought I heard—"

"Yeah, I thought so, too."

"Wait a minute! I didn't even finish my sentence. I thought I saw—"

"The tour guide from Scotland. Right?"

She fought to keep her jaw in place. "Right."

"I know. It wasn't him."

"You're certain?"

"Oh, yes. I'm certain."

She turned around again. She stepped up on the sidewalk. " 'Bathe a Beauty for a Buck,' " he said, reading the neon advertisement. There was laughter in his voice. And something about it touched her. . . .

She turned to look at him. He shrugged. "Poor things must be really dirty."

"I thought you were familiar with New Orleans."

"Too familiar. It's just that I haven't seen that particular sign before."

His hand touched the small of her back. She nearly jumped through the doorway. That was the way to want someone! she thought. The slightest touch, here, there, anywhere, in the night, in the morning, in pain, in pleasure . . .

Derrick saw them coming back in. He lifted a hand to Jade. "Hey, kid, saw you running." He nodded, acknowledging the man behind her. "Jade, I got you a fresh beer. Sir, what will you be having?"

"Whatever Jade's having works for me."

He nodded.

Jade smiled. "Derrick Clayton, this is . . ."

"Lucian. Lucian DeVeau," her companion said, shaking Derrick's hand.

"Lucian. Nice to meet you."

"Thanks. You, too."

Jade stared at him, sipping her beer, gulping it. Here he was, here at last. She should be calling the police.

He'd be gone before they ever arrived. She knew it.

He turned on his bar stool, watching the band. He seemed to like the music. She studied the planes of his face. Powerful, handsome. And arrogant. He knew his own strengths and abilities.

"Is it real?" she asked softly.

"What?" he turned back to her, his eyes as black as the night, with that vague, strange hint of red.

"Your name."

"Yes, it's real. Never changed to accommodate a new place or time, I'm afraid."

"It's French."

"Yes."

"I met you in Scotland. You said you'd come from there."

"Yes."

"DeVeau is hardly Scottish."

"People do move, you know."

"So where were your people originally from?"

"He leaned toward her. "France, most probably."

"Do you speak French?"

Now he hesitated. "Yes. I like the language."

She was frustrated, getting nowhere at all.

"You saved my life." She wasn't sure if it was a statement or a question.

"Yes," he said simply.

"But then you disappeared, and let everyone think I was a drug addict or a lunatic."

He sipped his beer, staring ahead at the bottles behind the bar, not looking at her. "They knew you weren't on drugs. They took you to a hospital. I'm sure they tested every fluid in your body."

"But you . . . just left!"

"I had to."

"But—"

"I wasn't in great shape myself."

She drew her fingers around the rim of her glass. "You knew what was going to happen," she accused him.

"No, I was afraid something might be about to happen," he corrected.

"You're not a cop."

"No."

"Obviously," she muttered. "If you were a cop, you would have stuck around to speak to the other cops."

"I told you. I was hurt myself."

"You know what? I don't think you're real. Even now. Even sitting there right next to me. You'll puff into thin air again any minute—"

"Jade! Lucian!"

They were suddenly hailed from behind. Jade turned quickly, astounded that anyone she knew might know Lucian. It was Daniel Thacker. She stared at Lucian, who shrugged. His eyes spoke eloquently: *See, I'm real, I'm here!*

Danny was a bit into his cups. He looked young and

flustered, blond hair a total wreck, green eyes a startlingly pretty color, they were so surrounded by red.

"God, is it good to see you two!"

He put an arm around them both. His beer was in his right hand. It sloshed perilously in his glass. She thought that Lucian's immaculate black jacket was about to get soaked in hops. The beer settled.

"Danny . . . ," Jade murmured. "You know Lucian?"

"Sure do." Danny set his beer down and offered Lucian a hand, grinning. "Hey, Jade, Luke here is thinking about writing. I think he should join our Wednesday group."

Danny leaned close to Jade, saying in a conspiratorial whisper, "He's loaded, you know. Old European aristocracy. We could use him!"

She arched a brow to Lucian. Was that true?

"I'd like to join your group. Sure," he said.

"We're not really a group," she said quickly.

"Oh, hell, yeah, suddenly she and Mr. Hotshot Durante are on all the best-seller lists, and we're not a group anymore."

"Danny, you are drunk as a skunk!"

"Yeah, kind of," Danny admitted, looking very sober for a minute. "Only, that could give a really bad name to skunks."

"Maybe I should get you home," Jade said.

"You get me home?" Danny protested. "No, you can't be alone. Even here, even in Derrick's place. There's bad stuff going down."

"Danny, it's New Orleans. I'm afraid we have lots of bad stuff going down."

"No, we have corpses."

"Dead people usually are corpses, yes, Danny."

"Usually," Lucian muttered. "You're right, Jade, we need to get Danny home."

"You don't know what I saw, Luke, Lucian." Danny's

eyes looked glazed. He punched Lucian lightly in the shoulder. "You don't know what I saw."

"I think I do," he said quietly.

Jade stared at him. "Tell you later," he said with a shrug.

"Will you?" she demanded. "Or will you just disappear?"

"I won't disappear."

"Damned right, I'm not going to let you disappear. We'll get Danny back, and then you'll come up to my place."

Lucian hesitated, his head lowered for a moment. When he looked up, she felt a strange flash of heat shoot down the length of her spine. The uncanny blaze, red against the darkness, had appeared in his eyes again. "That's an invitation, I take it?"

"It's an order!" she murmured, though she realized that he didn't take orders.

Not unless he chose to.

Danny put both his hands on Lucian's face, forcing him to look his way, into his eyes. "She has to be, like, really, really, careful, Luke," Danny slurred out.

"Danny, what the hell did you see?" Jade asked.

"It must have been a very bad day at the morgue," Lucian murmured. "Let's get you home. I think we're all pretty safe tonight."

"Oh, yeah?" Danny looked at him trustingly. "How do you know?"

"Intuition," he said.

Lucian stood. Danny wasn't small, but Lucian seemed to tower over him. Of course, Danny was falling down around him, almost as if he were boneless, or melting.

She'd known Danny a while. Several years. Through his trials, his romances, his heartbreaks—bad days at the job. They'd all been out together, drinking, celebrating.

She'd never seen him drunk like this.

She started to put money on the bar; Lucian had already done so. She stared at him.

He shrugged, a half smile in place. "The least I can do is buy you a drink."

Danny wagged a finger at her. "And he's going to protect you."

"From what?"

"The creatures of the night."

She stared at Lucian. "And how do I know that he's not one of the creatures of the night?"

Lucian stared back. "You don't. Shall we go?"

She didn't need to help with Danny. Lucian had an arm around his back, and Danny was clinging to Lucian's shoulder. His feet were barely touching the ground.

Outside, the jazz played on. Neon lights burned. Laughter filled the streets.

The BATHE A BEAUTY FOR A BUCK sign began to flicker.

The usual Friday-night cacophony reigned.

Sean Canady burst into the old family manor on the outskirts of New Orleans where he lived with his wife and child.

She was standing in the entry, waiting, as if she had been aware that he was arriving at just that moment.

Sometimes she still had that ability.

Her hands were folded before her; she was trying to appear serene. Her agitation was in her eyes.

He held dead still in the doorway.

"You know?" he said.

"I tried to reach you at the station."

"I was at the morgue."

"And the battery is dead in your cell phone."

"You could have tried Jack's number."

"I needed to talk to you first."

He strode across the room to her, lifting her chin. He loved his wife. God, he loved his wife. He kissed her lips long, hard, before saying more.

Then he drew away.

"They're back," he said simply.

She nodded.

"How do you know?"

"Lucian was here."

"Lucian?"

"Want a drink?"

"A big one."

She started walking toward the right-side parlor. He followed.

It was a hell of a fine mansion for a police officer to live in. It was Maggie's family estate, thought he would one day inherit his own. It was down the road a bit, inhabited by his father, who he prayed would live long, hale, and hearty.

She poured him a large Scotch.

He accepted it and walked toward the fireplace. "I was at the morgue all day because the automobile accident that's been written up in the papers wasn't an accident at all."

She poured herself a drink and sipped it. "Not an accident? The car went halfway through a tree; the kid had been drinking—"

"Oh, yeah. All kind of alcohol and drug levels in the blood. But he was dead before he went into the tree."

"But—"

"The head was nearly off because it had been serrated after death. Serrated with the broken glass from the windshield."

She didn't speak. Her mouth formed an *O*.

"Where's Lucian?"

She shook her head. "He wanted to talk to you, but you

didn't get back, and he was restless and insisted that he had to go. But he promised he'd be back."

"Is he worried about the MacGregor girl?"

Maggie frowned. "The MacGregor girl? The woman from New Orleans who survived the night in Edinburgh?" She shook her head. "He didn't say. He was there, as we suspected. He knows who . . . destroyed all those people in New York. He talked a bit at first, but he was in bad shape, and I made him rest. I thought you'd be home . . . and he was too restless to wait. I couldn't make him stay."

Sean set down his glass on the coffee table, ran his fingers through his hair. "Then he's gone to find her." He looked up suddenly.

"The baby?" He referred to their ten-month-old infant, Brent.

"He's fine, sleeping, secure in his room."

Sean exhaled slowly.

"Sean, Lucian seems to think that he's wounded this fellow badly. That he's hurt, in pain, and will have to move on somewhere else until he heals."

"Maggie, you're sure you don't know where he went?"

"No, he didn't tell me, but . . . Lucian could be anywhere, Sean. You know that. But he'll come back. He wants to see you. And he . . ."

"He what?"

"I think he, I think he needs . . ."

"You?" Sean queried tightly.

She shook her head. "I think he needs us."

Sean was quiet for a minute, hands on his hips. He flexed the muscles in his shoulders, trying to ease the strain.

"He's got to know," Sean said softly.

"Know what?"

He looked at his wife. "Just who the kid was who was killed in that crash."

* * *

Danny's little place was a studio above a sex shop—dining room, kitchen, and living room all combined. The bath was fairly large and nicely modern, and off to one side.

Danny dozed off a few times on the walk home. Lucian all but carried him. Jade pointed out the way.

The store windows in front of Danny's were full of impossibly shaped mannequins dressed in leather thongs and corsets. They carried whips and wore masks. Edible panties in chocolate, vanilla, and strawberry were advertised.

Jade walked by a dozen sex shops a day, every day of her life. She seldom gave them a second glance.

She found that she was doing her best not to stare at the windows, to pretend they didn't exist.

"Those stairs there," she directed. Her face felt as if it were redder than the heart-shaped, strawberry-flavored edible thongs on the mannequin closest to the stair side of the shop. If Lucian noticed her severe discomfort, he was tactful enough not to comment on it.

They brought Danny up. He began singing as they climbed the steps, carefully, one by one. At the top he laughed. "Come in, come into my parlor! And my kitchen, bedroom, and elegant dining room, too, of course."

Lucian carried him in. "Give me a sec—I'll get the pullout open."

Jade opened the couch. Danny crashed down on it.

Jade looked at him, shaking her head. "I've never seen him like this."

"All men have a limit; sometimes they have to lose control."

"Hm." She stared at him. "Tell me, do you ever lose control?"

"Not often. Shall we go?"

"Have you ever lost control?"

"Yes, shall we go?"

"Let me get his shoes off. And maybe you could pull him up. He's going to have an awful twist in his neck in the morning if we don't."

Lucian leaned over and picked Danny up, straightening his cramped length. Jade took off his shoes, then set them by the side of the bed.

"The lower lock will click automatically when we leave," she murmured. "I wish there were a way to turn the top bolt."

"He'll be all right."

"How can you be so certain?"

"Why wouldn't he be?"

"Because he's afraid of something."

"He's in his home, sound asleep. He'll be fine."

She wasn't sure why, but she believed him. She started down the steps again, aware of him behind her, aware that they had to pass by the sex shop, aware that she had the ridiculous feeling that she'd already been with him. Well, she had been, in a way, at least. He had admitted to saving her life in Edinburgh, and she had been found in a shroud, so he was certainly familiar with her.

All of her.

She felt her cheeks growing red again as they walked. He took her hand, leading her through the throng of people. There were more costumed party goers on the streets now. A weaving werewolf nearly crashed into Lucian, looked at him, and found much better balance. Jade felt as if she were with Moses—and the Red Sea were parting for them.

She stopped suddenly, the tug of her hand pulling him back.

People milled all around them.

"Why am I dreaming about you?" she asked him softly.

He didn't reply, then said lightly, "Because I'm devastatingly good-looking?"

"I've been dating a man who is kind and sweet and absolutely, positively devastatingly good-looking," she told him.

"But you don't dream about him," Lucian noted quietly.

She felt her cheeks warm again. She started walking past him. "I didn't say what I'd been dreaming," she reminded him.

"No, you didn't."

He followed.

She felt his closeness.

They reached her house and entered it through the upstairs hallway. He seemed to pause a minute in her doorway—not hesitant, just observing. He strode in then, toward the mantel. He looked at the pictures there. "Your sister," he said.

"How do you know?"

He shrugged, amused. "She looks just like you."

The tension in her shoulders eased a bit. "Can I get you a drink?"

"Are you having one?"

"Oh, you bet. Maybe a bunch."

"Whatever you're having."

She opted for wine, a rich cabernet that Matt had brought back for her after a publicity tour in California. Lucian accepted a glass from her gravely, seeming to study the deep, rich, bloodred color of the wine, then pointing to another of the pictures. "Your parents?"

"Father and stepmother."

"Is she a terrible, fairy-tale stepmother?"

"Not at all. My mother died when Shanna and I were in our teens. My dad was devoted to her until the very end. Liz came later. We have baby brothers—there they are.

Petey and Jamie. Names right off the old MacGregor immigration papers."

"Handsome little towheads," he remarked.

"They are. Just as cute as can be. Totally into their terrible twos. Why did you disappear when we were in Edinburgh?"

"It was necessary."

"You could have helped the police."

He shook his head. "No, I couldn't have."

"You could have told them who—"

"It wouldn't have done any good."

She stared at him, frustrated. "They've killed again."

"Yes, they have."

"In New York?"

"I believe."

"Why are you here, in New Orleans?"

He hesitated a moment, then shrugged. "Because of you."

Her heart seemed to slam against her chest. She didn't know him. She really didn't know him at all. Scotland.

A few really decadent dreams.

And now.

She approached him at the mantel. She set down her wine and stared into his eyes. They were so curious. Like the wild contacts opticians sold for Halloween: normal, deep, and very dark one minute, touched with bloodred fire the next.

"You're here because of me."

"Yes."

"And . . . you were in Edinburgh because of me?"

"No," he replied with a rueful smile. "I was in Edinburgh because I'd heard about a guide and an underground tour . . . and I suspected those who were involved."

"And you were right."

"Yes."

"And you're out to stop them?"

"Yes."

"But you're not a policeman."

"No."

"FBI?"

"No."

"Secret Service?"

"No." He hesitated again, then touched her cheek. "Let's just say that I'm the head of another group with a vested interest in what's happening."

"And what's happening?" she whispered. She felt his fingertips on her cheek. Nothing in life had ever felt so compelling. So seductive. She ached to feel more of that touch. She took a step closer to him. His knuckles brushed her flesh; he cupped her chin in his palm, meeting her eyes.

"What is happening?" he repeated.

"You said that you're here for me."

"Yes."

"Because . . . ?"

"You could be in danger."

"But I . . ."

Date a cop.

The words didn't quite make it from her lips. She had moved closer. Closer. Arched up on her toes. Logic reminded her that he was highly suspect; she barely knew him.

Instinct told her she knew all she needed to.

There was no question when his lips touched hers that either of them expected any other outcome from the evening than what occurred.

The heat of his mouth was delicious, white-hot, staggering. His tongue invaded like the smooth shaft of a sword, and her own was quickly wrapped around it. His kiss was passionate, hard, staggering. Before she knew it, her arms were wound around him, and he was lifting her against himself. She felt the pressure of her breasts against his chest, his groin against her hips, and that, like the thrust of his tongue, aroused her to a sweeping pitch. Her fingers threaded into his hair, working down his nape. His mouth lifted from her, moved to her throat.

For a moment it lingered there. . . .

And she could feel a pulse. A rampant pulse. The beating of his heart? No, her own. It was a thunder, a cascade. She felt as if the beat permeated her limbs, throbbed at a place between her thighs. She could feel the denim of her jeans against her flesh, the fabric of her panties, the air, the night, even the tick of time. He held her there, breathed in, breathed out, and the fire of his breath teased her flesh, her throat. . . .

Then he was moving with her, unerringly, to her bedroom. She didn't know quite how he got there so easily; she didn't care. She didn't know what she had become; she couldn't slip his jacket from his shoulders fast enough; her fingers clawed at the fabric of his shirt. He shed the garment himself, coming down against her on the bed, his shoulders broad, rippled with muscle, touched with the iridescence of the moonlight streaming in.

She was naked herself.

She didn't know how . . . didn't remember. Her clothing was cast into a tangle of cotton and silk by the bed. His jacket, shirt, and pants lay there as well. He was gorgeous, huge, powerful, encompassing her. His tongue was on her flesh. His fingers were gliding over her. An erotic brush of his teeth swept past her collarbone; his palm closed over her breast. The length of him seemed like molten steel, forming to her length, setting her afire to the same pitch of fire that burned within him. His mouth closed over her breast; she surged against him, white-hot streaks of desire flashing through her. She reached for him, felt the shaft of his erection, the fierceness of the heat that seemed alive with that wicked beat of her heart, her being. She touched him, stroked him, felt a shimmering burst of pleasure within, felt his kiss, his lips, his fevered hands, moving more, moving farther, moving deeper. His tongue teased at her nipple, slipped into the valley between her breasts, laved the tiny silver ring at her navel. She shifted with pure lust. His fingers stroked slowly down the length of her thigh. His head settled lower. He palmed the soft mound of her sex, parted it with his fingers, invaded it with his tongue. She shrieked, her fingers tearing into his shoulders, pleas on her lips, *no, yes, no, yes, oh, God, oh, God, oh, God, yes* . . .

She was limp when he rose over her, shaken, soaked, certain she could feel no more, do no more . . . but he moved into her, steel again, molten steel, invasive, searing, awakening . . . he *moved*, and dear Lord, the way that he moved . . .

She climaxed again, screaming, shaking, clinging to him. And again, and then at last she began to drift down from some exotic plain, and she was thinking that the dream had been good, but the reality, dear Lord, the reality . . .

She was still shaking, still *feeling*. The feel and sense and taste of him seemed imbedded within her. She would never forget, never want anything other, anything different; it was like life, and it was like death, like knowing the real feel of the heat of the sun. . . .

She jerked up suddenly, certain he would be gone.

But he was beside her, dark eyes hard on hers, and he was real enough, stretched beside her, the length of him smooth and powerful and sleek. Dark hair curled on his chest, whorled to a line at his waist, thickened again to a nest at his sex. His legs were long, powerfully muscled, his shoulders as broad as she had always suspected, his midriff as tight . . .

He leaned on an elbow, watching her.

"What?" he said softly.

"You're here."

"Yes," he murmured dryly. "Yes, I am."

"I did dream of you!" she whispered.

"Did I come up to par?" he queried.

She didn't reply. He was arrogant enough. She saw the scar then, long and white against his neck, shoulder, collarbone.

She traced it. "Old battle scar?" she whispered.

He caught her fingers. "Very old battle scar."

"You were in Desert Storm?"

"What?"

"Desert Storm. The Middle East—"

"No, different battle, different place."

"And you're not going to tell me about it?"

"No, not now."

"But you're not going to disappear?"

He smiled, touched her cheek, smoothed hair from her forehead. "Certainly not now. The cop could get over his cold."

She stiffened suddenly, lowering her head.

He caught her chin, lifting her eyes to his.

"How do you know my cop had a cold?"

He shrugged. "Sometimes I know all I need to know. Sometimes I don't. I can usually feel when—"

He broke off, shaking his head. "Tonight . . ."

"What about tonight?"

"It's quiet in New Orleans."

"Quiet? It's October, rowdy as hell—" It was her turn to break off. She studied him carefully. "You do know who killed people in New York. You're afraid for me, afraid they'll come after me. But you don't think they're here—yet."

"I don't think they're here—tonight," he corrected.

She touched his cheek, studied his eyes. She barely knew him. Knew nothing about him. She'd been dating a really great cop she had known fairly well.

And she was in bed with him. After the most decadent sex she had ever imagined.

At least I wasn't alone!

She turned away from him, trying to find some rationale for anything that had happened. He sat up, then crawled over her suddenly, pinning her down.

"You're not having second thoughts, are you?" he demanded.

"I don't think I ever had any first thoughts," she told him.

He smiled, pleased.

"I've never known anyone like you," she whispered.

"No, you haven't," he assured her.

"Never anyone . . . quite so arrogant," she said.

He laughed softly. "Well, that, I suppose . . . But no, you've never known anyone quite like me. Pray you never will," he added softly.

"Are you leaving now?" she asked.

"Not until morning—if I may stay."

"You're asking me?"

"Of course."

"Are you ever going to talk to me?" she asked softly.

She sensed his hesitation. "Of course. I've been talking to you."

"Talking—never really saying the truth."

"I haven't lied to you."

"Promise that you won't?"

"I promise I'll do my best to explain the truth, always."

His face lowered. He kissed her.

She was exhausted. Beyond exhausted. Sated. Drained . . .

His touch awakened her again. If she was dreaming, imagining, she never wanted to wake up. But he was real.

So real. She could see him, feel him, smell him, touch him, know him. . . .

Later he was curled around her. His arm was about her; she wrapped her hand around his, bringing it to her heart, between her breasts.

A soft sigh of happiness and pure, blissful satiation escaped her.

"This is so insane. I don't really know you at all. Are you a creature of the night?" she whispered.

Was he sleeping already?

Or did he answer her?

Oh, yes, definitely. I am.

I am a creature of the night.

Chapter Nine

The month of October.

It had become bigger business than Christmas.

Terror Town, a Halloween theme park in the middle of New England farmland, had been doing brisk business every season over the past twelve years.

People loved to be scared. It had started out as a Friday and Saturday haunted house on the weekend nearest Halloween. It had taken place with cheap effects inside a single barn. Then there had been the hayride, the "monsters" roaming the pastures and hiding behind the haystacks. The barn had next become a state-of-the-art building with special lighting, fog machines, piped-in music, a sprinkler system approved by the county fire chief, and more. Adult entertainers came in droves; college students vied for the "monster" job openings that now offered a fun income to be made every night in the month of October.

Darcy Granger, twenty-one, a Communications major at Holy Cross, loved her job working at Terror Town. The special effects had gotten really great, with the black lighting, the fog machines, the piped-in music. Her section had the theme "Transylvania Nights." She dressed up in black with fabulous makeup applied by Hollywood experts specially flown in for the month. Her job was to lie in a coffin. She appeared to be an effigy; then she scared people by rising, leaping out upon occasion, and whispering silly things like, "How about a kiss, sweetie?" or "Bite me, babe!"

It was fun. People screamed and then laughed. Darcy liked most of the people she worked with. Like her, they were making a few bucks and having a good time. They followed the rules. They jumped out, looked scary, tried to startle people into screaming—but they never tried to give anyone a heart attack.

Except for a few of them.

Like Tony Alexander. He'd gotten really pissed off the other night because a big kid had tried to scare him back. The guy had been an idiot, a real tough guy trying to prove his courage and make jerks out of the people working there. He'd been bad. Tony had been worse, hitting a light switch that darkened the place to pitch-black—and tripping the guy. The guy had turned around and complained. Tony had gotten yelled at—and he'd taken it out on every little kid who had come through the place since. Darcy had said something to him. "Parents shouldn't bring chickenshit little babies through here," was what he had told her. She'd warned him about getting fired. "Hey— I've worked here four years now, Darcy. Don't worry about me." The next night he'd pursued a kid, whispering that he'd kill him the next time the boy fell asleep—or the next time, or the next. The kid had left screaming. Tony had played innocent. Another kid had been fired.

No one had listened to Darcy.

Tony also liked to pitch the place into real darkness and assault his fellow employees—the female ones. He'd come after her a few times, then apologizing and telling her he'd been groping for the lights. Her sister had told her she could complain and get him fired for real, but Darcy had wanted to deal with it herself. She thought she was mature enough to deal with jerks like Tony. She'd also found out that Tony was a nephew of the owner. It was true—he kept his job because he knew somebody. Most things in life still worked out to one person's word against another. Her word wouldn't mean anything against Tony's. She really liked working at Terror Town. If she could handle the matter herself, she meant to do so.

Halloween was now approaching, and Terror Town was busy. Before the gates had even opened, people were lined up for what looked like miles. The employees were busy, from the college kids hired to give cheap thrills to the big-money organizers and managers.

Darcy was sitting in one of the makeup trailers when she first saw the newcomer. He had come in behind her, and sat at one of the dressing tables. She had watched him. He was tall and gaunt, but with surprisingly powerful-looking shoulders. His eyes met hers when she spun around at the sound of his entry. She felt a strange unease, but she was, by nature, compassionate, and she figured he might be uncomfortable here, his first night at this. She was sure it was his first night. There were lots of kids hired to work this place, but she knew them all, by sight and a smile, at the least.

"Hey, you look scared. Don't be. It's fun. Oh, you get the kids who want to impress their friends and their dates and try to scare you back, but not often. Most people want to have a good time."

He smiled. "Don't worry. I intend to have a good time."

"Good."

She turned back to her makeup.

"You like working here?" he asked.

"Sure. It's good money, lots of fun."

"It's fun to scare people, eh?" he teased. The way he said the last, she wondered if he was a Canadian. She loved the Canadian accent, with its long vowel sound on words like *cloud* and *about*. And she liked the little "eh" at the end of his question.

"Well, I don't want to scare anyone into any early grave or a heart attack. Just give them a few little shivers and some good fun."

"Good for you, then. Do you like vampires?"

"Do I like them? In pretend? Of course. They're deliciously scary and sexy, right?"

"You're very sexy," he assured her with a smile, but it was just a friendly smile, and his words were casual. Not like Tony's. She smiled back, then returned to her makeup. When she left her table, heading on toward her building, she touched his shoulder. "Good luck."

"Thanks. Happy hunting."

She went on into her building, waving to a few of the people she knew as they entered their little niches. She saw Tony going in; he was in an alcove before the long velvet black-lit hallway with "family" portraits that preceded her own area.

Lights were on. Thayer Harding, one of the technicians, greeted her. "Hey, Darce, how're things going?"

"Great, Thayer." He was checking out the springs on her pressed wood-and-cardboard coffin. "How are the wife and kids?"

"Fine, just fine. Thanks for asking. How is school, young lady?"

"Great. I think I made the dean's list."

"Good for you! Pop on in. Maybe the bosses will let us celebrate later. I'll take you out for a shake!"

She laughed. "But I did turn twenty-one. You can buy me a beer."

"Not if you're driving. Hop on in. We're about to open."

She grinned and crawled in, then tested the new springs and hinges he had just put in the coffin. Blue lighting on the ground was a safety measure, and she also knew where the switches were for the main lights and the sprinklers. The trail through the haunted house twisted and wove, and there were more kids up ahead in various little alcoves like her own. There were also walkie-talkies at blue-lighted areas along the walls, just in case there was ever a problem.

Other than with Tony, she had never heard of any problems. The place was a gold mine for its owner and his investors, but it was well run, with safety the number one priority.

"You in tight and snug, Darcy? That was it, my last repair. We're opening."

"I'm in. Snug as a bug. Take you up on that milkshake later."

"Great."

Thayer left. Darcy closed her eyes, shut into the velvety warmth of her pseudocoffin. She wasn't afraid of the dark.

She had a big speech coming up for English Lit. She began to practice, mentally planning the intonations in her voice, her gestures, and her movements. Time began to pass. She knew when people were coming. A little sensor caused a tiny red light to appear in her coffin.

People.

She sprang out. A mom with two ten-year-olds jumped and laughed delightedly.

The ten-year-olds screamed and giggled. She bared her teeth at them and made a noise. They giggled at her and moved on.

She closed the lid to her coffin and went back to practicing her speech.

Jimmy Erskine loved haunted houses. They were guaranteed to make girls shriek. And with Cassie on his arm tonight . . .

Such a cute little chicken. She had a thing for him to begin with. *Why not?* He was an upperclassman, tight end on a winning team, in the perfect frat. She had a crush on him, but she was reserved. Careful, a brain, so into her books for so long that she hadn't taken a lot of time to date. A waste. She was small and slim—maybe ninety-nine pounds, and according to the guys at his frat, it seemed as if ninety of those pounds must be breasts. She had cleavage that didn't quit. What it did to his libido and concentration was sad. So tonight was it—he'd even taken a bet on his abilities to get her to bed, so he had to come through. He couldn't afford to lose the fifty he'd put on himself.

This had been the right place to come. He was going to be the rough-and-ready hero, laughing his way through the horror house, holding her tight, making her cling. He'd started off by buying some Halloween Jell-O shots— blue, purple, and bright orange—to get her courage up, so he'd told her. She was wobbling and holding tight, and unaware of the way he was touching her when they began walking through the vampire place.

It could be pretty creepy. They had one girl who lay in a glass coffin all dressed up like a sleeping princess— except that she let real rats run all over her. Every once in a while she turned in the glass case and bared her teeth. The whole place was filled with fog, foam tombstones, black lighting, and characters that jumped out here and there. He teased Cassie all the way through, making sure she saw the dark, the fog, the eerie, the unreal, and then buried her head against his shoulder. He made a point of letting others get ahead of him, and falling back so that they'd be alone, so that a crowd of little wise-ass kids didn't come running in around them to spoil all the effects.

They turned around a curve, and for a moment he didn't see the coffin in front of him. It creaked open with a startling sound. The girl who appeared did so with a sudden burst of energy that caused him to jump.

"Oh, Jimmy!" Cassie gasped. He immediately felt stupid. His face turned red. He saw the vampire chick smile, aware she'd startled him.

"Bad teeth!" he muttered. "Bad dress, bad coffin, looks like a cardboard jewelry box!"

"Jimmy," Cassie said.

The girl just went back into her coffin and closed the lid.

"Come on," he told Cassie brusquely.

They started walking again. He was irritated. Things had been going so well.

Then he stopped dead. Up ahead there was a tall, thin guy dressed as a vampire, with the flowing cape, the whole stupid bit.

"Watch out, here I come," the fellow said. And he started toward them.

Cassie let out a little cry of fear, winnowing against him. It was just what he had wanted, but he still felt unnerved.

And now this idiot was actually reaching toward them.

He was almost on top of them. The air around him seemed worse than foggy. It was cold. Uncomfortable. And the guy's fingers . . .

The nails were long. Bluish, or black. *Weird.* He didn't like the guy. Not one bit. He'd like to sock him in that skinny jaw, take him down and beat him to a pulp.

"You're not allowed to touch me," Jimmy said.

"Really?" the guy inquired.

"Yeah, really," Jimmy said belligerently. "So get away from me, you fake-looking, slimy jerk! Did you get those fangs out of a Cracker Jack box? A gum machine?"

"A Cracker Jack box? A gum machine?" the guy repeated, and started to laugh. "Um, yes. The better to eat you all up, and lick my chops."

"I'm going to break your chops, moron," Jimmy warned.

"Jimmy, don't!" Cassie pleaded. "Don't. This guy is obviously some kind of a psycho. Let's just get past him."

But Jimmy was a tough guy. Everyone knew it. And he was mad as hell already because the other two-bit park employee had scared him.

"No," he told Cassie, shaking his head. "Come on, man. Come on. I play first-string tackle at State. You're a goner, buddy."

"You think?"

"I think. Come on. Come on, ass-wipe. Put your money where your mouth is."

"Jimmy, no," Cassie pleaded.

The vampire smiled—a wicked grin. "Poor little girl," he told Cassie. Then he spoke straight to Jimmy. "All right. All right, gonna take me on, are you? Yeah, yeah. A hotshot football player. A tackle, no less. You come on. Tackle me."

The creature's grin deepened as Jimmy fell for the bait.

Jimmy charged hard, and with true aim. He knew his business. He'd broken a few bones in play. Hell, he meant to take it to the pros.

But it seemed that the guy moved like mercury. Jimmy struck, but he struck pure air. He went flying himself, crash-landing hard into a pile of rot meant to signify a burial mound. His head had struck something. Dazed, he shook it. He rose. His opponent was next to Cassie. *Impossible*. No one could have moved that quickly across the narrow space. Not past him.

Cassie was standing dead still now, pale as a ghost, her eyes wide and luminous on the phony vampire. Jimmy let out something like a snarl. His girl was looking at this freak as if he were some kind of a god.

"You're really toast now, jerk," Jimmy threatened. He rose and charged the vampire, half afraid that if he didn't do so quickly, the fool would disappear into thin air again.

This time the vampire didn't move.

Jimmy slammed into him. It was like slamming into solid rock. Cold rock. He was instantly paralyzed. Every nerve in his body, every muscle, seemed to tremble with a strange, chilling numbness.

He'd broken his neck, he thought, and the concept was so stunning that he didn't even feel pain, grief, or horror at first.

Then he felt the creature pick him up. He felt something like a breath of fire against his cheeks. He saw the eyes.

And looked into an abyss—stygian fire, touched by a hint of bloodred flame.

The grin on the creature's face deepened. Jimmy was totally helpless. The vampire-thing opened its mouth. The Cracker Jack fangs dipped into his neck.

Jimmy never screamed. Warmth surged through his broken body. He could hear the creature slurping as the warmth was drained, as total cold set in.

Until the very end, he could hear the slurping sound. A lapping . . . Cassie . . .

Whimpering.

When he was finished with Jimmy, the vampire—refreshed, energized, renewed—lifted the football player as if he were a rag doll. He caught hold of the big head and the shoulders and twisted.

The head came off with a pop.

Cassie still stared, a low, terrified, monotonous whine coming from her open mouth.

The vampire tossed the pieces of Jimmy aside.

She was lovely.

Very lovely.

And so, with Cassie, he took his time.

The next group of thrill seekers who came through were a mother, father, aunt, three teenagers, and a great-uncle. They clung together, scared, having fun, ducking the wafting fabric that teased from above them, jumping from each spring-loaded special effect that popped up at them. They saw the body parts. They *ooh*ed and *aah*ed with delight. Terror Town had done a great job. It was so incredibly grisly. The blood and guts were so very real looking.

They walked through, unmolested.

There was a tap on her coffin.

"Darcy, come on out. We're closing."

Darcy popped open her lid. It was Tony. Garish makeup made his cheeks gaunt, his eyes large. He smoothed back dark hair. "I just got a call on the walkie-talkie. They're having trouble with the lighting, and someone thinks some kids are hiding out—they came in and didn't reappear. There weren't that many people outside, so they've given rain checks. Let's go. Give me a hand, honey. I'll help you out of there."

She could have gotten out okay, but rather than be blatantly rude, she accepted his hand. There were all kinds of nice guys working here; she just happened to have gotten stuck with Tony. He managed to brush her breast with his palm. The subtle grin he wore told her he had done it on purpose.

She ignored it. "Thanks," she told him, and started walking toward the rear exit.

"What's your hurry?"

"You just told me we're closing."

"Yeah, well. Soon. We could take a minute, you know. Fool around in the hay and the headstones."

"Thanks again, but no thanks," she told him.

Then she stopped, standing dead still. The new guy she had seen for the first time tonight was standing in front of her. He was in a sweeping cape. He hadn't put on any makeup, and still . . . boy, something about his eyes was really still freaky. As if he were a cat. With night vision. With glow-in-the-dark eyes.

"Darcy, Darcy, Darcy . . . ," Tony was saying.

Suddenly he grabbed her from behind, his arms sweeping around her. He apparently didn't realize that she had stopped for a reason—that their path was blocked.

He seemed to think that she wanted to take him up on his offer to fool around in the hay after all.

"Come on, Darcy," he said huskily. "Come on, please, just give me a break. I know how you feel about me, and that you shouldn't see a guy where you're working, and that I'm kind of like the boss, being who I am and all. . . ."

Tony was breathing heavily against her neck—slobbering on her nape. He still hadn't seen the new guy.

"What?" she said incredulously, trying to slide away from him. She answered him quietly, still staring at the caped figure ahead of her. She tried to whisper, not wanting the relative stranger to hear what was going on, although she wasn't sure why. Tony was acting like a jerk.

She didn't want to be left behind with him.

She didn't want to move forward.

"Tony," she murmured, "I really can't stand you, and I don't think that you're like the boss at all."

What was the matter with him? He was still trying to jump her bones, while there was something really wrong with the corridor. They'd added more props. Gruesome stuff. Heads, bodies . . . blood. She couldn't see well in the dim light and shadows. All she could really see were the eyes of the newcomer. They were so startling.

And suddenly he spoke.

"Hey, now, enough of that," the newcomer said. He spoke lightly, teasingly. "I'm the only one who licks necks around here."

Tony was badly startled by the sound of the voice when he had thought himself alone with Darcy. He straightened and tensed like a springboard.

"What the hell are you doing here? And who the hell are you?" Tony said angrily. "I wasn't told that anyone else had been hired for this section!"

"Ah, how sad. They just don't tell you everything. And here I am, in your section. Scared, there, little boy?" the newcomer asked.

"Scared? You ass! Move on, Darcy. The bosses are going to hear about this guy," Tony barked. "Go on—move."

"No, don't move, not a good idea, Darcy," the tall man said.

She wanted to move; oddly enough, at that moment, she wanted to do just exactly as Tony had told her—move, get the hell out! But she couldn't move. She felt frozen, completely frozen. She couldn't draw her eyes from the face of the newcomer. In fact, she had done nothing but stare at him since he had arrived—and so it was hard to understand how, suddenly, he wasn't alone. There was a tall, slim, dark-haired woman at his side. She was dressed much as Darcy was herself. She was beautiful. Some logical part of Darcy's mind thought, *Great contact lenses! And look! She's got them, too. Look at those eyes. So darned scary. Horrible, red, burning, compelling . . .*

"Darcy?" Tony said softly. "Darcy, is this some kind of a joke?"

"No," she said under her breath.

"A bunch of you being jerks, trying to get to me—"

"No," Darcy repeated. She still couldn't tear her eyes away.

"Oh, do shut up, Tony!" the man said.

"That one is mine, I take it, darling?" the woman cooed to her companion, laughing softly. She looked Tony up and down, licked her lips, and shivered with delight. Then those eyes of hers touched Darcy. A chill went down her spine like nothing she had ever experienced. She felt . . . as if she were touched. Worse. She felt as if she were being consumed. As if she were bared to the bone by those eyes. And the feeling was filthy, horrible. Those eyes . . .

They touched her with evil.

They seemed to strip her down. They were awful. They somehow touched her inside and out. Invaded her. Raped her with their evil . . .

"Not that I'm at all choosy as to sex," the female said, her voice low, guttural . . . so sensual. She compelled just as she repelled.

And I still haven't moved, Darcy thought. *I can't move! It's like being stuck in a bad B movie. The fog is swirling at my feet, the lighting is shadowy and purple, I'm surrounded by tombstones, and I know that they're only foam, but they seem real, as if they could be mine, and the sound system is working just fine, and they're playing that cursed music from* The Exorcist!

And . . .

They're there! She's hungry, you can feel it, so hungry, like a wolf licking her chops, looking at me, oh, God, oh, God, there's a coffin behind me, my coffin, and I'm going to die. . . . .

"Mr. Frat Boy goes first," the man said, "though I'm not that choosy as to sex either, my love. You know that. Ladies first, though. My little vampiress looks as sweet as chocolate. Powder blue eyes . . . I can feel her heart beating from here, like a rabbit, the anticipation is so, so sweet. . . ."

"She does look delicious," the female said softly.

"Darcy, go."

"Tony, no, you can't stay—"

"Go! You've got to go. Get out!" Tony insisted. But his voice didn't sound so assured anymore. *Still* . . .

"I know you!" he whispered to the newcomers.

He knew them? These were people he *knew?*

"What a memory, Frat Boy," the man said.

"How could he forget us darling?" the woman queried.

"Well, he'd been smoking a little weed, and jerking down hard on that Johnnie Walker," the man reminded her.

"Go!" Tony commanded Darcy. He suddenly pushed her. Pushed her hard. "Go, Darcy. Run like hell!"

He broke the spell the hideous eyes had upon her.

And he gave her the momentum to run.

Through the cold. For it was cold. Icy, icy, cold. She ran past the newcomer. Saw his eyes again. Saw the amusement in them.

If he wanted to, he could stop her. He could just will it, and he would stop her!

Yet something in his expression changed slightly as he watched her. The amusement was still there, but there was something like a shrug as well.

He was letting her go.

Yes, he had chosen to let her go!

Her lips were bone dry; her lungs were heaving. She ran in pure, blind panic. She saw an emergency exit ahead. She plowed toward it.

She heard Tony scream.

And she burst into the night, screaming hysterically herself.

Chapter Ten

Jade rose late on Saturday, waking with a start. He had been there; she had found him. He had been with her, in flesh and blood.

But when she turned to him, he was gone.

"Why was I expecting that?" she muttered aloud to herself.

She rose and showered and debated the possibility that she had imagined it all again. That she was losing her mind.

Whether she had imagined her erotic evening again, or whether it had been real, she was crazy either way. If it was real, she had spent the night with a virtual stranger, betraying one of the really fine and decent men in the world.

After she had showered, she dressed, made coffee, and

looked at her answering machine. No messages. Lucian hadn't called.

Neither had Rick.

When Rick called, what was she going to say? She bit into her lower lip, drummed the table with her fingernails, and then sipped her coffee.

She had to tell him. He was too fine a person for her not to be totally honest. She was going to sound like the worst human being in the world, but that didn't matter. Hurting him as little as possible did.

But what if Lucian DeVeau really had no interest in her?

He did. Somehow she knew it.

As the clock crept past one in the afternoon, she picked up the phone and dialed Rick's house. His machine picked up. She left him a message, saying that she hoped he was feeling better.

She had barely hung up when the phone rang. When she picked it up, she heard a woman's voice. She tensed, thinking that it might be the same woman who phoned and then hung up on her yesterday.

But the accent was different.

And this woman didn't hang up.

She asked for Lucian DeVeau.

Jade wound the phone wire around her fingers. "I'm sorry, he's not here."

"He's left?"

She stared at the phone, wondering how on earth anyone could have known that he'd been there, and then wondering why the woman sounded so distraught.

"He's not here," she repeated carefully.

"Look, I'm sorry to disturb you, but it's important that I reach him. Please, if you see him, have him get hold of Maggie. As soon as possible."

"If I should see him, I'll certainly give him your message."

She set the receiver down, perplexed. The phone call meant at least one thing, she told herself: Lucian was real.

She tried Rick's number again. Once more she got his answering machine. When the beep sounded, she left her message.

"Rick, it's Jade again. I won't call anymore, but if you're still sick, you need to get to a doctor. Call me when you can; let me know you're okay."

She tried the station, asked for Rick, and wound up patched through to Gavin. "He didn't come in, Jade. Apparently he's really sick. He's at home."

"I just called his house and got the machine."

"I think he's sleeping. He told me he just can't shake this bug he's got, and he's going to try to sleep it off today. He threw up all over the morgue last night."

"He needs to see a doctor."

"Yeah, we told him so."

"Well, thanks."

Gavin didn't seem ready to hang up. "Jade," he murmured hesitantly, "have you seen any news today?"

Someone was pounding on her door. "Can you wait a minute, Gavin? Just a second."

She set the receiver on the table before he could answer. It was Shanna at her door, a newspaper folded beneath her arm.

"Did you see?"

"See what? I haven't even looked at the paper yet. Give me a moment—I've got Gavin on the phone."

She picked up the receiver. "Gavin?"

"Yeah, I'm here. Jade—"

"Shanna just came in with the newspaper."

"Read it."

"What's up?"

"The cult members have struck again. There were more murders last night."

"Last night?" Her heart quickened. "Where?"

"Don't worry—not here. Still far, far away. Farther than New York."

"But where?"

"In Massachusetts."

"In a cemetery?"

"No. In a theme park. A haunted house kind of a place. It's front-page news all over the country. Take a look. Give me a call back."

He hung up. Jade looked up. Shanna was pouring herself coffee. The newspaper was on the counter. Jade seized it quickly, and began reading the article.

"Oh, God," she said softly.

"What?" Shanna demanded.

"Tony!" she whispered. "Tony Alexander was on the tour in Scotland."

"Whoa!" Shanna took her coffee and slipped into a chair at the dining room table, not even pretending that the news wasn't disturbing.

Jade started reading the article again.

"Why in the hell would he work in such a place—after what happened?" Shanna queried.

"His uncle owned it, according to this article," Jade murmured, scanning the words over and over again.

"Jade, maybe you do need a pit bull."

Distracted, Jade shook her head.

"Shanna, they were found . . . all over the place. Some of the people who had gone through thought that the body pieces were special effects!"

The phone rang again. The shrill sound made Jade jump.

"I'll get it," Shanna told her.

"Hello?" she queried. Jade saw her sister frown. "Lucian? Lucian DeVeau? I don't know any Lucian DeVeau—"

Jade grabbed the phone from her hands. "Who is this, and what do you want?"

"I'm sorry to bother you again," the voice on the phone said. "But it's really incredibly important that I reach Lucian. I thought he might have come back."

"No, he's not here. I'm sorry. And I have no idea when he'll be back."

"Please, if you see him, tell him he must get hold of Maggie right away. It's urgent."

"If I see him," she murmured.

"Thank you."

"Wait!" she said, aware the woman was hanging up. "Wait, you didn't give me a number."

"He knows where to find me."

The line went dead.

Shanna was staring at her. "Who is Lucian DeVeau? If you're so familiar with him, why don't I even know the name?"

Jade sat down. She took a deep breath. "Shanna, remember me telling you about the man in Edinburgh? The one on the trip? The one—"

"The one who rescued you from the tomb? And then disappeared?"

"Yes. Well, he's here and his name is Lucian DeVeau."

Shanna leaned forward. "He's here . . . where, here?" she asked suspiciously.

"In New Orleans, not right here, not this minute."

"So why is this woman calling here looking for him?"

"I don't know."

"Was he here?"

Jade hesitated. "Yes."

Shanna was silent a long moment. "Just how 'here' was he?"

"What do you mean by that?"

"You know what I mean by that."

Shanna was too close to her, too ready to read between the lines of what she was willing to say and what she wasn't.

"I ran into him and we had a drink at Drake's. Derrick was bartending. And Danny came along, drunk as a skunk. We got him home together. I couldn't have managed it without Lucian's help."

"And then he came here."

Jade hesitated again. "Yes."

Shanna shook her head in disgust. "And you had Rick, one of the greatest guys in the whole world."

Jade exhaled impatiently. "Shanna, you said it yourself—it wasn't right. If it had been right . . . Rick would have stayed with me. Maybe. I think. I don't know anymore."

Shanna's sudden sound of shock alerted Jade to the fact that her sister hadn't realized just how far things had gone with Lucian. "Jade! You didn't."

"Shanna—"

"A total stranger."

"He's not exactly a stranger. He saved my life in Scotland."

"Did he?" Shanna queried sharply, her aqua eyes sharply narrowed on Jade. "Or was he part of it? Don't you find it amazing, the way that he disappeared after it all? And now people are being horribly murdered in the States—and here he is again!"

Jade pushed the paper toward her. "He's in New Orleans. People were murdered in Massachusetts!"

Shanna fell silent. "What's his explanation?"

"He . . ."

Shanna threw up her arms. "Great. He doesn't have an explanation. So you invited him right over and into bed."

"At least I'd met him. What about you?"

"I went to the movies. And Dave didn't show up anyway," Shanna murmured. She stared at her sister. "He's sick, too. Like Rick. Rick Beaudreaux. Remember? That really great cop you've been dating.''

"I'm going to break it off, Shanna, as soon as I can."

"Great. He's at death's door, and you're going to break his heart."

"He isn't at death's door—he's just really, really sick."

Frustrated, Shanna just stared at her. "Where is this Lucian now?"

"I don't know."

"Oh, great. He just up and disappeared again."

"No, he was here a long time."

Shanna made a snorting sound. "Good to hear that he isn't just wham, bam, thank you, ma'am."

"Shanna, stop it. We had a drink, we took Danny home, he stayed."

"And then?"

"All right—and then he disappeared."

"Jade, Jade, Jade!" Shanna murmured.

They both jumped when the phone started to ring.

"I'll get it," Shanna told her.

"No, I'll get it." Jade nearly had to snatch the receiver from her sister's hand. "Hello?"

"Miss MacGregor?"

"Yes?"

"This is Sean Canady. Detective Sean Canady."

"Oh, yes. How are you?"

"Worried at the moment."

"Really?" She sank back into her chair.

"Who is it?" Shanna whispered.

Jade covered the mouthpiece. "Sean Canady."

"The cop?" Shanna demanded, frowning.

"Miss MacGregor, are you alone?"

She hesitated. "My sister is with me."

He was quiet for a minute. "Lucian is not there?"

Her heart quickened and then seemed to miss a beat. "How do you know about him?"

"Is he there?"

"Do you know a Maggie?" she cross-queried.

"Yes. My wife."

"Well, your wife is trying to find him, too."

"Yes, yes, I know that."

"What the hell is going on?" Shanna demanded in a whisper.

Jade shook her head, shushing her sister.

"I'm here with my sister. I don't understand why you're calling."

"I don't mean to alarm you terribly, but I thought you should know that you were acquainted with the young man from the automobile crash the other day."

"I was?"

More ice seemed to settle around her.

"You also need to be aware that it wasn't an accident. It was murder."

"I'm sorry; I'm very confused."

"You've seen today's paper?"

"Yes, just now."

"So you know that Tony Alexander was killed at his uncle's theme park last night."

"Yes . . . I, uh . . . saw it." Her fingers curled more tightly around the phone cord. Shanna's eyes were wide and on hers.

"Detective Canady, I'm not sure what that has to do with the young man killed here."

"It was Tom Marlow. You knew him in Scotland."

Tom Marlow. Another face and name rushed back to her. She saw him at the start of the tour, teasing Sam Spinder, Marianne. . . .

She moistened her lips, fighting a wave of panic.

"But I saw the newspapers here when the accident occurred. His name was down as Tad Madsen."

"Tad was a nickname. I believe he was using Madsen on purpose, as if he were afraid that someone might be looking for him. He had just transferred down here to LSU from a college in the north. Maybe he was trying to hide."

Jade slid back into a seat at the table.

"Look, I'm sorry to give you this kind of news, but I want you to be careful. Most important, watch out for strangers. Be careful when you go out. In fact, you really shouldn't go out at all. And don't invite anyone in, do you understand? It's really important that you don't invite anyone in."

Shanna had edged very close to her. Now she whispered, "I heard that! I heard what he just told you. Maybe you'd better tell him that you trashed his friend to go to bed with a total stranger last night."

"Shush!" Jade told her sister, covering the mouthpiece once again.

"Look," she told Canady, "I believe I must be in serious danger, since it appears these people have come to the States and are hunting down the survivors from last October," Jade said. "I can call a locksmith right away—"

"Yes, you can. But don't."

"But—"

"I'll explain when I see you. May I come over now?"

"Yes, I guess."

"No, no—wait. Meet me downstairs, at the French restaurant next door."

"Now?"

"I'm not at the station; I'm home. It will take me a bit to drive in. Meet me in, say, thirty minutes."

"All right."

She hung up.

"What?" Shanna shrieked.

"I'm going to meet him at the restaurant."

"The cop?" Shanna said.

"Yes, the cop, who else? Shanna, the auto accident the other day . . . It wasn't an accident. It was a murder."

"But his car went through a tree," Shanna reminded her.

"I don't know exactly what happened. I don't know how or why, but Shanna, it was another one of the kids from Scotland."

The sisters stared at one another.

"So," Shanna said after a minute. "You're going to meet with this cop next door at a restaurant—why not at the station?"

"I don't know."

The phone started to ring again. This time neither one of them wanted to answer it.

The machine picked up. "Jade, it's Gavin. Please give me a call as soon as possible. I—"

She swept up the receiver quickly. "Gavin?"

"Hey, kid. I'm sorry, I've got some really bad news for you."

"About the kid in the car accident. I know who he was, Gavin. I just heard. Why didn't you tell me about him this morning, too?"

"That's not why I called, Jade. Rick has been taken to the hospital. He's bad. Really, really bad. I thought that you'd want to know, that . . . that you might want to be with him."

She frowned. "Gavin, is it that serious?"

"Jade . . . they're pumping blood into him hard and fast. They had him packed in ice . . . and now they've called a priest. He's Roman Catholic, you know."

"Last rites?" she said softly.

"I'm so sorry, Jade."

She dropped the phone. She even forgot her sister as she snatched up her handbag and started out the door.

"Jade!" Shanna cried.

She paused long enough to stare at her sister. "Rick may be dying."

"My God!"

Shanna was up beside her.

At the street level they hailed a cab, both completely forgetting about meeting Sean Canady at the French restaurant.

Maggie.

She had been taking the baby's clean clothes from the dryer, trying not to think about Lucian or Jade MacGregor or anything that was happening.

She closed her eyes, doubting that she had heard her name so clearly.

Maggie.

Lucian's voice. He could still reach her. Even now.

Lucian, where the hell are you?

The cemetery. The vault. I could feel you. You've been trying to reach me.

Yes! Lucian, they killed in Massachusetts last night. And they've killed here. A murder they concealed. Lucian, I think your friend Jade is in serious danger.

Silence.

Massachusetts?

Last night. Sean has been desperate to find you, to tell you. One by one, they're attacking and killing the survivors from Scotland. I've been trying to reach you through Jade. I couldn't explain why I needed you. . . . Sean finally called her. He left to meet with her.

Thank God. Then she's safe for now.

For now. Lucian, you've got to stop them.

I know. Maggie, take care of yourself. They might suspect our connection.

Maggie looked around her den. There was garlic everywhere—huge cloves covering all the windows. She'd been out earlier, visiting the church—scooping up water from the baptism font. She had carved dozens of broom handles into sharp stakes, and placed them where she would have quick and ready access to them.

I know how to deal with the undead, Lucian.

But don't be careless, Maggie. Not in any way.

No.

Tell Sean I know what's happened—and that I'll find him. Maggie?

She smiled.

I'll tell Sean you called, Lucian. I know how much he loves me, and that he has a certain reserved respect for you. But I'd just as soon he not know you can still touch my mind.

Lucian was silent a moment. She could almost see him smiling.

When I see him, I'll tell him I called you.

Take the greatest care, Lucian, please.

I will, Maggie. You take care of yourself. And that baby. And . . . your husband.

There was someone on the porch. The mailman? Was it time? Liz MacGregor didn't suspect any danger. Her husband had inherited his beautiful Garden District home from his folks. He'd lived there all his life. He knew every one of his neighbors.

It would never have occurred to her to be worried.

She stepped outside, looking around.

"Hello?"

"Hello! I was getting ready to ring your bell."

He was tall and thin, with a charming half smile, wearing a gray uniform and carrying a black box and a clipboard.

"Mrs. . . . um . . . MacGregor, right?" he asked, checking his clipboard. He offered her a cheerful smile.

"Yes?"

"I'm the cable guy. Oh—not Jim Carrey. Please! Seriously, I'm from the cable company."

"Oh! Hi!" She shook his hand. "I didn't call; we haven't been having any trouble."

"No, I know, but we're testing out a new children's station. It's a family channel, but geared to young children. There will be great new shows for little people. We'd like you to be one of our test families, with your little ones. I'm telling you, I've seen some of the programming, and it's just great. Your kids will love it. If I could just see your box for two seconds—I'll be in and out in a flash."

Liz smiled. She had Disney and Nickelodeon, but there was never enough programming for little kids. *Good* programming for little kids.

"I'd be happy to sign on as a test family," she said. "Come on in."

She reentered the house.

Sean Canady reached the restaurant.

Jade MacGregor wasn't there. He sat down and ordered coffee.

And waited.

And waited.

They wouldn't let Shanna in to see Rick, only Jade, and only because the police had explained that she was the closest thing to family Rick had at the time.

She couldn't believe how quickly the virus had taken over. He wore an oxygen mask, and an IV dripped blood into his veins while another tube was bringing nourishment. She sat down at his side and took his hand. He didn't acknowledge her.

She was there about an hour before a doctor came. When he did, she bombarded him with questions. What was it? What was happening? Surely he was young and strong, and he was going to get better?

"Miss MacGregor, you're his fiancée, right?"

She hesitated—then lied. She had no intention of allowing anyone to throw her out of the hospital.

"Yes," she said.

"I'm glad you're here. He doesn't have any family."

"His folks died when he was young. He has cousins, I guess, but they all moved away. No siblings."

"Good, good, then I'm really glad that you're here for him. This thing just attacked him, drained him, dehydrated him . . . he needed blood in the worst way. We're still running tests. But I'm pleased to tell you he is doing better. He's holding his own."

"I'm grateful, but . . . what is it?"

"We still don't really know. I hate to admit that, but it's the truth. We've brought in several disease experts . . . tested for food poisoning, bacteria . . . anemia . . . we're still working on it. But we have stabilized him."

She nodded, thanking him.

"You can stay with him awhile? I'm willing to bet he knows you're here."

"I'll stay. Of course I'll stay."

She sat at his side, holding his hand.

Praying.

* * *

Shanna was stirring clumpy, powdered cream into a cup of overbrewed coffee when Sean Canady took the seat opposite her at the cafeteria table.

She straightened immediately, her eyes going wide at the sight of him.

"Lieutenant!"

"Hello, Shanna. Jade is with Rick?"

"Yes. I'm so sorry; we forgot all about you. They called about Rick—"

"I know."

"Let me get you some coffee."

He lifted a hand. "No, thanks. I just had about twenty cups."

"At the French restaurant?"

He nodded.

"I'm so sorry."

"It's all right."

"Well, at least, I'm sure, you had much better coffee."

He grinned. "Probably."

"They wouldn't let me in to see Rick. Only Jade. He's so sick. I just can't believe it."

"I wish I could see him," Sean muttered. He studied Shanna suddenly. "How are you feeling?"

"Me?" She straightened. "I'm fine."

"And Jade?"

"She's fine, too. Just fine. But that cold is going around, I guess. Cold! It's much worse than a cold. Poor Rick. I can't believe it, but they say . . . his life is in danger. They've had a priest in. He's had last rites."

"So I heard, but last report has it that he's doing somewhat better."

"I'm so relieved to hear that."

"Jade is still with him, right?" Canady asked.

Shanna nodded. He was so intense. And so good-looking.

All the married ones were, she thought with an inward sigh.

Except for the guy at the coffee shop. And he had been a no-show. Maybe he was as sick as Rick. She hoped not.

"I'm really sorry we left you stranded there," she told Sean. "We just forgot. Completely."

"It's okay. I understand." He hesitated. "But I need to talk to Jade. I think she's in serious danger."

"I thought I'd just wait here until she comes down. I won't let her be alone. We won't try to walk home alone or anything. We'll take a cab."

He nodded. "I'll just wait with you—if you don't mind."

She shook her head. "I don't mind at all."

"Do you play gin?"

"Sure. Do you have cards?"

"Well, not on me, but there's a gift shop."

"Great."

They played gin.

Poker.

Shanna relieved him of the twenty dollars he had on him. Then she felt bad about beating a cop out of his money.

"It's okay," he told her, grinning. "My wife is rich."

"She won't mind my fleecing you?"

"Nope. But I can win it back at chess."

"You think?"

"Yep."

He was good at chess. He won the first game, and the second.

But she was good, too.

The games demanded their attention.

Time wore on.

* * *

There was a strength and peace in the darkness and silence of the grave.

He'd sought this peace, aware of how he needed the perfect quiet of the darkness, the cool, sweeping comfort of the earth, the marble around him, the prayers of the living and the dead.

He needed to concentrate completely.

Centuries had given him the power to see well, to feel— a ripple in the order of things, a deadly maliciousness, aimed not even at the natural world, but at himself.

Aye, his senses were attuned. His eyes were those of a wolf in the night, his hearing phenomenally acute. He needed only to let it come to him. . . .

It hadn't always been that way.

His lessons had been bitter.

His retaliation even more swift.

But now . . .

They walked the earth again. In anger.

And in wrath.

Her turn. She wanted revenge. She thought that her time had come.

She didn't realize the depths of his hatred.

But then . . .

He had underestimated her power.

Chapter Eleven

Days passed upon the Isle of the Dead.

It seemed there was no beginning, and no end. Lucian didn't care. Life was strange, but he expected no less, realizing that he was among the undead, the shadow-walkers of the earth. Wulfgar remained with him, having fallen in love with the abused wife of the now-deceased farmer. The two had settled happily and worked the fields. And, as time passed, more men joined their company, casting their fate with the strange chieftain of the undead. Some were Scots; some were Irish. The Cornish came, Welsh, Norman, Flemish, Norwegian, Dane, and Swede. They settled.

And they sailed their great ships, when the occasion or need arose. They left those decisions to their leader, the man growing legendary across the seas as the strange king of the Isle of the Dead.

Igrainia came when the dawn broke.

In those days he would see her, feel her enter the darkness of his room and lie down beside him. He slept, knowing she was with him.

At dusk he would awake, and they would have their time together, and then, when he chanced to close his eyes, she would disappear.

"Why do you have to leave?" he would ask her.

"Why do you have to sleep by the light of day?" she would return.

"Because I am now a monster," he would tell her. "And you will never be anything other than an angel."

"There are many things between monsters and angels, so many shades of gray between black and white," she would tell him. "We are in no position to question too much," she would say, and he would be afraid to say more.

Sometimes a ship would arrive on the isle. Men would come to him. Vicious slayers would attack to the north, on the coast of Eire, down to Normandy, even in Scandinavia. Sometimes he would hear a petition, and Igrainia would listen with him, and she would tell him that he must go with the warriors, and fight their battles.

And so he would sail. And when he would fight such an enemy, he would meet his own new standard of savagery, and though others fought as ferociously, he wondered at what he had become. Wulfgar told him he was ridding the world of creatures far worse than himself.

He pondered his right to judge which men should live and which should die. Wulfgar reminded him that all men took a chance when they went to battle.

And still the plaintiffs would come to him, those who knew of the chieftain on the isle. He would sit in a carved wooden chair with Igrainia at his side, and they were like royalty, receiving those petitions, and the homage that came because of them.

And still, soon after dusk, Igrainia would be gone each night.

"She fell to the sea," Wulfgar told him one night. "And the sea brought her back to the surface. The Irish call her a selkie. What does it matter what name you give life, when you have the hours to share together? If you are a monster and she is an angel, what difference does it matter where you meet? I daresay your hours together are dearer than those shared by most men and their wives."

Their time was indeed precious, but lacking. Their home was the fishing cottage, darkened by day, and always smelling of the earth, for he had learned that he must sleep with native soil somewhere beneath him, in some form, even just a handful. When he did not, he grew weak—too weak to move, to rise . . . to ever approach daylight.

And he would not give up daylight. His wife, his angel, his sole reason for existence, came with the daylight.

And departed soon after dusk.

Still, far into the future, into forever, he would remember those days when, for whatever brief respites of magic it might be, he sat with his wife in the carved chairs, and they listened, judged, and ruled in their world of the damned. He could see it always, in his mind's eye. The chairs before the central open fire, the smoke rising to the roof flume high above, the furs they wore against the damp and cold, the swords laid before them, the warriors who came in rustic mail and armor, conical helms, horned helms, brooches of Celtic gold and silver . . .

He would remember her voice always, the way she greeted newcomers and old friends, the welcome she gave.

He would remember her eyes. The color of the sea. In fact, the sea seemed to churn in them—the waves rose and rushed, blue and green, sunrise and sunset, that which they both had gained, and that which they both had lost.

Aidan, a coastal king of Eire, came to him. Aidan was wary, afraid. Afraid of the legends he had heard that were false about the island, afraid that much of what he had heard was true. Lucian liked him when he appeared before him; he had the kind of courage that overrode his fear.

The Ard-Ri, or high king, the king of all the Irish who sat at Tara, had sent word that he was being besieged by invaders from the very far north—a place so deep into the ice and snow that even the Danes, Swedes, and Norwegians knew little about them. They were wild men, men with their own language, more depraved in battle than the worst of the berserkers. Their total disregard for human life had left the Ard-Ri at their mercy; the lesser kings sent back their regrets and made excuses. They could not come.

Would not come. They were afraid. Such things were not said aloud. That such an enemy seemed to have other-worldly powers was not mentioned either; Ireland embraced Christianity. It was just that old myths died hard.

It was Igrainia who listened to stories of how the children were killed, how women and children found no mercy at the hands of the invaders. When they were alone, he reminded her that creatures of his own kind were known to prey with the greatest relish upon the most tender, the most vulnerable, and the most innocent of humankind. He was angry that dusk, that twilight, that strange red afternoon and evening would prove the end of their time together each day. In listening to the tales of the attackers invading deep into the capital of all Eire, he was listening to the stories of the monster he was himself.

She denied that he could ever be such a creature.

He remembered when he had first learned that he must feast on blood.

But she wanted him to go, and so he would.

She left with the coming of total darkness that night, when the red orb of the sun disappeared from the sky, and the shadowland of deep night swept around the isle to give him his deepest power. He saw her as she walked to the sea, shed the garment of silk and fur she had worn, and dived into the ocean.

He had never watched her go before. Far out on the horizon he saw the flip of a dolphin's tail, and then another, and another. Sailors talked of sirens at sea, from the Greeks to the men he now knew. The bravest men talked of dragons that attacked boats. He had thought himself a sane man, a warrior chieftain, then a sailor as fine as the Vikings who had taught him the craft. He had never believed in such things. He had seen too many beached whales, dolphins, and even huge octopuses and squids. He had once loved the sea so much, loved the lash of the waves against his legs, even as frigidly cold as it had been in his Highland homeland. Now the salt was deadly to him, but he still walked the beach, and he loved the horizon, and he loved even to set sail, knowing that he dared not stand as tall against the waves as he might once have done.

And still he didn't believe in dragons. . . .

Sirens . . .

He turned from the coast. They sailed with the dawn.

The fierce enemies of the Ard-Ri were human—barely. They were a pagan tribe, dressed only in furs, armed with poisons as well as weapons of wood and steel. Their total disregard for life made their courage limitless; they feared nothing. They besieged the wooden walls of Tara; they butchered any they captured.

For Lucian, they were a feast. He had no qualms tearing into them, thirsting, drinking, glutting—his savagery was as great as their own.

They attacked by day.

He thinned their ranks at night. He was not alone. Among the many northern European nationalities of men were a few of his own number. He had come to recognize them instantly; indeed, he had come to know where they were in the world at large. He could see and command, and was proud of his power.

But even as their hungers managed to decimate the barbaric attacking army, and he said his good-byes to the Ard-Ri they had served, he felt a new disturbance in the darkness of what was once his soul.

Sophia!

He knew fear as he could not remember, fear, terror, anguish. In that fear he closed his eyes; in that fear, he willed himself to the Isle of the Dead, though the ship sailed hard and fast behind him.

He came to the fisherman's cottage, and the great carved chairs, and she was not there, and he ran to the shore.

The people were gathered around something on the beach. They saw him, and their eyes were filled with the deepest sorrow, and they gave way.

He walked across the sand. And there, on the shore, he thought at first that he saw a beached dolphin, for he saw the sleek and shimmering silver tail. Perhaps he blinked, for when he looked again, there was a woman's body, impaled through the heart with a fishing spear.

Not just a woman's body. Igrainia's body.

He fell to his knees beside her. Her hand touched his face. Her eyes, her sea green eyes, touched his, and her fingers just brushed his cheeks. "My love . . ."

Her fingers fell. Her eyes closed. Her sweeping thick lashes forever shadowed the aqua beauty that had been his world.

And when he looked up, in his agony, and his rage, he saw Sophia, saw her standing before Darian, and they were both so defiant.

"We were merely . . . fishing!" Sophia said.

She had underestimated the monster she herself had created. He threw himself at her, mind and body. He tore into her, flinging her to the earth, falling upon her, raking, pummeling, hating, hating. . . .

Darian was at him. He brought his sword down, doing his best to sever Lucian's head from his body. But an islander was there, a dwarf cast from his own society, valued here for his ability to read the runes and to spin a fine tale. Small and short and huffing and puffing, he brought a sword from the fisherman's cottage, and when Lucian was down, caught between the two, he dared the wrath of them both to bring the weapon to Lucian. He parried Darian's blows, even as Sophia leaped upon him, tearing hair from his head, flesh from his shoulders.

Darian nearly lost his arm as Lucian dealt a furious blow. Catching the dangling limb, Darian shouted to Sophia and leaped away.

Lucian caught Sophia from behind him with both hands; he gripped her with the strength of his maddened wrath, wrenched her up and over—and threw her from him. She landed on the beach, stunned and partially in the water.

Suddenly she began to scream. And it smelled like burned flesh. And he realized that he had thrown her into the salt water. . . .

Darian was there, sweeping her up. And though the unspoken law of the damned forbade him to destroy his own kind, Lucian walked toward them, ready to deliver the death blows, and ready to die himself. Destroying Sophia had been his sole reason for existence. . . .

But Darian reached her first. And even as she screamed in her agony, he was lifting her from the water and whispering and pleading. And they both turned to mist even as the fog from the sea began to roll in. . . .

He didn't die.

Or cease to exist.

He stood by the sea and fell to his knees and let out a scream. It was the haunted, lonely cry of the wolf at night, howling to the moon; it was the shriek of the damned, of a man lost, even what had been the remnants of his soul now taken.

His cry was bloodcurdling.

It danced upon the wind and rode the waves, and the heart of it was a shriek within a storm, and carried from coast to coast across the seas. The Irish crossed themselves, and said that the banshees rode with a vengeance that night. Even Norse kings, still certain they would sleep in Valhalla, cast up prayers to their ancestors and to their gods.

But by then, his ships of misfits and the mighty had come upon the Isle of the Dead. And when he might have cast himself to the sea salt as well, they overpowered him.

Daylight. He was exhausted. Tired beyond death, so far beyond.

Igrainia's body was bathed, adorned in silk and jewels and fur. She was set upon a bier, and with all the ritual due the greatest royalty, she was set aflame and cast back to the sea that had claimed her.

He slept, and Wulfgar convinced him that he must live. Sophia was crushed, and there was a world of madness that must be ruled. Aye, and he was part of that madness! For many years to come, he killed with far less compunction, and far less judgment. Indeed, he was a warrior, nothing more.

Aye, more, Wulfgar insisted. King of the undead. There must be sanity and reason. The farther they drifted forward through time, the more important it became that they keep their balance with the world around them.

And so he lived. Or remained undead.

And it would be more than a hundred years before he would sense Sophia wreaking havoc in the world of the living once again. . . .

* * *

His eyes flew open. He felt the darkness around him, the comfort of his lair. But against that shelter, he found what he needed.

He sensed the disturbance in the universe.

His universe.

Liz MacGregor busied herself in the kitchen while the nice young man worked with the cable. She could hear the twins laughing as he worked on the box in the downstairs playroom.

She glanced at the clock. It was growing late. She wasn't used to Peter being this late, but he had called to let her know that they were dragging out all kinds of research, going back through the archives.

She was worried, thinking about Jade. She loved both her stepdaughters. The morning with Shanna had made her aware that they were all very lucky. Things weren't perfect, but they really were something of a family.

And she had heard in Peter's voice that he was worried about Jade.

Well, no matter how late he got home, they'd talk about it. She'd gotten up really early with Petey and his fever and ear infection, but that didn't matter. She'd be awake when her husband got home. She was just so thankful that Petey, who had seemed so sick, had sprung back so well.

She could hear his laughter now. It was late for the cable man to still be working. He must like his job—and be pleased to be getting overtime, or something. He had worked a long time—and kept the kids happy and laughing.

Glad of their enjoyment, she dried her hands on a dish towel and walked out to see what was going on.

Petey and Jamie were both silent then, just staring at the television set as if they didn't know what was going on.

Frowning, she walked around the young cable man to look.

A gasp of horror escaped her.

There was porno on her television. Rough, brutal porno. People with straps of leather covering many different places—but not the places that should have been covered. Men with masks and whips. Women . . . doing what they were commanded. Sex organs exposed everywhere . . . people having everything imaginable done to them.

"How dare you!" she charged the cable man furiously, turning on him.

But there was something about him then. Something about the way he looked at her. She wanted to move. Her limbs were frozen. She wanted to scream. No sound would issue from her throat.

"Liz, Liz, what's the matter, Liz? You know, you are a pretty woman. And young still. Just a bit over forty. Peaking sexually at your age, that's what some people say. Let's have a better look, Liz. I think you'll enjoy it if you give it half a chance."

He set his hand on her shoulders, drawing her in front of him. She felt his hands at her neck. She still wanted to scream; she was in horror, but . . .

His hands . . .

On her neck. They felt good. His fingers were busy along her blouse. Undoing buttons. It seemed oddly okay.

He had her facing the television.

She suddenly felt . . .

Swollen. All over. Watching . . .

She wanted to be touched like that. And he was going to do it.

The twins were crying. She didn't care in the least.

Annoying little rugrats . . .

Rug, rug, rug . . .

She was lying on the carpet.

"Want me to get rid of the brats?" he whispered to her. Then he laughed. "For now . . . I'll just throw the little darlings in their cribs."

He was gone. But she couldn't move. She could only stare at the television. There was a reason she shouldn't be doing this. She couldn't begin to imagine what it might be. She struggled. It seemed she could see something far away. There was a man in her life. A husband. A good one. She could see his face, fine green eyes, dark hair with dignified gray at the temples. A man she loved . . .

He was so far away.

Mist settled over her. Deliciously sensuous . . .

She had no control over this. The cable guy was there, smiling through the mist. It was all right. He needed . . . something.

She heard moaning.

She was doing it. There was a sharp pain . . . somewhere. It added to the sensation. Sticky, she was sticky with . . . something. Something red . . .

But he licked it all away.

Later the television went to static.

Liz lay limp on the rug.

From their upstairs bedroom, the twins cried and cried.

"Hey!"

A doctor had touched her hand, awakening her. Jade jumped. She jerked her neck. There was a sharp pain in it.

She'd been sleeping over the bed in a twisted position. She was sore all over.

But she saw the doctor and straightened immediately. This was a different man from the one she'd seen earlier.

He was older, with long, wispy white hair, a mustache, and kindly blue eyes. He was smiling.

"You're the fiancée!"

"I . . . yes."

He offered her a hand. "Dr. Wainwright. I specialize in rare diseases."

"Jade MacGregor, Dr. Wainwright. How is—"

"Your young man is much better. Miss Jade MacGregor. You've been the magic touch. He's doing incredibly well."

"He is? Really?" She barely dared to believe it.

She looked at Rick. His coloring was much better. He was breathing smoothly. His eyes were still closed; he slept.

"You should go home and get some rest," Wainwright told her.

"You really think he's going to be okay?"

"What do you think?"

"I think he looks much better."

"His blood pressure is good, breathing is regular, and the blood is pumping through him right as rain."

"Maybe I should stay a little longer."

"Miss MacGregor, I don't want another patient in here."

"Do I look that bad?" she asked with a laugh.

"You look gorgeous, young lady. The red in your eyes makes them a fascinating turquoise color, and those dark shadows underneath certainly do enhance it."

She smiled. "I think I was sleeping."

"This is no place to really rest. Go home. Come back tomorrow. He should be much better by then."

"All right. Thank you." She hesitated, moving up by Rick's head, touching his forehead. He was so much cooler. His pasty white color had gone; he was a far healthier-looking pink now.

She kissed his forehead. "Keep getting better!" she whispered.

He didn't respond. She glanced at Wainwright. "Don't

worry," he told her. "He's not unconscious anymore; it's just a good, healthy sleep."

"Okay."

"Get going!"

She smiled at him again, then turned and left the hospital room. She yawned as she walked, barely noticing the nurse who was briskly moving along the hall with a tray of medicines.

"Good evening," she murmured.

"Evening," the nurse said.

Jade kept going. She turned back. The nurse was gone. Had she entered Rick's room? The doctor was still there, of course. Rick was much, much better. It was okay to go home.

She started down the elevator, thinking that she needed to leave by the emergency exit; the main doors would be closed and locked by now.

Shanna wouldn't still be waiting—would she?

Knowing her sister, maybe.

She headed toward the cafeteria, which was, of course, closed. But there was an area of machines for the night crew at the entrance to the main cafeteria, and she went there, worried that her sister might have waited for her.

She had.

And to Jade's surprise she wasn't alone. She was sitting there, her head slumped against the shoulder of Lieutenant Sean Canady.

Canady.

She had forgotten all about him.

"Lieutenant!" she murmured, hurrying forward.

Shanna woke up, startled. "Jade . . . Oh, my God, is he—"

"Better," she said quickly.

"Definitely better?" Canady queried.

"Definitely. Really, truly," she said, smiling. "The doctor

just more or less ordered me to go home. Lieutenant, I have to tell you, I am so sorry. I completely forgot about you until seeing you this very moment, I'm sorry to admit. When Gavin called me about Rick—''

"It's all right. I understand.''

"You've been waiting here all this time as well?'' she asked.

"Yes.''

"You think I'm in that much danger?''

"Yes,'' he said flatly.

"But—''

"I'm going upstairs for a minute; I'd like to take a quick look at Rick myself. Don't go anywhere without me right now, understand?''

"All right.''

"I mean it now. You wait here.''

She lifted her hands. "Of course. You waited all day.''

He still looked at her suspiciously, as if she might run out the second he left her. She looked worriedly at Shanna.

Shanna shrugged.

"I'll be right back,'' he said.

"I'll be right here, I swear,'' Jade promised. "I'm just going to get some coffee out of the machine.''

He left them, looking back every few feet until he reached the elevator.

Jade bought coffee, then sat down beside her sister. "Do you know what's up with him?''

Shanna arched a brow at her. "I know he's okay at gin, and a whiz at chess. He likes his coffee black. He adores his wife and kid.''

"But . . . he's so worried. I mean, what a great cop.''

"Yeah, well, let's not knock him. This isn't looking real good. Jade, it's really scary, what's happening.''

"I know,'' Jade murmured, sipping her coffee. She

squeezed her sister's hand. "Thanks! Thanks for waiting, too. You're a doll."

Shanna eyed her sister carefully. "Rick's a great guy."

"I know."

They sat together then in silence and waited.

When Sean entered rick's hospital room, the doctor was gone.

There was a dark-haired nurse, her back to Sean, fiddling with Rick's IV.

"Hey!" Sean said sharply.

She turned. She was an extremely attractive woman, but something about her made Sean uneasy.

"What are you doing to him?" he asked her.

She smiled with no humor. "Blood transfusion. Who are you?"

"Canady. Lieutenant Canady. Homicide."

"They're bringing in Homicide detectives on the flu now, eh?"

"Is it the flu?" Sean asked.

She gave him a strange look, then suddenly lowered herself over the patient.

She's going to bite his neck! he told himself.

He quickly pulled out the vial of holy water he'd kept in his pocket all day. He threw it at the woman. She rose, shaking herself off, staring at him. "What the hell are you doing? Homicide cop or not, buddy, you're going to have to get out of here."

She wasn't a vampire, he decided, feeling like a fool. She had just been leaning close to get a good look at her patient.

"Sorry, sorry! Really, un . . . we're working under a lot of pressure these days."

"So are we, Lieutenant, so are we," she told him wearily.

"I'm so sorry. Honestly."

"Well, you can't arrest any flu bugs, Lieutenant. And you can't drown them, either." She smiled again suddenly, this time a real smile, a warm smile. "He's doing so much better, really. He's going to be okay. You go on home, Lieutenant, and get some sleep. And quit squirting water at people!"

"Yeah, sure, thanks. Uh, good night."

Sean exited the hospital room and started back downstairs, barely noticing the women at the nurses' station as he left.

One of them, however, watched him depart.

Her eyes followed him until he reached the elevator.

She then turned and started toward Beaudreaux's room.

He arrived too late.

Lucian knew it the minute he came to the handsome house in the Garden District. He could feel that Darian was gone.

He entered the house, instinctively heading directly for the room where Liz MacGregor lay on the floor.

Her hair was short and blond, and billowed out beneath her head.

He placed his fingers at her throat, seeking a pulse.

He covered her with an afghan from the sofa.

Then he picked up the phone extension and dialed 911. As he listened to the wail of sirens, he went upstairs. The twins were whimpering, but they seemed uninjured. He didn't try to reassure them; help was coming. He could hear it.

He walked out on the porch. He held very still and listened. Darian couldn't be far.

He concentrated again, hard. Sophia might still elude him; after all, she had been his creator. But Darian . . .

At last he sensed the man. A form, near, not far, close . . .

He followed. He ran down the street, trying for physical impressions.

Blood . . .

The scent of blood.

It would be rich on Darian now.

He didn't know how far he ran, but he suddenly realized that he was coming back to the cemetery. He burst into it and stood still.

Silence. The sound of silence.

Blood. The smell of blood.

He started to move again, past praying angels and marble crosses, through the murky light of moonbeams and the shadows cast by moss-laden oaks. Broken stones littered his path. Grand mausoleums rose before him. Steps, urns. A marble child with a bowed head over a grave, an angel with its wings spread wide, the figure of Christ high upon a cross.

Remember what it is to pray! he mocked himself.

And suddenly a figure leaped out at him. There was a flash in the moonlight, and something struck him hard in the arm. He felt a surge of pain. A whistle of the wind told him Darian was returning, knife in hand.

The steel of the blade made a noise as it sliced through air. Lucian ducked and rolled, coming up behind Darian.

Darian flew at him again.

He leaped high, reaching for a broken iron rail that should have enclosed a tomb with the name Fontville etched upon it. The bar broke free in his hand. Darian sailed above him. He struck out hard with the iron, hoping that Darian would plow straight into him and impale himself upon the bar.

Darian nearly did so, but he saw the weapon and Lucian's intent just in time. He veered, screaming as the rusted edge of the iron bar tore across his chest, tearing cloth and flesh.

"You foolish bastard!" Darian raged. "She won't just destroy you. She'll make you watch every one of these fool innocents expire by slow death and torture, and then she'll bring you down!"

"You leave these people alone, Darian. Or when it's time for you, I'll pin you with a stake and cut off every one of your extremities before slicing off your head."

"Mad about the MacGregor bitch, eh? And that one was only the mother—the stepmother. But she was good, Lucian. So good. Have you forgotten how good? You, the so-called king of the vampires! Eater of gerbils! Have you forgotten what a woman tastes like? She was good, Lucian, really good. She gets it frequently, you could tell. She wanted me; she was like a gusher the minute my fangs touched her throat—"

Lucian struck out with the iron, catching Darian across the throat.

Darian clutched his neck, hissing and howling. Then he turned and ran, stumbling through the stones.

Lucian followed.

Help me.

He came to a dead standstill, amazed at the strength of the voice in his ears.

Help me!

It came again.

Sophia! Damn her, damn her, damn her.

Darian was gone. He had found shelter.

Easy enough, here in the midst of the dead. He closed his eyes.

Saw the hospital. Concentrated on it . . .

He was in Rick's room. The young cop's head was twisted to the side. Fresh, tiny puncture wounds marked his throat.

He pushed an emergency button.

"Code blue!" he shouted.

Hospital personal began filling the corridors.

He eased back into the shadows, watching as they went to work.

Chapter Twelve

Jade sat in the front of Sean Canady's car, staring at him as he awkwardly tried to explain himself.

"Do you understand?" he asked her.

She shook her head. He was a tall man, built like a linebacker, just beginning to go gray at the temples, and very handsome and appealing. His size alone should have made her feel secure. And she did feel secure with him.

She was very tired, of course, which didn't make it any easier to understand him. Shanna had tried to listen, but apparently it had been too much. She had fallen asleep in the backseat.

"Jade?" he persisted. "Are you getting this?"

"I'm not sure. There were some really terrible murders here a few years ago. Prostitutes, pimps . . . and the murders were solved. And it stopped. And these murders are very much like those, but, of course, it isn't the same murderer. But the murders must be approached in the same way."

"The killers are very dangerous."

"Um. I'd say that's fairly obvious."

He reddened slightly. It wasn't exactly a flush, but he'd reddened. "I wish Maggie were here," he muttered.

"Your wife? You wish your wife were here?"

"She can explain better."

"Is she a cop?"

"No. But if I try to explain, you're going to think I'm crazy."

"Oh, Lieutenant. I'm starting to think we're all crazy."

Canady hesitated for a minute. "What do you remember from Edinburgh?" he asked her.

She tensed and stared straight out of the window ahead of her. "A lot of blood and horror. There were coffins in the vault, and corpses that were just in their shrouds on the shelves. And they all suddenly seemed to be awake, coming after people. . . ."

"Corpses."

She shook her head. "I suppose they were rigged. It's so hard to remember. But I'm certain that the tour guide ripped open Sally Adams's throat with his teeth. I saw it, and it was no act."

"Your tour guide is busy again, Miss MacGregor," he said softly. "And . . ." He paused, looking at her, then back at the road. "And you're just going to have to take a few crazy precautions, that's all."

She stared at him. "You believe in vampires, don't you?"

"What I believe doesn't matter."

"Oh, great! You're going to give me that horseshit! I got it from a half a dozen cops and shrinks while I was still in Edinburgh—"

"What you do is what matters," he interrupted.

She exhaled, staring at the road herself. "Did you think that Rick Beaudreaux had been attacked by a vampire?"

He didn't answer right away, and she touched his arm. "Is that what you think has happened to him?"

He flushed, looking uncomfortable. "I . . . well, I . . . Rick really looked pretty good. I think he has an awful flu bug. He seems to finally be shaking it."

Jade sighed with relief.

They had reached her house. Canady parked in front, reaching back to shake Shanna's shoulder. "We're here," he said softly.

"Shanna has her own place."

"She's staying here tonight. So am I."

"Really, Lieutenant Canady. What will your wife say to that piece of police business?"

"It isn't police business," he told her. "My wife insisted I stay."

She could have argued with him; she didn't want to. She was really exhausted. She'd spent the night awake with a stranger in her bed. She'd spent the day awake at the bedside of the man who should have been spending his nights in her bed.

"Fine. I'll put Shanna on the convertible couch in my office. And you—"

"A pillow, blanket, and a floor in the parlor will be fine."

"I have a convertible couch there, too, Lieutenant. Unless you prefer the floor. Shanna!"

Her sister roused herself. "I hope you have an extra toothbrush, Jade. If not, I'll have to go home. I think I could bear a crazed killer before sleeping with my teeth, the way they feel!"

"I have toothbrushes," Jade said. She always had plenty. She was forever leaving them behind when she traveled.

Twenty minutes later she had both couches made.

"I'm still not sure why we're doing this," Shanna said, decked out in one of Jade's flannels, new toothbrush in hand. "My place is very secure."

"We're all to tired to risk more than one place," Sean said.

Shanna grinned and shrugged at her sister. "He does carry a big gun."

Canady was looking at Jade without saying anything. She had a feeling that he didn't believe that his big gun was worth much in this situation.

"Well, good night, all," Shanna said, turning toward the bedroom.

"Do you need anything else, Lieutenant?" Jade asked, watching him kick off his shoes to settle onto her parlor couch.

"No, I'm fine."

He removed his jacket. As she watched in amazement, he took a number of vials from his jacket pocket and set them on the coffee table by the couch.

He caught her staring at him and scowled.

"Holy water?" she queried skeptically.

"You got it."

"Can you really believe—"

"You were there in Edinburgh," he reminded her, lying down.

"Just so long as that gun is loaded, too," she said.

His eyes were already closed. "It is."

"Good night, then."

"God night. If there's anything . . . anything that bothers you at all . . . come get me."

"I will."

She went into her own room, leaving the door ajar.

It was too much. There was a cop in her parlor with holy water. Rick was getting better, but still barely holding his own. And she was so, so tired! Sean had called about Lucian; then he hadn't said anything about him, and her room still seemed to carry the sensuous scent of Lucian's aftershave. . . .

And she hadn't seen him since he had disappeared again, and the cop hadn't explained him in any way either!

She started to head back out to the parlor, then shook her head. Tomorrow. Tomorrow there would be plenty of time.

She crawled into bed.

At first she thought that her mind was going to be racing so quickly that she'd never sleep. Never.

But her eyes closed.

And almost immediately she drifted.

Peter MacGregor sat by his wife's side in the ambulance, amazed that anyone could have gotten so ill so quickly.

He held her hand, just staring into her face, seeing the ashen color there. He couldn't lose her. He couldn't. He'd loved Janie, his first wife, loved her with all his heart. And they'd gone through months and months of sickness, and he had stayed with her, and in his heart he had believed that she would get better, that just the strength of their wanting it to be so could make it so. She had been brave, Janie. Smiling her way through pain. Taking care always with what she said to him, and to her daughters. He would have loved her until the day he dropped dead himself, had she lived. He still loved her, would always love her.

But now Liz . . .

His mind fought against this.

It was just unfair. Totally unfair.

They reached the hospital. Liz was whisked from the ambulance and into the emergency room. He tried to follow.

A doctor stopped him.

"Sir, we'll do our best for her if you leave us to it right now."

The doctor was strong. Peter didn't realize at first that

he had been shoving him until he stopped doing so. "Really. Let us work," he said softly.

Peter nodded. The doctor pointed out a waiting room right by the door through which they had taken Liz.

He sat down, bewildered.

He had tried both the girls after the cops found him at the newspaper office. He'd tried Jade earlier, and then Shanna, because the two were so close, always together. He'd wanted his daughters to come home. There were too many murders across the country.

They were too much like what had happened to his eldest daughter, involving too many of the same people.

It had all been bad enough.

And then the discovery that right here in New Orleans a kid had been killed, and it hadn't been an accident, and that kid had been in Scotland as well.

He groaned aloud. He still hadn't reached the girls. The twins were with his next-door neighbor.

He didn't understand what had happened to Liz. Had she been attacked? Had she just acquired a fever and torn off her own clothing in a delirious desperation to get cooler? He ran his fingers through his hair. He needed to try his daughters again.

He dialed Shanna's number first. It rang and rang, and then the machine picked up. He set down the receiver. He groaned softly, getting ready to dial Jade's number.

He paused. There was someone standing in front of him. A priest . . . his priest, Father Dunwoody. He was sixty, gray-haired, and pleasant mannered. A great priest, a perfect priest, he wore the cloth well.

"Peter, are you all right? You look like hell." He even had the trace of an Irish accent.

"Liz is bad. She's in there right now."

"I just heard. Saw you here and asked. What happened?"

"I've no idea—I was working late. The police came for me."

"You didn't find her?"

"Me, no, I was at work."

For the first time it occurred to him to wonder just how the police had managed to find his wife. At the moment, though, it wasn't important. Liz was important.

"Where are the girls? They should be here with you," Father Dunwoody said kindly.

"I was just trying to reach them. They don't know. Shanna didn't answer. She sleeps like the dead. Of course, it's what? Middle of the wee hours of the morning."

"I'll stay with you—," Dunwoody began, but he broke off. A doctor was coming out. He looked grim.

Peter felt as if his heart had leaped out of his throat and was beating and bleeding in his hands.

"Doctor—"

"She's pulling out of it. We've got the fever down, and we've pumped a hell of a lot of blood into her. We're still pumping. She's asking for you."

"Sweet Jesus!" Peter exclaimed. He looked at Dunwoody. "Sorry, Father."

"It's all right, Peter." He winked. "I'll apologize to the Lord for you—and tell him you said thanks as well."

"Yes, thank God! Thank God!" He stared at the doctor, shaking. He almost fell. The doctor steadied him, as did the priest. "When you came out here," Peter tried to explain, "looking so very grim, I was afraid of the worst."

"Sorry. She's really doing well. It's just the second admission we've had like this today. Seems like there's some really awful disease going around, and we don't begin to know what it is."

"But she's all right?"

"She's holding her own nicely right now, I swear it."

"Thank God, thank God!"

"Amen," Father Dunwoody said. He watched as Peter followed the doctor in to see his wife.

A chill settled over him.

A strange disease . . .

Father Dunwoody crossed himself before starting from the emergency room. At the door he paused again.

And crossed himself once more.

Come. Come to me.

She was deeply, deeply sleeping, but still Jade heard the voice.

Come. . . .

Don't be absurd, she thought. *I'm sound asleep, in a thin cotton nightshirt.*

I need you. . . .

The voice was plaintive, desperate. She knew that she was still sleeping, that she was dreaming.

She thought she heard crying. Her heart quickened. It was a little voice, lost and scared. One of the twins? *Oh, baby, baby, it's okay, I'm coming. . . .*

Absurd. She couldn't hear the twins from here. She was in her own bedroom, in her own room. Dreaming. But if she was dreaming, it was okay. She could follow the voice.

It was a very strange dream. In her dream she knew there was a cop in her living room, and that he'd stop her from going. She left her bedroom by crawling out the window to the wraparound balcony.

She left the balcony by crawling over the bricks and precariously making her way down an old storm drain.

Then she was on the street, bare feet hitting the dusty pavement.

It had been a busy night on the streets of New Orleans. And the city never really slept, but this was probably the quietest time. She stepped over a few homeless, apologizing for wearing nothing but her nightgown, and for having no coins to give them.

"Lady, go home," one old down-and-outer with a crippled leg told her.

"I'm not really here. It's just a dream."

"My dream, or your dream? I mean, like, you're not an angel, running down the street in a trail of flowing white, are you?"

"No, this is my dream."

"Go home, lady. Dreams like this one are dangerous."

"It's all right."

"Wish I had some shoes to give you."

She smiled and kept going. The poor fellow on the street had been right. This was one dangerous dream. She'd lived in New Orleans all her life. She loved the city. She knew what streets to be on, and what streets to avoid. Her dream was downright crazy.

But the voice came to her again.

Please, yes, keep coming, come to me, help me. . . .

And then again she heard the cry. The baby's cry. Definitely one of the twins. She knew their little voices. She could usually even tell them apart. But right now . . .

Duck down that side street. There's a cop coming; he'll stop you, and you must come, you must come, please. . . .

She slid into an alley and waited. Then she started down the street again. She was moving quickly now, almost running.

She'd come to a main road just outside the Vieux Carré. She knew then that she was trying to reach the cemetery. Odd—the cemeteries were locked up at night. They were very dangerous. People loved the cemeteries in New Orleans, loved the aboveground graves, the fantastic mausoleums, and even the ovens, boxes on top of boxes that housed the poor.

A car passed on the street. Slowed down. "Hey, sugar, where you off to?" a man demanded.

"Leroy!" The woman next to him hit him on the shoulder. "You leave her be. You don't need no sugar but me!"

"Lola, poor thing looks crazy!"

"Then let the folks from the nuthouse come get her!"

Leroy and Lola drove on.

Her feet hurt. She'd walked over dirt, filth, spilled drinks, twigs, rocks, and even broken glass. She was surely filthy. The hem of her white nightgown was tinged with the dirt from the city streets.

But here she was. And the great gates were yawning open for her.

She didn't fear cemeteries. She studied them. She loved old churches; she loved tombstones. She wasn't afraid. . . .

She stepped in.

Instantly, it seemed, the ground was awhirl with a silver-gray fog. It drifted around her, arose like a sea of beautiful clouds.

The dirt of the city of the dead seemed cleaned away by that fog. Tombs arose from the fog as white as her gown. Giant edifices to different groups of dead rose like the great domed capitals of the living.

Angels seemed to fly.

"I'm here!" she called softly.

Come. Come closer. Come closer . . . please help. . . .

Come closer where? Had someone been locked into one of the tombs?

She started to hear the crying again.

"Jamie? Petey? It's all right, baby, Jade is here. I'm coming. . . ."

She stepped on a shard of stone and winced, pausing to grab her foot. It really hurt. She felt the dust and grime on her toes. It was very realistic for a dream.

It seemed that a winged cherub reached out from atop

a tomb and pulled at her hair as she straightened. "Let go," she muttered.

Jade, Jade, Jade . . .

She heard her name, and a terrible sobbing sound. She moved more deeply into the cemetery. The mist continued to swirl around her. It covered the exit. She turned forward again, seeing the rise of the tombs in the silver mist and the darker-than-death shadows. *Fool!* she accused herself, *walking alone in a cemetery at night. Asking for trouble. Any idiot, even in a B horror movie, would know not to wander like this. . . .*

But it was just a dream. . . .

Jade . . . !

She felt her name. Felt it whispered at her back. And the feel, as it streaked down her spine, was pure evil.

Jade, come. . . .

No! She started to run.

Run and run . . .

The gown was caught by the stillness and the breeze. It trailed behind her, along with the length of her hair. She ran in slow motion, propelled by terror, held back by the confines of the dream, by the force of the evil whispering her name. . . .

The twins were not calling to her, she realized first.

She had been tricked.

Summoned here by the force of evil.

She had to keep running. In the dream she could feel her heartbeat, feel the pulse of her life, the desperate, mile-a-minute thud, thump, thud. . . .

It was all so real. The earth beneath her feet, cruel, cutting, the snag of broken stones and overgrown weeds against her gown. She thought she knew the way from the graveyard. The fog swirled around her, far too gray and misty; she couldn't begin to find the exit. She knew that she was pursued; she could feel hot breath against her neck.

Jade, Jade, Jade . . .

She was grasped by the elbow, swung around, thrown atop a tombstone. She felt the hard, cold stone slam against her. She screamed, shrieking as loud as she could, flailing wildly with her fists. There was someone above her in the fog, someone dark, decked in a cloak, someone, some*thing,* a terrible, terrible evil. . . .

She screamed again, and wrenched hard away from the caped, mist-enshrouded figure bending over her. She staggered, nearly fell, clutched hard to a figure of the Virgin Mary, and made it to her feet. She started to run again. The winged angels seemed to move; a gargoyle sneered before her, seeming to leap into the path. A Grim Reaper, its head bowed, lifted from its pedestal and started walking by her, just behind a row of family mausoleums.

It suddenly strode out before her. It blocked her path. It waved its scythe toward her and started to lift its head.

The eyes were cavernous.

Worms crawled from them, over the skeletal face.

"Come. . . ."

It lifted the scythe again with one arm and beckoned to her with the other. She turned, ready to catapult in the other direction.

She slammed hard against a wall.

A chest.

She slammed her fists against it hysterically. "No, no, no!"

"Jade!"

Something had her. Arms were fiercely upon her, holding her steady. She kept screaming. He shook her. Her eyes opened. She saw his face.

"It's all right, Jade, it's all right! You're safe."

Lucian.

He was wearing a black silk shirt, dark jeans. His dark hair was combed back, blue-black in the moonlight. His eyes were darker than the night, studying her.

"It's all right—of course it's all right. It's a dream, it's a dream. . . ."

It wasn't a dream. She was standing with him in the cemetery. Her gown was muddied and dirty. Her feet were bare and raw. She was cold and freezing, and suddenly acutely aware of every angel and cherub, every death's-head, the poor men's ovens, the rich men's ornate tombs. A huge, winged dog sat upon a nearby crypt. He growled in perpetual silence, guarding a long-dead owner.

"My God!" she said softly, staring at Lucian, jerking away from him. "You made me come here!" she accused him.

"No, Jade, no, I didn't—"

"You bastard!" She spun around. The mist she had imagined had faded away.

The angels standing sentinel over the dead were all still. No voices beckoned to her.

She squared her shoulders and started walking away.

"Jade!" His voice was sharp. She kept walking. She rounded a corner, then started shaking. She thought she was at the exit. She knew this damned cemetery, dangerous as it was; she had played here as a kid. Her parents had never known, of course. But she knew where the crypt with the Egyptian symbols was, and where to find the one with the piano keys carved into stone.

She was walking through a cemetery in the middle of the night in a dangerous section of town. She felt again as if tiny hairs were lifting on her neck, as if something . . .

She started to run.

Footsteps followed. Lucian was behind her.

"Jade!"

She heard his voice.

No!

Lucian was before her!

Did she dare trust him, after what had happened tonight?

Did she dare not?

Whatever it was—cold, evil, a nightmare—it was right behind her.

"Lucian!" she cried his name. She was racing forward, faster, and faster. Now there was a dark figure before her. The Grim Reaper? Death, waiting to sweep her into his arms? Or . . . something darker, a creature worse than death . . . ?

She was flying forward, too late to stop . . .

"Jade!" It was Lucian, emerging from the mist and shadows. He caught her as she flew against him, lifted her into his arms, and started to carry her from that place of death.

"You called to me!" she accused him softly again.

"No."

"Then—"

"I have enemies."

Shivering, she lay in his arms.

"It wasn't you; it was never you?"

"No."

"He touched me," she said with horror. "He called, and I came, and . . . he touched me."

The cemetery wasn't so awful. It was just as it had always been. They were already at the gate, exiting to the street.

"You're lucky you weren't shot by a drug pusher, or picked up by a pimp," he said angrily.

She struggled against his hold. "I can walk just fine," she said indignantly.

He set her down. She winced, grabbing his arm as her tender, torn flesh came down upon pebbles. Her feet were killing her. He steadied her.

The moon had risen very high. He seemed larger than ever; his features very sharp and striking—and powerful.

"All right, so I can't walk very well at the moment," she whispered. She looked back at the cemetery walls.

"It was the guide from Scotland, wasn't it?"

"Yes."

She stared at him long and hard. "The guide from Scotland. He killed those people, then went to New York and butchered a group there. He came after Tom Marlow here, in New Orleans. Then he went to Massachusetts and ripped up the people there."

"Yes, so I believe. He's not alone, of course."

"Of course—the woman who came out of the tomb and ripped open Jeff Dean's throat is with him, right?"

"Yes."

"They must be chalking up some major airline miles!" she murmured, staring at him.

He started walking. Limping, she followed behind him. "Lucian!"

He stopped, looking back.

"You're going to have to trust me," he told her.

"Trust you? I don't know what you are. I don't dare believe what . . . what it seems your friends are!"

"They're evil—leave it at that."

"Are you?"

He was quiet a moment. "I'm not much better," he said. "But I didn't kill any of those people, and I am trying to save your life."

"Why?" she whispered. "Why are you so willing to fight—for me?" she asked.

"The color of your eyes," he said simply, and started walking again. She stood still behind him, watching him go. This time he stopped and turned back.

"Come on, we've got to get back."

"Back?"

"There's a cop in your apartment who is probably going

insane by now. Your sister is worried sick, and your father has been calling."

"My father—"

"Your stepmother is sick."

"My God, is she bad?"

"She can pull through."

Can pull through!

The tone of his voice angered her.

"How the hell do you know all this?" she demanded. She shook her head, forgetting the pain in her feet, and striding on by him. Then she stopped, spinning around into him. "Why am I asking? You knew I'd be out in the middle of the night, running around the cemetery. You know what my entire family is up to. You know there's a cop sleeping in my living room, and that my sister is there."

"Yes," he said, walking at her side.

She was scared. She wanted to strike out at him again, beat against him. But she didn't want him to leave her. She had never been so glad to see anyone in her life as she had been to see him. Even scared as she was . . .

She was secure this minute. He was with her. She had wanted to strike him. . . .

Just so that he would hold her.

"Lucian." she murmured.

"Yes?"

"Why do you mean so much to me?" she whispered. "Why am I tolerating this? Why am I not screaming right this second, and trying to get the police here?"

He smiled suddenly, a wry half smile that curved his lips, and touched his eyes. "That I don't know," he told her, drawing her to him. He held her shoulders, looking into her eyes. Then he cupped her cheeks and gently touched her lips with his own.

Yes, he was real, so real; the dreams were over, and he was with her. . . .

"Hey, buddy! Take it on home!" someone shouted from a passing car.

Jade opened her eyes, meeting his. She smiled.

"It's impossible, but I think I love you," she told him. "I don't even know you."

"Maybe you know enough," he told her, smoothing back a lock of her hair. "I've loved you forever."

And he started walking again.

When she tripped, he swept her up into his arms.

She didn't protest. The whole picture was absurd enough already.

They were walking through one of the most dangerous sections of town in the pitch dark of the night. . . .

But with her head against the fabric of his shirt and the wall of his chest, she wasn't afraid.

It occurred to her just how strange they must appear.

Him, extremely tall, dark, dressed in black, ignoring the darkness and the shadows of the night.

Carrying a woman in flowing white cotton, walking down the street.

And toward the dawn.

Chapter Thirteen

Peter MacGregor sat by his wife's side, holding her hand. She was back with him, trying to talk, but she was distressed and confused. She couldn't remember what had happened. Strange little snatches of visions would come to her, and she kept trying to make sense of them.

"Liz, Liz! You had a fever; you were terribly, terribly sick," he explained to her softly, trying very hard to be reassuring. "Honey!" Leaning close, he kissed her forehead. "We're lucky you're doing so well. We're . . . we're lucky you're with us."

"But the boys, Peter . . . they were in their cribs; they were all right, really?"

"Sweetheart, the twins are fine."

"Are the girls with them?"

"Um, they're with Jeannie."

"Jeannie from next door?"

"Yes, Liz, and they're fine, really. Perfectly fine. You

must have gotten them into bed when you started feeling sick.''

''But that's just it, Peter. I don't even remember feeling sick. I don't remember anything at all, except . . .''

She frowned, disturbed, trying to remember. She had managed to sit up. She'd combed her hair, washed her face, and brushed her teeth. That had made her feel almost human, she had told him. She'd been so weak when she had first come back to consciousness. The transfusions she'd been given had helped tremendously.

''What, sweetheart?''

''The cable man,'' she told him, shrugging. ''I remember the cable man.''

''A cable man came out?''

''Yes . . .''

''There was something wrong with the cable?''

''No . . . Peter, this is so awful. I just don't remember anything. Have you called the girls?''

''They aren't picking up yet. It's still early. I've left messages on both their answering machines.''

''Peter.''

''Yes?''

''If you don't get them, go to their apartments.''

''I can't just leave you—''

''I don't know why, but I'm worried about them. Please, it's more important to me right now that you find out if they're okay.''

''Lizzie, they didn't give you a hard time about anything yesterday, did they?''

''No!'' she told him, shaking her head vigorously. ''Shanna baby-sat for me. We had a great conversation. They're both sweethearts, Peter; I love your daughters very much. There's just something. Please . . .''

''Liz, Daddy!''

Peter turned, and his daughters were there.

"Liz . . ."

"Jade." Liz gripped Jade's hand, searching out her eyes. Jade squeezed back, glancing at her father. "I'm so sorry. Shanna and I were both here most of the night—my friend Rick Beaudreaux is upstairs. He was terribly sick, but he started doing better in the middle of the night. We were actually here, Dad, when you first called."

"You left this hospital alone in the middle of the night?" he demanded. They were both in their mid-twenties, college graduates, on their own, but he was still a father, their father, and would always be so.

Jade glanced at Shanna.

"Dad, I was here, too—"

"And I was with them as well."

Peter jerked around, recognizing Sean Canady. From his long-running job at the paper, he had become acquainted with the Homicide detective.

Canady's words, however, were not as reassuring as he would have liked. Great, the girls were not alone, they were being looked after by a tall, intelligent, muscular cop— who carried a big gun.

But why was it necessary that they have a big cop watching over them?

Canady was quick to assure him, striding forward, shaking his hand. "Peter, it's good to see you. And it's good to hear your wife is doing so well."

"We called on our way in," Shanna explained.

"You got my messages then?" Peter asked, feeling puzzled and not sure why. Then he realized that there was another man with the girls and the detective. Physically they might have been cloned; both were well over six feet, toned, and dark-haired.

"How do you do?" the stranger said, stepping forward.

"Dad, this is Lucian DeVeau," Shanna said quickly.

"Mr. DeVeau."

"An old friend, Peter," Sean explained. "I've been disturbed by the things happening. You know, the case in New York—"

"Yes, and that massacre at the theme park," Peter said. "We were working story angles on the murders all day yesterday. It was why I was out when . . ." His voice trailed. "Is there some danger to Jade?" he asked sharply.

"We're not taking any chances," Canady said.

Peter stared at Lucian. "You're not a cop?"

"No."

"He's a friend, Peter. Someone I've known—"

"Mr. DeVeau! Liz interrupted suddenly, smiling. "I've met you somewhere before, haven't I?"

"Who knows, Mrs. MacGregor. It's a small world," he said politely. But the tall, dark-haired man walked toward Peter's wife, taking her hand, placing a palm on her forehead. "You seem to be doing well. How are you feeling?"

"Better. Much better, thanks," she said. Her eyes were bright as she looked at him.

"So, Mr. DeVeau," Peter said, startled by the sharp coil of jealousy that sprang to life inside him. "Are you a doctor, then?"

"He's a writer, Dad," Shanna said quickly.

"Oh?" Peter said suspiciously. "You've just met?"

"I just met him, yes," Shanna said.

"Lucian and I met in Scotland," Jade told him.

He suddenly wanted to wrench his daughters and his wife away from the fellow. He wasn't sure why. Lucian DeVeau was staring at him with his dark eyes open and frank, as if he were ready to respond to any question.

Or challenge.

"I could just swear that we have met somewhere!" Liz said.

"Daddy," Jade said, coming over to him. She smiled and gently touched his cheek. "Daddy, you look like hell, which is understandable. I'm so sorry you couldn't reach us. But you need some coffee, some breakfast, something. Shanna is going to take you to the cafeteria for a few minutes, and I'm going to sit with Liz.''

"Jade, you should be sorry—the two of you had me scared silly. But I'm all right."

"Peter, dear, please, go—get yourself some coffee and something to eat," Liz told him.

"Come on, Daddy."

Shanna came over and took him by the arm. He looked back suspiciously as she led him out.

"I'll be right back!" he warned them all.

Why was he worried? His daughter was looking at him with her beautiful turquoise eyes wide and innocent.

He liked the cop.

He didn't know the damned stranger; that was it.

And Jade seemed to know him too well!

The minute her father was out of the room, Jade returned to Liz's side. "Liz, you're really feeling okay?"

"So much better."

Lucian was beside her, smiling, touching her cheek, twisting her head this way and that. Liz stared at him, allowing him to do so. "You're not a doctor, but I feel that I know you. And I feel that you did something kind for me."

"Liz, what do you remember?" Lucian asked her.

"Nothing. Nothing but the cable man."

"The cable man?" Sean said sharply.

"They're testing some new market," she said dismissively. "What does that have to do with anything? I was just sick, wasn't I?"

She stared at them all hopefully. Then she looked worried. "Because I can't quite place it, but I feel . . . I feel that something bad happened. I can't say it to your father . . . I don't even know what I'm trying to say.''

"Mrs. MacGregor," Sean said. "If you start to remember something—if you even think you imagined something—will you call me, please?"

She stared at Lucian. "Why do I think I know you?"

"Perhaps we met somewhere."

She nodded. "I do know you. I know that I do. Take care of Jade, will you?"

"I intend to," he told her. His dark eyes touched Jade's. "I intend to."

"Matt Durante! Get in here!"

Matt had been tapping at Jade's door when Renate made an appearance in the hallway.

Renate wasn't his favorite person at the moment. She had invited him in for champagne and caviar; then she had spent the evening telling him how he needed to join a gym and how his taste in clothing was disastrous. If he wanted to keep his head up among world-class and *literary* writers, he was going to have to shape up.

Writers, he'd told her, were supposed to be eccentric. They were supposed to come in all shapes, sizes, sexes, and ages.

She had waved him off and sent him packing. If he didn't want to be helped, well, then, she wasn't even going to try to teach him how to appreciate good caviar.

"Renate, what? I want to try to see Jade."

"She's not there."

"Oh? How do you know?"

"Because I saw her leave, you idiot."

"Oh." He felt like an idiot. It didn't make him feel any more kindly toward Renate at the moment.

"So she's out. Well, then—"

"Matt, damn you, this is important."

He sighed. "Oh, all right, what?"

"Come in! I can't stand here talking to you in the hallway."

She met him halfway down the hall, caught his arm, and dragged him into her apartment. When he was inside, facing her, she leaned dramatically against her door, as if she were afraid he had been followed and they were in grave danger.

"What?" he said.

"Jade is dating a vampire!" she said dramatically.

He stared at her for several long moments, then shook his head.

"Renate, let me out."

"I'm telling you the truth!"

"Jade is dating a cop named Rick Beaudreaux."

"Beaudreaux is in the hospital, probably dying from the bite of one of the head vampire's little vixens. Jade is sleeping with the head bloodsucker!"

He arched a brow, sniffing the air. "Renate, did you try to drink up all the leftover champagne on your own? Or is it vodka? I know you like a good martini—or two—now and then."

"Damn you, Matt! I have not been drinking at all! I am telling you the truth."

"And I'm leaving."

He started toward the door. Renate jumped away from it—not because of him, but because there was a knock on it.

"The vampires?" he asked.

"Danny. Danny Thacker. I've asked him over."

She swung the door open. It was Danny standing there, yawning. "All right, Renate, I'm here. Hey, Matt, how are you?"

"Leaving," Matt said.

"No, you're not."

"Jade's dating a vampire," Matt said, rolling his eyes.

"I thought Rick was a cop," Danny said.

"Rick is a cop!" Renate said, aggravated. "I'm telling you that she's sleeping with—"

"Luke?" Danny said, his eyes going wide.

"You know the guy?" Renate asked.

"Real tall dude, about six-three, dark, damned good-looking son of a bitch?"

"So he's real, not a vampire?" Matt said.

"His name is Luke ... Lucian. Yeah, he introduced himself as Lucian. DeVeau. Nice guy. He wants to be a writer. I think he's independently wealthy."

"He doesn't want to be a writer—he just wants to get close to us. He wants us all to invite him in—that's the way it works, you know. You have to invite a vampire in."

Both men stared at her. "I'm telling you the truth."

Matt grinned suddenly. "Okay, I got it. You want to start writing horror. You want to be a major commercial success—"

"No!" Renate cried with frustration.

"You'll meet this guy, Matt, I'm sure," Danny said. "He's really decent. I had one hell of a snocker going the other night, man; I was just about falling down drunk after spending an evening with that kid's corpse. They brought me home."

"They who?" Renate asked suspiciously.

"They—Jade and this guy Lucian. She met him in Scotland, I think. I met him here. In New Orleans. At a café. Separately from Jade."

"They brought you home!" Renate repeated.

"Took me to bed, tucked me in."

"You invited him in!" Renate charged breathlessly.

"Well, yeah, I guess. And I'm still walking and talking."

"And I'm wearing a cross!" Renate warned, pulling a huge silver cross from beneath her blouse.

"Good for you," Danny said with a shrug.

"Look at his neck, Matt. Go on—take a good look at his neck."

"You can both look at my neck!" Danny said, turning slowly around. Renate went closer, closer still. She studied Danny's neck carefully.

"If he's a vampire, he wasn't hungry the other night," Danny joked.

"He won't go after you, not if he's seducing Jade."

"Wait up, now, Renate," Matt said. "According to you, Jade is already sleeping with him."

"Yes, but . . . well, he probably wants to seduce her to his cause. I'm not sure what he's planning, or what he wants. I'm just sure that . . . he's a vampire, and terrible things are going on. And we have to protect ourselves, and Jade—"

"Well, hell, Renate, maybe we just need to save the whole damned world," Matt suggested.

"Don't you laugh at me, Matt."

"All right. But why do think this guy is a vampire?"

She took a deep breath, looking at them both. "Coffee?" she asked politely. "I have a lot to tell you."

Matt looked at Danny. "Fine."

Renate sauntered into the kitchen, more assured now. "First off, I'll explain. I've been listening to the police band on the radio."

"All right, so go on," Matt said, accepting a cup of dark chicory coffee.

"Good, we'll go back. Jade heads off to Scotland, and comes back in sad shape. Scared, thinned to the bone, in therapy."

"Imagine that!" Matt said to Danny. "She survived a

horrible massacre in a graveyard and went into therapy. What will they think of next!''

"She met the guy in Scotland. There is a terrible killing spree in New York, and another one of the survivors from Scotland is among the victims.''

"Then there's our kid in the morgue," Danny commented.

"What?" Matt asked sharply.

"You haven't read today's paper, have you?" Renate asked.

"The kid killed in the accident . . . it wasn't an accident, and it wasn't just any kid. He'd been using a fake name when he transferred down here to school," Danny explained. "And he was dead before he went through the windshield. After he went through it . . . someone did the job on his throat with a wedge of the broken glass.''

"Ugh," Matt said, sinking down to sit at the counter.

"He was another of the survivors from Scotland," Renate said, making an annoying tingling sound in her cup as she stirred one packet of Equal into her coffee.

"Then, in Massachusetts, people are not just murdered in a horror house—but dismembered!" she continued. "And one of them is also a survivor from the massacre in Scotland.''

"Well, the killers will be out of survivors soon, right?" Matt said, trying to sound hopeful. Then he realized what he was saying. "Oh, God. Jade is a survivor.''

"So far!" Renate muttered.

"Okay, so how does that make this guy a vampire?''

"Well, he's Scottish, I'm pretty sure.''

"DeVeau?" Matt muttered, shrugging at Danny. "Well, actually, he is Scottish. The name came from Normandy, hundreds of years ago, some shit like that.''

"There you have it!" Renate said.

"Renate, vampires are usually from Transylvania, aren't they?"

"How on earth would we know where they really came from?" Renate demanded. "That's my whole point! I've been reading, and the legends didn't just start with Bram Stoker! Vampires are ancient; they were in Syria, in Egypt, in Greece—"

"They're just about biblical, eh?" he interrupted.

"They can be anywhere," Renate said. "Look!" She brought out a book entitled *Strange Stories of the Americas.* "These are all cases that are documented in old town courthouses, right here in the United States!" she said, flipping through the pages. She started to read, " 'Beautiful young Sally Anderson fell in love with the handsome stranger from the start. But soon after their engagement, she sickened. A high fever and general weakness dragged down on her. A terrible pallor in her cheeks increased night after night. She died two weeks after her first meeting with her fiancé.' "

"So—," Matt interrupted.

"Shut up and listen!" Renate commanded. " 'Her tearful parents buried her; the tall, handsome stranger had disappeared. Two days after her burial, her younger sister fell ill.' "

"It was probably a contagious disease," Matt said.

"Matt!" Renate warned, and kept reading. " 'Her sister complained of Sally coming to her at night, begging entrance to the room, and then kissing her neck . . . and making her sicker and sicker. The younger sister suffered the same weakness, the same fever . . . the same strange pallor. A week later she too died, and was buried in the same graveyard.' "

"Renate, it's nineteenth-century superstition—"

" 'A third sister in the same household fell ill.' " Renate read loudly. " 'She, too, complained of being visited by her siblings. Her sisters wanted her to hold them. They wanted to be warmed and kissed. The third sister suffered the same mysterious illness, telling everyone of the visits she received from her deceased siblings.' ''

Renate looked up, staring dramatically at both of them.

'' 'Then she, too, died.' ''

"High fevers, pallor, could have been a number of things," Matt said.

"You haven't heard the end," Renate told them. '' 'Desperate to save the one daughter they had left, and an infant son, the family called for help. The local minister said that they must dig up the bodies of their lost children, cut out and burn the hearts, and sever the heads from the bodies.' ''

"Wouldn't they arrest us if we dug up corpses in such a manner today?" Matt said.

"You bet. They arrest you for just being in the cemetery at night," Danny said.

"Will you two please pay attention! There are records on this in a New England courthouse."

"They hanged eighteen people for being witches and pressed a man to death in old New England as well," Matt reminded her. "In 1692, to be precise."

"Matt, this happened right around the Civil War."

"When they were really enlightened," Danny supplied.

"What the hell makes you think we're so enlightened now?" Renate demanded. "Will you please let me finish? 'The mother and father dug up their daughters. The bodies looked as fresh as on the day they were buried. The mother wrote in her journal that she thought her oldest daughter opened her eyes, that she was ready to talk to her. But the minister wouldn't let any more evil escape the child—he staked her heart.' And do you know what happened then—as seen by a dozen townspeople?"

"No, do tell, Renate, do tell," Matt said.

"She screamed."

"Such things have happened," Danny said. "Renate, they find out more and more as time goes by about human physiology. Maybe gases were suddenly released. Maybe the corpse had been buried in such a manner that there was a reflex—"

"Maybe they buried the poor girl alive," Matt suggested. "Such things have happened."

"Edgar Allan Poe—'The Premature Burial,'" Danny said.

Renate let out a sigh of pure disgust. "I have more books. Here's one I think you should see, Daniel Thacker."

Danny looked at the book. "*A History of Scotland—Families in Peril?*"

"I'll show you!" Renate said. She took the book from him and flipped pages. "A number of current clan names date back to the Norman Conquest—and before. The very famous Scottish king, Robert the Bruce, was descended from a fellow who came north from England after the conquest; his family had come from Normandy. In the first part of the century, many of the family went by de Brus."

"So?"

"This book tells of bad blood between the Bruces and a family called DeVeau. There's a stirring tale of the DeVeau heir coming to fight at the right hand of Robert the Bruce just as they faced the English."

"Scotland was full of feudal warring. You've lost me completely. First we're talking vampires. Then we're into the history of old Scotland—"

"Look!"

She pushed the book toward them.

"The bad blood came about because of a madwoman sheltered by the de Brus family. There were rumors that she was a witch and a murderess, and DeVeau wanted her to stand trial before the king, and, it's said, be executed by being drawn and quartered."

"And what happened?" Danny asked.

"Well, there's nothing in this book about an execution. I can't find a name for her anywhere, or any other information. But you're not looking, you two—look, please. Look at the picture."

Matt stared at the page blankly. There was a man on a horse, clad in mail with an overtunic that bore a family crest. It looked like a red dragon or a wolf on a field of gold. He carried a standard and a sword. The painting was from a fresco created for a church near Edinburgh.

"I don't get it," Matt said.

"I do," Danny told him.

"What?"

Danny glanced at Renate and shrugged. "The guy looks just like this new friend of mind. The painting is a spitting image of Lucian DeVeau."

"He is a DeVeau. It must be a family resemblance," Matt said.

"Oh, you fools!" Renate cried. "He isn't *a* DeVeau, don't you see? He's *the same* DeVeau."

When her father and sister were back with her step-mother, Jade excused herself to go up a floor and see how Rick was doing.

She realized that Lucian was behind her.

"I could have done this alone," she said. "In fact, I should be doing this alone."

"You shouldn't be doing anything alone."

"We're in a busy hospital."

"I need to see your friend."

"He was doing much better. He might be conscious. He

and Liz have had symptoms so much alike, and she's doing so very well. . . ."

"Let's hope," he murmured.

She stopped dead, placing a hand against his chest. "Lucian, I—"

"You're worried about your friend meeting me?" he inquired, his fingers sliding around her wrist to pull her hand away, his eyes cold. "Do you really think you could just go back to the way things were?"

"No . . . yes . . . perhaps. You still . . . I still know nothing about you. You've just barged into my life—"

"You know everything there is to know about me. If you admit it," he said, walking by her. She felt chilled.

He knew the way. They reached Rick's room.

He was still in intensive care. A nurse stopped them from entering. Jade said that she had sat with him for hours already, and the nurse said, "Oh, you're the fiancée!"

Her cheeks reddened as she felt Lucian just behind her, but she said, "Yes."

"He's still unconscious, but holding his own. Go on, talk to him. Maybe it will do him some good."

Jade slipped in. Rick still looked pale. She gazed at the different monitors connected to him; his vital signs seemed stable enough. She squeezed his hand. "You're going to make it. You are!" she encouraged him.

Through the glass window to the room, she could see Lucian talking to the nurse. The nurse smiled, opening the door for Lucian to enter.

She stared at him. "What did you say to her?"

He shrugged. "Nothing much. I said I was a friend." He paid her little attention, but walked straight to Rick, observing his face, then searching his neck. He seemed perplexed.

"Bite holes, right?" she mocked skeptically.

He motioned to her. There did seem to be two little

pinprick marks in his neck, but not the big red circles she had seen in movies.

"Shouldn't they be bigger?" she whispered, thinking she was really losing her mind now.

"She's playing."

"What?"

"Sophia is just playing. He's holding his own, though. For the moment. But he shouldn't be alone at all. I'll tell Sean."

"I don't understand any of this. And I don't believe he's sick because of those little pinholes in his neck. This is crazy."

"Very," he agreed.

And he turned around and left her.

Chapter Fourteen

By the light of day, in the sterile and well-ordered world of the hospital, Jade felt as if she were letting the bizarre get the best of her mind.

She wasn't running after Lucian.

She simply wasn't going to believe so easily. There were always logical answers in life.

Sometimes they were just hard to find.

Stubbornly, she remained with Rick. She sat by his side as time ticked slowly by. She held his hand; then she gently touched his cheek. "I'm so sorry. I would never purposely hurt you. Never."

She looked outside the room again, thinking that maybe Lucian was waiting for her.

He was not.

A few minutes later she saw a handsome young man come, take a chair, and settle with a newspaper outside Rick's door.

She exited, looking at him. He rose, a friendly smile on his face. "Hi, Jade, is it? Jack Delaney; I work with Sean."

"Naturally," she murmured. "You're going to watch over Rick?"

"For now," he said cheerfully.

"That's good to hear." She watched his eyes carefully. "He isn't being hunted down by a mafia chieftain or anything. He came in here sick."

"Right. Well, he's a cop, and a good one. One of our own. I hope you don't mind my being here with him."

"Of course I don't mind. I'm glad."

"Good."

Jack Delaney wasn't ging to give her any more information. Nor was he going to wink in a conspiratorial manner and tell her he was well armed with stakes and holy water.

"I guess I'll go back to my family, since Rick seems to be in good hands."

He waved good-bye to her. She started down the hall and turned back. Jack was already engrossed in his newspater.

When Jade reached her stepmother's room, she found Sean and her sister waiting, but Lucian had left the hospital. His exits were becoming very annoying. Downright irritating.

"He had some things to attend to," Sean told her. "Maggie wants to meet you. I've asked your sister already. I hope you'll come to my house for something to eat and a few hours of rest."

Jade looked at her sister. Shanna looked perfectly comfortable with the arrangements.

"I don't know," she said, wondering why she felt so argumentative. "Dad, what about the boys? I have baby brothers, you know."

"They're fine for the afternoon, Jade," her father said. "Why don't you get some lunch, some rest. We may need you and your sister in the days to come."

"Sure, then. I'm just dying to meet your wife, Lieutenant Canady."

"We'll be back then," Sean promised her father and stepmother. As they left the room, Jade saw that there was a very tall, exceptionally good-looking black man outside the room. He was wearing shades, casual clothing, and carrying a book. Sean introduced him briefly as Mike Astin.

"My stepmother needs a guard?" Jade demanded as they left the hospital.

It was all just too strange. When they had returned to her place that morning, both Canady and her sister had been frantic. Her father had been leaving messages, and she was gone. Canady looked really ragged—trying to figure out how she had gotten past him.

She had tried to explain it. "I guess I was sleepwalking. Having bizarre dreams." Canady knew Lucian, and wasn't at all surprised that he had brought her home—carried her home, her white nightgown draping dramatically over his arms as he entered the apartment with her. Shanna, who had been ready to dislike him on sight, made an amazing turnabout, introducing herself, watching him, querying him, and appearing generally fascinated by him. All too strange, Jade thought again as Canady drove them toward his house on the outskirts of the city.

"How do you know Lucian DeVeau?" Jade demanded as they drove.

His eyes met hers in the rearview mirror. Then they touched the road again.

"He's an old friend of my wife," he said.

Shanna leaned forward. "Did they date?" she inquired.

"Shanna," Jade remonstrated.

"Not exactly," Sean said, and the way he said it, the case was simply closed.

Sean Canady lived with his wife in a stunning grande dame of a plantation. Exiting the car, Jade wished she'd met the Canadys at a different stage of her life. The place was terrific. She could have taken rolls of pictures, and written a history on the architecture and the owners through time. It was beautiful, and restored rather than refurbished. Walking up the steps, she couldn't help but move slowly and admire the old-fashioned elegance of the house, an elegance that belonged to a time long past.

At her side, Shanna whistled softly.

"Hey, we grew up in a very decent home in the Garden District," Jade reminded her sister in a whisper.

Shanna elbowed her. "Shush. Whispering is rude."

"So is gawking!" Jade admonished her.

They had barely climbed the steps to the front door when it opened for them.

A woman stood there with a toddler in her arms. She looked as though she belonged in *Vogue*. She was tall, elegant, and wearing a casual at-home outfit that might have been on a Paris runway.

The baby was unmistakably Sean's. He had curious blue eyes and a cap of curly dark hair.

"So my husband managed to lure you out here!" she called.

Great voice. Soft, low, sexy. Jade smiled. "How do you do," she said. "Thank you for the invitation." Had it been an invitation, or a summons?

"Thank you for coming," she said, smiling. "And you're Jade, and you're Shanna," she said, naming them correctly.

"Right," Jade said. "And this is . . . ?" She indicated the baby.

Maggie's eyes were luminous as she gazed at the toddler in her arms. "This is Brent. Mr. Brent Canady."

"How do you do, Mr. Brent Canady," Jade said, reaching out to the baby. He was at that age when he might have turned away, pressed his face to his mother's arm, but he studied Jade and let her take his hand and shake it. He let out a little laugh and gazed at his mother with pleasure.

"He's adorable," Shanna said.

"Thanks. We think so," Maggie said huskily.

Sean came behind them, meeting her eyes strangely at first, then greeting her with a kiss. They seemed to have said a million things with a simple look. That, Jade thought, was what life was all about.

"Late lunch is nearly on, or early dinner, whichever," Maggie Canady told her husband. "Please come on in."

The house was even more wonderful inside. A grand staircase rose from either side of the foyer to meet at a halfway landing, then split again to rise to a second level. Arches and molding adorned walls and doorways. The house was both elegant and lived-in.

It also had a strange . . .

Odor.

When they reached the kitchen, Jade realized that there were large gloves of garlic hung around the windows. When Maggie moved through the kitchen to set the baby down in his play area, she saw that the French doors there also seemed to be surrounded by vines.

Not vines. Garlic.

There were a number of wooden sticks or poles leaning against the door as well. Jade tried to inspect them without appearing to do so. They looked as if they should have been attached to brooms or mops.

They were sharpened at one end.

"Crawfish étouffée," Maggie said, pausing at a stockpot. "My speciality. I gave the housekeeper the weekend off."

It seemed she exchanged a strange glance with her husband once again.

"What can I get you all to drink?" Maggie asked. "It's early, but I make a great Cosmopolitan."

"I could definitely use a great Cosmopolitan," Shanna said.

Jade lifted her hands. "Sure."

"Sean, would you run down to the basement and get another cranberry juice for me, please?"

"Sure. Anything else?"

She shook her head, her eyes meeting his. He smiled. She adored her husband. Jade lowered her eyes, looking away.

Shanna wandered into the family room, talking to the baby. Jade leaned on the counter, watching as Maggie stirred her sauce.

"You're from here?" she asked Jade.

"Born and bred. And you?"

"Yes. I was from here."

"Maggie, I just realized you're the Maggie from the shop in the French Quarter," Jade told her.

Maggie flashed her a quick grin. "Yes, it's my store."

"It's been there forever, right?"

"A very long time."

"Maggie," Jade said softly after a minute.

"Yes?"

"There's garlic all over your house."

Maggie's eyes met hers. "Enough of it works, sometimes."

"Against . . . ?"

"Vampires."

"And the stakes?"

"They work as well. Though you should cut out the heart or remove the head."

Maggie Canady, tall, slim, totally dignified, was staring at her as if they were discussing her recipe for crawfish.

"And crosses?"

"They have some power, depending on the vampire.

Personally I always love a beautiful cross. I'm very partial to jewelry."

"I'm not sure what you're saying. And Maggie, how could you know what might or might not work against vampires? If such creatures indeed existed."

Sean was still below. As Maggie set down her wooden spoon and stared at Jade, they could hear Shanna talking away to the baby.

"Because I was once a vampire," Maggie said, and turned and walked to a cabinet for more salt.

Jade stayed where she was, feeling as if a chill breeze blew over her. Now she really was losing her mind.

"You were a *vampire*."

"Yes."

"But you're not anymore."

"No."

"You went from being a hideous, wretched bloodsucker to the wife of a cop?"

"Well, I suppose you could put it that way—"

"So it is a cult!" Jade exclaimed. "You were part of it, but you got out—"

"No. I was a vampire. And nothing is that black or white. I was never a vicious killer. The world is not so simple, not even the world of the undead. Some people are kind, and some are cruel. Some would give up their own lives to help solve world hunger, and some would slaughter in cold blood in order to steal a few dollars. Most creatures are the same."

"Vampires kill."

"Men kill," Maggie said flatly.

"Vampires can't really exist!" Jade whispered.

"They can, and they do," Maggie insisted.

"I can't believe this!" Jade whispered. Tears suddenly stung her eyes. "I can't. Because I think you're trying to tell me that Lucian DeVeau is such a person, that I really was with a group attacked by vampires in Scotland, that they're killing all across the country, that—''

She broke off. Maggie was just looking at her, listening. Watching, waiting for her to accept what she was saying.

Shanna, she saw, had risen, and was watching from the other room.

Sean Canady had come up from the basement.

"I think I should make those drinks now," Maggie said. "Thanks, my love," she murmured, accepting the bottle of cranberry juice Sean had brought up. She set it on the counter. "Jade, would you get the ice from the freezer for me?"

To her amazement, she did, getting a tray of ice, walking back to Maggie.

She gazed at her sister, at Sean, and then at Maggie again. "You *were* a vampire?"

"Yes."

"And one day you just said, 'I don't think I want to be a vampire anymore'?"

Maggie had been putting the ice, vodka, cranberry, and lime into a pitcher. She set it all down, placed her hands on the counter, and looked into Jade's eyes. "Nothing in the world is ever that easy. There are strange laws that govern all life—and death. I believe that God exists, I always kept a certain faith, and maybe that's why I was finally given something back."

"I don't understand."

"Long before the Civil War, I met a man. My father knew what he was; I didn't. He never meant to hurt me. He really believed that his love was strong enough to give us both life. My father killed him, and I was tainted."

"Right before the Civil War?" Jade said.

"If you want to survive what is going on now, I suggest you open your mind and listen to Maggie," Sean said.

"I am listening!" Jade said. "I don't mean to mock or be rude, but—"

"Jesus, Jade!" Shanna exclaimed suddenly. "Don't you remember what it was like in Scotland? I wasn't even there, but I remember *you* after it all happened."

Jade turned on her sister.

"This is all absurd!" Jade whispered.

"Extraordinary, but absurd?" Shanna said.

Sean came to her, placing his hands on her shoulders, meeting her eyes. "Jade! I was keeping guard in your living room, Shanna was there, and you heard a voice, and eluded us both by crawling down from the second floor to the street!"

"Yes, but . . ."

She was shaking, inside and out. She'd been anxious to get to the hospital that morning. She'd been willing for Lucian to look over her stepmother. She'd had to have known *why!*

"Are those drinks ready yet, Maggie? If not, you could just hand the vodka bottle over to me?" Jade whispered.

"Don't go for the straight vodka," Maggie murmured, handing her a glass.

She gulped it down, then handed the glass back. Maggie refilled it.

"I just can't . . . but . . . you really were a vampire. And you *wore* a cross?"

"A personal preference."

"So . . . is there any real protection?"

"I guarantee you Darian doesn't like crosses."

"Darian."

"The tour guide, of course. I'll have one more drink." Maggie filled her glass.

"The garlic must mean something."

"I think it will protect against Darian and Sophia, yes. It makes Lucian ill."

Jade lowered her head. "I can't believe we're having this conversation."

"Yes, you can," Sean told her.

"You believe it, Jade," her sister told her. "You believe it because of Scotland."

"Oh, my God!" she sank onto a stool before the counter. "This Darian is . . . the worst, the most vicious of the vampires, is that what you're trying to tell me?"

"Among them, yes. Sophia is actually the one who is the epitome of evil."

"Sophia—the dark-haired woman who was in the tomb?" Jade said.

"Yes."

"And she's very old as well, I take it?"

"Ancient. Older than Lucian."

"Is she stronger?"

Maggie hesitated. "Lucian is very strong. He is the one others turn to. He sees to it that the rules are obeyed."

"His is the king of the vampires," Sean said flatly.

"The king of the vampires!" Jade repeated, feeling hysterical.

"Listen, you've to realize that it all began in a different time, a different world," Maggie said. "Vampires are ancient, nearly as old as man. And all those years ago, men were as brutal as any other creature. The Romans conquered and enslaved everyone in sight, the barbarians eventually helped the fall of Rome, Tartars killed anyone they came across, Vikings sailed the seas . . . and God knows, few places were ever as cruel and horrible as medieval Europe. My God, torture is still practiced in hidden cellars in far too many places around the world."

"It's illegal and immoral to run around killing people today!" Jade exclaimed.

"Oh, yes, of course, we've grown more civil. Far more civil. And as man has evolved, so have other creatures. We share the world. We all have to find our niche in it. We're not living in a world of such violence and sudden death and . . . most of the undead have learned to live quietly as well. Human blood is still the greatest temptation, and God knows, vampires kill, but most are careful. They select the ill, the aged—"

"Oh! Kind creatures, practicing a fine form of euthanasia?" Jade demanded heatedly.

"Sometimes death is a kindness," Maggie said softly. "But I'm not trying to tell you that any creature has the right to play God."

"We've watched someone we love die of cancer," Shanna reminded Jade bitterly. "There are things worse than death."

"Being undead?" Jade suggested, staring at Maggie.

"My wife is trying to help you," Sean said. His voice was hard; he loved her, and he was defending her.

"This is a lot to understand, to accept," Jade murmured. "I just . . ."

"It's all right, Sean," Maggie said. "She's right. And our meal is ready. Will you still join us, Miss MacGregor?"

"Of course," Jade murmured. "I, um . . . what can I do?"

"The salad is in the refrigerator. Shanna, would you mind putting Brent in his chair?"

"No, my pleasure."

They set the table with casual, polite small talk suddenly taking the place of the conversation they'd been having. Sean sat at the head of his table, across from his wife.

He said grace before they ate.

Maggie passed the shrimp. Shanna was next to the baby, helping him with his mashed-up food.

"You really do believe in God," Jade said suddenly.

"I thank him every day for the life I have."

"But you also believe—"

"It's very simple, isn't it?" Sean interrupted quietly. "There is good and evil. Every schoolchild knows that."

"Was Rick attacked by one of these vampires?"

Maggie looked at Sean. Sean answered her.

"We think so."

"Our stepmother?" Shanna said softly.

"Yes," Sean said flatly.

"Oh, my God, then—"

"So far the two have just been playing, trying to cause havoc, to make Lucian realize that they can attack at will. So far they've not done tremendous damage. If they had really ripped into one of them . . . ," Maggie murmured.

"If they had," Sean continued, "the two would be tainted. They'd be themselves, but not themselves. They'd be cruel. Then . . ."

"A serious bite turns someone into a monster?" Shanna said, looking very pale. She glanced at Jade. *Dad won't be able to take it if anything really terrible happens to Liz.*

"If Sophia or Darian were to choose to really rip into someone, you'd probably have a real monster. We're not sure how, but it might even be some kind of a blood condition, and so when you have creatures with that kind of a vicious streak, you get another creature when the blood is invaded. I saw such a thing happen to a man once," Maggie said. "He was a respected soldier. He went mad and viciously killed the men in the field who were wounded."

"What can we do?" Jade asked. "My God, my stepmother and Rick are so vulnerable—"

"They're guarded," Sean said.

"But—"

"Sophia has been evil longer than anyone can remember," Maggie said. "Lucian has beaten her before. He must beat her again."

"If he is the king—," Shanna said.

"Sophia has always been in rebellion, and Darian is her creature from hell," Maggie explained.

"If they've done such horrible things, and were beaten, why weren't they destroyed?" Shanna asked.

"It is a law: vampires are not to destroy one another."

"Even men destroy evil men."

Sean lifted his hands. "Really? Capital punishment is no longer acceptable in many places."

Jade suddenly leaned forward. "Why are they attacking people close to me?" she inquired.

Sean shrugged. "Apparently they intend to finish what they started in Scotland."

"So they'd be after me. Why Rick, why my stepmother?"

"Why not torture you, and keep Lucian running ragged in the process?"Maggie responded. "They are after you. Very much so."

Jade shivered, feeling ill. Suddenly her memories of Scotland were all too vivid. "Because I saw their act in Scotland?"

"I don't know," Maggie said. "They might have put on that act in Scotland just for you."

"For me!"

Maggie hesitated. "You're very much like someone Lucian knew years ago. Sophia hated her. She saw you— and she hates you."

"This is very, very scary," Shanna said.

"Where is Lucian now?" Jade demanded.

"I'll take you to him soon," Maggie promised. She stood, ready to clear the table. Shanna instantly hopped up.

"Should I go with Jade?" she asked.

"Tonight you should stay here," Sean said.

"But my father, Liz—"

"Mike Astin is watching over them."

"And Mike knows . . . all this?" Jade queried.

"Mike has seen strange things before," Sean told her.

Jade began to clear dishes. Shanna asked if she could help with the baby. Sean took the garbage out. Jade rinsed at the sink while Maggie Canady loaded the dishwasher.

"When did you meet Lucian?" Jade asked her.

"When I became a vampire."

"He didn't make you a vampire?"

"No. But he . . . summoned me," Maggie said, her head lowered as she slid a plate in.

"Were you . . ." Jade couldn't quite bring herself to finish the question she had been about to ask.

"We're old, old friends now, nothing more," Maggie told her. She straightened, looking at Jade. "Lucian has had his times of bitterness, and he's certainly had his times of arrogance. He was the king, a teacher. I would have perished without him. I learned the rules; he still came to my rescue. I wouldn't be here now, with Sean, if he hadn't. He wasn't always good. He isn't necessarily *good* now. But he is reasonable, and logical, and he always had his ethics, though I didn't see how strong he was, even then. They say a true vampire has no soul. I know better. He is like a man, Jade. His world isn't all black or white. There are many, many shadows in it."

"Yes, but—"

"He wanted me once. He never really loved me."

"I wasn't asking—"

"Yes, you were."

Jade flushed. "I barely know him."

"Maybe you know him much better than you think."

"What do you mean?"

Maggie flushed then. "I don't even really know. When I met Sean . . . well, he had an ancestor—there's actually a statue in his honor in the city—who was a soldier in the Civil War. Sean reminded me very much of him. So much of him . . ."

"Yes?"

She shrugged. "I think maybe he was Sean."

"And you think that I might be someone who lived long ago?"

"Who knows? Maybe Sean and I are meant to be together. And maybe . . . well, Lucian was never really in love with me, but he was in love once. Years and years ago. More than a millennium ago." Maggie hesitated a moment. "I wasn't there for Lucian's extreme past. He is very, very old. He lived in the Highlands, and he was a chieftain there. And he had a wife. Igrainia. He was very much in love, and she was cast into the sea, where he could not go after her. Some say she survived, and some say she did not. But the story goes that certain powers within the sea returned her, for certain hours, to be with him. And still Sophia discovered her, and killed her when Igrainia had come to land, away from the waters that would have saved her."

"She came from the sea?"

"There are more things in heaven and on earth—"

"Oh, Maggie, this is all ridiculous!"

"But you're drawn to him, right? You're angry with him because he comes and goes, because there are so many unanswered questions—because you're afraid. But you're drawn to him, and if he were suddenly to step from your life again, you would be devastated."

She refused to answer that.

"But with Sophia—"

"She thinks that you are Igrainia. That you've come back."

"That's ridiculous. That was so long ago—"

"I'm telling you what I believe. And her rage is incredible. Long ago she came upon Lucian when she was with Vikings, terrorizing the coast of Scotland. She is obsessed. She saw him, wanted him, created him. No one refuses Sophia. She is beautiful, and she is powerful. But he despised her, because of Igrainia. She is obsessed. He has hated her forever, and so all that she wants now is to destroy him.''

Jade moistened her lips. "These are fairy tales."

Maggie shook her head. "The human capacity to deny what is in plain sight is simply amazing. As amazing as any of this!"

"I'm afraid to believe any of this. And I'm afraid not to."

"But you want to see Lucian?"

She winced, gritting her teeth, turning away from Maggie. "Yes. I have to see Lucian."

"We're finished here now. I'll take you to him," Maggie said.

"Are the others coming?"

"No. Your sister will be safe here, with Sean and the baby. And you'll be safe with Lucian."

"Safe. What a curious word. I'll be safe. With a vampire."

Maggie cast her a wry glance. "Yes."

She hugged her sister hard and close before she left.

They left the house together in Maggie's handsome BMW.

When they were on the road, Jade looked out the window, worrying that she had just left her closest relative and best friend in the hands of psychos.

"We are really trying to help you. I swear it."

She glanced quickly at Maggie, amazed. Maggie had read her mind.

Maggie grinned. "I still have the gift of getting into a mind now and then."

"I'm sorry, I'm just . . ."

"It's all right."

They drove in silence for several minutes.

Then Jade saw where they had come.

Back to the cemetery.

She stared at Maggie, fear creeping into her system.

"Maggie—"

"You asked me to take you to Lucian."

"But—"

"He's alone," Maggie assured her.

Jade looked outside. Dusk was falling.

"Maggie, a voice called to me last night. I crawled out of a window and risked breaking my neck only to find myself running around in a cemetery."

"It can't happen tonight."

"How can you be so certain?"

"Lucian is expecting you. He wanted you to really understand what he is."

"And what is that?"

"Dead. Undead. A vampire."

Jade moistened her lips, seeing the rise of elaborate tombs over the edge of the walls.

She remembered what it had been like, being here before—when she'd thought she'd been dreaming. But had it been a strange reality? Real in fact, or in her mind? Had she seen winged cherubs reaching out for her? Angels that appeared to fly . . . ?

Trust me!

She suddenly heard his voice in her mind.

The words were as powerful as if they'd been spoken aloud.

She opened the door to the passenger's seat. She looked in at Maggie.

"You'll be all right," Maggie assured her.

"And why is that?"

"He loves you," Maggie said simply, then reached across

the car to grab the door handle and shut the door. She revved the car and drove away.

Darkness and shadows were everywhere. Jade stepped into the cemetery.

This way.

She followed the voice.

Deeper and deeper into shadow, darkness, and the land of the dead.

Chapter Fifteen

Tonight she knew that she wasn't dreaming. She walked through paths of stone, over patches of grass, pieces of life and green trying to break through the inanimate and the dead. She passed a hugh winged gargoyle, a handsome family mausoleum, then another and another. A great tomb to Shriners, a small monument in Latin, dedicated to Italians. Deeper, deeper into the graveyard.

And then she saw him. He stood in front of a simple, majestic tomb that was handsomely carved, guarded by winged lions on either side of heavy doors. The doors were decorated with stained-glass windows, with scenes depicting St. George slaying the dragon, and Lazarus rising. He wore black, blending with the night, coming from the night. His shirt was a casual long-sleeved polo, his pants were pressed denim, and the tailored cut of his jacket seemed to emphasize both his size and his sleekness. He didn't move; he waited for her, perched upon the small wall where one of the lions sat.

She stood some distance from him, staring at him.

"So you've come," he said.

She lifted her hands in the air. "You summoned, didn't you?"

He studied her, then shook his head. "No, I didn't. You're here of your own free will."

"Why am I here?" she whispered.

"I wanted you to see where I live—or don't live."

He rose, walking toward her. She wanted to run away, because she didn't want to believe. But more, far more, she wanted to be with him.

"Come. I'll show you." He stood in front of her and reached out a hand to her. Slowly she took it.

The night seemed darker instantly. She felt the electricity in his hand. It was like a jolt sweeping through her.

He led her to the steps. Her conscious mind rebelled. He was going to drag her in, lock her in with the dead. She couldn't begin to imagine the corpses here. The temperatures skyrocketed by day. The aboveground tombs were customarily given a year and a day—within that time, a body encased in a coffin and stone would disintegrate as if burned; one occupant's bones and remains could be pushed to the rear to fall through to a holding area, so that a second body could be put in. She didn't know what happened in the mausoleums. Surely they were cooler. Coffins were kept cooler, bodies remained . . .

It was a mausoleum. She balked.

He opened one of the doors with its stunning stained-glass window. One wall was enclosed by coffins. There was an altar in the middle of the room, another stained-glass window above that: Christ rising from the dead. There was a single coffin on either side of the wall.

She read the name DeVeau on the altar.

"Relatives?" she whispered.

He shook his head, smiling. "There's not a soul buried

here. There is earth from Scotland in all of these, nothing more. Except for that coffin—clothing. I try to keep up with the styles, you know.''

She looked at him, then walked across the room, wondering if she was going to make an idiot out of herself, trying to lift the lid on a coffin that might have been sealed shut for ages.

The coffin opened. He hadn't lied. It was filled with clothing.

"And the other?" she asked weakly.

"I don't have to sleep here," he told her, coming to her, lifting her chin. He must have felt the way her heart was thundering. She could hear it. The pounding seemed to make the entire place pulse. It was as if she could even feel her own blood pulsing through her. "I come back when I'm exhausted, weak. When I'm injured and need strength. I do need native soil, and it is with me always, everywhere I go.''

She was alone with him here. He claimed to be a vampire. Wasn't he tempted?

"Yes," he said softly. She knew she hadn't spoken aloud.

"How do you not—"

"Free will,'' he told her.

"Can we leave now?" she whispered.

He held her face between his hands, studying her eyes. Night was almost fully upon them. She could see nothing in the tomb. She knew that he could see her.

"We?"

"Yes. If you don't have to stay here, could we go to my house?"

He nodded gravely. "For a while. Then I want to get back to the hospital. Though we don't have to worry right now. Sean will bring your sister in tomorrow with the first light.''

"Can Sean's friends really protect Liz and Rick?''

"More than anyone else."

"Do they believe—"

"They know enough not to deny what works," he said briefly. "But neither is under attack right now."

"How can you—"

"I would feel it."

"Of course," she murmured.

They walked from the cemetery. No mist rose that night. The gargoyles and angels stayed upon their perches and stared out at the darkness with blank eyes.

On the street, he hailed a taxi.

At her place, she walked in, waited for him to enter, and closed the door. She had barely done so when she was in his arms. His kiss was wild, a raging fever, a hunger, wet, so demanding. His mouth barely touched her, and she felt weak, wanting him. But she clung to his shoulders, drawing away.

"I am not—"

"You are everything." His fingers thread through her hair.

"Lucian, I am not someone you once knew!" she whispered. "I am just me, Jade, Jade MacGregor, and . . ."

He held her from him. "I want you very much, Miss Jade MacGregor."

She touched his cheek with her knuckle, studying his eyes. His jacket fell by the wayside, and he touched her in return, his fingers upon the buttons of her blouse, one by one, his knuckles brushing her flesh where it was bared and starting pools of sensation everywhere they touched, sensation that spread out like the ripple of waves in a pool. She cupped his cheek with her hand, loving the structure of his face, the way his eyes fell on hers. Her blouse slipped from her shoulder and fell to the floor, and he turned her, releasing the strap on her bra. He lifted her hair. She felt first the warm, sensual sweep of his breath against her nape, and then his kiss, liquid, hot, the dampness then touched by the swirl of air around them, and that as arousing as all else. His kiss trailed down the length of her spine; his hands then fell to the waistband of her jeans, circled it, found the zipper in front, pulled it down. He stroked low and lower on her abdomen, pushing down on her jeans. She groaned as the pressure of his touch brought a new throbbing into her existence. She turned into his arms, stepping from panties and jeans, feeling the hard length of his body, so very hot against her own. She met his eyes again, and kissed him, and the kiss seemed to touch her everywhere, and everywhere she was liquid and weak, and when he picked her up, she had never wanted anything more in the world.

He was at home in her bedroom, the perfect lover, arrogant and tender, knowing where and when to touch, eliciting, arousing, giving, never hesitating, always demanding more. She marveled at the feel of his flesh, the pulse of muscle beneath her fingertips, the leanness of his hips, the hardness of his size. She didn't want any more questions that night; she didn't want to think, to feel . . . or to fear.

"Are we safe—from *them?*"

"I don't think they'll make such a direct assault," he told her.

"But—"

"I can feel them when they move," he told her.

She closed her eyes. Could that be true? She could feel nothing but him, and she wanted nothing more. . . .

He rose over her, entered her, became part of her. He was a fire, and the fire burned, and in those moments she believed in magic.

* * *

"Get him, get him! Be careful, not Jade—him!" From somewhere in her sleep, she could hear people.

The voice sounded like Renate's.

"Will this do it? Are you certain?"

Danny?

"Yeah, we don't want to just piss off a vampire, Renate."

That was Matt.

Jade awoke, amazed at the whispers she was hearing, thinking at first that she dreamed them. Her eyes flew open.

She would have screamed were she not so stunned.

The very first light of dawn was just beginning to creep into her room. Enough so that she could see.

Renate, Danny, and Matt were aligned around her bed, big sticks in their hands, staring down at her.

"He's not here!" Renate cried.

Sticks.

Stakes!

Jade flew up, clutching the covers to her chest, looking desperately at her side.

Renate had spoken the truth. Lucian wasn't there. She stared at the trio circling her bed. "What the hell are you three doing here!" she exclaimed.

Renate sat at the end of her bed, sighing softly. "We've missed him. I told you we waited too late."

"Renate!" Jade said with a warning edge.

"Jade, dear, you're sleeping with a vampire."

Matt was flushing. "Look, I'm, uh, really sorry, Jade. Renate insisted that we come."

"I wouldn't have come if it hadn't been for the picture in the book," Danny said.

"We're going to help you kill him," Renate said.

"You're going to have to be a hell of a lot more prepared than that if you're going to kill a vampire."

Jade gasped. Lucian had returned. Up, showered, dressed, his dark hair smoothed back, his tailored shirt impeccable, he leaned against the door frame, his arms crossed over his chest, his ebony eyes filled with amusement.

Renate jumped to her feet, the stake raised high.

Lucian hardly seemed to move. But he was in front of Renate; then he'd seized the stake and broken it over a knee.

Matt and Danny instantly dropped their stakes, backing away.

"Never hesitate with a vampire," Lucian told Renate.

Renate stared at him. A small gasp escaped her. Her eyes fluttered. Then she fell into a pool at his feet.

"She's passed out!" Matt cried. He started for Renate. Lucian lifted a hand. "Allow me," he said quietly, and he lifted Renate, and set her in a stuffed wing-backed chair by the balcony window.

"There's ammonia under the sink," Matt said quickly.

"She's all right, isn't she?" Jade murmured.

"She'll be fine," Danny said. "I recognize a dead body when I see one." He caught Lucian's eye. "Uh, usually," he said awkwardly. "I mean, sorry, I—"

Matt was back, waving ammonia beneath Renate's nose. She came to, looked at Lucian standing over her, and slumped right back into the chair.

"Excuse me, guys," Jade said with a sigh. "You all deal with Renate. I'm going to hop into the shower very quickly—and get some clothing on, if you don't mind!"

Danny and Matt both looked flushed—and scared.

She'd almost reached the bathroom, encompassed in her sheets.

"Jade!" Matt said.

She stopped, looking back.

"You are seeing a vampire."

"I know! But it's all right. He won't hurt you," she assured him, and hurried on into the shower.

When she emerged, they were all sitting around the kitchen table. Someone had brewed coffee.

"There has to be a way to find out just who exactly she is," Renate was saying. She seemed much better—totally in charge of herself, and the situation.

Jade poured herself coffee. Lucian was sitting in one of her large, stuffed chairs. She perched on the edge of it. He absently set his hand on her back. It was an intimate and domestic gesture, and she felt incredibly fulfilled by that simple touch. As if she belonged.

"I know exactly what she is," Lucian told Renate. "Evil."

"Lucian has been filling us in," Matt explained, shaking his head admiringly. "Who would have imagined . . . ?"

"Not you," Renate reminded him. "He didn't want to believe me when I had facts to set right beneath his nose!" she said.

Lucian looked at Jade. "I've been trying to explain to your friends that they need to stay out of this. It is never so simple as finding a powerful vampire sleeping by light, and quickly driving a stake through its heart."

"But vampires can be killed," she said softly.

He nodded.

"Bram Stoker!" Matt said suddenly. "Everyone watches movies these days; they so seldom just read! Dracula is not killed with a stake at the end. They cut into his heart, and cut off his head." He looked at Lucian. "That's why the kid's head was nearly off in that accident. Except—well, this Sophia of yours must have been the one to suck him dry. So why did she take his head off?"

"Because he meant nothing to her. Nothing more than vengeance, and a meal."

"But she had killed him. And she is a vampire. So why destroy him in such a horrible manner?" Danny asked.

"Think about it. There are laws, unwritten laws; the natural world is governed by certain laws," Lucian said. "We're not to create more than two of our own kind in a century. If there were no such laws, imagine. There would be more and more vampires—"

"And eventually no people left—"

"And then no mammals, nothing," Lucian said.

The room was silent. Lucian lifted his hands. "You shouldn't be involved. It was wonderful that you tried to protect Jade from me. But you mustn't be involved. It will only make you susceptible."

"But we know what to watch out for now," Danny said.

Lucian smiled. "No, you don't. You can't begin to imagine what you're up against."

"Lucian, honestly, we can help."

"Look, I appreciate your efforts. I appreciate the fact that you no longer want to stake, decapitate, and burn *me* to cinders. But you're not cops or soldiers, you're . . . writers!" he finished a little lamely.

"Excuse me, haven't you heard? The pen is mightier than the sword," Matt said.

Lucian grimaced. "I'm afraid that I've seen at times that that isn't necessarily so."

"We read, Lucian," Renate insisted.

Lucian looked down at his hands and sighed. "Look, you're not up against some green, new being with a unmanageable blood quest. She's ancient. She has powers—"

He broke off suddenly.

"What?" Jade asked him.

"She must have the locket."

Renate hopped on that. "What locket? What is it?"
He shook his head. "Years ago . . ."

Sometimes there were advantages to being the undead. Such as when Conte de Brus first rode north to Scotland. He was a man more self-righteous, arrogant, and convinced of his own magnitude upon the earth than any other, even among the aristocracy. He practiced cruelty at his estates in southern England, made war on the border lords, and came north to Scotland, where the wily king of the Scots struggled to keep his country from the far-reaching grasp of William the Conqueror, and the Norway progeny to whom he would leave his vast holdings.

It was a time when men were beholden to their clans. When a man such as de Brus ruled the family who rode with him.

By then his original band of Vikings was long gone. Only Wulfgar remained with him, for the disease that had claimed him at a young age had eventually caused Lucian to grant him the gift—or curse—that had changed his own existence. He had promised himself that he would create no more of his own kind, no more to suffer the agonies of the blood hunger, to fear the weaknesses of light, shun the sun, forsake the sea. Wulfgar had remained ever loyal through the decades. They have moved about, seeing the world, but always claiming kinship with the DeVeau family, a name that remained in the area—unaltered, even as most Norman, French, Flemish, and Norse names began to adjust, entering the general mainstream of the Scots.

With a French-tongued king sitting on the English throne, it mattered little.

But while Scotland struggled to create and maintain her independence, Norman lords encroached from the south; upon occasion the Vikings still attacked from the north. And within the country, lords battled over petty arguments, or land, for riches. De Brus settled near Edinburgh, claiming the land was owed to him, severing the head of the rightful owner, and augmenting the huge stone edifice already begun there. Neighbor lords tried to fight him; great Highland clans came to the Lowlands to conquer him. His power seemed greater than that of the king.

Then Justin of Ayr, a priest, came to Lucian's Isle of the Dead. He came alone, a young man of the cloth with his own power. He brought a leather sack of gold coins and laid them before Lucian.

"I've heard what you are."

"And you bring me gold; you don't come to destroy me? How strange! A man of the cloth!" Lucian mocked.

"There is a cross upon the wooden mantel in the rear of your house," the priest pointed out.

"My wife is buried there."

The priest grinned suddenly. "They say there was a laird near here who hunted down the poor people who took his deer, and watched them strangle to death as he hanged them. The man disappeared when you returned from abroad."

Lucian shrugged. "I roasted him and ate him," he lied wryly.

"Will you do the same with this de Brus?"

The priest talked that night. Talked and talked. De Brus had a strange power. His own kinsmen feared him. Warriors who would besiege him were found maimed and decapitated on the battlefields the following day. Brave men ran from him. And it had come to where, in nearby villages, lotteries were held, and young women were chosen in that manner to be turned over to de Brus to go to the castle. He had taken a wife, it was said, or had a daughter of his own, a woman who gave him his power, and demanded human life in payment. She drank blood, and bathed in it.

"And how did you become involved in this?" Lucian asked carefully. He had feared that Sophia had healed, that she was back. There was much death and cruelty in the world, but few instances were as dark as this one at the de Brus property. And few created such a disturbance within Lucian, waking him even when he was weary, sated with blood, sleeping by high noon.

The young priest looked at him. "I came home from a pilgrimage to find that my sister had been taken."

Lucian looked at Wulfgar. The next day they traveled with the priest.

At the walls of the de Brus manor, he felt an almost overwhelming wave of her power sweep over him. He could not enter without being invited. He could wait outside for the next group of warriors brave and foolish enough to try to assault de Brus, but the priest was desperate, praying that he could still save his sister.

They watched the gate throughout part of the night. At dawn Lucian saw a woman in handsome apparel, with a cape of silk and fur, ride out from the courtyard unaccompanied.

He followed her. She came to a clearing, dismounted from her horse, sat upon a log, and wept.

He approached her.

She screamed and jumped up at his arrival, clinging to a tree for strength. "They warned me not to ride out, that I would fall prey to our enemies." She noted the hugh sword swinging from the scabbard at his side. "They

warned me that all of the family de Brus are in danger."
She lowered her head. "For the pact with Satan we have
made."

He walked with her, lifting her chin. "Is it Satan?" he
inquired.

"It is my father's new wife. They call her a de Brus. She
is not. She is spawn of hell. What you hear is true. I hear
the young girls screaming. . . ."

"Invite me in," he told her.

"Can you stop her? My father will kill you. And there is
a man with her who does her bidding, who shares in her
. . . debauchery. He sleeps with her as well, and they both
laugh, and my father cares not."

"Invite me in."

"You will die."

"I'll take that chance," he told her dryly.

"Dear sir, whoever you are, if you can stop this . . ."

He rode back with her, stopping for Wulfgar and the
priest.

It was daylight. Not time for his full power. But not time
for Sophia's deadly strength. Yet she knew. She knew they
were coming. She was in the great hall with the laird when
they entered, and she was instantly up, calling for men at
arms. "Stop him, kill him immediately!"

And men rushed at him.

He was sorry for the death he wielded, for they were
only fools at her command. The priest stood by his door.
He and Wulfgar, back to back, met each man as they came
at him.

"His head, you fools! Sever his head, wrench his heart
from his body!" she raged.

Then Darian was coming toward him, Darian who never
learned his lesson. But Darian had glutted on blood in the
past months. Their swords began to clash like thunder

across the hall. They walked the stairs, leaped from the great table, tried to cast one another into the fire. Lucian's arm was nicked; his waist was hit. He cut Darian deeply in the thigh, crossed his chest with his blade. Suddenly Sophia let out a sound like the wail of a cat, a banshee, and she flew forward with a staggering power, a sword in her hand. She swung it again and again, not tiring. When Darian would have attacked him as well, Wulfgar joined the battle. Sophia was like a whirlwind. Lucian could scarcely see anything else in the room, he was so busy fighting Sophia. Her power was staggering. He wasn't assaulting; he was defending. He had cut her several times; she didn't seem to notice, to falter. She battled easily.

She still wore her pendant. Her fingers closed around it.

There was a scream, and he turned and saw that Wulfgar had fallen to his knees. "Do it! His head, take his head!" Sophia cried.

It wasn't Darian who delivered the blow. Sophia pushed forward one of the de Brus men-at-arms.

Wulfgar's head was neatly disconnected from his shoulders. The de Brus fellow was an excellent swordsman.

No hacking . . .

Just a clean blow.

And Wulfgar was dead.

The priest rushed to him, praying over the body.

Sophia began to cackle. "Oh, holy Father, he is among the damned! He will rest in hell, and I will let you join him there!"

She started toward him. Lucian reached out to stop her. His fingers tangled in her hair—and into the gold chain of the pendant. It ripped from her neck with a good handful of hair. She spun on Lucian, shrieking, "Give it back, give it back!"

He looked at the power in his hand. Felt the object

burning there. He looked at Sophia. She was raging at him, her fingers clawing, tearing at his cheeks. He held fast to the pendant, and struck out at Sophia with his sword. He slashed her from throat to groin. She let out a garbled sound and turned. "Darian!" she cried.

She was real; she was mist. She stumbled from the castle.

He tried to chase her.

He stumbled and fell.

He thought again that at last, he might have died. But he awoke in the castle, and they told him that they had found Sophia, and the priest had said prayers, and she had been entombed in lead, and could not arise again. He went to her crypt. The ancient laws told him that he could not rip the tomb to shreds and tear her head from her body. The de Brus men were all terrified of her. They would not do so.

The priest was satisfied that she was gone. Her coffin was lead; a hugh silver cross secured the lid. She would not, could not rise.

The locket he had kept. It was gold, with a strange insignia engraved on it. The likeness of a cat was upon it; the eyes were in ebony.

The first night he slept with the locket he awoke with a raving hunger. He was still at the de Brus castle. A maid walked by his room, and he leaped out at her, and he nearly tore into her throat with savage intent. . . .

But he saw himself. Saw his reflection in a shield mounted on the wall. Saw the hideousness of his own reflection, the saliva dripping from his fangs.

He cast the maid aside, amazed at his own strength. He went to help her up; she was terrified of him, and started screaming.

It was the locket, he thought. It gave him greater strength, but fed upon his hungers, and his cruelty. An army of de Brus men stood before him, staring at him with horror.

"I need Sophia's body!" he raged.

The locket needed to be buried. Sophia needed to be destroyed.

"She is gone, she is gone, she is buried, she will not rise again!" Lady Gwendolyn, the daughter of the castle, told him. Unafraid, she came to him. "We will bury her evil talisman."

The strangely decaying remains of Wulfgar awaited him. He took his dear old friend to the sea, and a bier was built for him, set afire, and cast to the waves.

Before he did so he slipped the locket into what remained of Wulfgar's hands.

It should have burned, melted. . . .

And fallen to the bottom of the sea.

Lucian finished his story and looked around the room. They were all dead silent, as if spellbound.

Then Renate cleared her throat.

"What happened to the priest's sister?"

"She was found. She had been kept with other girls in a cell below the great hall."

"Alive?"

He hesitated. "Alive. Tainted, changed. She went to live with nuns at Reims."

"How sad."

"Very," Lucian agreed. He leaned forward. "But I should warn you as well—everything in my own existence has not always been exemplary."

Renate chose to ignore that. "What of the Lady Gwendolyn?"

"A happier ending. A few years later she went on to marry into the family of Andrew de Moray."

"A few years later," Jade murmured, watching him.

"Yes, a few years later," he replied.

"But now," Matt said gravely, "you think Sophia has the locket again?"

Lucian shrugged. "She came from a lead tomb, and she's had the strength to kill across the globe. I'd say she had some help."

"Darian."

"Obviously he is with her."

"Is she wearing the locket?" Jade asked suddenly.

He shook his head. "I don't know."

"There are things that we can do," Renate insisted. "Sketch the locket for us. We'll find it."

"How?"

"Progress and technology!" Renate said happily.

"She means we're going to search the Internet," Matt told him.

"And we've got to head for the hospital," Jade said.

Lucian looked slowly from Matt to Jade, and nodded. "To the hospital."

From her father, who seemed very confused, Jade learned that Mike Astin had been spelled on guard duty at Liz's door by Sean Canady. Liz was doing much better, but they'd probably keep her another few days for observation—she had been that close to death.

He had met Maggie Canady, who had come with Sean. He'd seen Shanna for a only a few moments, because she had decided to go get the twins and bring them back to Canady's house, and watch them there with the Canadys' little boy, Brent.

"So Shanna has the boys?"

"Maggie Canady says that they're welcome to stay at their house; apparently it's huge."

"It is."

"And she's well equipped for little boys."

"But she's here, and Shanna is at their house?"

"Right."

"Where is Maggie?"

"At the moment I'm not sure. Sean Canady came and let Mike Astin go, and he's been out there at Liz's door ever since. I don't know why Canady feels he has to stand guard like that," her father said, shaking his head with wary concern.

"Well, Dad, it never hurts," she tried to say casually.

Lucian was talking to Liz. Her father was staring at him suspiciously.

"She's doing really well, but she still doesn't really remember what happened. Something about the cable man, but—," he broke off, shaking his head again, at a loss.

"But what, Dad?"

"They didn't send anyone out that day. I guess her fever was just raging, I don't know, but it is upsetting. I should have been home. I've spent my life trying not to let work take over. When your mom was so sick, I learned that time and people were precious and fleeting. I should have been home. I wasn't."

"Dad, you don't work too much; you were a great parent to us; you're a good husband to Liz, and a good father to the twins. Liz is doing well."

"You know what I can't figure out?"

"What?"

"Who called 911?"

"Must have been . . . one of the neighbors."

"In my house?" he said skeptically.

"Dad, really, what does it matter? Someone called, and help came, and Liz is going to be all right."

"Do you think she imagined a cable man? Maybe someone broke in; maybe she was in real danger—"

"Dad, she's here."

He nodded; she kissed his cheek. "I'm going to run up and see how Rick is doing."

"Jade," he said, stopping her.

"Yeah, Dad?"

"You know how much you mean to me, don't you? I love you and your sister. You can't imagine how much."

"Dad, we know."

He hesitated. He seemed very tired, and very worried, and as if he knew that something was going on. And that he was powerless to stop the forces around him.

"Dad, Shanna and I are both delighted that you found Liz, and that you have the twins. And we love you, too, with all our heart." His eyes were still on hers, as if he waited for answeres she couldn't begin to give him. "It's going to be all right," she said. There was a lot of force to her voice, and that was strange—she was feeling very lame.

She managed to leave the room quickly then, before he could stop her again, and before Lucian could stop her— or join her, either. She told Canady where she was going, and took the elevator up a floor.

She found Maggie Canady. She had taken the place of the cop who had been watching Rick's door.

"How's he doing?" Jade asked.

"Great. He's been in and out of consciousness, but doing much, much better. Go on in and see him. If his eyes are closed, try talking to him. The doctors say it's important."

"Thanks. Maggie, Shanna and the twins are all right, aren't they?"

"Fine. They have a houseful of Barney, Disney, and Pokemon, Legos, Fisher Price—you name it. Shanna is fine, and the kids are fine. And I'll go back and spell her in a few hours so she can come and see your stepmom."

"Thanks again."

"Go see Rick."

Jade nodded and went to the room. Rick looked good. His color was pink. He seemed to be breathing easily. His heart monitor showed a fine line almost perfectly accented by little beeps.

She sat at his side and took his hand. No matter what, these days, it seemed she was tired. She held his hand in both of hers and rested her forehead on her hands.

"Hey, kid," she heard.

His voice was thick and raspy, little more than a whisper. He smiled, trying to raise his head, then giving up that effort.

"Rick, thank God!"

She stood and kissed his forehead. He closed his eyes again. "Thanks for being here, Jade."

"Well, of course," she murmured, sounding only a little bit awkward. "You really scared us."

"I think I was scared, too. I don't remember."

"You had an awful fever."

"I hear your stepmother is here."

"Yes."

"You should be with your dad."

"I was with him. Liz is doing really well."

She smoothed back his hair, looking at his pale, still handsome features, and his honest blue eyes.

"Rick—"

He shook his head, catching her fingers, his grip weak. He met her eyes. "It's all right. You don't have to say anything."

"But I do. I—"

"You're not in love with me," he said quietly. He even said the words kindly.

She was so startled by his words that she was dead silent for several long seconds. "Rick, I'm so sorry—"

"No, no, it's all right. I know that you wanted to be. But Jade . . ." He hesitated, then told her. "Something just . . . with this fever, well, I was having some pretty bizarre dreams. And you weren't the one in my dreams."

She smiled. "Oh?"

"A dream is a dream, but there was this woman I had met, and she was the one in the dream. And I was thinking . . . well, hell, people have fantasies in life; they have them before marriage, they have them after. In the end, rather sadly, we're all animals, but . . . then I realized, you want to love me; you just don't."

"Rick—," she began, but then she realized he was looking past her.

"I had met this woman. Casually, I was just giving directions. But she's the one I was dreaming about, Jade. If that makes you feel any better."

"Rick, I'm just sorry about everything. You are the greatest person."

She turned quickly. She hadn't heard him, but Lucian had come in.

Rick looked straight at him.

"Rick, this is Lucian De Veau," Jade said. "I met him in Scotland. He also happens to be a friend of the Canadys."

Rick offered a limp hand to Lucian, but then said, "I know you from somewhere."

"I've been in here a few times with Jade," Lucian offered.

Rick shook his head. "No . . . strange . . . I have this feeling that I know you really well. Do you live in New Orleans?"

"I have a home here," Lucian said vaguely.

"Maybe that's it. Maybe we've crossed paths, walking

around Jackson Square, downing a pint or two at a bar somewhere.''

"Maybe. How are you feeling?"

"Pretty good. Weak as a kitten, but otherwise pretty good. This thing is wicked on the bloodstream. But they've been pumping me up with the red stuff, and it seems to work.''

Lucian nodded, then looked at Jade. "Think I could talk to Rick a moment alone?''

She was startled—and not at all certain that she wanted the two of them talking alone. "Lucian, Rick isn't well—''

"And he isn't stupid; he knows the score.''

Rick suddenly squeezed her hand. "It's cool, Jade. Really.''

She walked out of the room. Maggie was in the hall. "You know, they're all shits, and that's simply the way it is.''

Maggie smiled. "Men?''

"You bet.''

She shrugged. "Well, I guess they feel we're all a pack of harpies.''

"He's involved me in all of this!'' Jade exploded. "These are my friends, and—''

"There's a lot at stake,'' Maggie said softly.

Jade lowered her head. "I think I need some coffee. Will you tell Lucian I'm in the cafeteria? No, never mind, he'll know that, won't he?''

"He'll be able to find you,'' Maggie said.

"Hm. Well, you know, maybe he shouldn't be able to find me.'' She walked back to Maggie, not at all sure why she was so upset. "Because you know what? Maybe I look like this Igrainia of his, but I'm not her. I'm not the reincarnation of some selkie—some fish! I'm not. So if he's looking for someone else . . .''

Maggie waited, just listening, allowing her to spew out her anger.

"I'm not a fish!" Jade repeated.

"The coffee in the cafeteria is fresh," Maggie suggested.

Jade sighed. "Thanks." After a moment, she added, "Maggie?"

"Yes?"

"I'm sorry."

"It's all right," she said softly.

Chapter Sixteen

"Damn, but I feel like you're someone I know really well," Rick said, still studying Lucian.

Lucian shrugged. "Who knows?"

"Did you go to school down here? I mean, obviously you're from somewhere else, but . . . that's not a French accent, is it?"

"Continental, I guess," Lucian said. "I was born in Scotland, but I did spend a number of years in France. Paris is a great city."

"Yeah? Maybe I'll see it one day. So, what happened? There was something going on in Europe, you were around during that whole Scotland thing, you ran into Jade, and, apparently, jumped her bones."

"It really isn't anything like that," Lucian said.

But Rick lifted a hand, cutting him off. "What am I going to do, try to crawl out of bed and beat your ass? Not today. But I'm still crazy about Jade—she's a great person—so if you mean to hurt her—".

"I mean to help her. And this is going to sound strange, but I need to know about the woman you met."

"I only slept with her in my dreams."

"Are you so sure about that?"

"Unless she really floated through my window."

"Could you tell me about her?"

"Dark hair, lots of it, dark black, and pale skin, really startling with that hair, makes her even more exotic-looking . . . boobs up to her eyebrows. I mean, the lady has a chest. And a waist. Great hips. All the stuff fantasy is made of—which is why I suppose I was fantasizing about her. I work with kids, families, drugs—I'm supposed to be familiar with the human psyche, and that seems to be about the best way I can analyze myself."

"Did she have a name?"

"Not that she gave me."

"How was she dressed?"

"She wasn't dressed. You're forgetting the nature of the fantasy."

Lucian shook his head. "I think your fantasy woman might be real. She sounds like someone I know who is probably here in New Orleans."

"Oh, yeah? If you find her, send her in. I used to have a girl. I don't anymore." For the first time, he sounded bitter.

"I really am sorry."

"I believe you. But, it's just still strange. I'd be more pissed at you if I didn't think I knew you from somewhere. Of course, if you had been a friend, what you did would have sucked more."

"Rick, you say that this woman was naked. Can you tell me, though, was she wearing jewelry, a locket of any kind?"

Rick thought about it for a moment. "No."

"You're sure?"

"Positive."

"How are you positive?"

"She was naked in my dream. And I was really studying her chest. If she'd had a locket hanging there, I would have seen it. But it was a fantasy, so what the hell difference does it make?"

"It might be really important. Thanks for your help."

"Anytime. See you around, my new friend—or my old friend, whichever you may be." He grinned, then winced. "Man, it would be nice to have some strength back."

"It will come," Lucian told him.

He left Rick. As he did, he hesitated and looked back. Then he kept going. Maggie was in the hall, sketching. Her fashion designs were truly unique; women came to New Orleans just to shop at her boutique. "Nice one," he told her.

She looked up. "You think he's going to be okay?"

"I don't know. I hope so."

"I just remember years ago . . . how tainted and terrible that old general became, killing everyone. Lucian, if someone like Sophia infects the blood . . ."

"Sophia made me," he reminded her.

She nodded. "I was having these terrible images of a cop gone mad."

"Hey," he said suddenly. "Does that cop remind you of anyone?"

She shook her head slowly. "No one I know."

"But you do believe . . . in people coming back," he said, stooping down by her chair.

She smiled. "You know that I'm convinced I knew Sean before. But I should warn you, Jade was very upset. She told me in no uncertain terms that she wasn't a fi—" Maggie broke off, determined to spare his feelings. "She told me she wasn't Igrainia."

"How does she know about Igrainia?"

"I might have mentioned her," Maggie murmured.

He rose. "I'll go talk to her. I was afraid Rick wouldn't tell me what I wanted to know if she was standing there."

Maggie arched a brow. He shook his head. "Sophia isn't wearing the talisman, but I know she has it. She's going back to it for her strength; she's using it to heal Darian when he's wounded. I have to find it somehow."

"Is it in New Orleans?"

"I don't know."

"Jade is in the cafeteria," Maggie said.

Lucian shook his head after a moment. "No. . . not anymore. She's gone to the chapel, thinking I won't be able to follow."

The chapel was modern and universal. The floors were white; the pews were brown. There was an abstract stained-glass window, and a simple altar. Jade was half sitting, half kneeling in the first pew, staring at the altar. She had prayed—for Liz, for Rick.

And for herself.

Or she had tried to. She had lost track of her prayer; her mind had just gone in circle after circle.

She was startled when Lucian sat down beside her.

"I didn't think you could come here."

He shrugged. "Some can."

She nodded after a moment. "Oh, I see. You're a good vampire, right?"

He shook his head. "No, I'm not a good vampire. I've told you—I've had my moments of extreme violence and . . . cruelty."

"But you're in here."

"Maybe because I do believe in God," he said simply.

"There should be someplace you can't come."

"I can't go inside anyone's home or life without being invited."

"I invited you?" she queried.

"Loudly," he assured her.

She looked away from him. "What happens if Liz or Rick dies?" she demanded.

He hesitated. "Both are doing well."

"But they have been attacked, right? I mean, obviously I wasn't sure I believed all this stuff at first, but . . . that is why you checked them both out—for fang marks, right?"

"Yes," he said flatly. "If that's the way you want to put it."

"If they do die," she demanded harshly, "do they become raving, maniacal killers?"

"No. If they die, we sever their head," he returned, his voice as hard as hers.

She was shaking suddenly. "I hate you. I hate that you walked into my life. I hate what you've done to everyone around me." She looked at him. "And I want you to just go away."

He was very still. "I can't," he said simply.

"Yes, you can. You walk out of here and you go wherever you've been for the past centuries."

"Jade, I can't change what you mean to me."

"Surely you can! You're going to tell me that there haven't been dozens, maybe hundreds, of women in your very long life—or death? What makes me any different? I am not your wife, in the flesh, in a dream, in reincarnation—out of the sea. I'm not her. You loved her, you lost her. But there have been others, obviously. The woman from the de Brus story, Maggie Canady. They're all part of your past. Let me be the past as well. Just go. Walk away."

"Jade, I can't risk your life."

"My life isn't yours to risk! It's my own," she told him. She was suddenly close to tears, overtired and overwrought, worried. About Liz.

About Rick.

About the future.

She had invited him in. Loudly. Yes. Something had happened that night in Edinburgh between them. Since he had touched her, she couldn't stand being away from him. She needed him. Needed the way his dark eyes touched her. Needed to lean against him when he stood tall and rocklike beside her. She loved his laugh, his strength, the tone of his voice. . . .

And he lived in a tomb.

"You can have your life back," he said, a very cool tone to his voice, "when I can be sure that you're going to have a life to live."

She didn't reply. She lowered her head.

He stood up and reached down a hand to her. "Come on," he said huskily.

"Where?" she whispered.

"To tell your folks we'll be back later."

"And then?"

"You're going to stay with your friends and see if the pen—or the Internet—is mightier than the sword. Under no circumstances should you invite anyone else into your apartment. Not the cable man, the electric man, the phone woman—no one. Understand? And you don't leave until I get there."

"Where will you be?"

"Ashes to ashes," he said softly. "I'm going where my strength is greatest, and I'm going to sleep—perchance to dream."

Renate had been very busy. She'd left the boys in Jade's apartment, working there, and returned to her own place to work at her own speed. She'd tapped into every source she could think of—Greek and Roman mythology, Norse mythology, Syran stories, the tale of the Golgotha, biblical stories, medieval witchcraft, the modern wicca, and Egyptian gods and goddesses.

Finally she found what she was looking for.

"Eureka!" she cried.

Just as she was about to leave her apartment and shoot down the hall to Jade's, the bell rang from the ground-floor entry. She hit the button impatiently. "Yes?"

"Ms. Renate DeMarsh?"

"Yes?"

"I have a delivery of books from a store. A bookstore, a place in St. Louis called Coffee and Crime."

Had she ordered books? She couldn't remember. Probably. She buzzed to open the ground-level door.

"Just put the books in the entry down there. Thanks."

She hurried out of her apartment and over to Jade's.

Shade, darkness, coolness, settled around him. Mist rose, swirled, settled. He allowed the mist and the sweet ebony feel of the dark to enwrap him, and he gave over to it. In his mind's eye he saw the talisman. The gold chain, the creature carved into the gold. The cat with eyes of ebony . . .

The way to catch a cat . . .

As a wolf.

There was a great lake of mist, woods, trees, shrubs . . . a forest by night. The wolf, eyes as red as a dying sun, loped through the darkness, following the trail. He slowed, paused, stood still, his muzzle lifted, smelling the air.

Eyes of fire . . .

The animal began to run again, racing along the trail in the woods. There, ahead, the moon cast down strange gold beams upon edifices carved in stone. The graveyard.

The cat lay ahead—he could see it, feel it; the ebony eyes were like a beacon. . . .

A pulse beating. Like a heart pumping.

There were moans, shrieks in the wind. The cries of those who had left unfinished business, the tears of those who had betrayed others . . .

The ghosts of the graveyard. Creating a banshee howl that rose in the night, that was part of the world of the shape-shifter, the wolf who came, who sought. . . .

A marble angel suddenly stood upon the roof of a mausoleum. The wings spread out; the white marble of the angle faded to black. The wings were a great sweeping cloak. Hidden beneath a hood of black, the face of the being turned to the wolf.

Where do the dead hide their treasures, wolf? Think, feel, smell the air, see it in your mind's eyes, you are chasing a cat, wolf, a clever, nimble cat. . . . Where do the dead keep their treasures, where, where, where. . . . ?

He felt his muscles moving beneath him as he ran, felt their power, and the power was good. He felt the cool air of the night, and the soft embrace of the moon above him. Running, yes, he had to keep running, because he could see it, feel it. . . .

Where do the dead keep their treasures . . . ?

He awoke in the darkness, aware that something had changed.

Day was gone; the sun had fallen. In fact, it was closing in on midnight.

The midnight hour . . .

And there was definite disturbance in the ebony of the night.

* * *

Jack Delaney had come to spell Maggie at about five.
Maggie had quizzed him, making certain he was prepared
for any strange visitors who might appear.

"Maggie, that Sprite bottle is full of holy water, I
promise."

She nodded. She sometimes wondered if, even being
Sean's partner and having seen everything he had seen,
Jack really understood. It scared her a little to leave, but
it scared her worse to be away from her own home too
long.

"Throw it first, ask questions later!" she told him.

"Yeah, I can just see my future. Stripped down to beat
cop again for throwing water at doctors in the hospital!"
he teased.

"Just do it," Maggie warned him.

"Yes, ma'am," he said with a grin. She loved Jack; he
was a great friend to them both. "Get going," he told her.

Shanna was tired when she returned to the hospital.

Her twin brothers were a handful.

Maggie's housekeeper, Peggy—a little old lady with
white hair and a tremendous energy that belied her appearance of age—had come in the afternoon, and the kids
had settled down for a nap. Shanna loved kids, and wanted
several of her own—even if she never found a decent guy
and bought the dad's genes from a sperm bank—but it
seemed that she hadn't had sleep in forever.

When Maggie came back to the mansion to spell her,
she was grateful.

And she was grateful to have the twins where they were.
Jamie had scared her, really scared her, more than anything she had seen or been told, when he stared at the
television and told her, "I like their TV. The cable man
came and broke ours. Broke it all up—and Mommy, too."

And he had started to cry.

His tears had made her wonder just what had happened.

And she prayed that Liz would never remember.

When she reached the hospital parking lot at last, she did exactly what she had been told, parking as close to the emergency exit as she could. She had Sean's car, and it had police stickers all over it, so she was able to park under a light, next to the door.

She exited the car quickly and walked to the emergency entrance. There was a man ahead of her, walking toward the same door. Her pace slowed, then quickened. He must have come from the corner lot, she thought. She was afraid, but her mind kept racing. This was a hospital. A public facility. Lots of people came to the hospital. . . .

"Let me get that for you."

She had felt him behind her as she raced the last few steps to the emergency room doors.

The doors at the pedestrian entrance did not automatically swing open. As she stood there, almost paralyzed in fear, the stranger reached past her for the bar to the door.

"There you go," he said.

She hurried into the hospital entry, then swung around to look at his face. She gasped, a sigh of relief exploding from her. It was Dave, the guy she'd met at the coffee shop—the guy who had failed to meet her at the movies.

"You!" she said.

"Shanna." He seemed incredibly pleased. "I'm so glad to see you. I've tried to call you; I couldn't reach you." He was smiling as she looked up at him. "I was so sick, I just couldn't make the movie. But I did mean to see you again. To call you."

He was apologizing. Still, he had stood her up. She needed to be a bit cool. "Well . . . ," she said. "Call me, then."

"You don't sound as if you mean that."

She dropped her attitude and smiled at him. "Seriously, call me."

"I'll still be welcome?"

"Yeah. Yeah, you'll still be welcome."

She studied him then, suddenly worried. "You're not here because you've gotten any worse, are you?"

"No, no. I'm here to see . . . to see an old friend. What about you?"

"My stepmother and a friend. It's been a tough time."

"I'm sorry to hear that."

"Thanks. I guess I should get in. I have to see my father, and then call a friend and let her know that I got here okay."

"Get going."

"I'm glad to see you're better."

"Thanks." They had come down the corridor to the elevators. "I'm going to two," she said.

"I'm going to three."

"We'll ride together."

They stepped into the elevator together. He was very close to her. Smiling at her. She was surprised to feel both a little bit uneasy . . . and, incredibly, compelled. He was cute. And charming. And standing next to him was somehow . . . *sexual.*

She was glad when the elevator came to a halt and gave a little beeping sound.

She stepped off, turned around, and smiled. "I'll be seeing you, I imagine."

"You bet. You can just bet you'll be seeing me. It's a promise," he said.

He smiled.

The elevator door closed, and Shanna turned around again and hurried down the hall to Liz's room.

* * *

When Maggie had gone, Jack sat down to keep vigil at Rick Beaudreaux's door. The hours passed. He read, did a crossword puzzle, then stood and stretched. He chatted with the nurses who came and went. An aide brought him a cafeteria hamburger.

He almost drank the holy water, but remembered that it wasn't really a Sprite and what its purpose was, and asked a night nurse for some coffee.

At eleven o'clock the shift changed.

A new night nurse came down the hall, carrying a tray of medications. She had a stunning face and a perfect figure; blond hair was tucked neatly under her cap. She was really something, wearing her nurse's uniform especially well. She should have been on the cover of *Cosmo*, he thought, or modeling bras for Victoria's Secret.

"Hi, there, Officer. How's my patient doing?"

"He seems to be doing really well."

"You're keeping out the riffraff, I take it?"

"Yes, ma'am, that would be my job."

"Well, then, it's nice to have you here," she said huskily.

He smiled and went back to his book as she went in to the patient. As he was reading, it occurred to him that she looked awfully, awfully good for a nurse. There had been something a little too high-fashion about her uniform and her hat. She had looked like a photo-shoot nurse. A movie nurse . . .

Not a *real* nurse.

He leaped to his feet. As he did so, he blinked furiously, staring down the hall.

He thought he had seen a wolf. There. In the hospital. Running toward him.

Man, he was overtired.

It wasn't a wolf. It was a man. Sean's old friend Lucian DeVeau.

And then he knew he'd been right. The woman wasn't a nurse. He didn't wait for DeVeau to reach him; he burst into the hospital room.

She was stretched out on top of her patient. She heard him enter and looked up at him. Her eyes were wild, stunning.

Hypnotic.

Blood dripped from her mouth. Blood from Rick Beaudreaux's throat . . .

"Lord!" he said under his breath.

He started to lunge for her. Lucian DeVeau went flying past him, tackling the woman, pitching her from the hospital bed. The IV broke and spurted fluid all around them. A tray clattered to the floor.

"The holy water!" DeVeau shouted.

He ran for it as an alarm bell began to ring in the hospital. It was a code call. Someone was coding out.

Yeah! Rick Beaudreaux.

The holy water. He needed the damned holy water.

But as Jack burst back out into the hall he saw that there was now a tall, red-haired man in the corridor. He was lifting the Sprite bottle Jack had come for, laughing.

"Looking for this, Officer?" he asked.

"Give that to me!" Jack commanded sharply. "I am an officer of the law—"

He had started for the man, but the man walked to him, took his arm, and sent him flying with no effort.

Jack fell hard.

Still . . .

He leaped to his feet. He entered the hospital room in time to tackle the fellow's feet.

He was able to make him fall. The Sprite bottle flew. Lucian was still engaged with the woman.

She leaped up; he followed. She backed away, stepping into the water that had spilled from the bottle.

She let out a terrible scream.

"Ass!" the man, grappling on the floor, turned and pounded Jack once in the head. Hard.

As the room faded to black, it seemed that the woman disappeared. Into thin air.

Renate was excited.

The others were still in Jade's apartment, waiting.

"I know I'm right. I just know I'm right. And there's a whole tale with it! The creature is the cat goddess, and she gives power. I can't wait for Lucian to get back here. Jade, when is he coming?"

Jade, slumped in one of the big chairs, yawned. "Soon, I imagine," she told Renate. How many times had she asked so far?

Danny had dozed; she had dozed. Matt had snored.

Renate hadn't had a seat for a single second.

"I have found exactly what he needs!" she said proudly.

The phone rang then. Jade came awake immediately, leaped up, and hurried over to it. "Jade?"

It was her sister.

"Shanna! Oh, my God! Is Liz okay?"

"Liz is all right, but Jade . . ."

Her voice sounded so funny.

"What, Shanna? What is it?"

"Rick is dead."

"What?" She gasped.

"Rick Beaudreaux is dead. They coded him, they tried resuscitation, but . . . he's gone, Jade. Rick is gone."

The world was spinning around her.

She dropped the phone.

Matt caught her, and she turned into his arms and cried as Danny took the receiver from her. "Hello, hello?"

Danny listened to Shanna.

"We'll have her down there in just a few minutes," he said quietly.

Rick had been cleaned up when the hospital officials let her see him. Among the police force, she was still regarded as his fiancée, the girl who had loved him, whom he had loved. There has been all kinds of questions at the hospital, and Jack Delaney had answered them the best he could. He had remained passed out on the floor when the hospital staff came running in on the code alarm; he had come to only later, and then he had tried to explain that a pretend nurse had come in to see Rick. The body had been held for police photographers and forensic people. They had spent several hours searching for prints, fibers, and more. But though there had been little drops of blood on Rick's hospital shirt, there had been no visible marks of foul play upon his body.

Some people suspected that Jack had been denied sleep too long, or that he had hit his head while trying to see about Rick's condition, and imagined the murderous nurse. Of course, a full autopsy would be done. Jack Delaney could have sworn that the woman had ripped out Rick's throat; there were no such marks. He had simply died of anemia brought on by fever and dehydration— that was what it looked like. Rick had been a cop, and a good cop. And Jack was a cop, too. He might need a leave, but his word would be checked out thoroughly. When Jade reached the hospital, Rick was just being wrapped for transfer to the morgue. His beautiful blue eyes were closed forever. His cheeks were whiter than snow. He was cold, so cold already.

He had died, she thought, just because he had known her.

She was sobbing when Sean Canady came for her, telling her they were going to the chapel. She found out that Lucian was there, and the first thing she did was rush over to him and slam her fists against him with all her fury. She threatened him—no matter what happened, he'd best not let his sick enemies get hold of her stepmother as well. He stood perfectly still for the longest time as she beat against him; then he caught hold of her wrists.

"Jade—"

"No, I don't want to hear anything from you. I don't want to hear anything at all."

She tried to wrench away from him, and found that that was impossible to do; Shanna came and put her arms around her and tried to calm her, though she was in tears herself. Jack Delaney came into the chapel and started apologizing. "I am so sorry; you trusted me, and you warned me. It was my fault, and the doctors here are still convinced we're dealing with a new virus. They think I fell asleep and dreamed up the woman who came into the room."

Sean had been sitting in a pew, his head in his hands. He got up. "Look, Jack, you're not at fault. There is a force here that . . . well, it's very powerful."

"But it seems I'll never be able to convince the hospital and the police powers that be that Rick was killed by . . . what? An ancient evil?"

No one replied.

Jade stood, too upset to stay among them.

As she started out of the chapel, her sister called after her. "Jade! What are you doing? You can't just go off—"

"Jack, can you follow her, then get back to Maggie's as soon as possible? Sean and I have a few things to take care of here," Lucian asked Jack.

Jade went dead still, swung around, and walked back into the chapel, hands on her hips as she stared at Lucian.

"What do you think you're going to do?" she demanded.

"You know what I've got to do."

She shook her head in denial. "You think you're going to go down to the morgue and slice off his head and cut out his heart. No! You're not going to do it! You're not!"

"Jade!" Lucian exclaimed, seizing her by the shoulders. "We've got to. You still don't want to believe what you've seen, but this has to be done."

"No! No! If he can come back, let him come back!"

"Jade, you don't understand—"

"What don't I understand?" she challenged. "He'll come back the same as you!"

"He could," Lucian said.

"And he might not," Sean told her.

"What do you mean, he might not?"

"Some people shouldn't come back," Lucian said.

"Jade," Sean said, "he could come back with a really vicious homicidal bent."

She put her hands on her hips. "Who are you to judge who should and shouldn't be allowed to come back?" she demanded.

"Let me tell you why he shouldn't come back!" Lucian said, his anger suddenly rivaling hers. "He was a hell of a decent guy. Do you really want him damned, thirsting for blood, hurting every day he doesn't take a human life?"

"Is that how you live?"

"It's how I lived for a very long time," he told her, then added, "then again, lucky me. I learned about blood lust in a time when war meant decapitating your enemy and slicing him to ribbons. Jack, take her out of here. Get her out of the hospital."

"Jade," Jack said. "You know, they're going to cut into Rick anyway; there's going to be a full autopsy because it will have to be determined just how he did die. The hospital is convinced that we have a new and deadly virus on our hands."

"Well, we do, don't we?" Jade murmured.

"Who the hell knows what we have! I—"

"Don't! Please, please, please, don't hack into Rick. Give him a chance. If he's tainted—"

"*If* he's tainted?" Lucian said, crossing his arms over his chest.

"He can be killed later."

"Not by me. Don't you understand?"

"Sean can kill him."

Sean groaned.

"What if he comes back with a tremendous capacity for evil?"

"He won't! I'm telling you, I know Rick. And damn it, Lucian, look at you."

"Um. Look at me. I've been a long, long time in the making, Jade. You don't know what I came back like, and you sure as hell don't know some of the horrors I created in my day."

"Rick will have you."

"I had a guide as well—," Lucian began, but he suddenly broke off, remembering what he had felt when Rick had talked to him earlier. *Damn, but I feel like you're someone I know really well!* Rick had told him, and there had been something so familiar about him, too. . . .

"What?" Jade said.

Lucian looked at Sean. "You're a cop, and you know this town, and you knew Rick. It's your call."

"You mean . . . ," Sean said.

"We can see what happens."

"But what will happen when they take him in for the autopsy?"

"He'll probably wake before then," Lucian said.

"Right. And give the coroner heart failure," Jack suggested.

"And chew out his throat, probably," Sean said dryly. "You awake with a terrible hunger, right?"

"Most of the time," Lucian agreed.

"It's dangerous," Sean said.

"Dangerous!" Jade exclaimed. "Sean Canady, Jack Delaney. The two of you are sitting here talking calmly with a man who claims to be—or admits to being, whichever you want—a vampire. A killer. The king of the wretched beasts, as it were. He hasn't seized either of you for a midnight snack. How can you even think about going down to that morgue to slice up Rick Beaudreaux?"

"Please . . . we should give him a chance," Shanna said, piping on in on the conversation. "I mean, maybe Sophia infected him, but it's true that she did infect you as well. You may need more help than you've got fighting her and Darian—human help is frail, as we've all discovered— sorry, Jack—and Rick was a very fine person."

"Jack?" Sean said.

"I wasn't fond of the idea of cutting off Rick's head," Jack said.

Sean looked at Lucian. "Let's give it a try."

"Rick Beaudreaux may not thank any of us," Lucian warned them.

"And then, of course, we've got another problem," Sean said.

They all stared at him.

"Somehow," Sean said, "we're going to have to steal his body and get him out of the morgue. Because he might not wake up in time, and then he'll be a chopped-up, pissed-off, and really hungry vampire."

Chapter Seventeen

They waited several hours.

Lucian felt sorry for the hospital administrators. Trouble in the blood bank, a very strange death, and now a missing corpse. It wasn't going to look good for them.

There was no help for it.

Rick's corpse lay on the ground level, awaiting transfer to the parish morgue in the morning for a complete autopsy. Only one attendant was on duty.

Lucian went down first and engaged the night man at the morgue desk in conversation. A few seconds later, when the night attendant was staring into space, he summoned Jack and Sean, now clad in hospital gowns. They wheeled Rick out on a gurney and to an empty room. There, quickly, they dressed him. Lucian and Sean each put an arm around him. It looked as if they escorted a drunk, as they carried him between them, and with amazing ease they departed the hospital.

"Where are we taking him?" Sean, driving, asked.

"It's almost daylight. The cemetery," Lucian told him.

"If anyone recognizes me stealing a corpse after insisting a woman who disappeared into thin air murdered the guy, my ass is fired," Jack said forlornly.

Lucian looked at him. "No one recognized you," he said.

The girls had been sent to Maggie's. Mike Astin sat guard now for Liz MacGregor.

They reached the cemetery, parked the car on the street, and maneuvered the corpse out. Jack felt queasy as the gates opened at Lucian's approach.

Lucian lifted Rick Beaudreaux into his arms and turned back to Jack and Sean. "You two don't need to go any farther. I can take it from here."

Sean nodded. "He'll sleep through the daylight?"

"If he awakes, which he might, he'll sleep again. He'll have no strength," Lucian said.

"What's next?" Jack asked. "Are the girls safe at Maggie's? Is Liz in greater danger now?"

"Sophia and Darian were both hurt pretty badly in that last scuffle. Holy water burns worse than acid on human flesh," he said quietly. "They could prey only on someone really weak, and they'll be desperate to escape the sun with such severe burns. I can try to find their positions. I found them last night, but . . . a little late. I think we've bought some time. And we need it."

"What's your plan?" Sean asked.

"I'm going to Scotland."

"Great. Vampires run amok in New Orleans—and you're going to Scotland," Jack said, shaking his head.

"I think I know where to find Sophia's talisman."

"But what will happen here if you leave?" Jack asked.

"I promise you, if I head for Scotland, the two of them will follow. They came here and purposely and methodically started killing the survivors from their murder spree in Scotland. The talisman must be in the bowels of the tomb there. I think that Sophia displayed it somehow that night and that they've come after these people because she doesn't intend to lose it again."

"But what good does it do her in Scotland?" Sean asked.

"It's in her possession, kept in a family vault. A very rich man doesn't hold his money, but it exists in the bank," he explained. "That's what I think."

"I still don't quite understand this, Lucian. You're the leader; the oldest, the best—the most powerful. Can't you command—"

"In the days when the world remained a test of arms, we went to war constantly, and any man could be drawn into battle. The Norsemen I knew still hoped for an entrance to Valhalla, and those Christians with remnants of souls clung to the hope that there could be forgiveness. Like men, my kind have changed with the times. During times of plague we feasted and, God knows, perhaps saved men and women from unimaginable agonies. In the Renaissance, we learned to take care. During the French Revolution it was easy to rid yourself of certain enemies, bloodsucking and human. We've moved into a new age. Most of my kind feed discreetly on the dying, visit prisons, help rid the streets of human vermin, and spend most of their time visiting blood banks. It's survival. It's what I've taught. It's why I'm kind. I haven't gone against nature; I've tried to tame it for the changing times. Sometimes a terror arises, such as Sophia. And then there is action. But I am usually the one to take that action, be that in a physical reprimand that leaves the offender healing for a century or two, or in enlisting the aid of human beings to see to the final deed—always a risky proposition, when you are among the undead yourself. There are those I can call on for help, but they all fear Sophia. No king commands subjects in rebellion, and that is what she remains. I usurped her power; I changed the order of the day. Leave me now. I'll see you again come the darkness."

Sean and Jack watched while Lucian carried the body of their friend into the depths of the graveyard.

"Let's go home," Sean said quietly. "To my house for now. It's safest—and we need some sleep."

"It's almost daylight."

"I know. My habits are changing," Sean said with a shake of his head.

"Do you think Rick's going to be all right?"

"All right?" Sean said. "Jack, Rick is dead."

"As the undead," Jack said quietly.

"I don't know. I don't know. God, I pray we made the right decision!"

Shanna worried about Jade; she had taken Rick's death badly. At Maggie's house, however, she had calmed down after having a cup of hot tea.

Jade was sedated, Shanna quickly discovered, but still quivered in a pile of tears and devastation that not even the twins could ease. She was put to bed.

Shanna stayed awake with Maggie for a while, then determined that she must get some sleep herself. The mansion was huge and delightful. Her guest bedroom had French doors that opened to a wrought-iron balcony and the garden below.

The doors, of course, were closed that night. The windows were closed. The house was secured.

She thought that she would never sleep, but Maggie must have slipped a little help into her tea as well. She dozed restlessly soon after hitting the pillow.

She was plagued by dreams.

Dave was in her dreams. *I'm not well; you know that. I really need some help. Some comfort,* he teased. It was as if they were standing just outside the hospital doors. *I meant to call you. I will see you again; oh, I will see you.*

"I have to go," Shanna told him.

Don't be mad. I'm sick. I need help tonight. Come on, please, let me in?

His smile was charming. He was so cute. But she shook her head firmly. "My friend died tonight. I have to deal with my family."

Let me in. Come on, Shanna. I am in already; I'm in your heart, your mind. Open these doors; get rid of those smelly garlic vine things Maggie has wrapped everywhere.

"No! Go away! I'm tired!"

She jerked up, realizing that she had spoken aloud. The French doors had come partially ajar; they were still half-closed by the garlic vines. She got up and secured the door again, muttering.

She heard someone crying. The twins were just next door, between her room and Jade's. She ran in. Jade already had little Jamie up and in her arms. She was soothing him. She looked like hell. "Jade, give me Jamie; get back to bed. You're in horrible shape."

"You're not in any better!" her sister protested.

"Better than you," she insisted. "Maggie didn't whack me with as much sedation."

Jade arched a brow, but wasn't really surprised or angry. She started to bring her baby brother to her sister, then wound up hugging him between them. "I'm scared. I'm so scared for Liz now, for Dad, for all of us. . . ."

"It's going to be all right."

"It is!" Jade said, handing over Jamie and smoothing a lock of wild hair from her eyes. "I'm going to make it be okay." She smiled, kissed Jamie, and left the room.

"All right, kiddo, how're you doing?" Shanna demanded.

"Bad dreams," he told her. "The cable man."

"The cable man isn't here; don't worry."

"He was."

"We're all right. You come on and cuddle with your big sister. We're going to get a few hours' sleep, and we'll be just fine; we'll protect one another. Okay?"

He nodded. "Shanna?"

"Yes."

"The cable man is gone now. But he was here. Really."

"I'm glad he's gone. Let's get some sleep."

It was very, very late when Renate finally got to bed. She had stayed at Jade's with the boys for a long time, and they had all grieved over Rick Beaudreaux, and thought about Jade, who was devastated.

"It's the guilt thing as well," Renate had told Matt and Danny. "Guilt. She didn't love him, poor fellow. And there he is—dead."

"There he is—dead. You don't need to be guilty to be upset about that!" Matt told her.

They were both so cool to her, she decided to leave them to their own wallowing. She might have tried to soothe them more, make tea with brandy, help them get some sleep. But she simply informed them she was returning to her own place, and that they should let her know if she was needed. They barely noticed that she left.

The night was almost over when she finally lay down.

In her dreams, she twisted and tossed.

And a man was in her dreams. She knew him, if only casually. She seemed to remember that she had told him he could come in before. He was good-looking, very good-looking, but he was hurt. He was suffering from cuts and burns. He whispered her name softly, so softly. His whisper was like the gentlest, most sensual touch of fingers feathering against her cheeks. She moved to that touch.

Renate, those fools, they don't appreciate what they have, some-one smart, kind, and gentle, someone who knows. . . .

"They're terrible," she murmured aloud. "Horrible friends," she agreed.

I need you. I need you so badly. Touch me, heal me, let me in, take care of me, I need you, I need your help so badly.

She smiled. *Great dream.*

He was so sexy.

So nice, pleading, wanting her.

He was on his knees before her. Her fingers fell into his hair.

I need you, Renate, I need you. . . .

"Sweetheart, I need you," she murmured.

And she tossed. And she turned.

And she wasn't alone.

Lucian, at last, rested.

He had gathered and prepared what he would need when Rick awakened, and he had given Rick the healing sanctum of his coffin, and so he lay on a topcoat and pillow before the stained glass, his eyes closed. He hated to allow himself such a vulnerability, but he closed his eyes and allowed the power of his mind to take flight again.

There was a room in the very strange darkness of day, and in the center were the chairs, the carved chairs that had stood in the center of the fisherman's cottage. And one was empty now, as it had been for hundreds of years, but sometimes he could still see her there—see the fall of her linen tunic, the cold chain of the elegantly crafted belt she wore about her hips. Her hair was free, or sometimes tied into little braids; her fingers curved over the arm of the chair as she listened. Her eyes were like the sea, blue and green in ever-changing waves, wide as she mused a situation and gave it careful thought that she might advise him. . . .

Her chair was empty. He sat in his own and summoned the powers around him. Ragnor, from the far northern isles, Yves d'Pres from Bruges, the Spaniard, Roberto Domano. Lisa Clay from faraway Seattle, her consort, the artist, Fucello. Jean d'Amore from Burgundy, Chris Adair from Limerick. More and more they appeared around him. It was Ragnor who stepped forward to say, "Of course she's returned. Sophia has escaped her lead tomb. We've seen it; we've feared it."

"Lucian, why not let her wreak havoc among the humans until they bring her down themselves?" Yves suggested.

"Easy," Lisa interjected. "She will create such turmoil that the people will begin to believe in legends, and when they believe, they will be ready to kill, and a furor will go out, and we will all be hunted down. Men can be such fools! Don't you remember the witchcraft burnings in Europe, the hangings in England and the U.S.?" She shuddered. "I barely escaped myself! I agree with Lucian. She will bring us all down."

"But we are hunters, warriors, wolves!" Yves protested. "It is our lot to hunt. Lucian. You are the mediator; you are the guide. You are the king of all our kind. That I would never dispute, but I cannot help you hunt down a fellow creature; she came before you. This fight is yours."

"Do you grow weak, Lucian?" Roberto demanded. "Too concerned for the fate of those who would hunt us?"

"I do not grow weak, Roberto. I have saved many of your lives by keeping you from the carnage that would be your ruin. I don't want any of you to help me bring Sophia down. Few of you are old enough to have known her, or known the extent of her power, her malice. This is what I do want—I want New Orleans kept safe from all our kind. There have been too many killings there. Too much that is too strange."

"Even for New Orleans?" Yves said, laughing.

"Even for New Orleans," Lucian told him.

"I will watch over your city, Lucian," Ragnor told him.

"I only warn you all not to join with Sophia and Darian; don't be fooled that they will bring me down, because they will not; I will not allow it. And if you care to join with me, then you are welcome. It is not a command I can give you, nor would I. But you are all aware of the turmoil, of the ripple in the darkness, of the danger we face. We do not destroy our own kind—that is the unwritten law, as ancient as the hungers that rule us. But times have changed, and the ways of men and the world have changed as well. When we are all threatened by the excesses of a few, it then becomes a war, and as I have ruled our kind these many years, I tell you that I have no choice now but to seek the justice that will let the rest of us survive. And to those of you who may decide to join with them, be warned: this is a war, and I will destroy anyone who stands against me. Are we understood? If the law is one of nature, and I burst into flames at such an act, so be it. I will not allow Sophia's depravity to destroy their world, or our own."

A series of ayes sounded from the group.

They lowered their heads. He released his hold upon them.

He looked up. Chris Adair remained.

"I will fight with you, Lucian."

"I am best off moving alone, or with a new man among our number, who will shortly awaken. Ragnor will keep watch here. And I will be grateful if you will keep watch among us."

Chris nodded. "Aye, Lucian. I'll keep watch. . . ."

* * *

"Whoa! Where the hell am I? I'm starving, man!"

Rick Beaudreaux was sitting up in the coffin. His eyes were wild, trying to adjust. They fell on Lucian. "Burning, man, I'm burning up. And starving."

He was staring at Lucian, all but salivating. He stumbled out of the coffin, rubbing his neck. "Dark in here, hot. Lucian. Man. Lucian, you look good enough to hug. In fact, you look damned good. Good enough to eat all up. What the hell am I saying? Man, I'm just so hungry. . . ."

"I'm not what you're looking for, trust me," Lucian told him dryly. "What do you remember?"

"The sexiest broad in the universe crawling over me, and . . ." Rick suddenly doubled over. "Man, I am in pain. So much pain. And I could have sworn . . ." He rose slowly, still clutching his gut, looking at Lucian. "I thought I was dead."

"You were."

Rick finally got a look around the coffin. There was little light; night was coming again. But he could see, and well. Night vision was one of the advantages.

"What's the matter with me?" He closed his eyes. "I want to come out of here and—man, I don't believe this. I desperately want to drink blood. Warm blood. Fresh blood."

There was a squealing from the rear of the crypt. Lucian had collected some of the largest, fattest rats he could summon from the length and width of the cemetery.

Not surprisingly, they had been plentiful.

"Rats?" Rick whispered.

"They'll fill the need."

Rick didn't seem to have the power to resist the smell and the warmth of the creatures. He staggered toward the rear of the tomb.

The squealing increased to a fever pitch. Rick Beaudreaux glutted on the rats. Then, looking at his hands in horror—before deciding they weren't so bad and licking his fingertips—he leaned back against the coffin and stared at Lucian again.

"I'm dead, and in hell. Or I'm not dead, and this is the worst nightmare I've ever had. Or this is real, and I'm a . . . vampire."

Lucian nodded. "I'm really sorry. I wasn't for this idea."

"You wanted to stake me, right?"

"Something like that."

"It's all right. Jade wouldn't let you, right?"

"It was a decision made by a number of them."

"Don't worry, DeVeau. She probably did it because she *doesn't* love me. But I'm glad. I'm telling you, I can . . . I can do this."

"You're doing better than I did at first. I didn't want to accept it. But I warn you, being undead—damned, if you will, has its true miseries. Remember that hunger you just felt?"

"I can do this. Well, I mean, you can do better than rats without hitting on people, right? I mean, it could have been a cow."

"Sorry—I might have looked a little strange dragging Daisy or Elsie into a family mausoleum in the middle of a historical cemetery at the crack of dawn," Lucian said, aggravated.

Rick grinned, lowered his head, then looked at Lucian again. "It's not what I was planning. But I can do it." He was quiet a minute. "I want to find the killers. I guess you weren't among them. I'd rather be what I am—a rat-eater at the moment—and able to do something. I won't freak out and start attacking people I loved, will I?"

"It has happened," Lucian said. "But I intend to be with you. There are rules, of course, laws in this world, but you'll have to learn them as we go. Time is all-important to us now. There are a lot of arrangements to be made. We need to move.''

Rick nodded. ''As you say.''

Lucian turned around to start out from the tomb, remembering that it would take Rick some time to learn the power of mist and movement, mind and matter.

Iron gates creaked open as he let them out into the night.

He started walking toward the gates, listening for Rick behind him.

He heard tears and hesitated. Up ahead, a young girl was kneeling in front of a freshly sealed tomb, crying.

She was about sixteen. Her hair was in a ponytail. As she sobbed, even he felt the pull of the long blue vein in her neck, made so visible by the height of her ponytail.

''Fight it,'' he told Rick.

''I'm cool; I swear it,'' Rick told him, and they walked on by, nodding sympathetically to the girl. ''I'm cool, chieftain.''

Lucian swung around. ''What did you call me?''

''I don't know. Oh, chieftain.''

''Why did you call me that?''

''Well, you're Scottish, right? Even with the name DeVeau.''

''I was. Once upon a time,'' Lucian said, studying Rick. ''Once upon a time, long ago.''

''And now . . .''

''Now, it's time to go home.''

At first, Jade was convinced that they had all lied to her. They had pretended to save Rick, and they had gone down to the morgue and cut him to ribbons.

She had slept most of the day. They all had.

Amazing how time could turn around.

But once she had awakened, she had read the morning news. Rick Beaudreaux, a popular police officer, had died in the night. A fellow officer reported a couple who had come in to attack the officer, however, they had mysteriously disappeared into thin air. The unnamed officer how had been guarding the sick Beaudreaux had apparently injured himself in a fall—the insinuation was there that the fall had given the cop much more than bump on the head.

To make matters worse, Beaudreaux's body had disappeared. Cleanly, completely. He had been in the morgue; now he was gone.

She wondered if her father had had anything to do with the story. No. Peter MacGregor would never have said or done anything to make matters any harder on Jack Delaney.

Her hands were shaking as she put down the paper and looked at Maggie. Maggie smiled. "They might not have agreed with you, but they wouldn't have lied to you, Jade," Maggie told her.

"So . . ."

"We'll have to hope that he comes back . . . decently."

They were alone in the breakfast room. Jade had checked on her sister, and Shanna was still sleeping with little Jamie curled into her arms.

Jade stared at her coffee cup. "I still don't believe any of this. But . . . if you were a really decent person, could you come back as a . . . as a decent vampire?"

Maggie didn't answer right away.

"Maggie?"

She shrugged and sipped her own coffee. "*Rational* is probably a better word. The urge is there . . . immediately. The urge to kill, to savage flesh, to feed . . . but it can be controlled. I'm sure he's told you. Lucian wasn't always quite so ... discerning. But even in the days when it appeared he was far harsher, sterner, and mocking of the daylight world, I don't think he ever enjoyed killing. Not even after Igrainia ... I think he wanted vengeance against Sophia. And when she was entombed ... he existed to keep order.''

The phone started ringing.

Jade jumped up. "I'll bet it's my dad."

"No, I called him and said that we'd bring you and your sister later this evening. I'll bet it's that pesky neighbor of yours."

"Pesky neighbor?"

"The writer. That Renate DeMarsh."

"She's been calling?" Jade said.

"Again and again."

"She's convinced she has the answer to the locket situation."

"Maybe she does. You should talk to her."

Jade answered the phone, and Renate was tired and cranky. "Where is Lucian?" she demanded.

"Look, Renate, it was an eventful night. I don't know where he is right now."

"Well, you've got to get him over here. Quickly. Listen to me, the locket is all about an ancient Egyptian cat goddess—"

"Bastet?" Jade said, trying to remember all that she might have learned at one time or another about ancient Egyptian deities.

"No. Bastet is one, yes. But this was a cat goddess, more like a panther. She was called Ura. There's not a lot known about her, because in the days when they went to the new religion, they destroyed everything pertaining to her— every engraving, every statue, everything, because she was a *blood drinker*. They used to sacrifice to her. When she was at last destroyed, legend goes, she was burned. But her ashes remained. If collected in a locket, they were said to give the possessor the power of pure evil. And unless the owner of the locket was destroyed in fire along with the goddess, the power would remain. So taking away the locket does nothing. Sophia has to be burned, and burned to ash."

"I'll call you, Renate. That's great information. You've been wonderful."

Renate sniffed. "Hmff. I wish I felt wonderful. I'm exhausted. I've had no sleep. How are you holding up?"

"I'm okay."

"Did you steal Rick's body?"

"No."

"Well, call me. Have Lucian call me."

"I will. Thanks again," Jade said, and hung up.

"She knows?" Maggie asked.

"She's a researcher," Jade said. "She'd look up all sorts of stuff on vampires, and she and two other good friends decided to save my life by staking Lucian."

"They failed, obviously."

"But he talked to them, and they're trying to solve this whole thing through careful study and research. And Renate does have an interesting legend to relate about a cat goddess and the locket—it seems Sophia has to be burned."

"That's probably much easier said than done," Maggie told her. "And then there is the whole thing about . . . vampires are not to destroy vampires. Hurt them, maim them, put them away for centuries, but . . . Well, we'll have to figure it all out. It will be night soon. Why don't you go ahead and shower and change and we'll go in and see your stepmother."

"I should wait for Lucian—and Rick."

"Lucian will find us."

"All right," Jade said. She hesitated, studying Maggie.

"Maggie, you do admire him, don't you? And you think that he can—that he can make this right?"

Maggie paused, answering her slowly. "Make it right? Lucian . . . yes, Lucian has an incredible inner power. He rose to become a power with which anyone must reckon. And yet . . ."

"What?"

"Lucian taught me a great deal. But not everything. Long before Sean, I was in love with a young Frenchman. He made me a vampire, believing that the commitment could set us both free. He was killed. My father killed him, seeking to save me. I don't think that Lucian really believed such a force could work—until Sean and I came together. Lucian is cynical and hard. Will he beat Sophia in the end? Yes. I think so. Unless he somehow falters."

"Because of me?"

"I didn't say that."

"You were thinking it."

"At the moment he needs to remain very hard and cynical—and maintain the power to best Sophia. Yes, I admire him. He attracted me when I hated him. He became a good friend when I needed his power the most. That's all you need to know."

It wasn't all that she needed to know, but it was all that Maggie intended to say.

An hour later Sean took her into the hospital. Her father was beside himself, terrified that whatever disease had taken Rick was now going to take Liz. Liz, on the other hand, was doing very well. She told Jade how sorry she was about Rick, and how horrified that his body had been stolen. "I know how badly this must hurt you, Jade," Liz told her. "And I'm not going to try to tell you it will just be okay. You already know what it's like to lose someone you love. It will hurt for a long, long time. But we're here for you. We love you." She flashed a smile to Maggie, who stood behind Jade. "Like you all were here for me and the twins. I'm so grateful."

"They're thinking about discharging her from the hospital!" Peter said, dismayed, runing his fingers through his hair.

"That's great!" Shanna said.

"What if—" He broke off, not wanting to speak in front of his wife.

"Your father is worried. Rick Beaudreaux was doing so much better—then he died. Your father is afraid that will happen with me."

"You should't be alone, of course," Maggie said. "And it's difficult to recover with little ones roaming about the house . . . I know. You should let them discharge you, and you should come out and stay with Sean and me."

"Oh, we couldn't!" Liz protested.

"Seriously, you should. My housekeeper is incredible. She's there with the kids now, and they adore her. And the girls will stay on a while, too."

"Maggie, can I talk to you in the hall for just a minute?" Jade inquired.

"Sure."

They stepped out into the hall.

"Maggie, this is crazy! If you bring my dad and Liz out to your place, they'll eventually realize that . . . that Lucian is . . ."

"Lucian hasn't been coming to the house," Maggie said. "I've made it really uncomfortable there for his kind."

"But—" Jade broke off, spinning around. There was a man she had never seen before standing guard in front of Liz's room. He was even taller than Lucian, maybe six-foot-four. His eyes were powder blue, his shoulders were bigger than those of a linebacker, and he had white-blond hair that streaked down his shoulders. He was wearing a polo shirt and jeans, and still . . .

She turned back to Maggie. "Who is that?"

"Ragnor. He's an old friend of Lucian's. A very old friend."

Jade turned around and stared at the man. She tried not to gape. He smiled suddenly. He had a slow, easy, confident smile. "It's all right," he assured her. "I will not chew you up into little pieces. Nor take one big hunk out of your throat, for that matter."

She smiled weakly. "Thanks."

"No one will get to your mother," he promised.

She smiled again. She didn't correct him and tell him that Liz was her stepmother. "Thank you very much."

He was studying her still.

"You are a lot like her," he said softly.

"Like who?"

"Igrainia."

"But I'm not—"

He lifted a hand, impatient with her denial. "No one will get to your family."

She thanked him again, then looked at Maggie. "Where is Lucian?"

"I don't know. We're to meet in the chapel at midnight."

Time seemed to crawl, but it was finally midnight, and she went to the chapel. Sean was there, and Jack. She, Maggie, and Shanna joined them.

She looked at Sean.

"Where's Lucian?"

"Jade, he's gone back to Scotland. He thinks he knows where the locket is. He intends to get it."

"But having the locket won't help him! He has to see that Sophia is somehow burned!" Jade exploded. "I don't believe you! He couldn't have just left! Left . . . me! Without saying anything, anything at all—"

"Jade, you were rather angry with him last night," Jack commented.

"But . . . but . . ." She spun on Jack. "That's just it. Rick . . . Did you all lie to me? Where's Rick?"

"With Lucian."

"That's not funny!" Jade cried.

"It wasn't meant to be," Sean told her, smoothing back his hair impatiently. He looked to his wife for help.

Maggie shrugged.

"Jade, you told him you wanted him out of your life. It was his fault Rick was dead. And he is worried about you and your family. He knows you'll be safe from Sophia and Darian, because as soon as they realize he's gone and what he's doing, they'll go after him. And . . . you're to stay with us. You and your family. Ragnor can watch over Liz where Jack failed because he was human. It was the best way for Lucian to do things, Jade."

She stared at Sean, feeling helpless, furious, impotent— and afraid and ashamed. She couldn't let Lucian go alone. She had to be with him.

"I'm going to Scotland," she said.

"Jade, that's ridiculous," Maggie told her.

"You're not going," Sean said firmly.

She lowered her head. *Fine.* She wasn't going to argue with them. She'd just agree with them—and then do it on her own. If they knew what she was up to, they'd have good old Ragnor guarding the door and she'd be nowhere.

"All right." She let the tears she was feeling well into her eyes. "All right. We'll all go to your place, Maggie. My family will be safe with you."

She left them in the chapel.

She walked out into the hallway, and they let her go.

She left them with her shoulders slumped, her head bowed. As soon as she was out of their line of vision, she started running down the hall to the pay phones.

Within a few minutes she was booked to London on British Airways, and then onward to Edinburgh.

Chapter Eighteen

Jade's phone rang. Matt reached over and picked it up without thinking. "Hello?"

"Hello?"

"Hello?" he repeated.

"Who's this?"

"Who's this?" he demanded.

"You tell me? Who's this on Jade MacGregor's phone?"

Matt stared at the phone, remembering where he was. "It's Matt Durante. Now who is this?"

"It's Jenny."

"Jenny?" he said blankly.

"Jenny Dansen, your writing friend. Remember me, slice of life, Erma Bombeck for the new millennium?"

"Oh, Jenny, what's up?" he said with a sigh.

"You tell me. What are you doing at Jade's?"

"Long story. Um, Rick got sick—"

"And died and disappeared, so I read. I hope Renate

wasn't guilty of murder, desperate to get a feasible plot line."

"Jenny!"

"Well, that's why I called. The woman is acting so weird. I called her to ask her if she knew anything about a memorial, or how Jade was doing, and a man answered her phone. And then he hung up, and I called back, and she denied that anyone else had ever answered the phone."

"Maybe you dialed the wrong number."

"Maybe—but I didn't."

"How do you know?"

"My phone keeps track of the number that was dialed. It spits out a report every so many calls. I definitely called the right number."

"Well, then, she's seeing some guy, and she doesn't want us to know."

"She's seeing some guy, and she may not want to be seeing him. Go check on her, Matt, please. She's just down the hall, since you are at Jade's. Why *are* you still there? Where is Jade? Why hasn't she come home?"

"She's with some friends, she's doing very well, and we're just here because—"

"We're? Who is we?"

"Danny is with me."

"Why does she need both of you in her apartment?"

"We're just here in case she needs us, Jenny. Oh, and by the way, I'm fine, thanks for asking."

Jenny sniffed. "I'm fine, too. I had a flat tire last night, and Bonnie broke her third toe. The dry cleaner lost my mother's best lace tablecloth, and a migraine is setting in. Thanks for asking."

"Bye, Jenny. I'll go check on Renate."

Danny was in the kitchen, starting coffee.

"Jenny seems to think that some guy is holding Renate

hostage.'' Matt told him. ''If Renate got lucky with some guy, she is not going to appreciate it when we barge in.''

''But I guess we should go,'' Danny said.

They walked down the hall to Renate's, tapping on the door. She didn't answer. ''Renate?'' Danny pounded then. He stared at Matt. ''Renate!''

Matt started to pound on the door.

It was flung open.

Renate was there. Her hair was smoothed back, she had just showered, and she was in a terry robe, brushing her hair. ''What?'' she demanded sharply.

''We were worried about you,'' Danny said.

''Oh, now you're worried about me,'' she snapped. She yawned. ''I'm just really, really tired. I need some more sleep.''

''Renate,'' Matt commented, looking into her elegant apartment. ''Your iron is on, flat on that shirt—and it's burning. Big-time.''

He strode past her into the aparment, quickly pulling the plug on the iron. He tried to lift it from the shirt. They were fused together.

The entire ironing board moved. ''Renate, you're going to burn yourself down here!''

''Well, thank you, thank you,'' she said, walking over to Matt. ''Now I'll thank you to get out. Out! I'm tired. And you call that meddling busybody Jenny Dansen and tell her to mind her own business!''

She put a hand on Matt's chest and pushed him out of the room. Danny had followed in behind him. She turned and gave him an evil glare. ''I'm going, I'm going!'' he said.

They were out in the hall.

The door slammed. ''Well,'' Matt said.

''Something is up, bad,'' Danny said.

''Why? How do you know?''

"I went and read what she was doing on her computer."

"What was she doing?"

"Checking airline schedules."

He looked at Matt. "Jade is on a flight for Scotland leaving out of New Orleans and connecting through Shannon, Ireland, in less than two hours."

Jade made it out of the house easily; she had gotten up, showered, dressed, and bothered with nothing more than a jacket and her handbag. Luckily she carried her passport, and it was in good order. She checked in for her flight, then bought coffee.

And waited.

She was insane. She was going off to find a man in a cemetery where she had almost been killed a year ago.

No.

She was going off to meet a vampire in a cemetery where she had almost been killed a year ago. But she had to find him. It seemed incredibly important that he know what there was to know about the strange cat goddess so evil that they had tried to delete her from history.

She glanced at her watch, anxious to board.

Then, before they gave the call, she bit into her lip with dismay.

She'd been found. Maggie, Shanna, Sean, Jack, and all three little boys were heading toward her from across the airport.

She stood up. Before they had even reached her she started talking. "Look, I'm going. Please, please, don't try to stop me. I'll scream. I'll pitch such a fit you won't be able to believe it. Even if you're police officers—"

"Jade," Maggie said. "It's all right."

"It's all right?"

"We realize we can't stop you. We'd like to stop you, though," Sean said.

"But maybe we shouldn't," Maggie said softly.

"I don't understand."

Jack grinned suddenly. "You've got company. Shanna and I are coming with you."

"No, no. Shanna isn't coming—"

"You can't stop me either, Jade. And Jack and I have tickets."

"How did you know what plane to get the tickets for?" she asked suspiciously.

"Danny and Matt," Shanna supplied.

"How did they know?"

"Renate had been tinkering with her computer," Shanna said. "They saw that she had somehow drawn up your flight information."

"But I'm still confused. It doesn't make any sense—"

"Renate is good with that thing. And apparently she was upset with Danny and Matt, and didn't want to share information with them anymore. They had gone over because Jenny had called her and gotten a wrong number. She's certain she did call Renate, but some guy answered. Or maybe Renate is trying to keep her dates a secret, I don't know."

Over the loudspeaker, the flight number was called.

"Shanna, you shouldn't come with me. And Jack, you don't have to do this either. Aren't you going to be missing some kind of therapy for having illusions in the hospital?"

"I'm on paid leave until they find the missing body," Jack said.

"Um. Didn't they tell you not to leave town?"

"If they did, I wasn't listening. Look, Maggie and Sean are staying here. Your folks will be with them. Ragnor will be keeping an eye on things here. Matt and Danny called us, insisting that we not let you go alone. We've talked this all out. I mean, what are you going to do, walk around a cemetery alone?"

"I was hoping not to be alone too long. I have to find Lucian."

"Well, it will be far better for you to look for him with eyes on each side of you, right? And now that I know what I'm up against, I'll bet I can wield a pretty good stake."

"The situation is not open for discussion," Sean said.

"And they're calling the flight," Maggie reminded them.

Jade suddenly stooped down to her baby brothers, who, with Brent Canady, had been amazingly well behaved for toddlers as they stood there, listening to the grown-ups talk. "Hey, you two little short stuffs. Give Shanna and me big hugs. And go home and be good little munchkins, because your mom isn't well. And Maggie is sweet, but there are three of you now, okay?"

Petey looked at her solemnly, put his arms around her neck, and hugged her tightly. She passed him on to Shanna, then hugged Jamie tightly. Then she hugged everyone else. It was time to head for the plane.

They waved.

Maggie was holding Brent. Sean Canady had picked up the twins.

They had just come past the flight attendant taking tickets and started down the runway to the plane when Jade heard Jamie crying. "He's going to be so upset," she told Shanna. "He loves me, but he loves you best."

"No, he's pointing at something . . . someone," Shanna said.

Jamie suddenly shrieked so loudly that they could hear him across the room. "Cable man, cable man, cable man . . ."

He couldn't say his *bl*s that clearly, and it sounded like he was crying 'cave' man. "Cable man?" Jade said to Shanna.

Shanna shrugged. "Remember? The cable man came when Liz got sick. Oh! I know that guy over there! It's that Dave I told you I had met. He pops up everywhere."

"It's a public airport," Jade said, distracted, watching Jamie. He had buried his head against Sean. Sean lifted a hand to assure them that Jamie was going to be okay.

"Girls, it will fly away without us," Jack said.

Jade turned and quickly walked toward the plane, wondering why she felt so disturbed.

"Jesus!" Danny cried. He was at Maggie's computer, and had been pulling the same illegal strings to get into the airline's records that he had used earlier to check out what he had seen on Renate's screen. He had broken in.

Yes, Jack and Shanna had managed to get tickets on the same plane.

But someone else was on it as well.

"What is it?" Matt demanded.

"Renate—that's what she was doing, trying to follow Jade."

"That idiot. She's going to get herself killed."

"She'll stick with the others, I'm sure."

Matt sat down, letting out a long sigh. "This is murder, isn't it? Sitting here, waiting. Wondering. We can't open the door to anyone; we have to be so damned careful . . . and just sit vigil."

"Yeah," Danny said thoughtfully. "Sitting vigil—over what? Jade is gone, Renate is gone, Shanna is gone. And Rick is . . . well, we really don't know too much about Rick yet, do we? But anyway, he's gone, and . . ." He stared at Matt. "We're here."

Matt stared back at him.

They leaped to their feet at the same time.

* * *

In Edinburgh, Lucian and Rick checked into the Balmoral. Lucian left word at the desk that they weren't to be disturbed. He was charming when he talked to the woman at the desk, explaining they were suffering from jet lag.

He'd managed to get Rick out of Louisiana with no difficulty, having logged on to a Louisiana state government computer long enough to give him a new name—Richard Miller. There were thousands upon thousands of Millers in the States, and tracking all the numbers and information he'd filled in for Rick would be next to impossible. He now had a legal identity not his own, but pieced together from various places.

Rick looked around as he checked in.

"Fine hotel," he told Lucian. "Great city. Are we dining on rats—or chambermaids?"

When Lucian gave him a glare, Rick grinned. "Just kidding. Though I admit to feeling more like Renfield than Dracula earlier. There was a fly buzzing around that was making me ravenous."

"We'll find a butcher shop later, and I assure you, once we trek out of the city for the old cemetery, you'll find plenty of rodents. Squirrels are plentiful in the area as well."

"Shouldn't we be heading out to this cemetery now?" He stumbled walking along the corridor. He was still nearly worthless in the light. "I guess not," he admitted before Lucian could answer.

"I don't really like having you with me at all—you're too green, no offense. But I was afraid to leave you in New Orleans."

Rick smiled at him, hands on hips. "I'd never hurt her. Never in a thousand years."

"Yeah, well," Lucian murmured. "There are times when you don't intend to cause harm. And you start to feel blood, feel the heat, the pulse . . . the hunger."

"I keep telling you, I'm going to be all right."

"You're going to have to be all right—and strong as hell. Sophia made you. She'll have power over you."

"She doesn't have power over you."

"She did. Once."

They reached their rooms. They were adjoining, a slender hall attaching them. He was pleased to see that Rick had remembered his native earth, though Lucian had seen to it to bring along Louisiana soil as well, just in case Rick hadn't understood.

But Rick had. For a new member of the society of the undead, he was taking things rather well.

"Get some rest," he told Rick. "You'll need it."

Jade, Jack, and Shanna landed in Shannon at dusk; their plane to Edinburgh came in well after dark. At the Balmoral, Jade was disappointed to discover that no one named Lucian DeVeau had checked into the hotel.

"What made you think he'd be here?" Shanna asked her softly.

"I don't know. I guess . . . he knew that it's where I stayed."

"Maybe he's not in a hotel at all, Jade," Jack suggested.

"Maybe not, but . . . he should be at a hotel, some distance from the graveyard, but close to the city to reach it easily. And he has Rick with him."

"Jade, there was no guarantee that we'd find him," Jack told her.

"Yes, well, I can find the cemetery."

"Yes, well, we're waiting for morning."

"Lucian will go by night," she told him anxiously.

"Jade! Are you so anxious to die? Let us prepare for what's going to happen." He took her by the shoulder, looking into her eyes with firm patience. "He left quickly, determined to get away before Sophia knew he was gone. He's accomplished that."

"Yes, but he doesn't understand about Sophia and the locket."

"He doesn't understand what Renate found out about Sophia and the locket. Maybe that's wrong, maybe—"

"Jack's right, Jade. We need to get some sleep; then we need to gather our weapons. The shops on the Royal Mile are still open for a while, right?" Shanna said.

"I think so."

"Brooms," Jack said. "Lots of brooms. We'll slice the ends into nice sharp points."

"We need a sword from somewhere," Shanna commented. "They have to be beheaded, Jade, remember."

Jade groaned. "Oh, we're going to look just like your everyday tourists, walking through the streets with spiked brooms and a sword. Think a taxi will stop for us?"

"We'll manage."

"We still need to find Lucian."

"Jade, he'll probably find you."

The phone rang suddenly. Jade sprang for it, hope high in her heart. It was Maggie, checking to see that they had gotten there okay, assuring them that Jamie was fine, and telling her that Sean was going for her stepmother first thing in the morning. "Oh, and Matt called. He wanted to know if you had tied up with Renate yet?"

"Tied up with her? No. She's here?"

"According to the flight records, she was on your plane."

"She never even looked for us!"

"Who, what?" Shanna demanded.

"Renate was on our plane—she bought a ticket for it, anyway."

"Wow. The airlines must have been happy. Man, we all spent big bucks, booking so late!" Jack said, shaking his head.

"Maybe she missed the plane and took a later flight," Jade told Maggie. "We never saw her."

"Well, keep an eye out. Matt is certain she's going to think she's the queen of mystery and get herself into some real trouble."

"We'll watch for her, Maggie. You haven't heard from Lucian, have you?"

"No, I'm sorry. I'll let you go now, but keep in touch."

"Thanks, Maggie. Thanks so much."

"Stay safe."

Maggie rang off. "Isn't that weird?" Jade said. "If Renate was on the flight—"

"She had to have missed it. I mean, it was a big plane, and it was pretty full."

"Knowing Renate, she might have been in first class, and maybe she wants to prove something herself before finding us," Jack suggested.

"Well, I hope we see her soon. This has got me worried," Jade said.

"I'm going to shave," Jack said. "Then we'll head out. Shopping."

"Jack, will you and Shanna do the shopping without me? I want to wait here in case Renate is trying to find us, or in case . . ."

"Lucian tries to find you," Shanna finished.

"I guess it will be all right," Jack said. "As long as you don't open the door. To anyone. No room service, nothing, Jade."

"No room service," she promised.

* * *

Rick Beaudreaux had his first lesson in the power of the mind that night.

"It's in what you see with your mind's eye," Lucian told him. "Think it, and you will be it."

"Think it, and you will be it."

"Move with the power of air and mist, and you *are* the power of air and mist."

"Think it, and you do it," Rick said.

"Walk on water," Lucian murmured. Rick was staring at him. "The first time I saw Sophia, I thought she could walk on water. She wasn't walking at all. I only learned that later."

"When you learned to walk on water?"

"Something like that. Tonight we need to move as one with the darkness."

"Is Sophia here? Could you feel it if she were?"

"She isn't in the cemetery yet. But it's open for a party. Tomorrow night is Halloween."

"Halloween," Rick said. He started to laugh, and the sound was finally just a little bit bitter. "Halloween. Well, trick-or-treat on me."

"I'm sorry."

"I intend to help you beat her."

Lucian was still. "She isn't here, but she knows we are. And she can move quickly. Tonight will be our only chance to search the tomb unhindered."

"What about Darian?"

Lucian was quiet again for a minute. Still. Dead still.

"Close. So we have to move fast. Think about the beauty and the grace of the darkness. Move with the mist, with the shadow. Disregard gates and fences and iron doors. So close your eyes. See a new backdrop. Feel the wind, hear the air, listen to every pulse around you. The whisper of the leaves around us, ants moving in the earth. The flutter of bird's wing. Feel yourself. The power of your muscles, the agility of your body. Feel the earth with your feet, and run. . . ."

They had purchased a dozen broomsticks, which hadn't been all that hard.

The shops were geared toward Halloween. Broomsticks were popular objects at Halloween. Witches were common at costume parties.

Jack had even found a decent sword at an antique dealer. They'd managed to get into the Catholic church—a miracle, since the doors had been closed. A priest had come along who sympathized with their story that since they were Catholics in a basically Protestant country, they would dearly love just a few moments to pray.

Shanna had asked the priest questions about Catholicism today, keeping his attention while Jack filled empty little liquor bottles from the plane with holy water. She also persuaded him to sell her several blessed crosses from the small tourist store in the church, despite the fact that it, too, was closed.

When they got back to the hotel, they called upstairs. Jade was in bed, watching the news. She sounded despondent.

She'd yet to hear from Lucian.

They ordered drinks at the bar. Shanna hadn't realized how much she liked Jack until she had spent all those hours on the plane with him. He was handsome, very Irish-looking, and he wasn't afraid—or if he was afraid, he forged foward despite his fear. She liked that. He was dependable.

And he liked her. . . .

She was glad that he was going to be right down that narrow little hallway between the two rooms tonight. She was afraid. And she'd been uneasy ever since they'd left home. Jamie crying out in the airport had unsettled her.

Shanna ran her fingers around the edge of her wineglass, thinking it would be nice to be here under different circumstances—there was a fire roaring in the hearth, the wine was good, the company very pleasant. But thinking about Jack made her think about the other guy she had met—the one at the coffee shop who had reappeared at the hospital.

And then again at the airport.

"What?" Jack said.

"I was just thinking, I guess. About people—about timing in life."

"To people. And timing," Jack said. He had settled for a nonalcoholic beer, and he lifted it to her.

She smiled. "It's so nice here. I was just thinking . . ."

Timing.

The cable man.

Jamie had dreamed about the cable man. She had dreamed about Dave. Jamie had been crying at the airport. She had seen Dave.

Rick had died at the hospital.

She had seen Dave there.

"Jack."

"What?"

"What did he look like?"

"Who?"

"The guy who came after you when Sophia was tearing into Rick. Was he tall?"

"Tall, lean, but muscular. Reddish-brown hair, good features—I didn't have a lot of time to study him."

"Reddish-brown, longish hair?" she inquired.

"Yeah, it was longish."

"He's here."

"What?"

"Darian is here. Somewhere. Somehow. I . . . I met him. I met him at a coffee shop in New Orleans. I made a date with him, but he didn't show. It was the night all those people were killed in Massachusetts. But then I saw him at the hospital." She hesitated, deciding against mentioning the dream.

He had tried to come into Maggie's house. Somehow, by the grace of God, she'd managed not to let him.

But he was here now!

She stood up. "Jack, he's here. We've got to get to Jade. Fast."

Jade had stared at the news without seeing it for a very long time.

She was exhausted, but couldn't sleep. She stared at the phone now and then. *Lucian, where are you? Where are you?*

When the knock came at the door, she nearly leaped out of her skin. She jumped from the bed and rushed toward it, then stopped dead. Would Lucian knock? Would he need to? No, she had invited him in long ago.

"Yes?"

She peeked through the peephole.

Renate was standing just outside her door.

"Renate!" She threw the door open.

"Yes, it's me. Aren't you going to ask me in?"

"Of course. Come in! What are you doing over here? I paid attention to everything you said; I intend to relay it all to Lucian. It's dangerous, what you're doing—"

She broke off because someone standing behind Renate pushed her on into the room. "Invite me in," he said harshly to her.

"Come in," Renate said mechanically, her eyes never leaving Jade's.

Jade backed away, wondering what possible weapon she

had on hand as she watched the man who entered behind Renate.

"Darian." It was the tour guide from last year.

He smiled. "So you know me now, Miss MacGregor. And look at the way you're looking at me! As if I were Satan himself." He smiled. His voice was light, the accent smooth and cultured. His features remained appealing, though he appeared somewhat pockmarked at the moment. Injured.

"What have you done to Renate?" Jade demanded.

"Not half of what I'm going to do to you," he told her. "You were the best. Definitely the best. I knew it from the moment I saw you with that group of kids at Edinburgh Castle. And you were so intrigued with everything. You really loved history, and Scotland. You were so ready to learn, eager to talk to people, eager to embrace the world. I watched your hair in the light. Watched your eyes, watched you smile. Sophia, of course, was the one who saw the resemblance to Igrainia."

"I'm not Igrainia," she said.

"Who knows? That cop sure is—was—a lot like Wulfgar."

"What cop? And who is Wulfgar?"

"Ah! There go your eyes, darting to the clock! Playing ignorant, stalling for time, hoping for help? Help can't come fast enough. Lucian's a fool. He should have taken your blood right away and given you this gift. But then, that's the pity. There's good old Lucian, king of the vampires, a monster with a conscience, refusing to *damn* people, as he sees it. Well, I just see the grave. Dust to dust. Ashes to ashes. There are the powerful, such as we—and the cattle. Such as you, dear. Although you are finest filet. There's hunger, and there's lust, and you've inspired both."

He started walking toward her, and she threw a pillow at him.

Naturally he laughed.

It fell to the floor, causing no harm. *Obviously,* she mocked herself. He kept coming. Renate stood inside the room, seeming to see neither of them.

"Renate, help me! Do something!" Jade shouted. Darian had almost reached her. She leaped up on the bed, bolting to the other side.

"Run!" he told her, his smile this time betraying the length of his fangs. "Run. I just love it when humans run. It makes the heart beat more strongly. The blood rushes with passion through your veins."

She grabbed a vial of shampoo from the counter and aimed it at him.

"Get away. It's holy water. And I know what it can do."

He came to a halt. "Get it from her, Renate."

Renate came at Jade, grabbed for her arm, and slugged her hard, hitting her first in the jaw, then in the stomach. Jade doubled over before responding, amazed. Then she straightened, still in pain. She struck back, catching Renate's jaw.

Hard.

Renate crumpled and staggered back.

But not before the vial of shampoo had gone flying. It crashed on the floor. Darian jumped back, fearing the touch of the liquid.

But then he saw the thickness of the solution spilling onto the floor, and he shook his head, grinning ruefully, as if she'd played a marvelously good joke on him.

"Jade, Jade, Jade! You've nothing at hand. Nothing at all. Lucian, the great protector, is off chasing windmills! And your companions have deserted you on their quest to find weapons—leaving you empty-handed. All alone. Waiting. Ripe."

"Lucian is here, you know," she bluffed. "He won't let you do this."

"Lucian can't keep up with Sophia and me, my dear. Go ahead, run. Get that blood pumping. And while you run, tell me more about Lucian. About the way he's suddenly going to rescue you."

"He knows that I'm here."

"No. I don't think so."

"You're wrong."

"No, I'm not. You'd better run, Jade. Run. Because I'm coming. Now. I've been waiting, but ah, will you look? The wait is over. Here we are, you and me . . . together at last." He licked his lips. Smiled.

His fangs glittered in the light.

She did run. She tore down the length of the hallway between the two rooms. She raced to the door, ready to streak out into the hall.

He caught her before she could open the door, spinning her around, slamming her against it. He touched her cheek. "You are a gem, you know. Something to be wanted, coveted. I loved your questions that night. I loved the way you tried to be so courteous and so polite, and yet I loved the way your eyes would roll when they would do something just incredibly stupid or rude. . . . You're quite entrancing. I can see the hold you've had on Lucian all these years. . . ."

"I haven't had a hold on Lucian for years. You're not going to wage war with him again on that account. I'm not Igrainia."

She felt the power of his weight. He was leaning against her at the door. She was held prisoner there. He brought his hand to her face again. She flinched; he smiled, rubbing his knuckles along the length of her jaw. "You know, you liked me the night of the tour."

"That was before I realized you chewed up college students," she said.

"College students. I wanted the little boy—the blood of children can be so very sweet. But thanks to old Lucian, the woman took the kids home early. Kids have the best blood." His eyes widened as he taunted her. "College students are a poor substitute. The girl was all right, though. I had intended to take my time with her. Lucian rather ruined that."

"Doesn't it bother Sophia that you go after victims in such a . . ."

"*Predatory* manner? Or sensual manner?" he mocked. "We are creatures of . . . shall I say . . . flesh and blood? Ah, Sophia and I are not jealous of one another. If so . . . well, her obsession with Lucian would have destroyed me long, long ago. Now there's a rather sad case. She wants him almost as much as she wants to destroy him. And she will in the end. She has the talisman."

He placed his hand on her chest. "Feel your heart!"

"Get your bloody hands off me!"

She shoved his hand away, pushed him, and stepped past him. Startled, and then amused, he let her go.

"You haven't tried screaming."

"I will," she promised. "I'll scream and bring every cop in Edinburgh down on you."

"No, you won't."

She didn't blink; she barely saw him move. But he was right in front of her again. Touching her. "It's time," he said.

"No!"

His fingers were in her hair; he had her head wrenched aside to aim his fangs directly into her jugular vein.

She could feel her own heart.

She could feel her blood, hot, causing her vein to throb.

She could feel his fangs, the heat, the saliva, his touch. . . .

Chapter Nineteen

Suddenly she heard the sound of shattering glass.

The window had broken. Sweet, Jesus, yes, it was real. The glass had suddenly, violently shattered, and now it seemed to rain down in shimmering slow motion.

They were on the third floor.

A wolf, huge and silver, came hurtling through the glass. It landed on Darian with a thunderous force that ripped the vampire away from Jade and sent him flying against the far wall. Darian crashed hard against it. Then he rose, racing with the wolf at his heels, back down the narrow hallway.

Jade ran down the hallway between the rooms.

The wolf was gone.

Lucian stood in the center of the room, challenging Darian. But Darian had gone for the limp body of Renate, dragging her to her feet, using her as a shield.

"She's . . . she let him in!" Jade cried in warning. "She's . . ."

"Not dead yet, not his creature yet," Lucian said, keeping his eyes hard on Darian. "And if he harms her further . . ."

Lucian started walking toward him, his eyes a black pit of fire, his jaw dead set.

"Lucian, keep your distance, and I'll leave you the woman," Darian said. Lucian ignored him, striding forward. But before Lucian could reach him, the door from the hall burst open. Lucian was momentarily distracted.

Renate fell to the floor.

Darian dissolved into mist.

Jack and Shanna came hurtling in, each carrying a broom with a hastily fashioned point, and a vial of water.

"Jade!" Shanna called out, running for her sister. She dropped her broom and threw her arms around her.

Jack Delaney stared at Lucian. "We didn't know where you were."

"I know," Lucian said. "I didn't think you fools would come to Scotland. You would have been safe back in the States. Sophia had to follow me here, and she knew she couldn't combat me alone. You would have been safe!"

"We came to help you!" Jade called out angrily. She was shaking. And her mind was still refusing to believe what her eyes kept seeing.

"You should have been smarter; you shouldn't have come!" he insisted.

"Jade," Shanna said, but Jade stepped around her sister.

"No. You needed us. Because you don't know everything! Power isn't always everything; Renate was right—knowledge is strength!" She brought her hands up in fists to pound against his chest. Her hands fell flat upon his chest, and he enveloped her into his arms.

She felt a beating, beating, beating. . . .

Her heart? His? Did he have a heart that could beat so?

Did it matter? The pulse and fever she felt seemed a part of them both.

"I heard you calling me," he said very softly. "I barely came in time."

Lucian was shaking.

"He got away," Shanna said. "Jade! I was so stupid, and so lucky. Darian is Dave, the fellow I met at the coffee shop. Jade, I could have wound up like . . ."

"Me?"

They all turned. Rick was standing in the doorway. There was grass in his hair, Jade noted. She broke from Lucian, running to Rick, hugging him fiercely. "Rick, I'm so, so sorry. You can't begin to imagine—"

"Jade," he said kindly. He held her away from him. "Some things, maybe, are destiny."

"Oh, Rick—"

"It's okay."

"It's not okay. You're really . . ."

"Dead?" he whispered. "It's not a four-letter word— oh, yes, I guess it is. People, we need to think fast for the moment."

"I beg your pardon?" Lucian said, scowling.

"Excuse me, but I still know law enforcement and the 'protect and serve' routine. Security is coming up—the broken window."

"What do we do?" Shanna asked.

"Play innocent!" Jade said quickly. "It just suddenly shattered. We figured something had to have been thrown into the room, but we can't find it."

"When did Renate get here?" Jack asked. "And why is she out cold?"

"Put her into the bed. I'll explain later. And Rick, Lucian—"

"We'll be in the bar," Rick said quickly. He grinned. "I can have a Bloody Mary, right, Lucian?"

Lucian groaned. "Get out, Rick."

"We'll meet you down there," Jack told him.

The two exited just in time. Two security officers with great, broad accents arrived. Jade showed them the window. She said she couldn't find what had done it. She was thankful they seemed merely perplexed—and apologetic. It was obvious that the window had been broken from the outside in—the way it had shattered was proof. They would need a new room for the night, so that the window could be fixed.

That didn't sound like a bad idea. They changed rooms, Jack carrying Renate and explaining how she was very, very tired from jet lag. Luckily she moaned, almost opened her eyes and smiled vaguely, and made them look legitimate.

"We're due downstairs," Jack said, when they were settled.

"What about Renate?" Shanna asked.

"Nobody's going to threaten her. She's really out."

"I guess she'll be okay for a few minutes, but . . ."

"We won't leave her long," Jack said.

When they made it down to the bar, it was amazing to see how well Rick looked. Amazing that his sense of humor seemed the same. Amazing that his eyes could remain so kind when he looked at her. He squeezed her fingers briefly as they sat across the table. "Thanks!" he said softly.

"Thanks? I involved you with . . ."

"It's a new direction for me, that's for certain." He smiled at her again, then turned to Lucian. "Is Renate all right?" he asked.

Lucian was quiet a minute. "I believe she'll be fine tonight. There's no reason for him to come back for Renate. She's served Darian's purpose."

"Which was?"

"To get Jade," Lucian said.

Jade sat between him and Rick at their bar table, watching both. Strange, it was as if they had been best friends forever, instead of forced companions for less than forty-eight hours.

"Bloody Mary?" Rick asked her.

"Rick—"

"I'm sorry. Really. Want wine?"

"A beer tonight, thanks."

"Seriously, why are you here, Jade?" Lucian demanded when the waiter had left. "I left strict orders that you were to stay—"

"You can't leave *orders* for me, Lucian, I'm not your subject."

He inhaled patiently. "Jade, it was foolish and dangerous for you to come. I had Ragnor there watching out for you, knowing that Sophia and Darian would have to follow me to protect the talisman."

"But you don't understand, Lucian. Renate looked up the talisman and there's a whole long history to the creature on it. It's the symbol of a cat goddess that received human—*blood*—sacrifices. The goddess was so terrible that her images were all destroyed; she was wiped away, no matter what the cost, what the labor. She was supposedly burned, but the talisman has her ashes, and it won't do any good to simply take the talisman from Sophia. Sophia must be burned."

He watched her as she spoke, and when she finished he looked down at his drink. Whiskey, she thought. Good Scottish whiskey.

He looked up at her again. "You came here to make sure I was aware of that."

"Well, of course. I said that. Knowledge. It can work miracles."

"Thank you."

"My pleasure."

"You shouldn't have, though. You really shouldn't have."

"But she did," Jack said. "And we're all here. And—"

"Tomorrow. Tomorrow, we'll go back to the cemetery."

"Did you look for Sophia and the talisman tonight?" Jack asked.

"We started to. Something called us back," he said, looking at Jade. "Someone."

"So you might have found the talisman if it hadn't been for me," she said.

"I didn't say that."

"You meant that."

"It wouldn't have mattered that much if I found the talisman. It still belongs to Sophia, right? According to what you're telling me."

"That's the information Renate found on the Internet."

"So we start tomorrow," he said softly, his eyes on hers.

He suddenly tossed a key across the table to Jack. "We've a double on two. Jade and I will take one of your rooms."

"That leaves me . . . that means I get . . . Renate?" Shanna said.

"Do you think she's safe?" Jade murmured, worried about her sister.

"Renate is safe. She hasn't turned, and she isn't in Darian's power. He left her—deserted her. Besides, we'll be in the next room. Tomorrow we'll have to figure out if we have to keep her with us for her safety, or if she'll be just too great a danger to have with us. For tonight we'll have a room with Renate and Shanna just down the hall, and Jack will be down the hall from Rick, and we should all be close enough if there were to be any . . . happenings. Tomorrow . . . ," he said softly, his voice trailing.

"Tomorrow. It is tomorrow, has been tomorrow," Shanna murmured.

"Halloween," Lucian said dryly. He lifted his glass. "Cheers, everyone."

They lifted their glasses grimly. "People will be out everywhere by nightfall," Jack said glumly.

"Children," Shanna added.

"Pranksters," Lucian murmured. "All Hallow's Eve. It's natural that tricksters will be out as well. Along with those who mean much worse harm."

He drained his drink. "Happy Halloween. One hell of a night. We'll need to be prepared for it, really prepared. It's late. My human friends, frayed by jet lag already—you need some sleep."

He left a note of Scottish pounds on the table and turned away. Jade looked at her sister and shrugged. "He has just a bit of a problem with this arrogance thing," she murmured.

Lucian had turned back. "Coming?" he inquired.

They all trailed after him.

In the room, Renate remained asleep on the bed. She was pale, but her breathing was even.

"She isn't going to turn into a monster in the middle of the night and bite my neck off?" Shanna asked in a worried whisper.

Lucian, studying her, shook his head. "She's tainted, like Rick was tainted. But he has not entered into her veins badly enough to bring about death. There are two ways to feed—one is to chomp down, drain the body, kill the victim, rip him to pieces."

"Charming," Shanna said. "And the other?"

"Steal a little blood every night. Enter the body and soul of the victim. Hypnotize, seduce, control. That was his plan with Renate. Now he's lost interest."

"Great," Shanna said.

"He's abandoned her. I think she'll be all right." He

looked at Shanna. "Are you all right? We could get another room, but I'd rather have you near."

"Oh, I'm just thrilled to pieces here," Shanna said.

"Shanna," Jade began worriedly.

"I'm all right. Seriously."

Lucian smiled at her. Jade thought her sister smiled back. She knew her sister's thought processes. *Go for it, guys; tonight might be the last night for any of us. . . .*

Shanna yawned. "Well, guys, good night."

Lucian kissed Shanna's cheek. She kept her head lowered, hiding her grin as he took Jade's hand, traversed the hall, and entered the second room.

He didn't say anything to her. Nothing at all.

With his knuckle, he lifted her chin.

He kissed her lips.

His eyes met hers. He undid the buttons on her sweater. His fingers slid around her nape and her collarbone, sliding the garment from her shoulders. His lips molded themselves to the flesh there. She felt the sweet burning. A sound escaped her; her arms were around his neck, and she was kissing him, holding him, tearing at the cashmere of his sweater, the tailored cotton of the shirt he wore beneath it. The bedclothes wound up on the floor, entangled with their own.

Her limbs were twined with his on the bed.

She craved the liquid fire of his kiss, his lips, so searing upon her flesh. She felt the power of his muscles, playing beneath her fingertips, moving so rhythmically against her. He rose in the night, his eyes on hers, an ebony blaze that burned into body and soul. Sleek, taut, the wolf in the night, the fierce protector, the force of the wind, rather than the predator of the darkness.

He is both, she tried to tell herself.

But it made no difference. She longed to make love, ached to make love. She burned for the feel of his nakedness against her, the slick pressure and friction of his flesh, the *feel* of him touching her, the sheer burn of him inside her, a fire that imploded and exploded, burned within her, and burned within the night. . . .

"You fool," he said, at one point, looking down at her with his coal eyes unfathomable. "You shouldn't have come. Why did you come? Why did you come?" And he held her close, not seeking an answer, but she gave him one anyway.

"Because I love you," she said simply.

His arms tightened around her. She felt the deep heat and erotic tension of his lips against her flesh.

"Lucian?"

"Hm?"

"Maggie says that . . . there's a way. If you love me, too, if you take my blood, drain me, to a point of death . . . the chemistry can combine, the stars can collide . . . something can happen that can . . . that can . . ."

He'd gone still. Dead still. He lay beside her then. "Something that can make me human again?" he inquired bitterly.

"Yes," she said softly.

He rolled, his fingers sliding against hers as he brought his weight atop her, his body and eyes pinioning her in the night. "And if she's wrong? If the chemistry, the stars, the feeling . . . the *heart* just isn't there enough . . . What if I'm incapable of giving enough . . . What if you're damned, and no more?"

She felt the power of his strength. His hold was almost painful. She didn't know if he meant it to be so or not. She didn't flinch. "I am willing to risk it."

He smiled slowly, then shook his head. "I cannot. I have been far too long damned, far too long a creature of the night. I know that you are suddenly the world, that I ache to be with you, long to be with you at all times, but is that love enough? I know that I would not do this to you, even to have you with me. And there is more. I can't fall from what I am now; I can't fail against my enemies. To let them loose upon the world with no restraints, no power strong enough to stop them, to allay them ... the world has changed. I am still what I am, and still with the mock title, king of my kind, with the only strength to stop Sophia and Darian."

She touched his face. "I would do anything for you."

He arched a brow. "You know me now. You don't know the man I've been in ages past. Or the creature, as it may be."

"I am supposedly so like Igrainia—"

"But you have no vision of a past, no memories, no flashes of a life gone by."

"No. I am Jade, and no one else. But Lucian, I do love you!" she whispered softly, stroking his face, suddenly hungry for something far beyond the moment. A life. Together.

He caught her hand. "I have told you. I will not risk your life, or your death."

"Then what have we?" she whispered.

"The night," he told her.

"And it's all you'll offer me?"

"It's all I can promise you."

"It isn't enough."

"Then—"

"It will do!" she whispered, angry, hurt, loath to want him so badly, when he offered her so very little. And yet she understood.

And maybe he knew that when his ebony eyes touched her.

He made love to her until they were both sated, exhausted.

Then he held her, his chin atop her head, his body

wrapped to hers. She felt her exhaustion, and knew he lay awake. He would leave her, she thought.

"You're going," she whispered.

"I need a different kind of peace," he told her. "When darkness falls again . . . we'll all need to be ready." He swung on her suddenly. "I will come tomorrow, before the darkness. Stay safe, stay ready. I will be back wtih you. You understand, Jade?"

"I'll be fine. They'll need to rest and be ready as well."

He was silent.

"You could take me with you," she reminded him.

His arms tightened. He did not accept her suggestion. She held him, almost trying not to sleep. She was not so much afraid of losing her life as she was afraid of losing him.

Shanna let out a shriek that could wake the dead.

Jade jumped out of bed, disoriented, spinning around. She started to run to Shanna's room, then turned back for Lucian.

But Lucian was gone.

Already. But she had known that he would leave; he had told her as much.

She wrenched the covers from the bed to wrap around her chilled and naked flesh and went flying down the hall.

Shanna was up, standing by her bed in an Eeyore night-shirt. She looked as if she were all right. Jade's eyes flew to the bed where Renate had been sleeping.

Renate was still soundly sleeping.

"Shanna?"

Shanna flushed. "I was dreaming."

"Dreams are dangerous. What were you dreaming?"

"I dreamed that Renate came awake and attacked me

with huge fangs. They were so big, she looked like a walrus."

"Should we check her out?" Jade asked in a whisper.

"Maybe we should get Lucian."

"Maybe we should, but we can't. He's gone."

"Gone?"

"You know Lucian."

Shanna walked steadfastly to Renate's side. Gingerly she touched Renate's lip, opening her mouth to bare her teeth.

She let out a long, soft, sigh.

Renate suddenly swung up. "What are you doing to me?"

"Just checking," Shanna said. "Just checking."

Renate looked around, frowning, disoriented. "Where the hell am I?"

"Scotland," Shanna told her.

"Scotland!"

"Good God, Renate, you crossed the Atlantic. You don't remember coming here?"

She shook her head. "I think I remember a . . ."

"Yes?" Shanna pressed.

"Nothing," Renate said with disgust. "Nothing but a delivery man. What is going on?" she implored Jade. "Why does my jaw hurt so badly?"

"Jade hit you," Shanna supplied cheerfully.

"Sorry," Jade murmured, staring at her sister.

"It's okay. You were trying to kill her," Shanna added quickly.

"Oh!" Renate cried, and suddenly touched her neck in panic. "Oh . . . am I all right?"

"We hope so," Shanna said. "At least as much as usual."

"Could you please explain?" Renate said imperiously.

The sisters looked at one another. "Long story," Shanna murmured. "I guess we're up for the day."

"Yeah. I guess so. I'll order coffee," Jade said.

"You might as well," her sister told her, pointing toward the window. "It's actually daylight."

She started for the phone and then stopped. "No room service," she told Shanna.

"I could really use some coffee," Shanna muttered. "Have you noticed how we never seem to be able to get any sleep around here?"

"I'll hop in the shower and go down for some," Jade volunteered.

"Where's Lucian?" Shanna asked.

"I don't know," Jade admitted. "Somewhere. To rest. Prepare."

She walked back into her bedroom and realized that this time, at least, he hadn't just left her. There was a note on her pillow.

Oddly enough, that note touched her deeply. She had nothing tangible of him, or from him. And now a note. His handwriting was large, sweeping.

It's an arrogant hand! she thought, but with no bitterness. In his world, arrogance had meant survival often enough.

He wrote: *Preparing for the evening; sun seems very bright today. I, your inhuman friend, need rest as well, as I told you. Stick together, carry holy water, wait for me. I'll be back in the light; we'll strike before dark. Once again, stick together. Take care of yourself. For me.*

He didn't sign his name; there was no "Love, Lucian" to finish off the note.

It didn't matter. It was enough. It had to be. It was all he intended to give.

Take care of yourself. For me.

She showered, meaning to be very quick. But as she stood there, light and water bearing down upon her, she was suddenly afraid.

The cemetery . . . she could so vividly remember the cemetery.

Old, with broken-down stones, rusting fences, barren trees with skeletal fingers. That had been the innocence of the place.

Then there had been the tomb.

Creatures rising from spiderwebs and shrouds . . .

And she was back here.

She had lost her mind.

She dressed in the warm, ankle-length knit skirt she had brought along and a soft black sweater. The temperature was cool outside, and the outfit was warm and would blend with the darkness this evening.

Night fell early now. Very early. Around four.

"Jade?" It was Shanna calling her. The room she shared with Renate was darkened again. So much for being awake.

"Yeah, it's me," she said. "I'm going down for the coffee."

"Do you think you should?"

"The hotel is a busy place, and it's broad daylight," Jade said.

"Come right back," Shanna murmured sleepily.

"Will do," Jade said. She left the room and started down the stairs.

She had been right. The hotel was bustling. The restaurant was a hotbed of activity. The place had really packed in just that morning, she learned from a waitress. "Halloween, you know," she'd told Jade.

The girl told her it would be a few minutes before they had more coffee brewed. Jade said it was all right; she'd just go down the street.

"That's a good idea; it's bright and beautiful out today. A perfect day."

"The sun is strong?"

"Unbelievably—for an autumn day in Edinburgh!"

"Good."

Jade stepped outside. When she closed her eyes she

heard the normal tenor of conversation, marked with the charming accent of the Scots. The sky above was touched with gray, and yet it seemed very light. She loved Edinburgh, even in the chill of autumn. And yes—the sun, for Edinburgh, was very bright.

Time for all evil vampires to be locked away in the earth.

The brisk air was refreshing. She loved the city, loved looking toward the castle and down the street.

A lone piper played a lament as shoppers and businessmen hurried along. The wail of the pipes seemed very charming. It felt good to be in the fresh air, to feel the sun, the heat of the light.

The innocence.

The *normalcy* of a bright, shining day.

She started for the contemporary mall down on the left side of the street. It was there that the piper played. His lament was eerily compelling.

A small, mobile stage, like a gypsy stage, had been set up on the concrete entrance in front of the modern formation of shops. A woman in an old hag's costume was hawking the show, walking about, enticing people to come before the stage. The people themselves were a show. Some workers walking the streets were in costumes, and half costumes. Cat whiskers and tails adorned some people in the crowd; costumed children in everything from Mickey Mouse to Frankenstein apparel were already roaming the streets.

"Come see, come see the show!" the old witch woman called, beckoning children around her. A man from behind the counter joined her. He was decked out like the cat from Puss N' Boots, Jade thought, and she found herself pausing to watch them.

He joked and teased with the witch. The witch hit him on the head with a pretend loaf of bread. He called for volunteers from the audience, and one little girl hit the witch on the head for him. There was a lot of laughter. The crowd pushed forward. She didn't know that she was part of it.

Then the cat was skipping around, and she watched, laughing. Volunteers! He needed more. A beautiful princess, with gold and red hair, sunset hair, to flow around her, and there would have to be a prince, of course. Or maybe a frog. Because everyone knew of course, that a princess had to kiss a lot of frogs to find a prince.

She was laughing when the cat-man came up to her with the loaf of bread. He caught her eyes, staring right at her.

And then, too late, she recognized the man. She saw the eyes behind the mask.

She opened her mouth to scream; she turned to run.

The bread came down upon her head. Except that it was no longer bread. It struck hard and she was falling. . . .

Volunteers, volunteers, volunteers. How hadn't she seen . . . ?

She fell into the cat-man's arms. He and the witch swept her backstage.

They finished the show with the children all laughing, thinking she was part of it all. Because when the princess kissed the frog, the story went, unfortunately, the frog didn't turn into a prince.

The princess turned into a frog.

The children laughed.

It was autumn.

Night came early.

It wouldn't be long before darkness would fall. . . .

Chapter Twenty

The sky was gray. The air was cool.

Lucian felt the rush of the wind around him, embracing him. He felt the truth of the image, and he came to the Isle of the Dead alone.

It was less populated now than it had been all those years ago. Lone farmhouses dotted the craggy landscape, and the sea still swept around the isle. The only way to reach the island was by ferry. A new church had been built over the remains of the old one by the sea, near the place where the old fisherman's cottage with the fantastic carvings still remained, dilapidated and in ruins. Historians came sometimes, and students. The population on the isle was too small to create a booming tourist trade, and those who lived and worked in the wilds of the rugged hills and cairns of the windswept isle were fond of the privacy.

He came there and sat by her grave, and remembered an earlier time. A time so long ago, when he had been naive in a way he couldn't even begin to imagine now. So much time gone by. So many years when he had been vicious and bitter. So many years of learning. And still, so much anguish, and so many times when he felt cursed and damned, and desperate to kill, to butcher, slaughter, tear into human veins and quench the thirst that burned in him, no matter how far he thought he had come, how civilized he might think himself . . .

There had been the wars for independence in Scotland. A time to kill and glut, and never be known, with enemies so brutal themselves that his deeds were not noted. Medieval Europe. Ah, and there a playground, with the righteous burning the innocent—again, a time when enemies were clearly seen, when it seemed his judgment was no less merciful than that of "goodly" men.

There had been his days in France. Many of them. A time of revolution—when a vampire was assuredly in as great a danger as any mortal man. A time of great risk. Wars, more wars, and a new age, a new time. To think back, to come here . . . so long ago. And yet, in all, this was the past strongest in his memory.

He hadn't really come there. Not in the flesh. He dared not use that kind of energy, that much of his desperately needed strength.

Physically, rather, he had come to Saint Giles, and found an old entrance below, to a cache of buried dead from the early sixteen hundreds. He wondered if the corpses were even known in the church records. They were from a time of trememdous cruelty, when witches and heretics were burned in Scotland, when the powerful had the right of life or death over the weak—a time, indeed, when the cruel appetites of a monster were often no greater than those of the goodly men who ruled on earth. Rick slept near him; his travel was in his mind, in his sleep. Lucian did not shape-shift as he traveled now; he saw. With his mind's eye. Saw the past, saw her grave. He grieved as if it were yesterday.

And he was ready to move into the future. Should there be one.

Suddenly his dream was broken. Black shadows, like the huge wings of a giant bat, fell over his vision.

Darian stood before him, a shadow of twilight, even in the darkness of his sleep.

I have her, Lucian. I have her again.

Worms seemed to gnaw at his flesh. The earth groaned.

I will kill you, destroy you, totally, utterly!

You think yourself so strong. You think that you are the lord of us all, that you govern the undead. You thought yourself safe today. Ah, the sun! To carry out our . . . dinner plans for the evening. Of course, you can change it all. Come to Sophia. Maybe we'll let her go. Give yourself up; bow down to her again. She is your creator. Give her back the power. And perhaps we'll let your mortal lover go.

The air shifted; a flapping of wings sounded.

Lucian's eyes flew open; he bolted up.

Rick did so, too. Unaccustomed to his position, Rick cracked his head hard against the church flooring above.

Far above him, a tourist shivered, certain that Saint Giles was indeed haunted.

"They have Jade," Lucian said.

Shanna had fallen asleep. Deeply.

She felt someone shaking her shoulder.

"Stop, stop, will you please stop!" She moaned. "I am finally getting some sleep."

"Shanna, where's Jade?" It was Jack; he was standing over her, his face tense.

"It's all right," Shanna said, yawning. "She just went for coffee."

"When?"

"I don't know. I don't think it was that early. Maybe around eleven . . . ?"

"Shanna, it's three o'clock. Nearly dark."

"Oh, my God!" Shanna leaped out of bed, horrified. "She didn't come back then. We've got to go find her. Oh, my God, Jack, surely they had to rest! Sophia and Darian must have needed some rest. The sun was bright. . . . They would have known we were coming tonight. They would have needed to heal. They would have needed strength. . . ."

"Apparently they are preparing," Renate said from the other bed. "They're preparing to meet Lucian. They set out to get Jade because they know that he'll come after her. What better preparation to bring Lucian down? It's a trap. For him."

She awoke to sounds. *Halloween,* she thought. But it wasn't little children she was hearing, and those who were shrieking and talking seemed to be doing so at a distance.

She smelled earth, dank and fetid. She felt a very cold hardness beneath her.

It was dark, but when she opened her eyes, she could see enough. The tomb was lit by burning torches secured along the way by ancient iron brackets.

She tried to shift. She could not. There was a scraping sound, a clanking . . . and she was shackled to . . .

Her blood ran as cold as the stone slab to which they had secured her. She had been here before. She was deep in the tomb, incredibly deep in the tomb where she had been just a year ago, when she had watched Darian tear four young people to ribbons in a horrendous blood-bath. . . .

She ached; the cold had seeped into her. Her head hurt,

her throat hurt, her body hurt. She tried to wrench her wrist free from what seemed to be a centuries-old shackle.

She turned toward the skeletal face of a long-dead knight. The empty eye sockets glared at her. Some type of worm crawled out of one. She opened her mouth to shriek with horror. . . .

Somehow she closed her eyes and swallowed the scream. He wasn't that horrible. He was almost all bones. Fragments rested by the sword with which he had been buried. She wasn't going to scream. Not yet. She had to take care. Get her bearings.

Free her hands.

They might be near. Sophia and Darian. They might be just waiting for her to wake up.

Then . . .

She heard Darian's voice.

"So you want to be scared, eh? Really, really scared? Keep coming, my friends. Keep coming. Deep, deep, deep down into the bowels of earth, into hell; do come, my friends, and I will do my very best to scare you."

She lay upon the outer rim of the burial shelves, next to the old knight. Corpses lay above her and below her. Coffins were also laid about the tomb. Sophia's coffin was as it had been before. It was open. Sophia was there, sleeping, resting, drawing strength.

And Darian was now leading a crew of Halloween partiers down. Down, indeed, to the bowels of the earth.

Jade inhaled, and spiderwebs teased her mouth. She breathed the scent of death. She hadn't been slain as yet, she knew, because tonight she was meant to be even more of the show than she had been before. Her heart was thundering wickedly. Surely Darian could hear the beat. Even in her coffin, Sophia must hear the frantic pulse.

It was dark in the tomb, but not dark enough. The

ghostly torches cast their bloodred sheen over everything in the chamber of the dead.

"Come, come, my pretty!"

Jade slitted her eyes open, twisting toward the coming group. Darian was leading a girl dressed in a harem outfit. The girl giggled. Her escort was wearing a Freddy Kreuger costume, looking fierce.

"Yes, scare us, Scotty, old boy. Go on. We're waiting."

"You fools!" Jade shrieked suddenly, no longer trying to keep silent. She couldn't bear to think of another slaughter; they had to be warned. She worked her wrists furiously, trying to swing out from the burial shelf. "Get out of here. Go on, tough guy, Jesus! Didn't you idiots read about what happened here before—"

"Ah, the undead! There she rises. Igrainia, they called her. Wife of the ancient chieftain, Lucian. She was not of this world herself. Mermaid, some men called her. Fish, others said. Alas, the beauty departed this world, and whatever she might have been, she became—dead!"

The kids started laughing. There were more of them behind the harem girl and the Freddy. "Get back, Igrainia! Get back for now! We're waiting for your lover, the mighty chieftain. Alas, he hasn't come. So . . . you'll watch Sophia at work one more time—and then it is your turn. Fear not, my pretty Igrainia. You are always most coveted."

Darian's hands were on her as he forced her back next to the dead knight. He smiled, meeting her panicked eyes. His grip was as powerful as pure steel. He touched her, and she could do nothing.

He slowly licked the length of her face. "Delicious!" he said softly. "Absolutely delicious."

"Lucian will destroy you," she promised, furious, desperate—and totally impotent against him.

"He'd best hurry. I'm quite disappointed. I thought he'd be here by now."

Darian licked his lips, then ran his tongue along her flesh again. . . .

"There is the question, my beauty. My friends! Will her avenging angel come quickly enough? Only time will tell!"

Jack walked determinedly in the lead. The girls followed on either side.

They carried their stakes at the ready. They all had vials of holy water tied at belts they had fashioned for the occasion.

"Cool! It's Buffy the Vampire Slayer and friends!" someone shouted in a thick low-country accent.

"Why, 'Arry, look at those bloody blokes! You are Buffy and crew, right on? Americans, at that! That's what you are, right?"

They were traveling the streets, walking by a pub. These particular happy Halloweeners were well into their beers. One witch wore a hat askew. A fake vampire had spinach between his fangs. An angel wore a halo that was far more than bent.

"Something like that!" Shanna called, and they hurried on. Jack was walking fast. Shanna had to run to keep up with him. They turned a corner around a shop into an alley.

"Jack!" she called out. "Are you sure you know where . . . we're going?" she finished lamely.

Yes, he had known where they were going. They were there.

An old church rose before her, cast in the moonlight, Gothic, spooky. There had been kids running around the cemetery. Some were just disappearing around the church, into the trees. A police car was just driving away. Had the cops come to make sure that no merrymakers met the same fate as before? Wild kids, intent on daring play, were escaping before the police could call their parents.

They arrived just as the car was disappearing.

And just as the other creatures among the living slipped away.

And there, in the silence, stillness, and darkness of the night, was the graveyard. Tombs and stones rising here, there, and everywhere. The moon shining down. Angels seeming to move, to pray with greater desperation. The wind rose, whispered, seemed to howl a low, banshee note.

"We're here," Jack whispered.

"Why hasn't Lucian shown up?" Shanna asked, very afraid.

"God knows what they've done to him. Or your sister. It's up to us to find them. To get them back. Somehow. If we can."

"Lord, Jack, what do you think he's done? Has he simply ripped out her throat to anger Lucian? Will I find her . . . decapitated?"

Jack stopped to reassure her. "Look, if Lucian hasn't appeared anywhere, it's because he knows that if he just gives himself over to them, they'll kill him and then Jade as well."

"But I thought they couldn't just kill him?"

"Sophia doesn't feel she has to follow rules. She has the talisman."

"Where's the tomb?" Shanna asked.

Renate suddenly pointed. "It's that one straight ahead. De Brus."

Renate started forward. Jack looked at Shanna worriedly. "Maybe we're . . . doing just what they want us to do. Coming here. Maybe Darian has more power than we ever suspected."

"We have to find your sister. Keep your stake ready to strike. You can't falter. Use that holy water."

"Maybe we should get help, call the police."

They both gave her a stare. "Shanna," Jack said gently, "the police would just lock us up for being crackpots, and you know it."

Shanna tripped over a tree root. She steadied herself on the stone of a tomb. A night owl shrieked.

Clouds drifted over the moon. The cemetery was darker than ever. Renate had run ahead of them. They followed.

They reached the de Brus tomb.

A mist seemed to emanate from it.

A red mist. Illuminated by a strange glow of crimson light deep from the bowels of the earth.

Or the bowels of hell.

The iron gate gaped open.

In the strange, shadowed moonlight, it seemed to beckon.

Jade winced with pain. She was cramped, cold, her bones aching. Her tongue felt like sandpaper. She felt . . .

Wounded.

A sharpness . . .

A weakness.

Darian kept smiling at Jade. "I've enjoyed every slightest touch. So tempting. But tonight Sophia awakes, and we seize the moment together.

"Hey, me beauty!" he called to the harem girl. "Come over here. I'll scare you. I promise—I'll scare you."

The girl was coming closer and closer. Jade wrenched very hard on her wrist. To her amazement, the ancient shackle cracked open. She reached for the old knight's sword.

"No, no, no, my lady!" Darian cried. He slipped his arm around her, pulling her out with such force that she wondered which would snap first—her other wrist, or the shackle.

The shackle broke. She was thrown down. She landed hard against a coffin.

Sophia's coffin.

The kids were laughing and shrieking. Darian was stroking the harem girl. Jade was dazed, and still aching from what they had done to her. "Don't you understand!" she cried desperately, trying to rise. "This is real. They're real. . . ."

"She's good; she's really good!" the boy in the Freddy Krueger costume said. "Better than you, buddy."

Behind the Freddy were a candy striper, a guy dressed up as a nurse with big boobs and very red lips, and two monks. There was also a Grim Reaper.

"Go, get out of here!" she cried.

"They'll never leave here alive. Not unless Lucian wants to show himself," Darian said. He came at her, catching a handful of her hair before she could begin to move away. "Call him. Call to him now. Tell him you're about to die. I will not taste and sample and savor your blood—I'll savage your veins until every last drop of your blood is gone— and your head is severed from your shoulders. Do it! Call him. Tell him you're dying now."

He practically had her hair ripped from her scalp. She gritted her teeth against the pain, but stared up at Darian. "Call him—so that you can destroy him and then us?"

He tightened his grip on her hair. "Do it! You can die slowly as well."

"Jade!"

She was amazed to hear her name called. One of the monks threw back his cowl. To her absolute astonishment, she saw that it was Matt Durante. From beneath his brown wool garment, he pulled out a long stake.

"Matt, no, what are you doing here?"

"She's behind you! Sophia is behind you," Matt called. "Get up. You've got to get away from Darian, and come to us. Quickly!"

Get away from Darian? They couldn't begin to imagine the power of his hands.

Jade twisted beneath Darian's merciless hold.

Matt was right: Sophia had opened her eyes, and now sat up.

Dark, exotic, as astonishingly beautiful as ever, she rose, smiling at Jade. "This time you're mine!" she said softly. She looked with amusement at the others in the tomb. "Darian, how droll. The silly fellow thinks she can just get away from you. I think I'll just kill her. Now."

"No!" Matt made a flying leap across the room with his stake.

He didn't make it.

Darian caught him with one hand, plucked the stake from him, and snapped it between his fingers.

The second monk let out a cry, racing forward. It ws Danny, Jade realized with sinking horror. Of course. Danny would have never let Matt come alone on such a mission.

But Danny fared no better than Matt. Darian simply lifted his hand, striking Danny with such force that he screamed with pain and was slammed back against the dank stone walls. Sophia stepped gracefully out of her coffin and walked toward Jade.

Jade scrambled up, gripping her hair to try to prevent some of the pain as Darian dragged her to her feet to face Sophia.

He no longer held her.

But she wasn't free.

Now she was trapped.

Darian remained behind her. Sophia was before her.

It was then that she saw Jack Delaney hurrying, stumbling, into the tomb. He was followed by her sister and Renate. He waved a vial of holy water in front of him.

"Let her go. Now. Or I splash it all over your face. Your head. If your whole head evaporates, you're dead, right?"

Darian turned to smile at him.

"I dare you—test it out, big boy!" Darian taunted.

Jack threw the holy water.

Nothing happened. Nothing at all.

"But—" Jack said.

"It's water, Jackie boy. Just water," Darian said. "Renate, my sweet. How good you were, how very, very good. How well you served me. Come to me, now, though. I need to twist your head from your body. I might have taken just a bit too much blood from you, and I'm not sure I like you enough for all eternity!"

Renate started walking toward him.

"No!" Shanna shrieked, pushing past Darian. "Get away from him, Renate; he's going to kill you. Stop her, Jack."

"Do you think Jack can stop her?" Sophia asked.

"I'll damned well stop her!" Jade cried. But Sophia snaked out an arm, reaching for her hair. She jerked it, dragging Jade back to her. She wrenched her hair so that her head was forced to a painful angle. "Now, now, now!" Sophia raged, but she still made no move. She started forward, dragging Jade with her, looking toward the entrance of the tomb.

"Call him. Call Lucian!" she commanded, pressing Jade forward to her knees. "You are dead, you wretched selkie, you are dead!" she said in a hiss. "I killed you once, and I will kill you again!"

It was then that the Grim Reaper, who had stood at the back of the crowd, came to full life. He was suddenly there, behind Sophia, and pulling her from Jade. Sophia, caught off guard, was swiftly seized by Lucian; she felt his grip of steel around her throat, and began to scream.

"Move, Jade, quickly, away from Darian!" he commanded.

Darian sprang into action and reached for Jade, ready to take over, but another corpse suddenly rolled from one of the slabs, pulling the linen that had shrouded him from his body. It was Rick. He came after Darian and they began to fight, fists lashing out, feet flying. It was a deadly, sickening fight. Lucian had Sophia in a fierce grip then; her arm was twisted behind her; she was forced to her knees in the middle of the room.

"A stake!" Jade cried. "I'll throw you a stake."

"He can't kill me!" Sophia cried with triumph. "The rules—"

"The rules are about to change," Lucian said. "You wanted to twist them; so shall we! *I* am the king of our kind, Sophia. Time and temperance have made me so. I will change the rules, as I so desire. You are a threat to all our kind. Even among our peers, Sophia, there must now be a kind of justice."

Jade was crawling for one of the broken stakes that lay on the hard earthen floor. Sophia struggled with Lucian's grip and began to chant—strange words that sounded like a keening on the wind, strange words like none Jade had ever heard before.

And suddenly other corpses began spilling from tombs.

And it was the way it had been before, battles raging, the dead coming alive, the dead attacking the living. . . .

And at last, at long last, the girl in the harem outfit began to scream.

"Get out, get out!" Jack was shouting, trying to push the girl ahead of him. A corpse wound bony, decaying hands around Jack's throat. He struggled with the creature.

A corpse kicked the stake Jade nearly had in her grasp out of her way. She saw the sword her old knight had been holding.

His bony fingers were twitching, as if they were about to come to life.

She seized the sword and thrust the old warrior's skull from his bony frame.

Lucian had Sophia by her hair then. She was trying to let out her chants, but he was dragging her so quickly that she could barely make a noise. He was moving with a sense and purpose Jade couldn't fathom as yet.

Despite her talisman, he was in control. At the moment.

But Darian had taken Rick down and was standing over him, reaching for a knife sheathed at his calf. Lucian kept his iron grip on Sophia, but kicked Darian with an ungodly strength. Darian wailed, his fingers crushed. The knife was sent flying from his hands.

Darian was down on one hand and his knees, scrambling for the knife.

The sword was in Jade's hand. She swung. Hard.

The blade sank into Darian's neck. She hadn't hit hard enough. She cried out, desperate, and swung again. He let out a scream of fury, spinning on her. She struck again.

His head bounced from his shoulders.

Jade started screaming.

And screaming . . .

Darian was gone. Dead. Decaying, turning to dust . . .

Sophia let out a howl unlike anything Jade had ever heard. She rose, nearly escaping Lucian's fierce grip. He jerked her back. She let out a venomous spiel of chanting.

Suddenly all the corpses in the crypt were coming after Lucian. And Jade.

"Move!" Lucian commanded, looking at Jack. "Get the others, get them the hell out!"

Jack pushed Shanna; Shanna pushed the harem girl. Freddy Krueger was still standing there, blubbering. Matt caught hold of him, then raced to the wall, catching Danny, who was still stunned, his face bleeding. The corpses were spilling around them, and around them. . . .

"The torch!" Lucian cried. And then Jade saw what he had been doing all along: forcing Sophia and Darian *from* the entrance to the tomb, while prodding the others *toward* it.

She saw what he wanted: one of the torches. It burned from a notch in the wall. She bounded for it, grabbed it, and raced back to him, terrified as she thrust it into the leprous face of one of the dead called forth to fight.

It backed away.

She came to Lucian's side. He suddenly thrust Sophia from him, flinging her far against the wall and into the depths of the crypt. He grabbed Jade's hand, ready to run. "You can't!" Sophia raged. "You can't kill me, you'll be destroyed. They'll come and kill you, others of our kind—"

"It's a new time, Sophia," Lucian said. "A new justice."

"He won't kill you," Jade said. "I will."

"Jesus," Lucian yelled, "get out!" He pushed her ahead of him. "Now—throw the torch!"

"What if it goes out?"

"It won't go out. There's peat packed down here. It will burn. And burn. Throw it!"

She did as she was told.

The place instantly burst into flames.

Flames so close that they nearly burned her cheeks.

He turned her about. They ran.

As they climbed the levels back to the iron gate that led out of the tomb and into the night, they could hear her screaming. Screaming, screaming, and shrieking. The sound was terrible. It was a death rattle.

They burst into the night.

Jade came to a dead standstill. Jack was there, Shanna,

Renate, Matt, Danny, and the harem girl and Freddy Krueger.

The tomb was beginning to blaze behind them.

But before them . . .

There was a strange array of people. Pale, stalwart, silent, standing their ground. There were perhaps twenty, thirty, or more of them. They seemed to be different nationalities, ages, sexes. They were dressed differently.

They were undead, Jade thought with rising panic.

But when Lucian came before them, a tall, dark man who looked like a Spaniard stepped forward.

"It's over then?"

"It's over," Lucian said resolutely.

Another man stepped forward from the crowd. Tall and light, with strange, searing green eyes, he nodded at Lucian, then to the others.

"The king has not turned to dust, and the threat is destroyed."

Lucian looked from the one man to the Spaniard. "I have not been beaten," he said quietly. "I said that I would destroy my enemies—and yours."

She felt as if they were waiting. All waiting.

"It's over!" Lucian stated more determinedly.

The Spaniard nodded. "Aye," he said at last. He looked at Lucian again. "Aye, and you're right. There must be an order, and a justice, even among us."

He stepped back, still staring at them.

A mist began to rise, sweeping, swirling around the tombstones, over them, blanketing the people who stood before them. . . .

"It's over then, all over, really over," Shanna whispered, her voice pleading. "Isn't it, Lucian?"

"Yes," he said softly.

Jade's knees started to buckle. He caught her before she could fall. She tried to steady herself. They were once again standing over the tomb with *MacGregor* carved into it.

"Let's get the hell out of here," Lucian said. "The police are on their way. And I don't want to try to explain any of this."

"Good Lord, no, we can't begin to explain this!" Jack said.

Lucian supported Jade. She still felt as if she could barely stand.

Weak, so weak . . .

She pushed away from the MacGregor stone, and Lucian led her from the place of darkness, evil . . .

And death.

Naturally they talked forever.

They found a great pub with a fine private room in the rear that had a huge fireplace.

Renate really thought that she was all right. She apologized over and over again for emptying the holy water while Shanna and Jack slept. She hadn't known what she was doing.

Jade thanked Matt and Danny with all her heart for coming over. "You could have been killed. You nearly were!" she told them.

"All in a day's work," Matt said. "After all, what a story I've gotten out of all this!"

"No one will ever believe you, of course," Danny said. "My version, however, will be subtle, toned down. I know it will sell! I'll describe it from the point of view of a medical examiner."

"Listen!" Jack said suddenly.

The pub television had late-night news on. The big story

of the evening was the cemetery fire set by a gang of kids. They knew it had been set—they weren't sure yet how or when or even what kind of fuel had been used, but the tomb had been sabotaged with an inflammatory substance prior to the fire's being set.

They all stared at Lucian.

"I still haven't found the talisman. I think it's in the tomb, but . . ." He shrugged. "I knew she had to be burned, but they had Jade, so I had to play it very carefully. And then, suddenly, you were all in there."

"But she's gone now, right?" Shanna said.

"Yes, she's gone."

They were all so wound up, they couldn't sleep. It was very, very late, nearly daylight when they returned to the hotel.

They hugged and kissed as they said good night.

And then Jade was alone with Lucian.

"Will you be with me in the morning?" she asked.

"Tomorrow morning, yes," he said, and that had to be enough.

She didn't care.

"I would be with you anywhere, you know," she said very softly. "I'd sleep in the dirt with you, in a coffin, among the dead. You can seriously bite my neck anytime."

He kissed her gently.

"That's a very serious decision."

"The way I feel about you is very seriously love," she told him.

But he shook his head and told her ruefully, "The way I feel about you is very seriously love. So . . ."

"So?"

"We'll wait. There are things you have to know."

"Maybe there's a way out. I mean, Maggie was a vampire, until Sean . . ."

"I'm not sure, Jade, that I can give up what I am. Not now. Not until I'm certain. Jade, I never actually found the talisman. And I can keep a certain power and order and sanity. . . ."

"I love you."

He smiled. "Do you? Really? Can you really?"

"Yes." She studied his face. "I don't believe that I'm your Igrainia come back. I really don't, Lucian. I'm Jade. Do you really love me—Jade?"

He touched her cheek. "I love you—*Jade*."

She leaned her head against him. He stroked her hair.

"We have come through the fire."

Jade hesitated. She felt slightly . . . *different*.

She didn't know if it meant anything or not.

Sometime in the night, he would know. He would see the tiny puncture wounds in her throat, left by Darian when he touched her in the crypt.

In the morning Jade phoned home as soon as she woke up. She heard a female voice at the other end.

"Maggie?"

"Yes, Jade? I can hear you perfectly. Is everything all right?" Maggie asked anxiously.

Jade was still in bed. Lucian lay behind her. He wound his arms around her.

"Fine. I'm worried about you all there. My dad, Liz . . ."

"They're fine. Liz is doing very well."

"And the twins are there?"

"Yep. My Barney and Pokemon tapes are about worn out. Everything is fine here, really fine."

"Thank God. Thank God. Maggie, please, tell . . . Dad and Liz that we love them, and that we're fine. And tell Jamie for me . . ."

"Yeah?"

"Tell him we've gotten rid of the bad cable man."

Lucian's arms tightened around her. He took the receiver from her. "Hey, Maggie. Everything is really, really all right. The old cable guy is gone, the bogeyman is dead. We're all right. We'll see you soon." He was silent a minute. "And thanks, Maggie. Thanks for everything."

He hung up the phone.

And he looked at Jade. And his finger ran down her throat. His eyes were coals, shielded, so dark. "I'm sorry. So very sorry. I knew that if I showed myself as he wanted, he would have killed me, and then you. I—"

She put her fingers to his lips. "There was nothing you could have done. But . . . what does it mean? Am I just . . . tainted? Will I simply heal?"

"Probably. And maybe . . ."

"Yes?"

"I don't know."

"But . . . you'll be with me?"

He smiled slowly, and nodded.

He meant so much to her. Everything. So quickly he had become her world.

And she still didn't believe that she'd known him before, that she could be his long-dead Igrainia. He was simply everything to her now.

His lips touched her. Fire woke her spirit.

"I will be with you," he said. "Who knows? I hear they're having a shortage of policemen in New Orleans. It might be as good a place as any to work toward the future," he told her. And then he lifted her hand and kissed her fingers. "But for now . . . have I told you," he queried, "that I really do love Scotland, that it can be one of the most beautiful places in the world? Gorgeous, colorful . . . wild, rugged, a passionate land! When the wind blows, and the waves beat against the cliffs . . . it's like a heartbet. So sensual . . ."

She smiled and kissed him back.
She might not have loved him before.
But she loved him now.
And she would do so into eternity. . . .

Read on for a sneak preview of
the next Heather Graham novel,

DEEP MIDNIGHT,

coming in July 2013!

Available from Zebra Books.

The moon was full. Huge in the sky, a brilliant, iridescent orb that seemed to stare down mockingly at the earth.

Though his night vision was excellent, it helped him to see.

From the Campanile, he had chosen to survey the city. He looked out at the dazzle of the evening; at the people milling about, at the clear beauty of the dark sky far above, and he felt his tension and awareness increase.

Carnevale.

Venice.

The first true night of celebration. The first night of the grand balls . . .

Fat Tuesday.

The delirium of it all.

Tonight. They would strike tonight.

For far below, crowding the streets, alleyways, and canals, were all manner of masqueraders. Musicians, entertainers, stilt-walkers, rich and poor, all were out for a night of pretense, playacting, charades. The world here now was shadow, despite the lights that spilled forth in the city, despite the lanterns so many of the players carried.

Fat Tuesday . . .

The feast before Lent.

Yes, they would seek to feast tonight. And they would do so. Glut themselves . . .

Unless . . .

Silently, with the grace and skill of the natural born predator, he left his perch.

And entered the city.

Jordan Riley threw open the shutters at the window in her room at the Hotel Danieli, looking out at the loud and festive world around her. From her vantage point, she could see the waters of the Canale di San Marco, and down toward the Grand Canal; she could see the vaporettos, gondolas, and streams of people coming and going from the docks. Across the water was the magnificent dome of the church of Santa Maria della Salute. And, stretching her body out the open window, she could see, to her right, the beginnings of St. Mark's Square, the site of unbelievable revelry. The night was wild with the sounds of laugher and music, and everywhere there was camaraderie, joviality. The pre-Lent celebration might be well known and loved in other great cities as well, but Jordan didn't think that anyone else, anywhere, knew how to celebrate Carnevale quite the way the Venetians did.

No matter how strange, they were elegant as well.

"Jordan, ready?"

She turned around. Her cousin Jared was standing in her doorway, though, if she hadn't known it was Jared, she wouldn't have had the least idea that it was he. He'd come as the dottore, a popular costume here. Plagues had once consumed Venice, so the dottore wore a mask with a huge nose, usually beaked—reminiscent of the covering doctors had worn to combat the fetid vapors. The masks were elaborate, frightening. Jared wore a voluminous, hooded cloak as well; he hadn't been inclined to dress in anything as foppish as a Renaissance costume. The cloak and mask were easily donned; maybe that was why the costume was so popular.

"Ready? Yes! I can't wait. It's incredible out there!" She'd been to Venice several times before, but never for Carnevale. This year Jared and his wife, Cindy, had talked her into accompanying them to the festival. She felt a little awkward, being with the two of them but on her own at tonight's costume ball—unescorted. She felt just a bit like a fifth wheel. She spoke enough Italian to order room service and find her way around, but though it was true that many Venetians spoke English, she was afraid she'd find herself seated next to strangers with whom she couldn't begin to converse. Still, the excitement of the trip had outweighed the fear.

"Thank God! I thought you were going to try to weasel out tonight!" he told her.

"Me? Weasel out? Not on your life!" Of course, she was lying. She'd been thinking of doing exactly that until darkness had fallen, the music had begun, and the sheer vibrance of the evening had awakened a spirit of total devil-may-care adventure in her. Surely, there would be someone with whom she could talk, dance, and while away the hours.

"You're smashing, by the way," he told her.

She walked from the window and dipped a curtsy to him. "Thanks."

She'd rented her costume at the last minute, but it was spectacular. Renaissance—a popular era here—and festooned with sequins, faux jewels, and an overlay of lace. The gown had been available because Jordan happened to be petite—five three, standing very straight—and an even hundred pounds. The dress had been made for a young woman who'd had to cancel about a month ago, and no one the right size had arrived since.

"Smashing—and you look taller."

"It's the shoes," she told him, showing him the period shoes she wore. She wondered, however, if they'd really worn such wretched heels in times gone by. Surely, this kind of heel was a modern nod to women's vanity.

"Let's hope you don't shrink like Granny Jay. You'll be down to nothing."

"Go ahead. Be cruel because you got all the 'tall' genes," she told him. Strange. He was so tall; she was so petite. But they had both inherited very deep green eyes from their Granny Jay. That, and her penchant for new places, people, and cities such as Venice, with its truly unique character.

"Down to nothing," he repeated with a teasing sigh. She thought that he was grinning behind his mask. "Can you walk in those?"

"Um. I practice in heels a lot," she assured him. "It's the only way to see over counters, and manage to climb up on a bar stool, when necessary."

"Hey! You two, let's get going—it's late!"

Cindy, dressed in black Victorian mourning, came to the doorway. Like Jared, she was tall.

"Jordan! Great shoes. Maybe people won't think you're my child tonight!"

Jordan groaned. "Cindy! You're going to torture me, too?"

"Torture *you*. I'm only five years older—and people ask me if I'm the mother!" She shuddered.

"You're both smashing!" Jared said. "Two of the greatest beauties . . . there. That's said and done. Now, shall we go?"

A few minutes later, they passed through the centuries-old lobby of the gracious hotel. Even the bellmen carried masks, and everyone greeted everyone. It was a night for compliments, fun, and eternal smiles.

They left the hotel and came out on the walk before the canal. The pavement was thronged. People jostled people, and apologies were given in dozens of different languages. Jared, tall as he was, craned his neck to see over the people. Water taxis, vaporettos and gondolas all used the docks in front of the Danieli, and the place was simply packed.

"Girls, wait here just a minute. Our launch might be around the other side," Jared told them.

With a sweep of his cape, he walked away.

Jordan and Cindy moved toward the canal, away from the stream of pedestrian traffic, and waited while Jared went off to find the private launch which was to bring them to the ball. An annual event, the ball was always held in an historical palazzo, and was always one of the most prestigious events of the night. Jared's surname was Riley, just as Jordan's, but his mother had been a Genovese. Loving all things Italian, he had become the Venetian rep for a major American travel firm. He spent almost as much time in Italy now as he did in the States. His Italian was excellent.

Jordan wished hers was better. A man jostled her, paused, tipped his hat, and went into a long apology. Having no idea what he was saying, she smiled and nodded and told him, "Prego, prego!" Literally *I pray you* in English, it was, in Italian, a catchall for almost anything. He smiled, tipped his hat again, and went on.

"I'm going to have to keep a good eye on you all night!" Cindy told her. "That rat was trying to pick you up!"

"Cindy, that was mean. How do you know he was a rat?"

Cindy laughed, shaking back her long blond hair—very different tonight from its usual sleek cascade down her back, since she was wearing it in tight little ringlets. "He was dressed as a rat, Jordan, weren't you paying attention?"

"Oh!" Jordan murmured. "No, I saw the tail and the gray felt on his shoulders, but . . ."

"Rat," Cindy warned. "Renaissance rat, but a rat just the same. We'd best be careful. I imagine that there are a lot of rats out tonight. And wolves. And you look like prime bait."

"Girls!" Jared said, hurrying back over to them. "We've got to move down by St. Mark's Square—our fellow is way in back in the launch line, and he thinks he can get us easier ahead."

"Um, we need to move. The rats and wolves and basic slime-buckets are after Little Red, here."

"Little Red?" Jared demanded. This time, Jordan thought that he was frowning with confusion as he looked at her, but he was still wearing his mask, so she really couldn't tell. "Her hair is as black as pitch, what's little 'red' about her?"

"Never mind—he's no sense at all for fantasy," Cindy told Jordan, shaking her head with rueful affection. "We simply need to take care of your cousin, dear. She's far too delectable looking this evening."

"I guess," Jared murmured, and she knew he was staring at her. "Maybe you're right. Jordan, are those boobs all yours?"

"Jared, how rude!" Cindy protested.

Jordan laughed, her hands on her hips. "Yes, Jared, they are. How about you? What's behind that cod-piece?"

"Thank God we're in Italy and everyone on the street isn't understanding the two of you!" Cindy exclaimed. "Can we get going?"

They made their way through the crowd. Jordan was glad that Jared had such a firm hold on her arm; she could look around, stare, enjoy the sights and sounds.

The weather was crisp and cool, the city was wonderfully alive. Lights dazzled on the water, and each reflection caught in the shimmering canal was more beautiful, more colorful, and more fantastic.

Even the absurd was stunningly beautiful. The costumes ranged from elaborate period outfits, to fantasy, to animal. Birds strutted incredible plumage, cats were sleek and bejewelled. Newscasters from around the world interviewed people here and there; cameras whirred, music blared from the Square, voices and laughter rose above it all. They might celebrate in other places, Jordan thought again, but Venice was unique in its love of the sheer sophistication of dress-up; natives and visitors alike vied to be gorgeous.

Jared led them to the landings directly in front of St. Mark's Square. Jordan turned, feeling as if someone were watching her. She looked up. The Lion of Venice sat atop his high marble pillar, staring down at her. She looked around, at St. Mark's Basilica and the Doge's Palace. By night, shadows seemed to dance, as if they were real entities, hiding behind gargoyles, proud equine statues, and other fantasy creatures set upon splendid architecture by some of the greatest artists who had ever lived.

A church bell tolled in the evening.

A dozen church bells tolled. Jared gripped her arm, leading her over the dock to their vaporetto, and soon they were shooting through waters as heavily laden with revelers as the streets of the city.

Ah, there, ahead—our palace!''

She tried to remember everything she had heard about the event tonight. The ball was given by Nari Contessa della Trieste, a woman with a heredity as rich as that of the city itself. She was very wealthy, having married well—several times. Her first love, however, was the arts, and the Palazzo Trieste, far more of a palace than a castle, featuring the archways, architecture, stone and marble work of a building planned as a residence rather than a fortress from the very beginning. Beautiful, wrought iron gates allowed entry from the canals; there were elaborate, semicircular steps at the entry, where costumed footmen came to help the ladies and gentlemen from their conveyances.

Within the grand foyer, with its white marble staircase, they were greeted by their hostess. Of medium height and surely, a *medium* age, she was stunningly beautiful, dressed all in white, with huge white feathers sweeping the hem of her gown, an elaborate and very regal collar made of the same, and a mask of even longer feathers. She wielded her mask with experience, comfort and composure, nodding to the guests at her side, smiling, turning to greet the new arrivals. Jared, benvenuto! Cindy, ciao, bella!''

She drifted across the floor, greeting them with kisses on both cheeks. Then she took both of Jordan's hands, stretching away to survey her. "Oh, la, the cousin, Jared! Bella, bella, bella, cara mia! You speak Italian, a little? Poco, eh? Grazie, grazie, bella, for coming to my little soiree, eh? Grazie.''

"Grazieanche ei" Jordan told her. "Mille grazie.''

"You do speak Italian!''

"No," Jordan replied. "A very, very little, I'm afraid.''

"Ah, still, dance, be merry. Most here speak English, but then, sometimes it's much, much better when a man *cannot* be understood, eh?'' She grinned, expressive dark eyes sliding over Cindy and Jared. Jordan felt the strangest sensation of unease, wondering if their hostess weren't more familiar with her cousin than he had ever suggested. She quickly dismissed the thought; Jared and Cindy were very much in love, the perfect couple.

"The buffet is upstairs, the champagne is here!'' the contessa said, reaching out for glasses from a passing waiter. "And the dancing, the dancing is everywhere.''

As they moved on, Jared excused himself to her. "Jordan, I won't leave you alone for dinner, I promise. There are a few business associates I have to see . . .''

"He doesn't mind deserting me—just you," Cindy teased.

"You know people here."

"Does anyone really know people here?" Cindy queried, as they walked to the buffet table, looking around. The costumes here were even more brilliant than on the street—elegant and extravagant, costing thousands to tens of thousands of dollars, Jordan imagined. She began to feel underdressed in her sequins, faux jewels, and velvet. Too many women were wearing real gems. On one medieval gown, Jordan was certain she could see the sparkle of dozens of real emeralds.

"Jordan, sorry, that peacock with the chubby butt and big fan is Mrs. Meroni. I must say hi to her quickly. Come with me—"

"I'll wander," Jordan assured her. "Go talk."

"But—"

"I'll be fine."

"Watch out for the rats."

"If I go for any wolves, I'll make sure they're very wealthy," Jordan assured her.

"And young," Cindy advised. "Or else, old enough to keel off immediately and leave you filthy rich in your own right."

"I'll keep that in mind."

Cindy walked away from her.

He saw her walking idly to the buffet table.

She was small and perfect. A petite woman with dark, wavy hair curling over her shoulders, and drawn back from her forehead with a pair of slender braids in concession to the Renaissance style of the deep crimson gown she wore. Others might be more richly dressed; none wore a costume with such natural elegance.

As many here, she carried her mask, a silver and gold creation, on a wand. She pulled it away from her eyes, sipped her champagne, and studied a certain problem in regard to the buffet table—how to hold the drink, the mask and a tiny shrimp.

He left the balcony, and came down the stairs, studying her all the while. He joined her at the table, addressing her in Italian at first, but when her eyes immediately hit his with a certain confusion, he switched to English. "Good evening. Excuse me for being so impertinent—" he paused, lowering his voice—"I believe one is supposed to have an introduction here, but as you seemed to be in some difficulty, I thought I would be of assistance." He reached out a hand, offering to rescue the champagne glass, the mask, or both.

She looked up at him, green eyes that rivaled any gem here, alight with a sparkle, a slow smile of rueful amusement curling her lips.

She spoke softly, too. "I'm not so sure I can accept your assistance. I've just assured my cousin-in-law that I will watch out for rats and wolves and all predators of the night, I believe."

"Ah, unless they should be filthy rich," he murmured.

She laughed, the sound a bit guilty as she looked around, the slightest touch of a frown furrowing her brow.

"Well," she murmured, looking him up and down once again. "You are a wolf."

"A wolf?" he said with mock distress.

She indicated his costume. His mask was leather, with

carved nose and teeth. He wore a black cape, but beneath it were worn strips of fur.

"But perhaps I'm a young, very wealthy—filthy rich—wolf. Take a chance. Dance with me. Well," he amended thoughtfully, "have a shrimp, finish your champagne, and then dance with me."

"Ah, but—"

"Live recklessly. This is Venice. Carnevale."

Her smile deepened. She handed him her mask, quickly finished a shrimp, swallowed her champagne, and nodded. "I will do my best."

In a minute, they were out on the dance floor in the rear, a terrace that looked over another section of a canal. The moonlight captured on the water reflected the dancers. They played a waltz; she had warned him she was an American and frightfully behind in the etiquette of dance, but she seemed to waltz as if she had been following his lead for years. She glided, she laughed, she stumbled, and grimaced. "You're a bit too tall," she told him.

"You're a bit too small. But we shall manage."

"You're not Italian?" she told him.

"A wolf—and not even Italian," he admitted.

"But you're not American."

"A citizen of the world," he told her. "But you are, of course, American."

"I might have been English," she told him.

"Not in the least."

"Ah, but perhaps I'm Canadian."

"You've the clear mark of an American," he assured her.

"Oh, do I?" It was true; everyone always seemed to recognize Americans immediately. Before they spoke. It was as if they wore the word American tattooed on their foreheads. "From Charleston, South Carolina," she admitted. "And you?"

"Italy is my home away from home. At the moment. There are few in the world as warm and welcoming as the Italians."

"But you were born . . . where?" she inquired, curious green eyes bright on his.

He smiled, deciding not to tell her. There was little reason to do so. After tonight . . .

He shouldn't have danced with her. He shouldn't have spoken with her. The mayhem was coming. But she had caught his eye; she had awakened his senses, perhaps his instincts. Then, it seemed, she was capable as well of charming the mind.

And the soul?

Sir? Excuse me—Sir Wolf? Where are you from?"

"Far, far away," he said lightly, sweeping her in a circle. Then he paused at a tap on his shoulder. "Signore, per piacere . . ."

A Victorian gentleman, clearly English, broke in on him.

He acquiesced, bowing low. "Care Americana," he told her. "Ciao, bella. Ciao, bella."

She smiled at him, regret in her eyes, he thought. Or was it only that he could not help but hope?

He watched her dance away.

Her feet hurt—she had practiced in heels, but these were high. And the night was far from boring. First— the wolf. The enigmatic, very tall, oh-so-charming wolf. She hadn't the faintest idea of what he really looked like. He wore his mask. And yet, his height was hard to hide. Would she recognize him again? She would know his scent, she thought. Certainly. Very nice. An aftershave that was clean and woodsy but . . . with a very sensual, musky undertone.

After the wolf—the Englishman.

Then a harlequin, or joker.

He complimented her gown, then her eyes and her hair. Then the length of her neck.

She laughed, kept her distance. "You are too effusive, sir."

"Ah, never. Such lovely white flesh. The way your pulse . . . beats."

Just when she was beginning to feel uncomfortable, a Grim Reaper in brown leather and silk broke in on her. He was a Spaniard, tall, attractive. He commented on her wonderful energy, the ray of light that seemed to flow from her.

She thanked him. His features were colored with gray makeup, but his eyes were very dark and intense. *Sexy,* she thought.

Cindy, you're right, there are wolves everywhere. Tempting wolves . . .

As they spoke, a mummer in crimson tights and jacket came up on the terrace, ringing a bell, followed by a midget, clapping paddles together.

He spoke in Italian, at first, but translated for himself as well, to benefit all the guests at the ball. "Hear ye, hear ye, the masque begins! In days long, long gone, Odo, Conte of the Castello, had no son, but brought forth to the earth a daughter so glorious that the greatest of the nobility thought him rich. But Odo decried his lack of an heir, seizing his wife—"

He grabbed a middle-aged woman in a twelfth-century headdress, inquiring softly if she would play. She nodded, laughing, all for the game.

"Seizing his wife, he shook the poor wretched creature!" He pretended to shake her. "And gave her the kiss of death!"

It appeared that he whispered to the woman; she went limp, he set her down.

"So!" the crimson-clad mummer went on. "He married anew! But this wife, also, failed to give him a son!" From the growing crowd around him, he found another matron who eagerly nodded her assent to act out the part of the Conte's wife. He whispered to her; she went limp. He carefully let her fall to the floor.

"And again, he took a wife!"

He seized another woman, who was giggling and nodding before he could ask. She went the way of the first two women.

"Alas, he went through more wives than Bluebeard!" The mummer waltzed about the room, taking woman after woman.

Then he paused, dramatically shaking his head.

"But still, no woman gave him a son! So! He offered up his glorious, glorious daughter!"

The mummer came walking through the crowd. He, too, was tall and powerful, Jordan thought, muscles straining the form-hugging clothing.

He was walking toward her, she realized. She backed away. "American!" she said softly.

"No matter!" he told her. He reached out a hand to her. She started shaking her head, but he had her already. She was a guest; she didn't want to be rude.

"So he offered his soul to the very devil to find the man who would be his daughter's husband, and take on the family name! Ah! And where was the devil?"

As the mummer walked around the room, looking for the devil, guests laughed and moved about.

And then Jordan saw the crimson spill coming from beneath the head of the first woman who had fallen to the floor.

Blood.

She gasped, drawing a hand to her mouth, and began to scream.

The mummer saw her reaction, and snatched her up. She shrieked, trying to fight him off. He was stronger than she had imagined. And then, to her horror, she saw that the room suddenly seemed to be full of . . .

Beasts. Demons. She was seeing things. Surely. Men clad in furs, capes, coats . . . women suddenly let out shrieking cries, displaying . . . fangs.

"Let go!"

She fought wildly, kicking, screaming. She found herself dragged to the far end of the terrace by the mummer.

His crimson coloring as dark as the blood that had spilled . . .

Suddenly, the mummer was wrenched away from her, and she looked into the eyes of the wolf.

The mummer snarled, hurling out vindictive words in a language she didn't know. The wolf responded. The mummer struck at the wolf; the wolf ducked and fought back.

Jordan began to scream again and again as the force of the blow sent the mummer's head dangling to the side of his body, his neck broken.

All hell seemed to be breaking loose within the elegant palazzo.

Jordan stepped back, dazed.

Beasts were spilling from the house. *Beasts! Creatures*

in all manner of costume! Animals, with huge long teeth now, with blood dripping from those . . . fangs.

Then she started to scream again because the wolf reached for her. She ducked low, but he was incredibly powerful.

He bounded from the terrace . . .

Into fog! Sheer fog. A mist that had formed in the night, so rich, so thick, they seemed to jump into a black hole, into eternity . . .

His feet thumped down hard upon something. A launch. It rocked wildly with the impact of their weight. Jordan screamed with delayed terror; she could have fallen upon stone, upon marble, she could have broken her neck . . .

She could have just fallen forever and ever, into the mist, into hell.

He set her down in the small launch, then looked up at the startled oarsman.

"Row!" he thundered. "Row, row, now!"

The fellow sprang to life.

Then the wolf sprang from the launch to the pavement.

And turned.

And was swallowed into the mist.

Books by Bestselling Author
Fern Michaels

___The Jury	0-8217-7878-1	$6.99US/$9.99CAN
___Sweet Revenge	0-8217-7879-X	$6.99US/$9.99CAN
___Lethal Justice	0-8217-7880-3	$6.99US/$9.99CAN
___Free Fall	0-8217-7881-1	$6.99US/$9.99CAN
___Fool Me Once	0-8217-8071-9	$7.99US/$10.99CAN
___Vegas Rich	0-8217-8112-X	$7.99US/$10.99CAN
___Hide and Seek	1-4201-0184-6	$6.99US/$9.99CAN
___Hokus Pokus	1-4201-0185-4	$6.99US/$9.99CAN
___Fast Track	1-4201-0186-2	$6.99US/$9.99CAN
___Collateral Damage	1-4201-0187-0	$6.99US/$9.99CAN
___Final Justice	1-4201-0188-9	$6.99US/$9.99CAN
___Up Close and Personal	0-8217-7956-7	$7.99US/$9.99CAN
___Under the Radar	1-4201-0683-X	$6.99US/$9.99CAN
___Razor Sharp	1-4201-0684-8	$7.99US/$10.99CAN
___Yesterday	1-4201-1494-8	$5.99US/$6.99CAN
___Vanishing Act	1-4201-0685-6	$7.99US/$10.99CAN
___Sara's Song	1-4201-1493-X	$5.99US/$6.99CAN
___Deadly Deals	1-4201-0686-4	$7.99US/$10.99CAN
___Game Over	1-4201-0687-2	$7.99US/$10.99CAN
___Sins of Omission	1-4201-1153-1	$7.99US/$10.99CAN
___Sins of the Flesh	1-4201-1154-X	$7.99US/$10.99CAN
___Cross Roads	1-4201-1192-2	$7.99US/$10.99CAN

Available Wherever Books Are Sold!
Check out our website at **www.kensingtonbooks.com**

Romantic Suspense from
Lisa Jackson

See How She Dies	0-8217-7605-3	$6.99US/$9.99CAN
Final Scream	0-8217-7712-2	$7.99US/$10.99CAN
Wishes	0-8217-6309-1	$5.99US/$7.99CAN
Whispers	0-8217-7603-7	$6.99US/$9.99CAN
Twice Kissed	0-8217-6038-6	$5.99US/$7.99CAN
Unspoken	0-8217-6402-0	$6.50US/$8.50CAN
If She Only Knew	0-8217-6708-9	$6.50US/$8.50CAN
Hot Blooded	0-8217-6841-7	$6.99US/$9.99CAN
Cold Blooded	0-8217-6934-0	$6.99US/$9.99CAN
The Night Before	0-8217-6936-7	$6.99US/$9.99CAN
The Morning After	0-8217-7295-3	$6.99US/$9.99CAN
Deep Freeze	0-8217-7296-1	$7.99US/$10.99CAN
Fatal Burn	0-8217-7577-4	$7.99US/$10.99CAN
Shiver	0-8217-7578-2	$7.99US/$10.99CAN
Most Likely to Die	0-8217-7576-6	$7.99US/$10.99CAN
Absolute Fear	0-8217-7936-2	$7.99US/$9.49CAN
Almost Dead	0-8217-7579-0	$7.99US/$10.99CAN
Lost Souls	0-8217-7938-9	$7.99US/$10.99CAN
Left to Die	1-4201-0276-1	$7.99US/$10.99CAN
Wicked Game	1-4201-0338-5	$7.99US/$9.99CAN
Malice	0-8217-7940-0	$7.99US/$9.49CAN

Available Wherever Books Are Sold!
Visit our website at **www.kensingtonbooks.com**